Dirty Magick: New Orleans

edited by Charlie Brown

luckymojopress.com

Contents

Cover art by Trent Oubre (http://trentoubre.com/)

ACKNOWLEDGEMENTS

To Dave Robison for creating the RoTaNoWriMo Facebook group and for all of his tireless efforts. Glad to find such a wonderful community of support and talent.

To Veronica Giguere and Paul Cooley for lending their vocal talents to the Balticon reading.

To Mickey Finn, for promotion and recruitment way above his pay grade.

Introduction: Hiding In Myth's Shadows: New Orleans's Complicated Relationship With Truth

by Charlie Brown

On a moonlit night in late fall, the fog lowers onto Jackson Square, clinging to the street lamps and bathing the ancient cobblestones with a soft ambience. These moments show how magical New Orleans can be, how it is a world separate from the known.

On any night and in any part of town, those same streets can be bathed in revolving red and blue glares, police creating a barricade to investigate violent crime, maybe multiple-victim murders of wasted youth.

The sad truth about New Orleans is everything that makes it great simultaneously makes it awful. The *laissez-faire* attitude can devolve into lawlessness, the celebratory drinks carried through the streets can flip into fistfights and the culture's uniqueness can squeeze itself into parochial arguments about who and what is authentic.

But one fact remains. New Orleans is about the show. Bourbon Street's constant carnival draws visitors eager to drop cash on illicit pleasures. Fancy restaurants offer service so perfect that it's impossible to tell when that water glass refilled. Few weekends go by without some sort of parade.

And yet, we keep many secrets. We're free with the house wine, but reserve the good stuff for ourselves. The best meal may not be served by the black-coat-white-shirt set, but out of an old woman's kitchen deep in back of town. And this is where the magick happens.

Nobody embodies this public-private dichotomy better than the city's most famous magician: Marie Laveau, the voodoo queen.

History has declared her the most powerful practitioner of voudun, the American importation of the Yoruba religion which, when mixed with

Catholicism, also resulted in *santería* (Cuba) and *candomblé* (Brazil). But this Haitian version made its way to the Crescent City after the island's slave uprisings, quickly becoming part of the local color.

Laveau may have come by her religion naturally. Her parents were mixed-race free people of color, firmly within the social construct of black Creole. Her husband, Jacques Paris, was a Haitian immigrant (such a connection should be noted), and they stuck to Christianity enough to be married in St. Louis Cathedral, the celebration supposedly performed by Père Antoine himself.

But while the Widow Paris (as she was better known in polite society) was only ever proved to have been a liquor importer with a business in the Faubourg Marigny, her legacy is too large for there to be no truth to her practicing some sort of underground ceremonies. And, hey, they used a lot of rum in their rites. Why not make a profit from it?

But these rituals, reported to be moonlight bacchanals on Bayou St. John and Lake Pontchartrain and conducted first by Marie and then by her eponymous daughter Marie Laveau II, were mostly for rich white women. The matrons of a very rigid society must have reveled in their liberation from whalebone corsets and bustled dresses, finally ridding themselves of the "vapors."

(As an aside, the condition known as the vapors was gas, plain and simple. Maybe Marie Laveau profited so much in this world because she let fussy white women fart freely. But that is my own conjecture.)

But, again, her St. John's Eve and other wild celebrations were a show, another party framed as mystical experience. While they may have followed true ritual, were they what Laveau herself practiced in private? That is something no one will ever know.

But while voodoo is a real religion with its own beliefs and practices inherited from Africa, another figure looms large over the supernatural landscape of the city, especially the gothic imagination bathed in night.

When Anne Rice first created Lestat in *Interview With The Vampire*, he was a malevolent figure, pure evil out to torture the soul of the young gentleman Louis. But as the novel series continued, the writer became entranced with her character, morphing him into an anti-hero whose vile actions could not only be explained but atoned for.

Rice was so close to her creation that he became real, at least in her mind. Flush with cash from book and Hollywood sales, she wanted to buy the building where Lestat buried himself at the end of her second novel. But Al Copeland, the tackily *nouveau-riche* owner of the Popeyes franchise, had beaten her to it. As he readied one of his "upscale" cafes, Rice attacked him in the press, saying his brand of glitz wasn't right for tony St. Charles Avenue (she said this while not acknowledging that the brick monstrosity was once a car dealership).

Copeland fought back, feeling safe his deed would render her point moot. The final shot was a letter written by Lestat himself (so Rice claimed) published as a full page ad in the local paper. Most everyone agreed that the author was a loon and sided with the fried chicken magnate.

Her eccentricities aside, Rice's fiction created a major groundswell of interest in the city. Other writers like Poppy Z. Brite took up the mantle, adding their own tales to the dark side. Goths flocked to the French Quarter, wrapping lower Decatur Street is swaths of velvet and leather.

In that hoariest of clichés, the city was now a character in a leering, purple exploitation novel. Historical sites of horrific violence like the LaLaurie House became mere stops on the ghost tour. Haints and ghostly presences sprouted, and customers can even know ahead of time if a property they would like to buy is haunted. The grand romantic tale has become a parody.

But it shouldn't be surprising that New Orleans, a "print the myth" town if there ever was one, shadows accuracy for an entertaining tale. But, like the street violence plaguing its daily life, truth has a way of exploding in ugly fashions. And so these following stories are fantastical, unreal, the products of imagination. But they also have roots in reality, the gritty streets, even if the sand shifts beneath them. Somewhere in all these lies, there's shards of honesty. But's it up to you, dear reader, to find them.

KNOWLEDGE IS POWER

BY RHONDA EUDALY

Janna Allen breathed in the heady scents of flowers, humidity, and spicy cuisine as she stood on the curb outside of Place d'Armes Hotel in New Orleans. The front door closed behind her on its own. She nodded to the hotel's ghost, a translucent, bearded gentleman in Victorian style dress.

Armed with a tourist guide, phone, and camera, Janna headed toward St. Louis Cathedral and Jackson Square. Her goal was mapping out which museums and libraries she wanted to visit after the cathedral, but first things first: a beignet and coffee at Café du Monde.

Janna sat at the corner and breathed in the rich smells of powdered sugar, fried dough, and strong *café au lait*. She formed a quick incantation and sent the sensory message off. Almost immediately her phone rang.

"Hello, Amie."

"I want to call you so many bad names right now." Amie sounded both annoyed and amused.

"You were the one who thought I was stupid to come here on vacation." Janna tried to sound sweet and innocent – and failed miserably.

"I didn't say that, and it had nothing to do with the *food*. I only thought it was crazy for someone who deals with magic all day every day to vacation at one of the magical centers of the country – heck, the world. I just said if it were me, I'd find a deserted beach somewhere and get a tan."

"Yeah, I have no melanin. A beach would be painful – all that time applying sunscreen."

"That's what cabana boys are for. Don't you know anything?"

"And where on a *deserted* island would these mythical cabana boys come from?" Janna asked.

Amie snorted. "You're the Theurgist. Conjure one."

"A beneficial magic though that would be for *me*, it's not how it works and you know it. How's Copperfield?"

"Does your cat *always* get you up at 5 a.m. to be fed?"

Janna sipped her *café au lait*. "No. Never."

"Then I guess I'm special."

Janna checked the time. "Oh, I gotta go. St. Louis Cathedral closes soon. I'll check in with you later."

She shut down the call before her well-meaning friend could take her on another conversational tangent. She didn't really need to rush, but she was on vacation and didn't want to continue defending her decision to spend it...here.

Janna strolled the brick-paved lanes through the Cathedral's grounds. Andrew Jackson kept watch from his horse as she wandered the centuries-old property. She had time for the self-guided tour of the cathedral before heading to the Old Ursuline Convent.

The aromas of beeswax and incense infused the air as she studied the intricate details inside the building. The murals and friezes gleamed with vibrant and restored color and gilt details. She paused in front of the mural of St. Louis, King of France, sending troops off on a crusade at the back of the church. She could almost feel the history in the walls, the power of believing souls raised in worship gave the place power.

"Special Agent Allen?"

The heady sensory experience shattered. Janna turned, wary, to see a middle-aged balding man in a priest's collar and black suit approaching. She had no idea who he was, though his rounded features seemed vaguely familiar.

"Can I help you, Father?"

"I think maybe I can help you."

"What makes you think I need help?" she asked. "Father...?"

"Leloup. Richard Leloup. I saw your name on the registry. You were scheduled for the museum tour, yes?"

"Yes." Janna kept her voice neutral. "Excuse me for being blunt, but do I know you?"

The priest smiled. "Of course you wouldn't remember. I was but newly ordained when you and your team recovered a relic–"

"St. Vincent's, yes, now I remember, we retrieved a werewolf relic. It was my first case out of the Academy. I'm glad you're doing well, Father. The priesthood becomes you."

"Thank you, Special Agent. I suspect you're here to see the Grimoire Exhibit. I assure you, the great Books are secure."

"I have no doubt, Father, but I'm not here in any official capacity."

"You're not?"

Janna smiled. "I'm here purely for the historical factor. I'm on vacation."

"That's a relief. As a thank you for all your hard work, may I offer you a private tour?"

Janna blinked. "That would be amazing."

The priest led her through the cathedral to the Ursuline Convent. They passed docents gathering other tourists for their tours and passed through the rope barriers into the Grimoire Exhibit. Several plain grimoires lined the walls, but a spotlighted, high-tech glass case in the center of the room drew her eye. Inside, an ornate leather-bound book with gilt accents and trim lay open to an illustrated page covered in hand-lettered Latin.

"Is it safe to have the book open?" she asked.

"Oh, don't worry, Special Agent..."

"Please, I'm on vacation. Call me Janna."

"No need to worry, Janna. The page is an innocuous crop spell. No one would want to cast it, and there's no way for anyone to move to a more dangerous spell."

"Why not?"

"The case has a state-of-the-art pressure switch alarm system. The glass is impact-resistant up through large caliber projectiles, and the whole area is warded against spells, hexes, and other magical incursions. The *Arcanus Magus* is perfectly safe, and so are all who view it."

"I feel better already, but I'm a bit surprised the Church is hosting this exhibit."

Leloup waved her off. "Magic is a gift and a tool. Besides, it's our duty to protect and guide souls. How better than to know thy enemy?"

"Interesting perspective. The *Arcanus Magus* is spectacular."

"The great books always are. Despite being a book, it holds elements of power."

"I feel it." When the priest gave her a startled look, Janna shrugged. "Part of my talent – and my job."

"Yes, that would be beneficial in your line of work."

As Janna moved around the Grimoire, her attention focused on the case. Her fingertips hovered just out of range of the glass. "But *this* is living history, dark and palpable. The temptations must be...difficult."

"We study it as an artifact. Pure faith protects us."

"Of course, Father. It's been an honor to see the book."

"We have a few more artifacts you might like to see. This way."

Light streamed through the hotel room windows, triggering a blinding headache. Janna blinked. Maybe not choosing the interior room was a mistake. She remembered wandering the French Quarter as the clubs opened up. The rest was a blur. The pounding increased in volume and insistency until she realized it wasn't her head. Someone was knocking on her door.

"One moment." Janna stumbled out of bed and slipped on her robe. Maybe she'd ordered breakfast before falling asleep?

Room service wasn't on the other side of the door. Surly looking men in sports coats and badges stood behind a nervous-looking hotel manager.

"Janna Allen?" the lead jacket asked.

"Yes?"

"We need you to come with us," he said.

"Not until you identify yourself." Janna took a solid stance. "You know better."

"NOPD. Detective Eli Medina. Please come with us, Ms. Allen."

"Why?"

"The *Arcanus Magus* was stolen last night. We have questions."

Janna's eyes widened. "Give me an hour to shower and dress–"

"You'll come with us now, Ms. Allen. We'll use handcuffs if necessary."

Being on the suspect side of the interrogation table felt weird. Janna tried to breathe normally, but couldn't stop her rising anxiety. The room didn't help, with the bare cinderblock walls and steel furnishings. At least she'd been able to put on real clothes, if not shower. The door squealed on its hinges. Detective Medina stalked in and dropped a file folder down on the table.

"You know I'm on your side, right?" she asked.

"We're looking into your background, *Agent* Allen. But that doesn't mean you're above suspicion. In fact, your skills with the Federal Special Investigations makes you uniquely qualified to pull off this theft."

"Why on Earth or Ether would I steal the *Arcanus Magus*? I know what that book can do."

Medina glared. "That sounds like motive to me. Planning to use it? Magical terrorism? You were at the convent."

"That's ridiculous. I'm on vacation. I visited the exhibit because the Grimoire is a piece of magical history. I admire it like artists admire the 'Mona Lisa' at the Louvre."

"But no one saw you on any of the official tours. How do you explain that?"

"Father Leloup gave me a private viewing." As soon as the words left her mouth, she realized how bad it sounded.

"So you admit to having access." Medina leaned forward. "You want to give me means? Tie it all up for me?"

"I assume you're searching my hotel room right now?" Janna's annoyance over the accusations burned away the anxiety. "You won't find it, because it's not there. I didn't steal it. I know magic – I wouldn't mess with something that dangerous."

"Why are you in New Orleans, Ms. Allen? The real reason."

"Vacation *is* the real reason, Detective Medina. I heard this town had great food. I wanted to see for myself.

"Where were you last night?"

"French Quarter. Being a tourist."

"Places? Times?" Medina persisted.

"Um...not sure. French Quarter? Tourist? Pretty sure there's surveillance and credit card activity. I don't carry a lot of cash. And you don't have anything to hold me."

"We'll look into that. Don't leave town."

"So what are you going to do?" Amie asked over the phone.

"I'm going to find the *Arcanus Magus*, Amie."

"But the police–"

"Aren't interested in clearing me. And they don't know how dangerous the *Arcanus Magus* is. If someone tries to handle the Grimoire without the right precautions, they could get really hurt."

"Isn't there a branch of the FSI in New Orleans? Can't they take care of this?" Amie asked.

"Probably. But they're not as motivated as I am."

"Be careful, Janna, this is...weird."

"Thanks, Amie. My stay may be extended. Take care of Copperfield for me until I get back?"

"Of course. Be careful."

"Thanks, Amie." Janna clicked off the call and stared at the convent front door. She wanted to see the scene – how the Grimoire had been stolen, but uncertainty stopped her.

"Agent Allen?" Father Leloup appeared out of nowhere. Her gifts told her he was coming – but also he moved as quietly as the wolf he was named for.

"I didn't steal it, Father."

"I know."

She gave him a slight smile. "Thanks. Do you know who did?"

The priest shook his head. "If I did, you wouldn't be here. They masked their scents. They were good. Are you going to find it?"

"I have to, Father. The police think I took it. Can you... will you help me?"

The priest scanned the area, as if checking for witnesses. "You are one of the good. Whoever took this...they are bad. Evil. I can give you some resources. Contacts. But I can't actively participate. The Grimoire was under my charge. It was stolen on my watch, and the Church has a much more... thorough investigative process. I will not be available to help you. But I will pray for you, Agent Allen, for your success and for us all."

The cab ride to Tulane University shook her sense of direction. In the Crescent City, nothing was set on straight lines, which was probably why magic congregated here. The cab dropped her in front of Tilton Memorial Hall. She took a couple of deep breaths before heading in to the Amistad Research Center. Though renowned for collecting and cataloging African-American culture, they also housed a significant magical collection known only to a few. Janna had heard rumors and reports, but only now had them confirmed.

A tall, dark, and lean man in that indeterminate age between thirty and forty-five met her in the lobby wearing khakis and a research facility logo emblazoned shirt.

"Ms. Allen, Father Leloup told me to expect you. I'm Keith Hughes, curator of the Arcane Collection. If you'll come with me, please."

She shook his hand as they fell into step and felt a familiar tingle of power. He would have to have some talent or gift to work with a collection like this. "Thank you for seeing me on short notice, but time is essential."

"If someone stole the *Arcanus Magus* with the intention to use it, you're likely right. May I ask why you didn't come with the police? They were just here."

"In fact, we're still here." From a side hall with a restroom icon on the wall, Medina stepped in their path. "What are you doing here, Ms. Allen? This is an official investigation. You wouldn't be obstructing it, would you?"

"I would never get in the way of a local investigation, Detective. Besides, who wants to work on their vacation?"

"Good, because I'm not convinced you're in the clear, no matter how many people vouch for you. Stay out of our way. *If* we need help, we'll call our regional branch of Special Investigations." Medina stomped past and out of the library.

Hughes studied her. "Not officially here?"

Janna blew out a frustrated breath. "That detective thinks he can do this on his own, and he'd be wrong."

"Then I'll tell you what I told them. If the Arcanus was stolen to be used..."

Hughes' voice trailed off.

"The Great Fire spells were in the *Arcanus Magus*. Do you think we'll be seeing more of those?" Janna asked.

"I think it'll be worse than that. The fire spells were set by lower level practitioners at the times. Anyone willing to go to this much trouble is probably powerful enough to cast one of the more dangerous spells."

Janna felt a chill. "Anyone that strong would be monitored by the Special Bureau. Trained. Tested."

"Someone like you?"

"Or someone I work with, but we'd know if someone went that dark." But Janna couldn't help the niggle of doubt.

"How well do we know anyone?"

Janna ignored the philosophical comment. "Apparently you know the *Arcanus* on an academic level, and if the fires aren't the worst we can expect, what can we?"

"Katrina and Rita were weather spells from a similar Grimoire. Add those to the power of the fire spells, and you'll be getting close. I can't even begin to calculate the destruction of both infrastructure and life." Hughes shivered.

"Then the book needs to be found quickly."

Hughes gave her an eyeroll worthy of any teenager. "You think?"

Janna pulled a card out of her pocket. "My cell number is on the back. If you think of any other information that might help narrow my search, let me know. I still have some resources that the local law enforcement may not."

"There's someone else you should talk to."

Janna stepped off the bus on Rampart Street. She checked the address and headed down to the Voodoo Museum. The small building seemed cluttered and charming. But she felt the power behind the artifacts.

"I'll be right with you," a resonant and Caribbean-accented voice called from the depths of the two-room museum.

Janna studied the brightly colored, mostly hand-made exhibits and displays. She soaked in the history and energy of the room.

A young, African American woman with rows of braids and a dress of brightly colored and patterned fabrics bustled out of the second room. "What can I do–" She stopped abruptly. "You're a practitioner."

Janna nodded. "You have an interesting place. It's more than a museum, isn't it?"

"Voodoo is a legitimate and ancient belief system." The caretaker's tone turned cool and stiff.

Janna raised her hands. "I didn't mean to offend you. It was just an observation. My name is Janna Allen. Father Leloup and Keith Hughes thought you might be able to help me locate something before it's put to its darkest uses."

"Is this an official investigation? You are Special Investigations, Agent Allen." The woman crossed her arms, suspicion pouring off her. "You were on the news."

"No, it's not official, but it's vitally important. Please?"

"I'm sure, if the old wolf sent you to me. I'm Odette Bouvier. You can call me Odette."

"Janna. I will take any help you can give me. You know the local area – and the local power. I need information."

"Let me close up, then we can talk."

Odette moved quickly but efficiently to shut down the museum and drew Janna farther into the small building.

"Tea?"

"What kind?"

Odette smiled. "I have many varieties, depending on what you need. Today, I'm thinking a nice Sencha. Or even a decaf. Come with me."

Janna followed Odette into a homey kitchen adjacent to the museum. Natural light filtered through sheer curtains over a steel farm sink. Odette set a kettle to boil on an antique gas stove. She settled at the thick, hewn wood table with mismatched chairs covered in hand-sewn cushions.

"What can I do to help?" Odette asked.

"I need to know who locally might be tempted to take and use the *Arcanus Magus*." Janna decided it was best to just lay it out.

Odette drew back as if slapped. "That's dark magic. We don't–"

Janna had to backpedal once more. "I'm not implying that you or your people took it. But Father Leloup thought you'd have information or contacts through the voudun community that I could never tap. Someone has to know something – a whisper, or rumor, something. I will take anything. This is too important."

Odette sat back with her mug. "Leloup is misnamed. He should be a fox, not wolf. He flirts with the edges of his vows, I think."

"Confession or magic?"

"He's a licensed counselor. So am I. We have a professional...bond. We see similar kinds of people. I like Richard, and if he sent you...let's talk."

Janna gave Odette a summary of her conversation with Hughes. Odette went a little gray and gripped her tea mug with an ever tightening grip. "What is it?" Janna asked.

"I need to make some calls. This is..."

"Beyond bad, Odette. If someone you know is involved, they're in danger. We all are."

Janna strode down Chartres Street toward the Pharmacy Museum. Armed with a shopping list, she moved with purpose. She had a feeling time was running out. She needed to move fast.

She pushed open the museum's polished wooden door. The bell over the door announced her entrance. The building was the first licensed apothecary in the United States. Janna was counting on the museum being more than collections of herbs and bottles, as with the Voodoo Museum.

"The tour doesn't begin until 1 p.m.," the aging matron behind the desk said, not looking up from her tablet. "Feel free to look around."

"I'm not here for the tour. I hoped I could see Dr. McLean?"

The woman looked up, suspicion sparking in her blue eyes behind retro-chic cat's eye glasses. "Leloup sent you, didn't he?"

"Actually it was Odette Bouvier."

"I'm Robbie McLean. Who are you and what do you want?"

Janna sighed and introduced herself. She told her story as quickly and concisely as she could, all the while telling herself that she didn't have time to keep going over the same things. Not with so many lives at stake. But at least the dour woman behind the counter seemed less suspicious. As Janna told her story, the woman straightened and took off her glasses.

"I'm hoping you could help me acquire some unusual elements for a spell so I can find the Grimoire."

"Are you serious? Someone's about to use the *Arcanus*? Here? In New Orleans? I told that old wolf of a priest putting that book on display was a bad idea. He didn't listen. What do you need?"

Janna handed over her list. McLean put her glasses back on and scanned the page, frowning as she did so.

"If you can help me with any of these," Janna said.

"Oh, we have access to all these things. We are much more than a museum. It's...I sold almost this exact list a few days ago."

Janna's interest spiked. "To whom? Do you have a receipt or surveillance recordings?"

"I'm afraid not. None of these elements are controlled, so I had no reason to flag the purchase, and the person who bought them paid cash."

"Male or female?"

"I couldn't tell. Loose clothes. Hat. Sunglasses. Didn't say much, but sounded like he or she had a cold. Their voice as low and harsh." McLean snorted. "And I've been trying to get upgrades to our surveillance for years."

"I understand. Thank you, though."

"I hope you know what you're doing. These elements work for more than location spells, depending on how they're blended and manipulated. I'll get what you're asking for, but please be careful. Spells are like medications. There can be side effects, interactions that can be deadly."

"I promise to be very, very careful."

Janna didn't like the looks of the dark alley between two shotgun houses with warped boards and peeling lavender paint. Odette's calls and information sent Janna to the Tremé neighborhood just the other side of Rampart Street from the Quarter. Odette's information and her locator spell had taken up the rest of the daylight and led her to this spot and told her this creepy alley was where she needed to be. It also made sense – whoever stole the Grimoire wouldn't want to move it far.

The cab driver tried to talk her out of stopping. She paid and ignored him.

Standing in the mouth of the alley, she felt and heard...nothing. The alley felt muted, like it was blanketed.

"Veils." She pushed forward and met resistance. "And wards. At least they're not completely stupid."

But you may be.

The threat whispered through her mind like a breeze. She shivered and scanned the shadows. Two sections of dark broke away from the depths and moved independently of any light sources. Whoever took the Grimoire had enough power to use Shades as sentries, and Janna tried to swallow her spike of fear around the lump in her throat.

Janna took off running, sensing that the shadows followed. She needed to find light, the brighter the better, before the Shades caught up. She turned onto what should have been a main road artery. It was a dead end.

"Stupid, aggravating crescent street patterns!" She turned to backtrack when an arm pulled her into an alcove. An involuntary shriek threatened to rip from her throat until she saw Detective Medina holding a finger to his lip. He pulled her farther into the darkened doorway.

"Sunlight spell," he said into her ear. "You know one?"

"I do. How do you? You're not a practitioner."

"I'm a New Orleans cop. Give me some credit. Now come on. Sunlight spell, before those gremlins or whatever they are figure out where we are."

"Let me focus." Janna did her best to calm her mind and let the words of the incantation flow.

"Focus faster. I hear them coming."

"I'm doing it now." She cupped her hands and whispered the words. A ball of light formed in her palms. As the Shades scrabbled to the mouth of the alley, Janna tossed the ball into the air.

"Cover your eyes!"

The light shot up and seared away all the darkness. The Shades' squeals faded as the light disintegrated them.

"The light won't last long." She clutched Medina's arm. "We have to go, in case more shades come."

Service weapon drawn, Medina stepped in front of her. He checked the road, then pulled her out with him.

Janna yanked her arm away. "What are you doing? The *Arcanus* is the other direction."

"They know we're coming. Going in now would be suicide. We come back in the daylight when they're weaker. Right now we need light and crowds."

Janna followed Medina's lead to Rampart, near a bar with a brass band and a laundry decorated like a tiki bar. She slowed her pace until the revelers common to New Orleans no matter the time of year separated them. She dashed back the way they came. Medina's plan had merit, but if they lost the *Arcanus* now, they wouldn't pick up its trail again until it was too late.

She didn't get far before footfalls followed her. Determination kept her moving. Medina fell into step beside her. "What are you doing?" he demanded.

"I may not have my gun, or my badge or jurisdiction, but I'm not defenseless. And, frankly, I know magic better than you. I can't risk losing the Grimoire."

"But–"

"I'm going in now. You can't stop me." Janna put more speed in her stride. She didn't look to see if Medina stayed with her.

"If you get us killed, I'll haunt you for eternity, because this is a *stupid* idea."

"Fair enough."

Janna led them back to the alleyway. The wards and veils remained in place. She pushed through with Medina right behind her.

"You're sure this is the place?" he asked. "It's...empty."

"Trust me." She looked over her shoulder at him. "I don't suppose you have a backup on you?"

Medina looked like he would say something snarky, but thought better. He took a small semi-automatic from an ankle holster and handed it over. Janna checked the magazine and chambered a round. She pointed to a solid-looking door set off to the side at the end of the alley. Medina nodded.

The door was locked. When a couple of sharp shoves followed by kicks from both of them failed to budge the door, Janna motioned for Medina to step back. After a whispered charm on the barrel of her gun, two suppressed rounds blew out the lock.

In textbook procedure, they cleared each room, all as quiet as the alley. Deeper in the building, the glow of electric/candle light came from a cross-corridor. Janna held up a fist to stop Medina. She leaned in close.

"Voices. To the left. The suppression wards stop here. They won't be far. Stay alert and be careful."

Medina nodded. As they hurried down the corridor, they kept low and ready, the voices getting louder as they headed into the light. Janna stopped them before they blundered into a wide, open floor plan room. She pressed back against the wall and eased around the corner.

The ritual area was laid out perfectly for a major working. The circle on the floor had candles at the points of a pentagram. The *Arcanus Magus* lay open on a pedestal in center. A practitioner in a black robe with silver embroidery stood in the center, the hood obscuring the head and face. Janna sent out her senses to gauge the practitioner's power.

The hooded robe jerked upright and turned in her direction. The hand looked nearly skeletal in comparison to the wide sleeve as it swept toward her. Five burly human minions in dark clothes came out from behind crates and boxes to move toward them. Janna couldn't tell who or what they were.

"So much for stealth," Medina said. "You okay with blazing glory?"

"We can't let that spell be cast, no matter what."

"I'll take care of those guys. You get Merlin." Medina didn't wait for her agreement as he stepped into view. "NOPD. No one move."

The classic identifier only propelled the minions to move faster. Medina shot two before having to go hand to hand.

Janna turned away and headed for the practitioner. She began chanting a spell to rip though the shields certainly raised around the circle. She was most of the way through when an imp popped up in her path, disrupting the incantation. With barely a misstep, she shot the imp in the chest and kept going. Supernatural or not, most creatures went down with that kind of shot.

She restarted the incantation, focusing only on the circle. The mage in the center bent over the book, muttering a spell. Janna picked up the pace, nearly shouting the words of her spell. The magic shimmered and shattered. Janna bounded over the circle and plowed into the mage.

The two fell in a pile of fabric with wild yells. As the mage squirmed and struggled, Janna tried a number of submission holds and spells. A few elbows and blows landed, nearly breaking Janna's concentration. Something about the way the mage moved was familiar, as if he or she knew what Janna would do and how to counter.

The hood fell back, and Janna skittered back as if hit by a stun gun. "Amie?! What the... how could...? It was you?"

"I tried to talk you out of coming here."

Janna wanted to scream. This was her best friend. "You're possessed. That has to be it. I know a priest here. He can exorcise whatever it is. You won't be held accountable."

"I'll be more than accountable, dear naïve Jenna. I'll be the one who resets the *world*. A brighter future, Jenna. Clear the corrupt and start over. Be better. It's what you've been trying to do your whole career. I can do it in one try."

Janna couldn't believe what she was hearing. She'd known her friend was a crusader, but to go to these lengths? "I can't let you do it, Amie. Do you know how many innocents will die to accomplish what you think your spell will do? Stop this now! Before it's too late!"

"It's already too late, Janna. The spell has begun. There's only one small thing left to do. It's a blood spell. I was going to use one of my minion's blood, but yours is much more righteous. I am sorry, my friend, but you'll still be part of greater good."

Amie jumped to her feet and rushed at Janna with a wicked curved knife. Silver lined the runes etched along the blade. Amie shed the robe in one practiced move. Her training kicking in, Janna rolled out of the way. Unfortunately, she'd taught Amie most of the same moves, thinking her friend should have a way to defend herself. Amie anticipated Janna's actions and pinned her.

"You always wanted to save the world, Janna. Too bad you weren't visionary enough to do what needed to be done."

"And you always focused on your pet causes to the point of tunnel vision. You need to see the bigger picture."

"Really? Snark when you're about to die? How is changing the world not seeing the bigger picture?" For a moment, she seemed like the Amie Janna knew.

"One, you'd know that I wouldn't take kindly to your leaving my cat alone. And two, you'd think to wonder if I came alone or not."

Amie snorted. "Who would you bring, Janna? You even went on vacation alone."

"Maybe she met someone new."

Amie spun around as Medina fired his gun. Janna watched her friend drop, bright red pooling around her from the gaping hole in her chest. Janna hesitated – torn between rushing to her friend and throwing herself on the Grimoire.

"Secure the book!" Medina shouted, jarring her into action as he pulled out his cell phone.

Janna scrambled to the pedestal. Dark power radiated off the pages. She had to contain the magic. She tried the simple measure of closing the book, but the cover seemed fused the pedestal. A containment spell might help do keep the destruction in check, but her mind was too rattled to focus.

"Problem, Allen?"

Medina's voice cut through her doubt and fear. She reached deep to find the power and voice to cast the containment spell. A mystical blanket smothered the dark cloud rising from the book. In a moment, Janna was able to close the *Arcanus Magus*. She backed away from the pedestal and turned to Medina. He'd covered Amie's body with the robe.

"This is officially the worst vacation ever."

Janna sipped a strong cup of coffee at Café Beignet. She'd considered going back to Café du Monde, but couldn't without thinking about Amie. She'd tried to enjoy the beignet the café was named for, but found herself leaning on the brass railing of the table trying not to think.

"You know beignets are better eaten warm, right?"

Janna looked up from the depths of her coffee. "You're both here?"

Leloup and Medina took the extra seats at the table and signaled for coffee. Leloup cocked his head at Medina. "The detective told me the mastermind behind the theft was your friend. He thought you might need to talk."

"I'll be okay."

Medina sipped from the cup the waiter brought. "You did good in there. Thought you should know. The Local SIs found where she was staying. She's been researching and planning this a long time. We might not have found her in time if not for you."

Janna snorted. "Thanks."

Leloup pat her hand. "He's right. I studied the wards and veils, I think your connection with...her...let you get close enough to stop her. You saved a lot of lives."

"And the Grimoire?"

"Safely locked away in a secure vault. It won't be on exhibit again. Ever." Leloup looked chastened. "It's been so ordained by the Holy Father in Rome."

"Well, I guess there's nothing left to do but go home and get on with life." Janna picked at the beignets.

"Or you could stick around and let some residents show you what New Orleans is really like," Medina said.

"I haven't had any Cajun food yet – or met any."

Medina twitched. "Creole. The people are Creole. Not Cajun, and so is most of the food. You need a guide. Come on. And if you're good, we'll find you a gator."

Janna almost smiled. And that, at least, was a start.

Blood Debt

by Terry Mixon

Al Blake stepped off the train and into the humid summer heat of New Orleans. He'd waited for the crowd to clear the platform before leaving his private compartment. As an assassin, he liked crowds well enough, but preferred to keep any connection with his newest client under his hat.

It wasn't hard to spot his ride. The beefy man in the ill-fitting suit screamed "mob goon." With a disbelieving shake of his head, Al gestured for the porter to follow him and headed over. He extended his hand to the large man. "I think you're expecting me."

The enforcer's eyes shifted to the porter who wisely stood too far away to overhear any of the conversation. "If you're Blake, I'm your guy."

"That's me. Where you have me staying?"

"I'm Charlie. The Boss got you a room at the Roosevelt. Classy. Come on. I got a car up front."

He'd have rather bedded down somewhere with a lower profile, but these mob boys would take that as some kind of insult. Al wasn't sure why a guy like Sam "Silver Dollar" Carolla needed an outside assassin, but the money he'd offered just to talk was good. If Al took the job, his payout went up significantly.

He looked around the platform one last time. No one was watching them, not even the porter.

"This the place where Capone got his hand slapped?" he asked after a moment. He'd heard whispers about a confrontation between the Chicago boss and Carolla in the dark corners of the bars he frequented.

Speaking of bars, he made a mental note to hit some of the jazz clubs while he was here. He might never have another chance to hear some of the greats playing live.

A friend had recommended he seek out the Young Morgan Band if he wanted to hear what Heaven sounded like. Since that was about as close as Al would ever get to that fabled place, he'd make every effort to find them. If he had time, he'd also take a swing through the French Quarter. Who could visit New Orleans and not see the French Quarter?

Of course, the band might not even be here anymore. Ever since jazz had caught on, places like New York and Chicago had lured the best players away. Al felt a sense of satisfaction that men of color were finally breaking out into the public consciousness. It was about time.

The mob guy grinned. "Yeah. Ballsy bastard showed up with some of his toughs to force the Boss to ship him some booze. He wanted to cut Aiello out of the Chicago bootlegging. The Boss broke his guys' fingers and sent them all packing. He don't take to out of town big shots thinking they can throw their weight around."

His tone and expression made clear he personally included Al in that category.

"Is that so? Let's get a few things straight. I'm here because your boss paid me to come. I can hop right back on that train just as easy and you can explain why I'm moving on."

The goon looked unimpressed. "So? That's one thing. Give me another."

"Insulting a blood mage assassin might not be good for your retirement plan. We have long memories and savor grudges like fine wine. And we make examples of people to keep the rest in line. Me, I'd rather keep things civil. Fewer bodies that way. Your call, though. How's it gonna be?"

The enforcer stepped back and raised his hands. "Hey, I didn't mean nothin'."

Satisfied with the belated fear in the other man's eyes, Al smiled. "We shouldn't keep your boss waiting."

Two cars waited for them out front. The Model A coach with more mob goons was far less interesting than the sleek black roadster pulled up to the curb.

Al gave it an appreciative whistle. "Man, this beauty set someone back a pretty penny."

"A hell of a lot more than a penny," the goon said. "Climb in. The boys will take your bags to the Roosevelt while we go see the Boss."

Surprised, Al turned to the mob tough. "This is yours?"

The big man grinned. "Sure is. A Mercedes-Benz SSK. Almost hand made. Real rare. And fast. Real fast."

Impressed in spite of himself, Al nodded. "She looks it. You must do real well down here to afford something like her." A lot better than he'd thought possible for anyone in the mob, other than the men at the very top. Silver Dollar Sam could afford one. One of his goons? That seemed…unlikely.

The big man climbed behind the wheel. "You want to know something? I bought this baby off what I made in the stock market. A bunch of us are doing real well. I can give you some tips, if you like."

Al made a mental note to get out of the stock market. He'd been getting jittery for a while, even though it was a good place to hide his assets. Everyone seemed to think the only direction for it to go was up. Al had to admit that his investments had made him a pile of cash, but when a mob thug made more off the market than crime, it was time to get out. He'd call his guy tonight.

The car pulled away from the curb with a growl that spoke of power to burn. Everyone watched them as they moved through the crowded streets. Another good reason not to have one. Al didn't like people remembering him unless he wanted them to.

He expected them to go to a house, but they stopped outside a club. The Sazerac. It looked like a bar, but that wasn't likely with prohibition. Though booze was available for the right people, no doubt .

The inside of the club was packed, many of the patrons drinking right there in the open. Al followed the big man as he threaded his way toward the back. "I'd have thought people would be more discreet. Aren't you worried about the cops?"

"Nah. See that guy? That's the Kingfish. He comes here a lot. They started calling this place his office. The cops aren't going to bust them."

Al slowed to give the man in question a longer look. So that was Huey Long, the Governor of Louisiana. If Silver Dollar Sam thought Al was going to whack someone like him, he was dead wrong. Nothing but pain came from killing big name politicians.

Long wasn't much to look at, a little portly, well dressed, and loud. Just like any populist politician. He had a herd of people hanging on his every word, though. His kind loved the sound of their own voice. And an audience.

The sound level dropped when Al and his guide went through a door at the back of the room. This was more like it. Quiet and out of sight.

One of the offices had two men guarding it. They let Al and Charlie pass. The office was well appointed and full of mobsters, with the man behind the desk obviously in command. Sylvestro Carolla had the look of a pureblooded Sicilian from the old country. New Orleans attracted a lot of them, he'd heard. The climate was similar to home. Poor bastards.

It amused Al that the man needed to put on a show. All these people were supposed to intimidate him. It was flattering, really.

Silver Dollar Sam stood and gestured toward the door. "All of you guys get out of here. I got business to discuss. Charlie, you stay outside so that you can give the man a ride."

"Sure, Boss." The big man followed the others out as the mob boss rose to his feet.

"You want something to drink?"

Al shook his head. "It's a bit early for me. Thanks, though. This your place?"

"I'm a silent partner. I picked up my interest when The Kingfish started coming here regular. The people he has trailing him around make for good information." The mobster poured himself something, sat, and gestured Al into a chair. "I want to thank you for taking the time to come see me on such short notice."

"Happy to. Besides, you made it well worth my while." Al settled into the seat. "Forgive me if I skip the chit-chat, but I'm curious why a man of your means even needs someone like me. You have plenty of people to handle your problems."

"Straight to the point. I like that. My boys can handle almost any problem, but this issue is more up your alley. Somebody killed Luigi Russo, one of my lieutenants, a couple of days ago. He was inside one of my buildings where no one could get to him."

"And you think one of your people took him out?"

The mob boss knocked back his drink. "Nope. I know they didn't. They found him with blood pouring out of his eyes and other places. Like it boiled inside his body." His eyes grew cold and hard. "It was magic. Now you see why I called for you."

He did. The mob rarely used blood mages. They were too dangerous. The tiniest bit of blood meant they could kill you almost literally by looking at you. Crime bosses tended to be more than a bit paranoid. The two didn't mix well.

"So you want me to track down your killer and what? Bring him in to you? That's chancy. Blood mages are dangerous." He should know.

Carolla leaned back in his seat and gave Al a steady stare. "You got a reputation. You always carry out a contract. I don't know who killed my guy. If it was revenge, I might never know who was really behind it. If you tell me you killed the bastard, all I'll have is a body. And your word. I'm willing to live with that."

"Going after a blood mage will cost you more. The Order allows me to do it, but this is going to cause me grief somewhere down the line. And I have rules that might limit my ability to take out your killer."

The mobster nodded. "So I heard. No women. Well, it just so happens that we've been developing rules of our own. We decided that killing cops is bad for business. So, I can accept that you have your own quirks. If you can't make the killer pay for what he did, will you promise to give me his name? If so, that's how we'll play this. I want the bastard who caused this to scream and bleed."

Al nodded. He could do that. The chances the killer was a woman were low. Most blood mages became healers because they couldn't stomach seeing what their magic did to a human body when they killed. That ruled out most dames in his mind. If it wasn't a case of revenge, he didn't see a woman behind this business. If he was wrong, well, that was Silver Dollar Sam's problem.

"Sure. I can work with that. Tell me about Luigi. Why him? Why not you?"

"That's a question I've asked myself a lot these last few days. If the killer could get to Luigi, he could've probably gotten to me. I figure it had to be something he did. He made someone mad enough to pay top dollar to whack him. If I don't come down on this hard, that bastard in Chicago will think he can do the same."

Al crossed his legs and settled back in his chair. "Capone. Could this be a test to see how the other bosses react?"

"Maybe. That's why I need results. Public, messy results, if possible. Make this a message."

"What did Luigi do for you?"

"He ran my girls. We got a couple of houses where the cops look the other way for a price. He made sure things ran smooth there."

That surprised Al. As distasteful as prostitution was, it was low on the pecking order in the mob. Not very respected, even though it earned them a steady income. Not exactly the kind of target he imagined someone probing Carolla's organization for a weakness would hit.

"I'll need access. To the place he was killed, to his operation, to his place."

"You got it. Charlie will see you get whatever you need. I want this taken care of as soon as possible. If you get it wrapped up in twenty-four hours, I'll tack on a hefty bonus to your fee. Charlie!"

The big man opened the door. "Yeah, Boss?"

"Take Mister Blake to the henhouse. Give him whatever he wants."

"You got it, Boss."

The trip to the brothel took about twenty minutes, out to the center of the city near the cemeteries. Al took the opportunity to gawk at the bright colors on some of the buildings on the way.

The brothel wasn't that much to look at. The three story wooden building needed some paint and a few boards in strategic locations. The stairs from the street led up much higher than houses Al was familiar with. It almost looked like there was room for another floor there.

"Why do the stairs go up so high? Flooding?"

"Some, yeah. The river can get pretty wild. Scary wild. Back in '27 I thought it was gonna get us. They had to blow out the levee south of the city to keep the water out. Some houses are built high enough to have a basement where the ground floor should be 'cause the ground has too much water. Whoever built this place did that. We use it for a pantry and laundry."

Al stepped out of the roadster and put his hands on hips. "It looks a bit run down. Is that because the customers don't care?"

Charlie shook his head and adjusted his hat. "Nah. Business was down and Luigi decided it was safer to skimp on the house than to short the Boss."

"Not that it's any of my business, but that might cost you in the long run. If the place puts off the customers, it will make less money."

The big man shrugged as he headed up the stairs. "I don't know nothin' about that. You should tell Frank. He's in charge now."

Two skinny guys sat in the entrance hall. Both stood quickly when they came in. Charlie barely gave them a nod. He stomped up the interior stairs with Al at his heels. The inside was in better shape than the outside, but not by much. The plaster could use a touchup and the paint was peeling in places. It was clean, though.

The mob enforcer went to the third floor and knocked on the first door. A muffled voice told him to enter.

Al noticed the office was two steps above the rest of the house. Freshly painted, too. The smell was still in the air. The furnishings were fancy and expensive. Dark wood glossed to a high polish. The desk looked imported.

The silver-haired man behind the desk rose to his feet. "Gentlemen, welcome. Charlie, I have it from here. If you want to wander down to the kitchen, I'm sure one of the girls will fix you something."

"Sure, Frank. I'll leave you two to talk." The mobster closed the door behind him on the way out.

Al examined the mob lieutenant closely. The older man was well dressed, but he didn't overdo it. He also didn't look like a Frank. Maybe a Franco.

The man held out his hand. "Francesco Bernardi. You must be the specialist the boss brought in."

He shook the man's hand firmly. "Al Blake. I appreciate your help. First, where did the attack take place?" He suspected he already knew the answer.

"Right here. We found Luigi on the floor about where you're standing. It wasn't pretty. I've seen some bad stuff, but nothing quite like that. There was blood coming from everywhere, plus a few places I wouldn't have thought could bleed without a knife."

"Can you describe it?"

"I can do better than that. We had a guy come in and take pictures before we cleaned up." Bernardi opened the desk drawer, pulled out a folder, and handed it to Al.

Al knew at a glance that Carolla had been right to call him. This was blood magic all right. The mage had literally caused the man's blood to boil. A terrible and painful way to die. Much simpler to cause someone's blood pressure to spike until they had a stroke or heart attack. Someone wanted the man to suffer. Or he wanted to send a message.

He examined every photograph carefully. He found the cut he expected on the man's forearm. That spoke of a crime in the moment. Otherwise, the killer would've found a way to get the blood without directly confronting his prey.

There was a void in the blood spatter. Something or someone had been between the dead man and the door. Probably a person. Based on how the drops hit everything else, the mobster had already been on the floor when the worst of the spell had taken hold. That made the size of the void an unreliable measure of the killer.

One thing it did speak to was the assassin's experience. A blood mage learned fast to stay out of spatter range. This killer was relatively inexperienced. An oddity, considering the spell was very difficult. Perhaps it was someone who normally used their powers to heal.

"So, you think it was voodoo?" the mobster asked. "Luigi had a thing about voodoo."

"You mind if I sit?" Al sat at the man's gesture. "I think it's magic, but not voodoo. It feels like blood magic. Who might have hated him enough to hire an assassin?"

"That depends. How much are we talking about?"

The mobster laughed when Al told him. "Nobody. Not for that kind of money. They'd have just shot him."

"Where did he stay?"

"He spent most of his time here. This was his little kingdom. He ran it his way and he liked being here."

"How long was he in charge of this operation? Does anyone else want it?"

"Four years. And plenty of people would like to have it. This is cushy duty, if you know what I mean."

Al nodded. "Did you want it?"

Bernardi laughed again. "Sure. About twelve years ago. I ran this place before Luigi took over. I've moved up in the organization. I'm only watching over things until the Boss finds a replacement."

"I see. And the people who might want this job probably don't have the money to afford someone like me. You have any competition? I heard Capone was sniffing around a while back."

"Nah. We got this town pretty well locked down. Capone was more interested in booze than girls."

"The place looks a little rundown. Business bad?"

The mobster's expression closed down a little. "I don't think we need to get into that. It's not important to what happened."

Al considered the mobster. "We don't know what's important yet. If it was easy, you wouldn't need me to check things out."

"Yeah, business is down, but I'll get that turned around. I have some guys coming out to get the place fixed up next week. How's that relate to someone killing Luigi?"

"I don't know that it does. Did he pick the furniture in this office? It looks pretty expensive."

"Yeah, he did. He liked the pricier side of life. So what? He paid his share."

"Just getting a feel for the guy. Maybe he had a gambling problem or something."

Bernardi shook his head. "No way. We'd hear about something like that. His vices didn't cost more than he could afford."

It made sense they'd keep track of stuff like that. "Okay. I need to have some time alone in here. I may be able to divine something about the killing. It would've been easier if there were still some blood, but I'll try."

He fixed the mobster with a level stare. "And I need total privacy. This kind of magic is sensitive. No interruptions and nobody here to screw it up. I might not get a second chance to get it right."

The mob lieutenant didn't look too happy with that, but he rose to his feet. "The Boss said you get whatever you want, so fine. Come down to the kitchen when you're done."

Al waited for the door to close and then locked it. He didn't want suspicious people watching him snoop. Solving crime was the opposite of what he did. He killed people for a living. He hadn't ever had to worry about finding a murderer. It made him feel like he was betraying one of his own.

Someone had wanted the man dead in the worst way. Something important might still be here. He'd also look for any blood the cleaners had missed. The stuff could get into the oddest places when someone started shooting it out every orifice.

While Al didn't understand a lot about financial matters, he looked at the books first. Money was always a likely reason when people killed one another. Blackmail could make someone pay big for a kill. Especially if they had a reason to hide the things they were doing.

If there was a list of customers, he couldn't find it. That would've been too easy. And frankly, most people wouldn't be worth blackmailing over women of negotiable virtue. Maybe the Kingfish would kill if someone caught him whoring around, but that seemed unlikely. He'd have plenty of women throwing themselves at him.

One thing that stood out as he went through the office was that everything seemed impersonal. Only the things required to conduct business. No pictures. No mementos. This office was for show. He'd need to see the man's rooms to get a sense of him.

Someone had scrubbed and bleached the floor. He found no sign of blood out in the open. His luck changed when he looked under the edge of the desk. There was some under the leg. Not much, but perhaps enough to get a sense of what had happened.

He grunted with effort and lifted the desk enough to wipe the stain with a handkerchief. The amount of blood on the pristine cloth was depressingly small.

Al laid it out in the center of the desk and rolled the chair away. He placed his hands to either side of the handkerchief, closed his eyes, and focused his will on it. The spell that attuned him to the blood wasn't overly complex, but it was delicate.

So the pounding at the door totally disrupted his concentration. The backlash was relatively mild, but it still hit him like a hammer between the eyes.

He staggered back and cursed. It took a few moments before he could see straight. He marched over to the door, yanked it open, and glared up at the hulking mob enforcer that had brought him here.

"I said I needed to be left alone."

The big man held up his hand. "Sorry. You need to come with me right now."

"Yeah? Why? I'm working on a spell that might tell me who the killer is and I don't have a lot of blood to do this again."

"You want more? I got more. Someone just killed Frank in the basement. He looks just like Luigi did."

Okay, that was a pretty good reason for the man to interrupt his spell. "I want this house sealed. No one gets in or out. If anyone is missing, I want their name. Take me to the body."

Charlie gave orders to the men behind him and they scattered. He led Al down to the basement through the kitchen. The cooking staff looked terrified. They probably thought they'd catch the blame. Well, one thing he could do was settle who was guilty or innocent with a simple test. The only way the killer would escape would be to get out of the building. And that was an admission of guilt, too.

Francesco Bernardi lay sprawled at the base of the stairs. Half a dozen women and children huddled beyond the spray of blood under armed guard. They looked about twice as frightened as the people in the kitchen. If they'd seen the mobster die, they'd likely seen who did this. Or perhaps one of them might be the killer.

This kind of magic took fierce willpower and concentration. It also took training. Having blood magic wasn't enough by itself. Most people with the talent didn't have the strength to kill. Healing small injuries was the most common and benign manifestation of his art.

The fresh blood made his shoes stick to the steps as he made his way down to the body. A look around confirmed that the base of the stairs was where the attack had taken place. Blood spatter didn't lie.

"How many ways out of the basement?"

Charlie, who hadn't come all the way down, answered him. "Three. This one, another for the laundry, and the outside doors they use to bring in supplies. They're locked from the inside. There's only one key and Frank had it."

"Someone check to see if they're still locked."

One of the men guarding the laundry workers partly raised his hand. "I checked them. The chain and padlock are still there. Nobody snuck in or out that way."

"So, whoever it was snuck in through the kitchen or laundry. Someone probably saw the killer. If they aren't still right here."

He examined the dead man for cuts. Someone needed blood for this dark charm, the fresher the better. He found a gash on the back of the mobster's right hand. The killer had stood right here, cut the man, and cast the spell. Another crime of the moment.

There wasn't any gap in the blood spatter, so the killer had backed up as the man started convulsing. He'd learned.

Al smeared a drop of blood onto his fingertip and closed his eyes. With an effort of will, he summoned his talent. Blood called to blood. He felt it scattered all around him. He dropped the closest spatter from his awareness. The further out he moved his senses, the less there was to find. Eventually, there was only one source left.

His breath rushed out and he opened his eyes. It came from behind the guards. Much too far away to have come from the attack.

Everyone moved out of his way as he walked over to that side of the basement. The response came from near the exterior doors. He took a moment to check the chains and lock. Yep, still locked up tight.

The spell led him to sacks of flour. He moved some with a grunt and saw a bloodstained knife.

He pulled out another handkerchief–one could never have too many– and picked it up. Small bladed and short, it looked like a paring knife. One suitable for peeling apples or potatoes. Blood stained the blade.

"Found the knife." He turned to face the crowd of people staring at him. "I want everyone taken upstairs. I'll question them one at a time, starting with the people down here. And nobody needs to worry if they didn't help kill these men. I'll know the truth. Blood never lies."

He returned to the office and pocketed the handkerchief he'd left on the desk. One of the hired guns brought in a trembling woman. Short and dark, she had prominent bones in her face that gave her a somewhat skeletal look. Her clothes were worn and well-used, but professionally patched.

Al motioned for her to sit. "If you had nothing to do with the killing, you'll walk right back out that door with no problems. Understand?"

She nodded and shook harder.

Al pulled a small leather wallet from his vest pocket. He extracted a pin stuck in some cork. "This won't hurt much." He took her hand and pricked her finger until blood welled up. He caught some on the tip of the pin and cast a truth enchantment. He would know if she lied or told the truth, based on what she believed.

"Did you kill either Luigi Russo or Francesco Bernardi?"

"No," she said, her voice wavering in fear.

Truth.

"Do you know who killed either of those men?"

"No."

Truth.

"Do you know of anyone that can cast blood magic?"

"No."

A lie.

Well, sometimes magic was too literal.

"Do you know of anyone who can cast blood magic other than me?"

"No."

Truth.

"Do you know anyone who wanted either of these men dead?"

"Yes." She looked at the guard.

The man frowned. "I didn't want nobody dead."

"I think she's afraid to talk in front of you," Al said dryly. "Wait outside and don't even think of causing her any trouble later. You would deeply regret it."

The man scowled, but stepped out of the office.

Al leaned against the desk. "Who wanted either of those men dead?"

"Just about all of the woman wanted Luigi dead. He beat us, raped us. If anyone complained or tried to quit, they got hurt real bad. The man was a monster. I'm glad he's dead. If I could have killed him the way Mister Bernardi died, I would have."

Truth.

The words had poured out of her in a flood of venom. She sat back and waited for him to drop the hammer on her for daring to hate one of the dead men.

"I don't know the man and I won't defend him. Scum like that deserves exactly what he got. What you said will stay between us. Please go with my apologies for the terrible experience you've had today and the part I played in it."

With a look of astonishment that she was still alive, the woman fled the room. The guard looked at him with a raised eyebrow.

"She didn't say one word about you and she's innocent. Send someone else in."

He went through the kitchen and laundry staff. No one had a hand in the deaths or anything more than suspicions about who might have wanted the two dead.

By all accounts, Bernardi had been a gentleman. Particularly compared to his successor. The freshly killed man had been well liked. In fact, almost everyone had been hoping that he would come back to head the operation.

With the staff cleared, he started questioning the working girls. Their views were just as stark as the staff. Luigi was a bastard and no one missed him. They respected Francesco. He had continued frequenting the girls after he'd moved on, but they had no complaints about his behavior.

Once Al finished with the girls, he went through the mobsters and guards. Nothing. They might have disliked Luigi, but none of them seemed to have been involved in either of the deaths.

Stumped, Al considered his options. Everyone who had been in the building had been accounted for. None of them had committed the crime.

Well, perhaps if the adults didn't know anything, one of the kids he'd seen around did. He disliked using even benign blood magic on kids. It felt dirty. Yet he didn't have a choice. One of them might have seen something.

Charlie rounded up the kids. There weren't many. Three belonged to members of the laundry staff and two were children of working girls.

Honestly, Al was surprised there were so few, considering their line of work.

He started with the boys and quickly eliminated both of them from consideration. He tagged the two girls who had been down in the basement next. No joy. That left the daughter of the working girl.

Al had the guard bring her in and sat her in the chair. Dark of complexion, she had the look that he associated with Creole. He guessed her age at about ten. She clutched a stuffed bear close to her chest. The staff said that her mother had died a few weeks back and they'd been taking care of her while they tried to find a more suitable home for her.

"What's your name?" he asked gently. "I'm Al."

"Marie."

"Well Marie, I need to ask you some questions about what's happening around here. I'm going to use a pin to draw a little blood from your finger, but you won't feel much pain."

"Why not tell me I won't feel a thing? Isn't that what grown-ups do?"

He considered her questions seriously. "I could've said that, but even though it's a harmless fib, I like to tell the truth where I can."

"Are there times you can't tell the truth?"

Al smiled. "Sure. You don't get into my line of work without needing to keep secrets."

"Is it true that you kill people? With magic?"

He nodded. "It's true. In my defense, I kill people who deserve it. Let me get my needle and we'll get started. If you've done nothing wrong, there won't be any consequences."

"And if I did something wrong? Will you kill me?"

His smile faded. "No. I don't kill women or children."

"You don't need to use your magic. I killed them."

He considered the little girl gravely. "That's an extremely serious thing to say. One that I don't believe to be true. Let's humor me and do the test."

He wiped the pin clean and heated it in the flame of a candle he'd lit after he questioned the first woman. The girl held out her hand with an expression that defied him to do his worst. He pricked her finger and created the link between them.

"Did you kill Luigi Russo?"

"Yes."

Truth.

Al sat back on the desk, shocked. "How did you kill him?"

"With my magic."

Truth.

"You have blood magic? Did your mother have it too?"

The girl nodded. "She could heal cuts and bruises. She taught me to do that when I was little."

Truth.

That was extremely unusual. Most people with the talent didn't manifest until after they reached puberty. This girl was too young.

"How old were you when you used magic the first time?"

"Four."

Unbelievable, but she thought she was telling the truth.

"Did your mother tell you that was how old you were?"

She shook her head. "I remember it was right after my birthday. I was four."

Truth.

Inconceivable. The youngest person to manifest the talent had been eight. And that had happened before the United States rebelled against Britain and become a country of its own. Frankly, he'd never even believed the legend was true.

Blood magic manifested earlier in people who would one day be powerful mages. Al had come into his talent when he was eleven and he was one of the strongest in the Order. If what he was hearing were true, this girl's power would one day dwarf his. Hell, she'd be more powerful than the High Mage.

And he'd sworn to kill her or turn her in to a man would without a moment's remorse.

"Why did you kill Luigi?" he asked after a long pause.

The girl's gaze narrowed with hatred. "He killed Momma."

That would do it. Strong emotion could make up for a lack of formal training.

"What happened?"

"Momma didn't want to live here no more. She cried all the time. Told me that she didn't want to visit with men no more."

While that might piss Luigi off, the story really didn't hold water. Women left brothels like this all the time. She could've run off. Gone to another city. The mob wouldn't have chased her.

"What else did she say? Did anything happen right before she died? Even if you don't understand it, it might mean something to me."

The girl's brow furrowed. "Well, the bad man said he wanted to get to know me better. That's when Momma got really mad. She hit him and he punched her. I ran for help, but no one would come. He hurt her real bad. Then he told someone to beat her up again and she died."

Al's blood ran cold, then hot with rage. He wished he could've killed the bastard himself.

He took a deep breath and forced himself to calm down. His training made that possible, if not easy. "I see. And Mister Bernardi? Did you kill him, too?"

"Yes."

"Why?"

"He left Momma here to die."

Something clicked in his head. "He was your father."

She nodded. "Momma said he used to live here. She told me not to be mad, that she didn't blame him for moving on, but he left her here so the bad man could kill her. So I killed him. He yelled when I cut him and ran. Then he screamed when I made him burn inside."

Not exactly fair, but understandable. Al had killed men for less. So now he had a problem to solve. He'd made a promise, but he also had a duty to protect the raw talent that this youngster had manifested. Two diametrically opposed situations.

Yes, he could lie. He'd never done so about a job, but the Order would forgive his lapse. They would celebrate it. Yet, he hesitated. If he did, he'd never be able to swear his honesty and read as true. His career as an assassin would be over.

"Do you know who Luigi told to beat your Momma?"

"They called him Renaldo."

Al rose to his feet and opened the door. "Go get Renaldo."

The guard frowned. "That's me."

"Get in here."

The thin man came in readily enough and Al closed the door behind him. He couldn't avoid what happened next. He sent a prayer to the God he didn't believe in that he wasn't making a terrible mistake. "This girl killed your bosses."

The man stared at him as if he'd sprouted a second head. "That's crazy!"

"And yet it's true. She had good reason to want them dead, but that doesn't matter, does it?"

"Hell no." The man pulled out his pistol. "I'll take her somewhere and lock her up."

"I have one question, first. Why did you kill her mother?"

The man half-turned and gaped at him. "What?"

"She says you beat her mother to death a few weeks back. I'd like to know why."

"Luigi said to rough her up because she tried to escape. I got a little carried away."

"I'd say killing a woman for trying to escape someone like Luigi qualifies as an overreaction. So, let me run this past you. If you hadn't killed this girl's mother, she probably wouldn't have killed your boss or Frank, would she? If Luigi hadn't wanted something no man should even be considering from her daughter, that woman wouldn't have tried to escape, would she? Did you know what Luigi wanted?"

The man nodded. "Sure. He had a thing for young girls. Sick, but he's in charge."

"I see. Your boss created this situation, but arguably, you caused the deaths of these people."

"That's bull!" He turned toward Al, bringing his gun up.

Ready for his move, Al twisted the gun from the man's grasp and jabbed him with the pin he'd just cleaned. The man jumped back, swearing.

Al smiled without humor. "There's a lesson in this, Marie. I want you to pay close attention. Actions have consequences, even when you think you've done something for the best reasons. And someone always pays a price."

He focused his will into the man's blood and cast the same kind of spell the girl had used to kill the men she'd held responsible for her mother's death. It took every ounce of his skill and power to do so without using a ritual and pre-charged implements. It amazed him that Marie had killed with her will alone.

The man screamed and clawed at his eyes. "No! Please! Mercy!"

"I have no mercy for you. Have some justice instead."

The man spouted blood in every direction and collapsed into a twitching heap. Al wiped his face. Small droplets of blood covered him from head to toe. Marie hadn't escaped the spatter either. It felt fitting.

The door burst open and Charlie ran in with his gun drawn. He took in the situation with a glance. "What the hell happened in here?"

"This man was behind the deaths. I've made him pay for his crimes as I agreed I would."

The mobster gaped. "That mug? No way!"

Al smiled tiredly. "You'd be surprised. People can sometimes tap into raw talent no one expects of them."

"How is that even possible?"

"I can't explain because that touches on the deepest secrets of my Order. The uninitiated may not know of these things, on pain of death. I'll explain everything that I can to your boss, but I have stopped the killings and know everything I need to about why they happened. This matter is done."

The other man holstered his weapon and scratched his head. "I have no idea what that means, but that's between you and the Boss. I need to call him."

"You do that. I'll need a few minutes, then you can have someone start cleaning this room. Again. I'll also need a place to clean up and someone will need to bathe the girl. She's coming with me."

He closed the door behind the puzzled mobster and turned to face Marie. "What I said was true, as far as it went. You will join our Order. The uninitiated are not permitted to know the kind of magic that you've done. You're a danger to yourself and others without training. Your path forward lies with the Order."

It was her turn to look at him as though he was crazy. "People like me don't join no orders. Whatever that is."

Al smiled. "I'm quite aware that your people are discriminated against, however that doesn't matter. The Order takes in everyone with the talent, no matter their sex or color. Under the skin, we truly are brothers and sisters. You will be welcomed with joy and find that they don't care one bit what you look like.

"I'm not saying that everyone is going to be all sunshine and light, but you won't find a better group of people to protect you. They would willingly die before they let an outsider hurt you."

He took a deep breath. "Now for one last bit of unpleasantness. When we promise something, we deliver. I delivered the letter of what my contract demanded, but I have to fulfill the spirt, too." He went to the fireplace and built a fire. He imagined one wasn't needed all that often down here on the southern coast. Certainly not this time of year.

Once it was crackling brightly, Al stood and looked at the girl. "I promised to make the person behind this pay. To make them scream and bleed. I already made you bleed. I'm sorry. I hope one day you can understand and forgive me."

He snatched the stuffed bear from her hands and cast it into the flames.

Marie jumped up, screaming. "No! My Momma gave her to me!"

Al caught the girl up and headed for the door. She beat on him and wailed as though her very world had ended. It crushed his heart, but she needed to learn this lesson in a way she would never forget. Power came with a price. And debts must be paid in full.

Silver Dollar Sam could keep his bonus. He'd earned a treasure far more valuable. The girl might hate him with all her heart, but he'd keep her safe until he could meet with the Order. He hoped she'd understand one day and forgive him, but he'd do right by her no matter the cost. That was his blood debt to her.

Stigmata

by Scott Roche

Willie "Sparkles" Evans looked up at the edifice of the Church of the Immaculate Conception. It had been a number of years, almost half of his twenty six, since he'd set foot in a church. He didn't know what the hell he was doing approaching this one. He did need sanctuary, and he'd heard holy ground was always supposed to be a safe place, even for a drugged-out, hung over hedge wizard like himself. He started across the street without looking both ways, traffic non-existent in the muggy pre-dawn. There were a few lights on inside the house of God, showing off the beautiful stained glass.

He reached into one of the pockets of his faded green Army surplus jacket and pulled out two blue tablets. He popped the pain killer in his mouth and pulled a battered silver flask from the same pocket. The cheap whisky wasn't what he wanted to chase the ibuprofen with, but it was what he had. *Cafe au lait* would come after he knew he was safe. He grimaced and pushed on the door.

"Locked? When did they start locking churches?" A sudden sense he was being watched made him want to be anywhere but outside. He touched the door's lock with his finger. "Open, says me." There was a click and he rushed through the now-unlocked door into the cool air of the nave beyond. He made sure the door was locked behind him before moving on.

The lights overhead were turned almost all the way down. Candles flickered here and there. He grabbed a few brochures from a rack near the door, hoping they would tell him something useful. He scanned them, and they gave a brief history of the building, but that was all. He didn't need the history lesson right now and tucked the brochures into his other jacket pocket, next to what was left of last night's spliff.

He took a moment to look around. The ceiling was crazy high, and the benches were gorgeous things made of wrought iron. He walked past the font of holy water and dipped his fingers in. He flicked the water into his own face, hoping it would wake him up a little. "Hello? Anyone in here?" His words echoed back to him. The place was deserted. "Maybe I can catch a few winks and go to the nearest crowded café." He still wasn't sure why he was being chased or who was chasing him. It could have been nothing more than his own personal demons, but drunk or straight he had never been this paranoid without reason.

If he could just spot who it was, he'd call his sister, the detective. She'd ream him out in good fashion, but then she'd listen and maybe he could crash on her couch for a day or two while she looked into it. Until he could identify them, it wouldn't do any good. She'd chalk it up to his penchant for telling stories and ask him when he was going to get his shit together.

Halfway down the center aisle, he saw the crucifix. They were the creepiest fucking things. Christians complained about Islam being a religion of violence, but they seemed to forget that a man on a massive torture device hung in the middle of theirs. He looked closely at the artifact. He'd always thought Christ was supposed to be naked. This guy was wearing all black. He had the crown of thorns and blood-smeared face Willie always heard about, but the blood looked wet in the candlelight.

When he smelled blood and shit, he realized this particular torture victim was flesh and bone and not a wooden representation. Now he had a reason to call Helen. He just had to find a phone.

The phone in the church office worked and inside of fifteen minutes Willie found himself looking down the barrel of two police-issued handguns. He had no idea what kind they were, but they would kill him just as well. "Fellas. I'm the one that called this in. If you let me reach into my pocket."

"Not a chance." The big black cop waggled his pistol a little. "Jerry, you get whatever it is."

Jerry, a smaller white man, whined a little. "Why is it I always gotta go digging in the junkie's pockets?"

"I'm not a junkie. Needles are bad news."

Jerry holstered his pistol and pulled on a set of black cut-proof gloves. He gingerly patted Willie down first. He found the flask and the spliff. More importantly, he found Helen's card. It was the "Get Out of Jail Free" she gave out to some of her helpers. Willie was always careful to say nothing about their relationship. "Call her. She knows me. She'll clear me."

Jerry called into the station and asked them to page Detective Helen Evans.

"What the actual fuck, Willie? How do you get into this shit?" Helen was gorgeous when she wasn't angry. When she was righteously pissed that beauty sharpened into a weapon that could drive any person to their knees. Her black hair was tied back into a tight ponytail, and she wore a dark gray suit made of light linen to combat the New Orleans heat. Cat eye sunglasses, not needed for at least another hour, were pushed back onto the top of her head.

Her partner, Detective Sparrow, was pissed for entirely different reasons. "Why don't you just throw this joker in the river and be done with him?" A good six inches taller than Willie or Helen, Sparrow should be more imposing. He was skinnier though, and an arrogance in him defused fear. Instead of being afraid, people subjected to his presence just got pissed off. His light colored suit was rumpled, and Willie could smell dried up sex on him.

"It's not like I asked for this. I was just looking for a safe place to crash."

"What were you doing in the CBD?" Helen put her hand dangerously near her service pistol.

It was a fair question. The Bywater or St. Roch was the usual hangout for junkies and losers. "I had…" He knew Helen wasn't going to like this one bit, "…a vision."

"A vision? What the hell does that mean?" Sparrow pulled out his handcuffs. "I should just put these on you right now."

"Surprised your boyfriend isn't still wearing them," Willie snarled. He didn't care that Sparrow was gay. He just hated the man wouldn't admit it.

"You two shut up." Helen's voice was tired. That was almost as bad as angry. "Tell me about this vision, Willie."

He sighed. "It wasn't anything precise." He ignored Sparrow's snort. "I just knew something around here was dangerous. I needed to find out what it was. It's old and carries a shitload of bad juju. I was nearby, communing with the spirits."

"Fucking getting high." Helen filled in the blank.

"Potato, fucking potato. I was communing by getting high. I saw some things. They started to chase me. I wound up here and saw him." Willie pointed his thumb at where Father Macumber, the Jesuit priest, had been hanging from his hands and feet. The killer had even shoved something long and sharp into his side. That explained the smell of feces still hanging in the air.

"We'll call you." Helen started to turn.

"We're not going to haul this waste of space downtown?" Sparrow put his handcuffs away.

Helen whirled on him. "You seriously think this fleabag killed the priest, crucified him, hung him up there by himself, and then called the cops?" She didn't wait for an answer, opting to go talk with the crime scene people.

"It's a valid question."

Sparrow whirled on Willie, ready to backhand him. When Willie flinched, Sparrow smiled and punched him twice in the arm. Then he followed Helen.

Willie walked out of the church and stood, looking in the direction of the rising sun. "Thank you father for blessing us with warmth." He turned to where the moon would have set. "Thank you mother for keeping me safe." He pulled out his flask and poured a drop out onto the sidewalk. It was all he had. He hoped the luck and blessing would help this day turn out better than the last.

He started to walk towards the smell of frying food, when he realized something. When he did the blessing, he should have felt something. He was standing on holy ground after all. That usually gave spells a little extra oomph if it was a boon. The killing had desecrated the church. It wasn't just the method or who had been killed. The goodness that had soaked into New Orleans's soil over the life of this building was dried up. The thousands of prayers and all of the little graces, not to mention the faith exhibited here, should have kept this place charged up for a block in every direction.

He pulled out the brochure and looked at it. Why would someone want to desecrate this particular church out of all of the hundreds in the city? He had some digging to do. The best place to do that was his favorite cafe. It was a hell of a walk and two bus transfers, but it would be worth it.

Soul Brews was a funky little place just off Esplanade Avenue near City Park. It could seat fifteen people and had a space up front for a two piece band or someone reading bad poetry. Willie stepped up to the counter and smiled at the gorgeous blond wiping it down.

Brenda, his favorite barista in New Orleans, smiled back at him. "Hey, Sparkles. The usual?"

That was part of the reason he loved her. When she looked at him, she saw a regular, not a bum. "Yup." While he waited for his large pour over, he looked around. "Dead today, huh?"

Brenda didn't look up from weighing out the grounds. "Yeah. Trying to figure out why. We're usually packed right about now."

That was good. He wanted to set up shop here, but he hated to do that when they were crowded, since he was going to nurse the coffee for at least an hour.

A man walked up to the counter, a high school jock gone to seed if Willie was any judge. He still had the build, but some of his muscles had turned to jelly. He wore an expensive suit and cheap cologne. "Large latté, half-caff. And hurry up."

Brenda nodded. "Be right with you, sir."

Half-caff looked over at Willie. "Shouldn't you be at the shelter?" He chuckled to himself.

Willie just smiled.

Half-caff watched Brenda as she turned to tamp the espresso. His eyes drifted downwards.

Willie had to admit that Brenda had a fine ass, but the band on Half-caff's finger said he should probably keep his eyes to himself. Willie coughed into his hand and pointed his pinky at the heavy set dude.

"Fuck." The man shook his left hand like he'd just grabbed a hot pan. The ring came off of his finger and bounced off of the tile floor, stopping when it was under the nearest trash bin. He scrabbled after it.

Willie enjoyed watching his gyrations.

"Sparkles." Brenda called. "Here's your pour over."

Willie took the coffee and smiled a thanks. She'd never know what just went down. Wouldn't believe it if she did. But Willie treasured the thought that she might be grateful all the same. He walked over to the nearest booth and took out his iPod. He used it to connect to the shop's wifi and opened the browser. There were a few sites he could check regularly that acted as reputable conduits for information on New Orleans' supernatural activity. He knew which ones to believe and which ones not to. It helped that he wrote for a few of the better ones when he had something to say.

He had just gotten the first site up when he felt a presence to his left.

Half-caff stood there, looking down. "Don't you think you should move along, Sparkles?"

Willie turned slightly in his chair. "I'm a paying customer, sir. I've a right to be here. Just as much as you."

"That's the problem with this city. Too many low life druggies think they're entitled to the same things real people have."

"Hey, get out of here." Brenda's voice cut through the funky jazz coming from the speakers.

"See? She agrees with me."

"No, I meant you, assclown. Willie is a regular customer. He brings in business. You come in here and act like you own the joint. Your four dollars only buys you the best latte in New Orleans. It doesn't buy my respect. Go on."

The man looked a little cowed and began to redden. "I'm going to tell your manager about this. Where is he?"

"The owner will be here tonight after six. If you want to stop by, I'll tell her to keep an eye out for you. In the meantime." She made a shooing motion.

Half-caff looked like he was going to have an apoplexy on the spot. He snorted and stomped outside.

"Thanks for that, Brenda. But I don't want you to get in any trouble."

She smiled. "Don't worry about that. We close at six on Mondays. Dumb shit won't have anyone to report me to. Besides, she's good at smelling bullshit, and that guy reeked of it. Drink your coffee, hang out, and let me know if you need anything."

He nodded his thanks and watched her walk away. He wished, not for the first time, that he had the gumption to ask her out. He turned back to his web browsing. An hour of slurping coffee and combing the net led him to understand that the church in question had a history of supernatural events. There were a series of murders in the late 1920s attributed to vampires. Some of those said vampires might be buried underneath it.

He sent off a few emails to people who would know more and finished his coffee. He got up to leave.

"Hey, Sparkles." Brenda called to him. "Come here."

Willie dropped his cup into the trash and walked over. "Yes, ma'am."

She handed him a cup of coffee and a brown paper bag. "Got you some bagels and a refill."

He took them. "I... I can't pay for this."

"Refills are free, and we donate all of our bagels to the shelter once they go past a certain point. Those aren't due for another few hours, but..." She gestured around the still empty shop.

"Thanks." He smiled. "These will go down nicely." He paused, wanting to say more.

"Need anything else, Sparkles?"

"Would you like to go out some time? I mean to a movie or something?" She looked a little uncertain.

"Never mind. Thanks again for the bagels." He turned and started to walk away.

"Hey Sparkles, I'd like that. Swing by here on Wednesday. I get off at three."

He turned around and walked backwards, pleased to see her grin. "Wednesday. Three o'clock. I'll be here." He turned just before he got to the door. The cool air of the cafe gave way to the humid blast of mid-morning heat. When he saw Half-caff standing across the street looking at him, all the good feelings evaporated.

Usually a runner, Willie decided if this guy wanted to have a go, then Half-caff would just chase him down. He looked both ways and crossed the street.

Half-caff nodded at him. "Hey, homeless Joe. I saw you had a little moment with your girl in there. She even gave you breakfast. How sweet."

"Do we have a problem?"

The big man cocked his head as though listening to something far off. "I don't think so. I just need you to come with me. Now. If you don't, we might."

Willie cradled the bag of bagels in the crook of his right arm and fished one out with his left hand. It was chocolate chip, made with Mexican chocolate and cinnamon. He was beginning to think Brenda knew him better than he hoped. He ripped a chunk out of it with his teeth and chewed thoughtfully. While he did, he really looked at Half-caff. Most often when he used his third eye, he closed his brown ones, but he didn't think it would pay to shut his eyes around this mook. Using his physical and mystical senses at the same time was disconcerting. What was more disconcerting was the fact that Half-caff wasn't human or wasn't alive or both.

Willie swallowed the bagel and took a slurp of the coffee. "I don't think we have a problem. As long as you don't intend to cut my head off and suck out all of my blood through the stump."

Half-caff didn't so much as blink at the odd and graphic caveat. "I don't intend to, but you never know what might happen." He smiled broadly. "Let's take a walk. My van is right around the corner." He put a hand on the back of Willie's neck and exerted a small amount of pressure. It was enough to let Willie know that if this thing exerted itself, his neck would snap like a pretzel.

"You drive a creepy van? How not surprising." Willie walked ahead of Half-caff, feeling like a petulant child who'd been collared by his rage-fueled father. There was no way he was getting in any kind of vehicle with this guy, but the few little spells Willie knew were meant more to ease life and annoy strangers than to poleaxe supernatural brutes. They'd gone ten steps when he noticed the manhole cover just ahead. This would take some real effort, but he felt like he could use a variation on his lock pick spell to his advantage. It was no more than focused telekinesis, after all.

Willie envisioned a hand on the underside of the metal disk. When he crossed it, he envisioned the hand pushing with all of its strength on one edge.

Half-caff stepped onto the edge of the metal disk and his foot went through. The manhole cover flipped up and Half-caff's following foot also went into the hole. As a result, the metal edge caught the big man right at the junction of his legs.

Willie didn't know if the dead had working gonads, but apparently all of the right pain sensors were there. As soon as the huge mitt was off the back of his neck, Willie broke into a full-on run. Random lefts and rights, and one street crossing complete with honks and hurled epithets, took him to what he hoped was a safe distance from his would-be kidnapper. He realized that somewhere during the run he'd lost his coffee and the bag of bagels. The Mexican chocolate pastry was still firmly held in his left hand though. He took another bite and considered his next move. Who would want him in their clutches?

He really wanted to do nothing more than go to his crappy little apartment and crawl into bed. By now he'd been awake for something approaching twenty-four hours. His energy level, even with the marvelous coffee in his belly and the shot of adrenaline thanks to Half-caff, was at an all-time low. It wasn't meant to be though, not yet. The man who would have the info he needed was across town. It took a long time to get there by city bus. The bus ride did allow for a brief power nap. By the time he got to Hunter's Books on Magazine Street, the boost had worn off.

The jingle of the bell announced his presence in the occult book store. Like most of its competition, the air of this store was permeated with incense and old paper. Unlike those other stores, Hunter had the real deal. Sure, there were cheap crystals, books on how to tune your chi, and ones that guaranteed to help you find your Celtic Zodiac sign. The man had to do something to keep his doors open. If you knew where to look, or if he knew you, all manner of real mystical treasures could be found. Thankfully, Hunter knew Willie.

Willie hadn't made it five steps in before the big man came out from behind a beaded curtain at the back. "Willie, how are you?" Hunter's broad face was split by a wide grin and his light brown, thick hair was tied back in a ponytail.

"I feel like the ass end of a long bender. Oddly enough, it isn't because I'm at the ass end of a long bender."

Hunter held up a finger and turned around. In a minute, he came back out with a steaming mug. "This will fix you right up." He pushed the mug into Willie's hands.

"This isn't coffee."

Hunter shook his head. "Hell no. Coffee will pick you up and slap you back down. This is a tea blend we're going to sell in the shop. It has all kinds of good, healthy things in it. I don't know what all, but it tastes good and should give you a boost and help you feel better."

Willie took a tentative sip. It did taste good. A little sweetness from honey, some mint, and something earthy. The warmth also helped. He curled his toes and took a longer drink. He could feel the energy from it working its way into his body. "This is damn good."

Hunter clapped him on the shoulder. "Only the best for a good customer and a friend. What brings you by?"

"Better have a seat. This could take a bit, and I might need you to look up some things for me."

Unlike a lot of folks in the magical community, Hunter was something of a techno-wizard. He'd digitized a lot of the more authentic records of New Orleans magical history. In addition to that, he also had a number of spells, rituals, and recipes in his system that were easier to cross check. They weren't anywhere online. He didn't want just anybody to have access. The right people could peruse them for a fee in the shop, or he would answer simple questions for free.

Hunter pulled out his laptop and fired it up. He pulled a wand from a pen holder on his desk, passed it over the keyboard, and muttered a few phrases under his breath. It beeped at him, and he looked at Willie. "What are we talking about?"

"There was a murder at a church early this morning. The priest at the Church of the Immaculate Conception was killed and crucified. Hopefully in that order. I could tell it was part of a ritual to desecrate the church and the land around it."

Hunter nodded and typed as Willie talked.

"I read about some murders in the area back in the twenties and read rumors about vampires being buried on church grounds."

Hunter nodded again. "Drink the rest of your tea. I'll see what I can pull up in the meantime."

Willie went back to sipping the warm tea and let it work on his body. The aches from being up long hours on his feet or on the run began to ease. He wanted to lay down on the floor right now and sleep. He wasn't tired anymore, but his soul was weary from what he'd seen. "Oh and there was some big mook that I ran into at Soul Brews. He tried to take me somewhere, against my will. He was either dead or wasn't human."

"That fits what I'm seeing here." Hunter pointed to the laptop. "There was a vampire who also happened to be a warlock running around New Orleans in the late 1800s. His name was Anton Krev. He came over here from what would have been Bohemia in those days. That's the Czech Republic now. He may be old enough to have been buddies with Vlad Tepes."

Willie almost dropped the mug.

"Yeah. That's the rumor anyway. What I know for sure is that he and four of his acolytes were put down by the Knights of Columbus about the time that Immaculate Conception was being built. They figured being put under a church would be permanent. According to the unofficial official record, one of his followers was able to free them in the twenties. They killed over a hundred people over the course of two years. Turned more than a dozen into blood suckers. They were defeated again and this time the powers that be ground them into dust, mixed them with concrete, and put them back under the church."

"That should do the trick, shouldn't it? I mean general wisdom is once you dust a vampire they stay dust." Willie counted his lucky stars he'd never run into a vampire in person that he knew of. There was this one chick he met at a rave, but she could have just been really into the Goth scene.

Hunter nodded. "Usually, yeah. Krev was no ordinary bloodsucker, though. He was also a heavy hitter in the magic arena. There are rituals that could bring him back, under the right circumstances. Step one would almost certainly be desecration of the area."

"Fuck me. So we need to keep that from happening."

"We?" Hunter raised an eyebrow.

"Yeah, we." Willie put down the mug. "You'll help me, right?"

Hunter closed the lid on his laptop. "I'm a businessman, son. You able to pay me to incur this risk?"

Willie shook his head.

"I'll give you as much information as I reasonably can for free. But there's no way I'm going to get mixed up in this. Not even out of the goodness of my heart."

"What if they manage to raise him?"

"That's a big what if. The magic they would have to do to make that happen would have been easier fifty years ago. You know as well as I that magic is on the decline. You can barely manage a halfway decent light spell. I don't know three people in this country who could pull off half of what would be needed to do something like this. I'm one of them, and I'm not involved."

Willie stepped up to the counter. "Then tell me who the other ones are." He smacked the glass with his open hand. "Do something to help me."

Hunter scratched his chin. "You could go talk to some of the voodoo people around here. They might point you in the right direction. You could consecrate the grounds. You could call the police and tell them that they'll need to watch out for vampires."

"If I wanted to be mocked, I'd just go to Helen."

"Sorry, Willie. What I'm trying to tell you is, don't sweat it. Someone may think they can get away with this. Here's what's gonna happen. Your sister is going to catch these fuckers. They can't very well do whatever it is they're planning if they're in Orleans Parish Prison. And if what I do know is any indication, they would need to act soon. They wouldn't kill this priest and wait a week. Leave this to people whose job it is."

Willie wanted to scream. So he did. "There is no one whose job this is. The people who put these creatures in the ground aren't around anymore. We need to do this. I need to do this."

"Why? To prove you're more than just a dabbler? You've got talent. There's something about you that tells me if you really applied yourself you might be able to do great things. But you haven't and there's not enough time to make up for what you've lost. You get mixed up in this and, even if the people stand no chance of completing this ritual, they have a pretty good shot at killing you. They got damn close this morning."

Willie nodded. "They did. They got close. I'm not kidding myself about that. I'm probably kidding myself about being able to stop this, but my sister won't believe me if I tell her some ancient Czech psycho wizard vampire is going to come back to life along with his cronies and start killing people. Or barring that, that some group is trying to make that happen."

Hunter rubbed his temples. "Lie to her."

Willie opened his mouth to argue with whatever point he thought Hunter was going to make. His mouth clacked closed.

"If you think this is going to happen and you think that your sister has to be the one to help you, then you have to lie to her. Tell her whatever you need to in order to get her there. Then the two of you can take them down."

Willie held up a finger. "Yeah. Maybe I can do that. Question is, where do I go to stop them? I'm not her. I'm no detective."

Hunter shook his head. "No, you're not. You are a halfway decent wizard. What did you see when you looked at this guy? What clued you in that he wasn't human?"

Willie closed his eyes and thought. "There was no life energy in him. He wasn't a construct. The colors would be different. He'd been human once. But he wasn't a vampire either. The sunlight would have weakened him. He was a ghoul."

"That makes sense. He's in thrall to some vampire, somewhere. That would give him the strength you described and the different aura." Hunter opened his laptop. "There's no social media gathering spot for the undead, and they don't have a directory, but any vampire willing to bring an old one back to life has to be young and stupid. That narrows things down a little." He tapped at the keys.

Willie nodded along. Older vampires tended to be anti-social when it came to their own kind. The four acolytes the history spoke of would have been ghouls or vampires subjugated by his will. An old one would be too smart to risk bringing someone that powerful back.

"Some of the local hunters point to vampire activity at New Orleans Country Club. You could go poke around there and see what you find."

Willie nodded. "If I'm going to do that, having a car sure would help."

Hunter reached under the counter and came up with some keys. "Here." He tossed the ring to Willie. "You can take Queenie." He pointed towards the back of the shop. "I've also got some holy water and stakes in there."

Willie chuckled. "Why on Earth would you have those things ready?"

"They both have other uses. And in this city, it pays to be prepared."

Willie went to the back of the shop and grabbed a plastic flask filled with a few ounces of clear liquid. It was labelled as being blessed by Friar Spence. He put it in his breast pocket. The stakes looked like little more than wooden tent pegs. He grabbed a couple and tucked them through his belt. As he passed by the counter, he nodded at Willie. "Put it on my tab."

Hunter shook his head. "This one's on the house. Besides, you're never going to pay me off anyway."

"Queenie" was a VW Thing that Hunter had restored to its original appearance. Red paint made what was already an ugly vehicle stand out all the more. He'd have a tough time tailing anyone, but that wasn't the plan. Speaking of plans, his idea of a plan didn't included hunting around a country club at the edge of the parish for hours or days trying to find any vampires who called it home. He had a more direct approach in mind.

He pulled out into traffic and headed back to Soul Brews. He didn't think he'd run into Half-caff, though if he did that could make it easier. He parked across the street and ran into the shop.

Brenda smiled at him. "It's not Wednesday yet."

Willie returned the smile. "I'm looking forward to it when it gets here. But I had a question for you. You know that guy that was hassling us earlier?"

She nodded. "I run into my share of assholes here, but he's one that would stand out. Why?"

Willie raised an eyebrow and smiled. "Well, it appears he has it in for me. I don't know why and I want to find out. How did he pay?"

Brenda poked at her register. "He paid with his card. Ordinarily I wouldn't share this information with anyone, but I don't like people picking on my friends. His name is Brandon Jenkins. Looks like he paid with a corporate Visa. He works for Biggs Construction."

"I could kiss you."

She winked at him. "That will have to wait for Wednesday."

"Now I just need to use your phone."

She reached under the counter and produced her cell phone.

He took it and their hands brushed. "It'll just be a minute." He walked over to the corner and called Helen.

"Detective Evans." There was a note of question in her voice.

"This is Willie."

"Whose phone are you calling from?"

"A friend's. Look I don't have much time. I was accosted and almost kidnapped by a guy this morning. I think it's related to the killing. I saw this guy outside the church last night. Didn't think anything of it until he collared me. He must have followed me. His name is Brandon Jenkins, and he works for Biggs Construction. I'm positive he's involved."

There was a pause. "This had better not be one of your lies. I can tell when you lie, always have been able to."

"I swear this guy is dirty as they come." He wanted to add that the man wasn't exactly a man, but that would sink the whole deal. "He said something about taking me somewhere to deal with me. We find him and it will tie this whole thing up in a bow for you."

"We? There is no we."

"Helen, look. I need to be in on this one. I can identify him for you. Then you can pick him up."

The pause this time was longer. "Alright. I'll come get you."

"I'll be outside of Soul Brews." He gave her the address.

"I'll be there in ten minutes." She hung up.

He took the phone back to Brenda. "Thanks."

She took it and put it back under the counter. "What was all that about?"

He didn't see any reason to get this relationship off with a lie, but he couldn't tell the whole truth. "I work with the police sometimes. Had to call a detective I know. The guy we saw this morning is a person of interest in a case they're working on. I knew I recognized him, but didn't put it together until a half hour ago."

There was a new look in her eyes. He'd just gone up a peg or two in her estimation. "Alright then. Well you be careful out there, Sparkles. I don't want you to get hurt and miss our date."

"Not gonna happen. Can I get a cup to go?"

Five minutes later he was standing outside, waiting for Helen. When she pulled up in her nondescript police issue sedan, he was pleased to see that her partner was absent. He climbed in the passenger's seat. "Where's Sparrow?"

"When I told him I was coming to get you to ask you a few questions, he remembered that he had some legwork of his own to do." She put the car in drive. "I made some calls on the way over. This guy works for Biggs in a security role. Why would someone like that kill a priest?"

Willie shrugged. "I have theories, none of which you'll like."

She looked over at him. "You may as well tell me. If it will help us get this case wrapped up quickly, then I'm open to hearing almost anything."

"This guy moonlights as muscle for a group who's trying to find something on or under the church grounds. I did some digging online, and it looks like there's some kind of treasure rumored to be buried in the church's foundation. I figure the priest knew something, and they were trying to get the information from him. When they did, they killed him like that to throw off any scent. Make it look like some crazy serial killer did it and no one would think to finger them for it."

Helen shook her head. "That sounds like another one of your funky dreams. But it's more than I had to go on earlier. The priest is clean. Nothing points to this being personal. And if it was, who kills someone like that? We'll find this guy and ask him a few questions. Then we'll go from there."

Willie nodded. This was why he'd gotten his sister to come along. She had the skills he needed. "How do we find him?"

"I looked up some of his pertinent details in our database. He's clean as far as major criminal charges go, but he did have a couple of parking tickets and one charge of simple assault. The assault was a couple of months ago. I have his address. I figure we stop by and see what happens." She gunned the engine, zipping in and out of traffic.

"When we find him, what then?"

"You stay in the car. I go and talk to him. Lean on him a little. I can tell him that we have someone who's filed a charge against him, and we're investigating it."

He didn't want to stay in the car, but there were things he could do from a distance if he needed to. It didn't take long for them to get to his address.

Interestingly enough, he lived in the last section of Orleans Parish before it became Metairie, just on the other side of the cemeteries and only a few blocks from the country club. Willie filed that away for later. A dark blue panel van was parked in his driveway. There were no markings on it, so it wasn't a construction company van.

Helen parked across the street. "You wait here. I fucking mean it." She poked him in the chest.

"Pinky swear." He waited for her to turn her back, and then he fluttered his hands, linked at the thumbs, imitating a bird in flight. He blew across his thumb knuckles making a low whistle.

Helen closed the door, but a piece of Willie's soul traveled with her. She walked cautiously up the drive, her right hand on the butt of her pistol. No sounds came from inside the house. She knocked on the door and waited. No one answered.

Willie sent his mana bird through the door and could immediately sense a problem. Death permeated the place. He didn't see anyone, but the further his invisible drone got, the harder it was to see anything. Bracing himself, he got out of the car and walked towards Helen. That allowed his spy to get further in. When he saw the bodies, he took in a sharp breath.

Helen spun on her heel at the noise. "What the fuck? I told you to stay in the car." Then she saw the look on his face. "What's wrong?"

"There are dead people in there. Lots of them."

She shook her head, but somewhere, somehow she believed him. She turned and pounded on the door. "NOPD. Open the door." She tried the knob, but it was locked. "Would I realistically be able to see any of the bodies from a window?" She asked over her shoulder.

Willie nodded. "There are a few you might could see."

Her nostrils flared. "You smell that? They've been dead for a while." She lifted a foot and after three solid kicks the door banged open. "NOPD." She shouted into the empty house. A thorough sweep indicated that no one alive remained inside. The bodies were mostly children. It was hard to place their ages as decomposition had set in. Willie ran back outside, taking deep breaths of clean air and trying not to puke. He knew Helen was still inside calling for backup and taking stock.

When the van's engine roared to life, Willie startled. He hadn't thought to check and see if Half-caff was inside.

Rather than backing up, the van lurched forward headed towards Willie.

He leapt to one side and landed on the front yard's lush grass. Not trained in any formal martial art, he'd been thrown around a lot and knew how to take a fall well. He came back up to his feet quickly. He made a slashing motion at the van's rear and the stems on both tires fell to the ground. They slowly began to flatten.

"Son of a bitch." Half-caff snarled through the now open window. He pointed a large revolver at Willie.

When the sound of the shot came, it wasn't from the van. Helen's service pistol barked three times. Two of the shots found their targets in the man's forearm. The other gouged a hole in the van's front quarter panel.

Any normal man might have at the very least screamed in pain. Half-caff grunted. He dropped the pistol and shouldered the door open. There would be no escaping with the air leaving his tires. Blood trickled down his arm, the healing powers and resistance to pain given to ghouls by their masters ensuring he wasn't out of the fight.

"NOPD. Get on your knees and put your hands on your head." Helen now aimed for his chest. Her hands were rock steady.

With a roar, Half-caff lunged at Helen. He closed the distance with speed that shocked even Willie. Helen got a shot off, but he batted her gun aside and punched her square in the face.

There was a loud crunch and she left her feet and landed half in and half out of the still-open front door.

Willie clenched his fists. He wanted to say something eloquent about how nobody could get away with hurting his sister. Instead he roared and thought about the wail of a bean sidhe.

Half-caff clapped his hands to his ears. Blood trickled from between his fingers and leaked from his eyes. He fell to his knees like he'd been poleaxed.

Willie grabbed the plastic container of holy water. He had no idea if it would affect a ghoul in the same way it would his master. He thumbed off the lid with a motion practiced on a hundred bottles of hooch.

"In the name of the God whose church your masters' defaced," he flicked his wrist and a stream of water spattered on Half-caff. The man screamed in pain. Willie took another step forward. "The son whose death you mocked." Another stream of water and the sound of hissing. "And the Holy Spirit who gives men wisdom." He now stood in front of Half-caff and upended the bottle. What was no more than water from a tap ate at the ghoul's flesh like the most caustic of acids. "I send you to the hell you deserve." He pulled the stake from his belt and jammed it into the man's throat.

Ghoul or not, eighteen inches of sharpened oak to the trachea proved fatal. Half-caff fell to one side, clutching at the stake and gurgling.

Panting, Willie dropped the plastic container and stumbled back from the spreading pool of blood. "This is gonna be a tricky one to explain." He looked towards his sister. She still lay in the doorway. He moved to make sure she was still breathing. Satisfied that the powerful punch hadn't killed her outright, he thought about what he could say when she woke up.

He slid his hand down the outside of her leg and pulled out the knife she wore strapped to her calf. The six inch blade was a mean looking piece of work, black on every surface except for its keen edge. He walked over to the body and yanked the bloody stake free. Even in death, the wound wanted to close. He jammed the knife into the hole and worked it around. A small part of him hoped that the creature could still feel it.

That done, he reached into his pocket and pulled out a blank business card. With a jittery hand, he wrote today's date, 9:15p.m., and the address of the church. He tucked the card into Half-caff's pocket. Sirens wailed in the distance. Sticking around would make the whole thing more than just a little awkward for them both. He trusted that his sibling would be able to work it all out.

Before he had gone two steps, he heard her groan. She was sitting up.

He looked back at her with a raised eyebrow.

Both of her eyes were already swelling shut and would leave her looking like a raccoon for weeks. Those eyes were still sharp though. "I'll take care of this." She stumbled to her feet and over to the body. "You get the hell out of here." She put her hand on the knife's hilt, but didn't pull it free.

Willie nodded. His being attached would only bring suspicion on the case and he'd wind up hurting Helen. He jogged across the street and made his way quickly out of the immediate vicinity.

Willie walked into the Church of the Immaculate Conception. They'd cleaned up a bit since last time he was here. Had it only been two days? He could smell bleach, but in spite of that he thought he could almost make out the tang of blood and feces. Before he'd set foot into the building proper, he made sure that the grounds had been sanctified. According to Helen, the police had a proper stake out the night they'd found the bodies. They caught half a dozen people in the sweep. He felt pretty sure they were normal humans. The buzz on the internet was that they'd nipped it in the bud. The right elements wouldn't be in place for another decade at least.

He dipped his fingers in the font and crossed himself. He thought he had it right, having researched it thoroughly by screening Nuns on the Run.

"Can I help you, son?"

Willie nearly jumped out of his skin. He turned and saw someone who looked a bit like Sean Connery from the end of Robin Hood. He wore a long black robe and a white collar peaked out from under a short silver beard. "Just came in to get out of the rain. I'm meeting a friend in a little bit..."

"You're the one who found Father Macumber's body, aren't you?" The man's bushy eyebrow raised like it had been pulled by a very long hair.

"I can't very well lie to a priest." Willie smiled.

"You'd be surprised." The priest smiled back, though there was a sadness in it. "Thank you for helping. I know what you prevented from happening. I can assure you we've taken precautions so that it won't come that close again."

Willie nodded. "That's good." He wasn't sure what else to say, so he looked at the space where the crucifix had been.

"If you ever decide to take a more active role in policing the evils that roam the city..."

Willie held up a hand. "I'm not an action hero. I help in little ways, but I leave the running and gunning to the people who are cut out for it."

"You and your sister have done a lot for this city."

Willie's mouth hung open a little. "Sister?"

The priest held up a hand. "If a priest can't keep a secret, who can? I was involved in your adoption. You're both far more special than you know. If you ever need anything, let me know." He held out a hand.

Willie shook it. "Thanks..."

"Father Hite. And you're welcome. Have a good night."

Willie nodded again and walked out into the soggy night. He didn't want to keep Brenda waiting.

All The Pretty Little Horses

by Michael Ashleigh Finn

It was always about the music.

The first time I'd heard New Orleans's special blend of jazz, I had been sent to the city by Winesap to look into the man behind a string of murders in 1919, in which the music played a pivotal role. Ever since, I'd made sure that if I came anywhere near the city in my travels, I'd swing by to get an earful before going on my way. There's a soul to the sliding bend and weave of the notes that's just mesmerizing.

On one such visit, Baba Ghede found me.

I was tasting the local spiced rum and enjoying a slow rendition of an old southern lullaby being crooned out by a woman, accompanied by bass and sax.

Hush-a-bye, don't you cry,
Go to sleepy little baby

A slender man slid onto the seat next to me, skin dark as pitch with a cocky demeanor and a grin nearly splitting his face in two. "Why, as I live and breathe, is that a Wormwood I see before me? What Christian name are you using these days?"

I looked sideways at the man. "Josiah, same as the last time, Baba." His family and I go back a ways. "You're looking in good spirits."

He spread his arms wide, barely missing someone juggling drinks away from the bar. "Have I no reason to be?"

I took a sip. "In my experience, meetings with you and yours are seldom accidental."

He cocked his head and peered at me, some of the joyous demeanor dissipating. "I remember you being more fun."

He wanted something and was trying on the charm of a salesman. It didn't suit him. I took another sip. "What can I do for you, Babaco?"

His hands made placating gestures. "Alright, alright. We do need your help. But not here, we need to discuss this in private."

"I like this seat. Spill."

He leaned forward and hissed in my ear. "The Loa are missing."

I slipped off my stool and followed him into a back room.

"It's been happening quickly, over the past month," Babaco continued, once we were away from potential eavesdroppers. "Their *chevals* started noting that they weren't appearing at all, to anyone."

"The...what?" I knew some of the lingo, such as the term Bokor meaning a male wizard gone bad. This word was new to me.

"*Cheval*. Those they ride. The horses."

Ah, horses...those I knew. Voudon horses weren't equine; they were humans who willingly let themselves be possessed by the Loa. It's not like involuntary demonic possession, more of a matter of lending their bodies to the Loa to ride about for a brief while. Pass messages. Dance about a bit. Let loose on the mortal plane.

"So, their followers noticed they left. Maybe they all went on vacation? Buggered off back to Haiti or Africa or wherever?" I'd done them a few favors over the years, and I figured we were probably pretty even at this point...but it's always good when the local embodiments of Death owed you instead of the other way round.

"Ah, *mon frere*, me and my brothers are also Loa, did you forget? We'd know of such a, how you say, vacation. No, they have just fallen away. No one knows where. And now even my family seems affected. Nibo has gone missing. Kriminel and Papa know of my longstanding association with you, and asked me to approach when they heard you were here. Find our brother." He clapped me on the shoulder. "In doing so, you may find the others."

I considered the rewards inherent in saving the majority of a pantheon of gods. Alright, they were not really gods...more this religion's versions of angels, reporting to the Big Bon Dye of Mysterie Beyond Human

Understanding. But if you've ever met an angel of any stripe, you'd know that a host of them is nothing to sneeze at.

Then I considered the reprisals of whatever force was nasty enough...and crazy enough...to mess with the Loa en masse.

Hell. I'd had my time in the sun, if it came to that. No risk, no reward.

I finally answered, "Do you have anything of Nibo's I can borrow?"

The Ghede are unusual for the Loa; they can manifest without possession, although it drains them somewhat. Still, they get to skip having to wait for someone to ride. Purely a guess on my part, but I suspect they manage it because, unlike most of the other Loa, they were once human beings themselves.

Nibo was the guardian of those who died in places not known to their loved ones. Baba and I were hoping that if we found him, he might be able to find the other missing ones. It was a longshot...the others weren't dead and were always Loa, but maybe that skill set would translate. Nothing to lose by finding him first.

Locating him wouldn't be overly difficult, given Baba had provided me with a shovel from Nibo's collection. Yes, the guy collected shovels. He's a gravedigger. Work-related hobby, I guess. I had to shoo Baba away so I could work.

"Why can't I stay and watch, Jo? Maybe learn a few things myself."

"What I'm about to do isn't in your bailiwick. And I don't need the distraction. Go. I'll call you when I find him."

While all of that was true, the fact of the matter was Baba was acting a mite peculiar. I couldn't quite place it, but something was off. He was never the best liar, and if he was holding something back, I'd rather not have him around. A lack of difficulty in this task did not equate to "perfectly safe" and I'd rather not have him as a distraction.

So I got into my dusty white Edsel and drove to my hotel, got to my room, sat on the bed, and held the shovel.

People expect a practitioner to have all the trappings...the runes on the walls, the magic circle, perhaps a familiar. Most needed things like that to focus and direct the energies. My own skills didn't require that sort of gimmicky *lagniappe* for something as simple as this.

I drew in a deep breath and concentrated on the shovel. Eyes closed, I could still see the old dirt on the edge of the spade, compacted so hard it was practically a part of the metal. That could be distracting, as dirt carries so many connections, so I undid the bonds and it sloughed off, falling to the carpet. I focused on where it had been touched and felt for my own residue. Discounted that. Felt for where Baba had touched and got...nothing. I frowned, trying to remember if he had been wearing gloves. He hadn't been.

Curiouser and curiouser.

I searched for others who may have left a trace of themselves behind and...the nausea nearly overwhelmed me. Tossing my cookies on the one link to Nibo would seriously cramp my style, so I managed to choke it down, regain focus, and tried to analyze it. It was...oily. That's not quite the right word, but English doesn't have terms for this sort of thing. It was slimy and dark in my mind. It smelled wrong, so to speak. And it was actively trying to slither away from my attentions.

I only knew of a few types of entities with the nasty qualities who could pull off that particular trick. It didn't tell me who I was dealing with, but it did give me a direction of how to ward against the culprit.

I set aside the task of finding Nibo for now and concentrated on isolating this bugger. If I put that off, I might not find this trace of him again.

It felt masculine. Don't ask me how I could tell. That ruled out a few more choices for possible glyphs.

After more gag-inducing attempts, I managed to isolate the foul residue and move it down to the metal end of the shovel. Sadly, as I unbound the molecules, this scored the wood where it was removed, but that couldn't be helped. I try to keep myself from using those particular abilities, so I don't have the fine control I once did. Using them can attract unwanted attention from powers I'd rather not have looking at me. Especially since most of the people who knew of my old line work believed I was retired.

I set about carving sets of particular glyphs into several bullets from my sidearm. The warding glyphs would then be filled with essence of ick to help lock in the spells.

I was just transferring the last of the ick from the shovel to the carved glyphs when a knock came at the door.

I grabbed my backup from my ankle holster and threw a sheet over the shovel and bullets. That would be difficult to explain to almost anyone if left out in the open.

"Yes?" I called.

"Room service."

Really? Seriously?

I palmed the pistol as called "Come in!" There was the noise of a key in the lock, which meant this wasn't just a casual con to get into the room. Then a busboy entered with a cart, a Creole who may have still been in his teens. As he started to roll the cart into the room, I squinted behind him. "Close the door, please. I'm agoraphobic." Hey, it was a spur of the moment excuse.

He looked momentarily confused, but did as I asked. Unfortunately, when he turned back around and saw my gun pointed at him, he merely looked amused. Not a good sign.

"Josiah. It's me."

"That's helpful. Most people are themselves."

"Not in this case."

I squinted. Still didn't recognize him. Wait....

"*Cheval*. Name the rider."

"It's Nibo." Ok, that was unexpected. Still, I had no way of verifying that unless I invoked the Rule of Names.

"Officially. Name yourself officially."

He sighed, and said "I am Ghede Nibo."

I lowered the gun. The thing would only harm the poor guy he was riding anyways. And why the hell was he riding someone? He didn't have to do that. Ghede can just appear pretty much anywhere they want. In their own body.

"Why didn't you just show up in my room?"

"Respect."

"Ah. Why the sneak?"

"Wariness."

"Ah." He wanted to show up incognito, in case I wasn't alone.

We stared at each other a while.

"How did you know I was here?" I asked.

"You have my shovel. The connection flows both ways."

Of course. That was idiotic of me. I thought about the foul stuff in the bullets. Crap. I hope they didn't allow for a two way bond. They shouldn't... but I wasn't sure what I was dealing with. Well, nothing to do but forge ahead.

"You don't know whether to trust me or not."

"You have shown to be a friend in the past. But you are not one of us. Something outside has deemed us prey."

"Which means you need someone outside to help, looks like. Otherwise you wouldn't be hiding from the other Ghede."

"There are no other Ghede. They've been taken like the rest, all save Babaco. And I do not trust him to be himself."

I blinked. "You think someone is riding him like a horse?"

"Worse."

After hemming and hawing, Nibo agreed to sneak out to my car, get in the back, and lay low. A bit later, I slid into the driver's seat with a mind to head up Esplanade towards one of the larger cemeteries in New Orleans. Nibo had been taciturn about what he wanted to show me there, but it was clear it had spooked him.

After a few turns, I called to the back seat, "We're safely away. You can sit up now."

A large man, dark as midnight, sat up in the back seat. I nearly had a heart attack, but it was just Nibo is his normal form. He'd left the bus boy back at the hotel.

I still couldn't stop a flinch and exclaimed "Gah!"

He chuckled, the only bit of humor I'd seen from him the whole time. Which was understandable, I guess.

"So, why are we going to this cemetery?" I pried. "You got a clue to where everyone's at?"

"Not a clue. Know."

I eyed him in the rear view mirror. "Then why all the mystery?"

"You'll see," he said quietly. "You'll see."

I did indeed see...and understood. Pieces started to click into place.

In New Orleans, the dead do not simply go into the ground. There's only one spot in the whole city not below sea level, and I think the keepers of the zoo would start taking offense if people tried to bury anyone there. No, they go in crypts designed to bake the flesh off the bones over the course of a year. When that's done, the dearly departed's bones mingle with other family members in the crypts, and the slab is laid bare for the next member of the family to join them.

Nibo had directed me to St. Louis Cemetery Number 3, larger sister to the cemeteries housing more saintly denizens and the infamous Marie Laveau. It also houses larger marble crypts than its smaller, older siblings. We parked the car, and he led me down the aisle to one of the roomier crypts, where there would be room for us and the body inside. It was just past sundown, and the place should have been oppressive in the heat. Instead, it was fairly cool, and the body on the slab was still breathing. Out cold, but still breathing. "Which Loa is this?"

"Petro Danto."

"She's not going to be happy when she wakes up."

He looked at me sharply. "Do not joke. You can wake them up?"

I squinted at the energies I saw surrounding her. I could see the trap that held her in stasis, the spell that kept the crypt from becoming an oven, and something else I couldn't finger. "How many are there around here?"

"All of them. Save Papa, who laid low like me."

I looked up, blinking. "They're all here?"

He nodded and inclined his head towards the door. "Spread out in different crypts. Randomly, I think. One per crypt."

I squinted at the woman again, and more pieces slotted together. The spell component I couldn't finger...it was part of a larger spell. They were all part of a larger whole. Which means their placement wasn't random like Nibo believed, but part of much bigger...holy Hell. Our mysterious bad guy was using Loa as spell components. As if they were nothing more than bits of chalk and salt and chicken feet.

We could probably rule out the trickster gods. Even they weren't that arrogant. Damn, they were the easier ones to deal with.

"Nibo, all we need to do is disrupt the spell on a few of them. When I manage to find out who's behind this, I need to break his connection to them, and the whole shebang will fall down, allowing them to wake." I showed him how to disrupt the spell, fairly simple for a Loa to pull off. A human practitioner would be hurting after one or two, but these guys? Piece of cake, once shown how.

"She's not waking up."

"And she won't until we get Mr. Mojo to tip his hand. But without disrupting the spell by removing a few connections here and there, I don't think we can get him to wake them. You can move through the shadows to the other crypts, right?" He nodded. "I'm stuck to physical travel, so you get to do the lion's share here. Just pop around. Order doesn't matter, but try to spread out. If you concentrate in one area he'll notice and pop up before we're ready. Go."

He extinguished the light and was gone. Which meant I was sitting there in total darkness. Lovely.

Of course, that meant I could see clearly when I emerged from the crypt, so I spied the spider at the center of this web, waiting for me as I exited. His teeth glowed in the light from the near-full moon.

Baba Ghede leaned against another grave's masonry. Crap. If he was here before we did any damage to the spell, that meant the ick from the shovel was likely from him. He must have traced me here by following it after I transferred it to the bullets.

He grinned at me, all white teeth, jovial and sly. "Hey, Jo! What did you find in that crypt?"

I shot him in the face.

The glyph on that one was meant for various Tricksters, and probably wouldn't do much harm. The grin turned rictus, white marred with blood and gore. His voice was slurred, as the jaw was askew. "But Jo-Jo, we were getting along so well...."

The second shot, the silver one carved with cabalistic symbols, took him in gut. He seemed to implode for a brief moment, the various parts of his body collapsing inwards in ways that suggested broken shale more than living flesh. Then the moment was gone, and he straightened, eyes fierce. A bee crawled out of his mouth, from the mangled side, and his voice sounded like the roar of a hive, slur gone.

"You shall not...." Then he looked perplexed, trying to take a step forward. His eyes narrowed.

"You're trying to use the Loa as a source of power to open a gate? Where?"

"You know you can't keep me long, Horseman," he buzzed. "I'm impressed you even got this far." Then his scowl turned to a look of bemusement. "You still haven't recognized me, have you?"

"You're not Babaco. I started to work that out when you couldn't keep my name straight. He's only known me as Josiah. You, on the other hand, seem to know who and what I really am."

He chuckled, a low, throbbing sound that made my fingernails itch. "We've crossed paths before, yes."

I waved the gun to swat another one of the bees away. He was playing for time, refusing to be direct. The longer we gabbed, the more his will overcame the binding in the silver bullet embedded in his sacral chakra. "Whatever. What the hell were you thinking, using the Loa in this way? How did you think there wouldn't be repercussions?"

He laughed outright at that, a bark of derision. "Are you serious? They're not even proper gods. More like what you used to be. Why did you give up your mantle?"

"This isn't about me. What had you planned to do, bokor?"

"Oh, please. You must think me daft. They're not even worthy of contempt, just tools to an end! You know I'm no priest of this pointless religion." He spat the title as if it left a bad taste in his broken mouth. "If I was able to capture them in their pretty little ponies, you know I'm no mere bokor."

He wasn't going to tell me his grand plan, so I extemporized. "You were setting them up be be used as loci of power to open a gate. Why here? Why not, say Pittsburg? Detroit?"

He waved my words away. "Their followers are right here in New Orleans. This is where their ponies are. Besides, the government between here and there frowns on human trafficking in this century."

That movement told me I didn't have long left before he freed himself. "So why the hell approach me with the case in the first place? Why set me on your tail? Were you so bored you had to create difficulty for yourself?"

A snort. "You are not a difficulty. You are a momentary distraction. Centuries ago, you gave me a run for my money! Now? Bah." The tone of the buzz suggested more anger than the indifference he feigned. "To be honest, I thought Papa Ghede had brought you down here to investigate the missing Loa. By the time I realized you were here by accident, I had already, as they say, stuck my foot in it. Had to see it through. I had access to something of Nibo's so I sent you after him."

"The Watchman at the Graveyard. The one who keeps the dead souls where they belong. The first victim of violence, as the stories go."

"Exactly. With him at the center, I can better funnel the deaths of the horses." He shrugged. His jaw drooped a little more from the motion. It didn't affect his speech. "He isn't necessary, but he will make the gate wider. More...effective."

"And Babaco is dead I take it?" My own eyes narrowed now. I shifted slightly as I saw a small motion in my peripheral vision, to draw his eyes away from it. "You used his blood as the binding agent to put the horses to sleep, I take it?"

He spread his hands. "Just so. Since the stories have Papa Ghede as the first man who ever died, he would have been the best choice. Damn man was the only one who saw through my Babaco disguise and went to ground, taking Nibo with him. So, for the binding I used their weaker brother. He was easier pickings. His blood worked almost as well."

"Shame you don't know where Nibo is. You might have guessed I'm not going to track him down for you."

He narrowed his eyes again, and buzzing turned from a roar to a knife's edge. "Oh no. You'll be dead soon. What happens when I overcome this ward, little Horseman? How many of these trapping bullets do you have? You will run out. I have time immemorial."

"You can't kill me any more than I can kill you."

"Ah, but I can. You gave up your mantle centuries ago."

I left the gun on him, but idly chewed at the fingernails of my other hand. "Now, what makes you think I did that?"

He waved the thought away. "Everyone knows that...." His voice had returned to the bass roar. He paused, blinked at me, implication setting in that my wards may be doing more than simply holding him still. "You're bluffing."

Another motion in the corner of my eye, a spade held aloft. "Maybe I am, maybe I'm not. Point's rather moot, as you're not going to get a chance to open that gate."

"You don't even know..."

"I know just fine. It's a complicated spell to pry open the gate sealing Azathoth's Children. The layout of the Loa in their Horses in each crypt draws out the points on a summoning glyph. I can't make out which glyph from down here on the ground, but it's not rocket science."

The rage in his voice brought the buzz to almost incomprehensible misalignment. "How could you know? I am a mystery to you!"

I looked up from my fingernails. "I was a little slow out of the gate, but come on...there were few suspects capable of this. And so I carved different bullets with different wards to cover all my bases."

"You said you did not recognize me." His voice quieted, the thrum of cicadas before a dixie storm. "I know you did not lie."

I shrugged. "You look different from the last time I saw you. That's your nature, though, isn't it? To hide in plain sight, taking on a form no one knew you as before? That was the first clue. Second was that it'd have to be someone so full of themselves they'd think the Loa were simply playthings for their own amusement. That points to either one of the particularly nasty Trickster gods, or an Old One. So I carved those bullets. The first one didn't work, so that ruled out the Tricksters." I raised the pistol and my voice. "I name thee thrice, Messenger!"

Eyes ablaze, his jaw distended and a swarm of bees poured out to stream towards me. I resisted the urge to duck, though the gun wavered. "I name thee thrice, the Alhazred's Lament!" This was going to hurt.

The blade of a shovel took off the Old One's jaw completely as Nibo swung in from the left, and the bees became a directionless swarm. I steadied my aim. "I name three thrice, Tempter in the Dark!"

The third bullet, the one carved with Egyptian hieroglyphs of unbinding, caught him square in the chest. Both he and the bees disappeared in an explosion of swirling mist. The mist formed tendrils, with a brief glimpse of flailing tentacles. The wriggling mass quickly returned itself to the form of the impostor Ghede Babaco. Healed.

Shit.

He golf clapped. He had just started to say something when Nibo took another swing at him. The haft of Nibo's shovel was caught and flung away. "You," he intoned, voice back to human, "I have plans for. After I deal with Wormwood." Slow but steady, fighting what was left of the wards, he advanced towards me.

The crypts exploded.

Flying masonry was mixed with masses of butterflies so dense that "swarm" was an inappropriate word. "Torrent" faired better. They streamed out of the ruins of the crypts, winding up in the sky. The false Babaco, now named Nylarthotep, screamed rage so pure that it threatened to peel the skin from my face.

As figures stumbled from the crumbling ruins, Nylarthotep's voice faltered. Throat raw, he exclaimed, "They cannot be free! How can you have unbound them, you were right h...." His eyes swung to Nibo, who simply gave him a small grin.

The figures...the remaining Ghede and the horses, the Chevals with their Riders all present, all turned their eyes to Nylarthoptep.

I swear the Old One gulped. It may have been my weary imagination, but I swear I heard it from thirty feet away.

Then the entire pantheon of Loa roared with one voice. The ground shook, the air vibrated...and the gathering mass of butterflies all descended on Nylarthotep.

I backed away as quickly as I could. Even being in the same town as the Loa was dangerous right now. I didn't want to be anywhere near the object of their pissiness. Remember how I mentioned that having the gratitude of a host of angels would be a good thing? Imagine them all wanting to smite you at the same time.

They couldn't kill him, but they could make him pay. And there was a high possibility of indiscriminate backlash. I got the hell out of Dodge.

Shortly after dawn, with freshly carved bullets in two separate guns, I peeked back into the cemetery. One gun was in case Nylarthotep had managed to inexplicably escape. The other was in case Danto and some of the other Petro family of Loa were still lashing out. Several of them are famous for their long tantrums. I had no illusions of taking on several (or even one) angry Petro, but I had no qualms about binding one and running away until they calmed down and someone had a chance to tell them I was one of the good guys.

I needn't have bothered. I found Nibo digging a grave for a skeleton, picked clean. Apparently there was still something in the brain case, as a lone bee was trying to fend off several butterflies protecting an eye socket. The bee wasn't just outnumbered, it was putting up a hopeless fight. Blue and gold butterflies were pouring into the other socket. Brain eating butterflies. Somehow that outdid the concept of flesh stripping, bee-eating butterflies.

I may never be able to look at a pretty bug again without getting the shivers.

Nibo gave me one of his rare grins and leaned on his shovel. "Josiah," he offered.

"You know he'll just pop up somewhere again, right?"

"Yeah, but it won't be here. Or anywhere we hold sway. Not after what we did to him."

"Fair enough. And the Loa?"

"All back to doing what they do. Save for poor Baba. He'll have to find his own cheval to visit this world again."

"All the Loa know I was not involved in their capture? Misunderstandings can be a bitch."

The grin widened. "*Mon frere*, they know you helped free them. They're in your debt."

I sighed, relieved. "That's payment enough." At my age, favors owed are worth more than gold. As I started to wander back to my car, Nibo got to digging again and started whistling.

I recognized the tune, and got shivers down my spine. It was that old southern lullaby again.

Way down yonder, down in the meadow,there's a poor wee little lamby.
The bees and the butterflies pickin' at its eyes, the poor wee thing cried for her mammy.
Hush-a-bye, don't you cry,
Go to sleepy little baby
When you wake, you shall have all the pretty little horses.

Everything Has Strings

by Claudia T Smith

"Dammit, Jesus!"

That's the sound of the Right Reverend Pastor Timothy Michael Nelson as he realizes the control he had over "his" spirit was fleeting – if it ever existed in the first place. In a minute there will be screaming, followed by begging, and then the sound of something ripping a body apart. And I'm going to let it happen, because the bastard deserves it. Then, once he is good and thoroughly dead, I'm going to send the spirit back to the Hell that spawned it because that's what I do.

My name is Violet Le Chance and I am a paranormal investigator.

I've lived in New Orleans for twenty years now, and this city is like nothing else out there. Forget the tourist shops and forget the self-styled High Priests of the Forgotten Gods That Should Stay Forgotten. Forget the seafood and forget shops like Marie Laveau's Poser Emporium. There is real magic on the streets and I find it. If it is friendly, I let it keep on going. But if it is not… well, the results usually speak for themselves.

I'm not the most talented magic slinger around here, but I know when to use salt as opposed to antimony. I have only one real talent besides a bit of magic – I can see patterns. I know how to link events to see the real links underneath, and how to get to the center of the issue.

Which is why I was on the case when the hookers were dying.

There was a client – lovely lady, goes by the name of Shugah on the street. She hangs out in the Lower 9th, but she's been known to dress up to go to the Vieux Carre. She came to my office on a Tuesday morning, so I knew right away that something was very wrong. Shugah rarely gets up before noon, especially since she works all night.

"*Bon jour! Com é çava?*" I greeted her as she came in. I knew it was serious, but we have a thing.

"If you ever learn to say that right, I'll be amazed. Coffee?" She planted herself in the seat I keep out for clients while I went over to start up some coffee.

"If I ever learn to say it right, I'll be amazed myself." I paused to let her get her bearings, but plowed on. "How bad is it?"

"Ebony died last night. So did Sapphire. So did Madison."

I paused filling the coffee filter. "All three of them? What? How?"

"Can I have some coffee please? I'm gonna tell you, but…" As she paused a couple of tears started streaking down her cheeks. "Please?"

I nodded and finished setting up the pot. The scent of brewing coffee filled the office, a surreal counterpart to where my mind was going. Ebony, Sapphire. Madison. No pattern in the names. They had all been hookers in the Lower 9th though. Maybe the same john? No, I needed more data.

The coffee finally finished and I gave her a cup with a bit of creamer in it. She stirred it five times – she always stirred five times – and threw away the stirrer. She took a sip and let the warmth fill her for a moment before beginning. "I don't know what happened. They weren't stabbed. They didn't get hit. They didn't have the same guy. They were each on a different call last night."

"Any changes to how they got…clients?"

"Say 'johns' honey. That's what they are."

"Johns."

"And no. Same as always. Walk around, wait for someone to notice, try not to get picked up by a pig."

"Common johns in the near past? All coming down with the same cold? All ate at the same restaurant? Hell, did they all wear the same shade of lipstick?"

"Nope."

I thought about it some more while I made my own cup of coffee – black, no additives. When I sat down at the desk, I considered Shugah some more. "I'll take it."

"You know I ain't got a lot to pay you."

"We can trade later. Get with all the women you know. If anyone else has died, I'll need to know. I'm taking a trip to the coroner."

She sipped her coffee. "I'll see what I can do. I just wish I had a way to protect myself."

"Yeah, me too. I figure something out, I'll give it to you."

"Like the tattoo on my ankle?"

"Just like that."

"Should I tell the other girls about this?"

"Not yet, but you probably will soon. But I need to see what I can find out."

As we finished our coffees, she took a couple twenties out of her purse. I waved it off and told her to keep it until I was officially on the job – it might just be one of those weird coincidences we have around here (although I doubted it).

At the coroner's office, Boris was happy to show me the bodies. I'd done some work for him involving a poltergeist some time back, so he usually let me see what I needed to see. The bodies were in good condition – no marks, no bruising. Other than the standard blood pooling, no visible indications that it was anything other than a normal, natural death. But when I pulled out the pendulum, it moved in huge circles. There was definitely some magic going on there.

It was time to hit the library. I got Boris to promise to call me with the cause of death, and headed down to La Rue.

The La Rue library started as a plantation-style mansion just off the Garden District, but got renovated through several different "lives." It had been a commune before being bought by the city and converted to a library. People could take books out to the upstairs porch to read them, or enjoy some coffee in the tiny kitchen. It was old enough to have a personality, but fortunately that personality was more like a kindly aunt than anything else.

As I drove to the library, I passed a handmade sign advertising (yet another) tent revival. It looked like it was going to be in that big field off I-10. Great. Another dog and pony show to get people riled up over nothing.

The newspapers at the library didn't have anything about the dead girls, but that didn't surprise me. Unless the deaths are lurid, sensational, or happened to tourists, they never cover the stuff about the "undesirables." It was time to work my version of magic.

My ability to see patterns seems supernatural to people when they hire me, but it isn't. I just have a knack for connecting events. Given enough information, I can see the synchronicities and relationships between things where others can't. It's like people who can tell when someone is lying or always know what direction is north.

There was definitely something here, but it was time to talk to the girls. They had to have seen something – even something insignificant. Even if the only connection was that all of them had had bacon for breakfast, it would be something that might lead me in the right direction.

When I interviewed the girls, most of them hadn't seen anything, but the stories of the ones who had were odd.

Siren called it a shadow and described it as moving. "It was pretty cool, ya know."

"Cool?"

"Yeah. You know that with my job it's sometimes hard to be enthusiastic about it, but I loved it that night. I remember I saw a shadow move past the streetlight and suddenly my john was throwing money at me and I was tearin' his clothes off and …mmmmm, mm. Best sex I evah had!"

I looked her up and down. "How long have you been doing this?"

"'Bout seven years now."

"You ever enjoy it like that?"

"No, honey, but that don't mean I can't enjoy it."

"I know. But with a … john?"

"Ain't happened very often. That's why I remember. There was a shadow, and I remember looking up and then I was all… horny. And the guy I was with seemed to be feelin' it too, 'cause next thing we was in the alley and it was the best."

"Wow."

"You said it." Siren smiled serenely. "I don't know what that was, but I could use some more."

Heather and Bon had similar stories. Both had been with a john when they saw something – Bon said it was a flock of birds, which was weird because it was too late for the starlings to be flying – and both suddenly had the greatest sex of their careers. The johns had given them everything in their wallets, which was nice, but it was the sex angle that had me worried. Maybe some sort of lust spell?

Back at the office, the coroner's report was waiting in my inbox. After reading it, I had to call him.

"What the hell is this, Boris? Chewed?"

"Hi, Violet. Yes. Their uteri were chewed."

"Like an abortion?"

"Like someone had eaten them from the inside."

As I was hanging up on him, my friend Heather walked in, grinning like the proverbial cat. "You have to come with me! It'll be fun!" Heather pretended to be a little stupid as part of her act as a dancer, and sometimes it rolled into real life. But she had done me a lot of favors, so I put up with her excess of enthusiasm.

"Where? For what? A subject might be in order, sweetie."

"I'm going to the revival!"

I remembered the signs I had seen driving around. "Are you kidding? What the hell possessed you to go to a revival? You're ostensibly Catholic."

"I don't know, but after last night, I want you to come with me. You'll have a blast! They start near sundown."

"Heather, you know I love you, and I would do anything for you since you introduced me to Sister Angelica, but have you…" I suddenly realized that there was a pattern here. I couldn't see it all, but it was definitely forming. "You know what? I'm in. I'll pick you up at 5:00."

It was a tent, plain and simple, filled with chairs in a chevron of rows. It was starting to fill and I was intrigued to see that I knew several of the people there. A few hookers, a couple of pimps, some people who were obviously not as well off as the others, and a smattering of the devout. I could see by the way the street people carried themselves they were happy to be there, which was weird because the last time Tiny Ben had been in anything like a church had been at his christening. But there he was, with several of his girls, arranging themselves in the middle row.

I found a seat near the back and waited.

At about an hour before sunset, the preacher arrived. He wandered through the crowd a bit, introducing himself, shaking hands and god-blessing everyone. I shook hands when he came close, but it was not fun. His hands were clammy and I got the feeling he was more used car salesman than holy man. There was also something that hit my reptile brain, making it yell out that I needed to get away.

He started his show, and I listened closely while watching the audience. The people were enraptured (even Heather) and followed every word he said, amen-ing and hallelujah-ing in the right places. But the sermon was wrong. He talked less of love of God and more of how Jesus loved him and that the people should be glad to be part of his flock. He didn't quote as much Bible as I would have expected either.

But there was something about his voice. Even though part of me kept trying to get me to flee, I found myself nodding in the right places and whispering an amen here and there. His voice would have been soothing if I had not been on the alert. I pinched myself between thumb and forefinger, and for a moment it went away and I really SAW him for what he was: a normal if slightly weedy looking guy. But as the pain faded, I found myself fighting his voice again, until I reached into my left pocket and started poking a thumbtack I keep in there.

As it got close to sunset, his assistants opened the front of the tent and I saw it: a wooden statue of Jesus that he had erected on a pole. It was high enough that the dying sunlight cast a shadow into the tent, covering most of the people there. I was far enough to the back and one side that it did not touch me.

I knew this was part of the pattern, and I squirmed a bit to make sure there was no way in hell that shadow would touch me. Preacher Nelson led the crowd in a hymn and they all stood and swayed and sang together, obviously getting into the spirit of things. Part of me wanted to join, and only the continual pain of the thumbtack kept me from joining my off-key voice to theirs.

The sun dipped down as the hymn reached its crescendo, and the light changed as the shadow of Jesus spread over the congregation.

I guess being in this business makes you wary because as the shadow spread, I kept moving out of the way until I was near the rear exit. As the song ended, and the congregation belted out the last lines at the top of their lungs, I saw the shadow gather and leap up, off of the people, and into the night.

The congregation clapped and stamped their feet, excited and happy. There was still a shadow over them, but as the last of the sunlight disappeared, lamps were lit in the tent. The preacher's assistants wandered up and down the rows with pillowcases, and the congregants put money in. I watched as people literally emptied their wallets into the kitty, or dumped in any jewelry or watches they were wearing. Heather was smiling while tears streamed down her face as she pulled what was obviously at least two days take out from somewhere and dropped it in the pillowcase. Tiny Ben was also crying as he dropped a roll of bills in that was at least two inches across.

When the assistant came to me, I gave a dollar, and shrugged. "Wish I had more, *mon frère*." He just nodded and went on.

The service over, the congregation started to leave. Heather and Tiny Ben found me and started talking about how amazing the service was. I told them to go on without me and that I would see them later. I had to figure something out.

I wandered outside, melding with the congregation as they filtered towards where they were parked. While walking, I made sure to go past the statue of Jesus that had been put up on the pole. Something about it was off.

When I got close enough to get a good look at the spot-lit statue, I realized what was wrong: the wooden Jesus had a woodie.

A part of the pattern clicked together. I had to talk to an old enemy – or maybe friend, I usually couldn't tell.

Say what you will about tourism and how annoying it can be, but there is nothing on this planet with the power of a New Orleans graveyard. The ground is full of spirits, age and stories. The one everyone goes to is St. Louis Cemetery #1, but years of tourism have taken the edge off of it. The real power is in Odd Fellows Rest. St. Louis is older, but Odd Fellows has the real power – if you know the way in.

It was nearly midnight when I was finished with my preparations and was able to sneak in. I cast a circle of amaranth and dandelion, and put the offerings at the cardinal points: Bread with black beans and rice, black coffee, sweet apples, and the cheapest cigars I could find. This was not the first time I had talked to the spirits, and while everyone knew about the peppered rum, I needed someone specific.

I don't do rituals, exactly. I put all the right ingredients together, concentrate, and keep repeating the thing that I want. Maman Brigitte once told me I was rude, but she was the only one. She is a true lady, so I don't blame her. I set my duffel outside of the circle and intoned Ghede over and over, concentrating as hard as I could. He kept me waiting for almost an hour before he arrived, short and stocky, with eyes that twinkled with a wicked sense of humor.

"Nice hat," I said by way of a greeting. "It might be taller than the last one even. Who is your haberdasher?"

"Ah, sweet Violet. You are as charming as ever, cher." His voice was a straight razor whetted by velvet and I had to shake my head. I've always been a sucker for the dangerous ones.

"No flirting tonight, Papa Ghede. There are people who will die and you know how I am when I am on a mission. But, I do have a gift." I reached into my duffel and brought out a special potion that he had enjoyed before: Old New Orleans Cajun Spiced Rum with sweet apple juice and ghost peppers.

He licked his lips as he eyed the bottle, his tongue just long enough to dip below his chin. He raised his eyes to mine and smiled a smile just a bit too wide to be truly human. "Oh, you know me, darlin'. Pour and I'll give you the usual three."

"Give me three straight answers, and you can have the entire bottle."

"Deal, my sweet."

I pulled a highball glass out of my duffel and scuffed the line of the circle. The circle couldn't contain him anyway – it was more a thing to concentrate my focus. Spirits are different than what people think. It doesn't take much to bring one to you – it's getting rid of them that can be a problem.

"Some of my friends are dead," I informed him as I poured him a full highball of the mixture. "I need to know what it is. And I think that it's related to the new Salesman for Jesus that's on the edge of town."

He took a long swallow and I watched his throat move as the liquor went down. For a short guy, he had a nice neck. "Mmmmm…you always know what I like."

I nodded but did not start the conversation. Papa Ghede was fascinating, but under the fascination, I knew that this spirit could kill me if I said the wrong thing. He was every cliché you ever read: a cobra to my mongoose, a wolf to my dog, a flame to my moth. But we had talked many times before, so I was mostly sure he wouldn't kill me – not tonight anyway.

"You want to know about the preacher man, or something else?"

Now it got interesting. I could ask three questions, and he would answer. But I had to hit the right ones, or his answers would be useless. He would tell the truth – he always told me the truth. So I nodded. If I didn't ask a question, he might give me something, just to get me to ask.

He laughed, and sat next to me. He smelled of sweet cigars, rum, mint and earth after a rain. He grabbed one of the cigars I had offered, and the end lit up without any visible effort. "Let me tell you a story, sweet Violet. I like the offering and I don't like what I see happening these nights, so I will help you punish a spirit who should not be here. Will you take my story?"

I couldn't help it. I dropped down next to him, set my head on his shoulder, and let him curl an arm around me while I nodded. This case must have affected him in some way, or he wouldn't be so free to offer information.

"There was a small, small man in the City of Angels that had ideas. He knew how to make numbers dance, but he was a small man in a huge city, and there was nowhere he could use his numbers to get what he really wanted – power. He wanted to have the things that he did not have as a boy: women, influence, and most of all, money.

"So this small man decided to try a couple of tricks with his dancing numbers and, once he realized the tricks he could pull, he went to the desert to the City of Light and Noise. There, he set the numbers dancing, and they brought him some wealth. It was a good feeling.

"But there is something about when you get what you want – you want more. So he made more numbers dance, a shake here, a wiggle there, an occasional ballet in a pyramid or a mambo in a hotel. And every time he got more, he wanted more.

"Hunger attracts hunger, cher. And there was a Hunger in the city that saw in him someone it could use. So the Hunger set on him, and taught him more tricks. It taught him how people would give him wealth if he used the Voice of Hunger to talk. It showed him how to say the right words, make people listen and love him.

"And it learned his numbers. It learned how numbers work, and it learned about things that could happen that had not happened yet. It learned how numbers can predict and how numbers can satisfy a hunger if used right. The knowledge made it stronger, and it learned to work through him to feed more and more."

We sat in silence for a few while I pondered his words (and enjoyed the strength of his arms – make no mistake). He finished his highball and handed it back to me for refilling. As I refilled it, I pondered how to ask the right questions.

"A mathematician from Los Angeles went to Las Vegas. He counted cards, played a lot of games, and every time he won, he got greedier. And a Hunger…" I trailed off. I'd heard of these, but, "He attracted a spirit. There have to be a million spirits in Las Vegas. It's got a magic like we do here."

"Not quite like here, sugar," he growled and suddenly his arm was tight around me.

"No, not quite. There is nothing that can compare to the Barons, and I know it."

He turned his head to give me a quick, rum scented kiss on my cheek. "You know how to flatter an old spirit." But his arm loosened and I could breathe better.

"So a spirit of hunger grew on his greed. And it taught him to speak – he's the preacher. But it learned numbers from him. Spirits don't do numbers. Math is science and science is the opposite of magic."

"Not this time."

His answer was too short. I had to ask. "What exactly happened? I know the spirit has to be able to possess him to make him sound like he does. But what happened in the other direction? Be specific."

"I'll try, sweetling, but you know the game."

"I'll sweeten the deal. I can't let my friends die."

"Every spirit feeds on something. Some feed on blood. Some on a good rum." He raised his glass. "Some demand sacrifice, and others just want to enjoy a ride. But there is something for every spirit. And a Hunger spirit has to eat."

"But they all eat something different. Please, give me one word that will help me figure out what this one is eating! Why is it killing prostitutes?"

"Potential."

I sat there, thinking furiously. Potential. Everything had potential. But in Las Vegas, all potentials were constantly being realized: hold some dice and you could roll snake-eyes or sevens. Until you turned over the cards, you had a potential blackjack with just two cards. The spinning wheel was a jackpot until you hit that button. And the spirits there were very, very hungry.

Math was the art of manipulating potentials.

Parishioners were a potential jackpot.

And there were other potentials.

"And now, he has brought this spirit here. To our home." I straightened up and he released his arm from me. "I have my final question. If I summon you, on your own home, without binding, can you defeat this thing? I've seen a part of what it can do, and I know that I can't."

"Of course, little one." He leaped to his feet and offered me a hand up. "But if you let me go without any bindings, you know you will owe me."

"I know."

He looked me up and down, very slowly, taking in every inch of every curve that was and was not showing. His eyes were like a tongue, tasting me. "Oh you will owe me so much, cher. But I think we can come to an arrangement."

I stared into his eyes for a moment, and grinned with inspiration. "Oh, yes. I think we can."

He laughed. "You know that I see the future. This will be done. Take this." He threw me a small bone. "Break it when you need me, and I will be there. But be sure of where the spirit is. If I don't have a fight, I will take other compensation for coming – and no, not our arrangement that you are going to be working on. If there is no fight, then I will take a ride."

There were more deaths that night. Seven women in Tremé while I had been talking to the Baron. When I visited Boris, he showed me the preliminary report, and I started to tear up a little. I knew two of them. They were good people. Say what you will about the cliché of hookers, hearts and gold, but some of them were actually kind people who were just trying to make things work. I was going to miss them.

The uteruses had been "chewed" on like the first ones examined, and Boris saw no reason to think it would not be the same person.

The Hunger spirit was eating women. Why?

Potential.

I needed confirmation, so I had Boris do some searching. Sure enough, there had been a couple of deaths in Lafayette three days before, and one two days before that in Beaumont, Texas. There had been seventeen in Houston four days before Beaumont, and six in San Antonio three days previous. Before that in Fort Stockton, two, El Paso had four, and three in Tuscon, nine in Phoenix and...there it was. Las Vegas.

Boris just kept shaking his head as he found more and more, but I was looking at something else. All had been hookers. And after a bit of searching, we were able to place a traveling preacher in each town. Arriving the day before the deaths started, leaving the day after they stopped, and with reports of people who only had fuzzy memories of why they had given the preacher everything they could.

Potential. I had it.

Lust is a type of hunger. For closeness, to be with someone, to give yourself to them, and yes, to have sex. It is one of the strongest emotions we have. And every encounter has potential outcomes. People fall in love or don't. People can murder or cherish each other. People can experience emotions or spread disease.

And if all the circumstances are right, sometimes a woman will conceive.

I remember the first time I saw a spirit enter a baby when it took its first breath. It went from a potential human to a real being in one moment, and the spirit who entered it would help determine what it would become.

Maternity wards are painful to me because I can see all the spirits waiting for someone to be born so that they can enter the world. There is potential for everything in that moment.

I thanked Boris and swung by my house before starting the drive to the revival tent. I considered: as great as the potential of that birth is, there is more. Before that spirit enters the body, that body has the potential to house any of them. And before that, it might or might not be born. A fertilized egg might or might not implant. The potentials were enormous. And every stage in the process grew it.

This thing had been eating potentials in Vegas, but when it learned how numbers really worked with Nelson, it saw new way to feed – this time on the potentials of people and what happened when they had sex. It wasn't lust. It was the after effects.

This spirit must be huge by now.

And where it touched, a side effect. What the spirit contaminated would also hunger on a deep level of the soul. And people always go to religion when their souls are hungry. And the preacher had been taught to feed just enough of that hunger to take them for everything they had – even if they didn't have it.

Bastard.

As I pulled into the revival lot, I saw at least four times as many cars as the previous night, even though it was a full three hours before the show. People were gathering in little groups, some talking eagerly about what it would be like, others enjoying the camaraderie and carnival atmosphere. No one paid attention as I walked over to the cross and bowed my head for a moment before looking up.

Jesus was not on the pole. I half expected this, but it was going to make things a bit more difficult. Before trying to find the Jesus, I decided to lay down some insurance. I had to be careful not to be seen, but a circle and path of binding powder later, I was ready. That shadow was going to be very limited to where it could move.

I scanned the area and discovered a couple of small tents set apart from the main one, under some trees. It didn't take long to discover the Jesus statue in one of them, guarded by the same guys who had been collecting for the preacher. I avoided them and circled around again so I could approach from a different angle. A bit of cherry bark, chicory, and amaranth on my hands, a quick invocation to any air spirits that might be listening to shield me, and I was inside of the tent, considering the Jesus statue.

Most people wouldn't feel it, but it was not friendly. The spirit housed inside was aware of my presence, but not afraid. It knew I did not have the magic to even think about taking it on.

But it didn't know that I am tricky, nor did it understand that binding powder does just that – it binds. Almost anything within it.

The work of a minute cast a circle around the statue. It started to rise, a shadow like black syrup, but I was too fast and chained it to the proscribed area. After finishing with the invisibility powder, I snuck back out and made my way to the revival tent where I waited in the back.

It didn't take long. Preacher Nelson made his way through the tent, glad handing and god blessing, but there was something slightly off. I was not the only one who noticed the salesman this time. People shook hands, then surreptitiously wiped them on their slacks or skirts. The eyes of the congregation followed him, but quizzically, as if they couldn't quite believe this was the same person as before.

Preacher Nelson noticed, and started to launch into the sermon, but it was obviously off. This wasn't the same magic of words from the past, just a slightly seedy guy trying to have more presence than he did. And it was not succeeding.

It only took a few minutes for the congregants to decide that this was not what they had come to see and start to file out. He tried to keep them there, haranguing a bit as they streamed past him out the front exit, but it didn't make a difference. The magic was not there.

Preacher Nielson turned to one of his helpers who had just come in. "Put it up! Put it up!"

The one addressed just shrugged. "It's not time."

"Do it anyway!"

The guy shrugged and went out, presumably to do what he was told. That was when Preacher Nielson saw me, hanging back. "What do you want?"

I smiled, strolling down the aisle between the chairs. "I just wanted to hear what you had to say. You were really good last night."

"You're the only one who thinks that."

"I'll just get out then. Maybe I'll see you later." I tried my friendliest smile.

"Whatever." He turned away from me.

I exited the tent and immediately ducked to the side so I could watch what was going to happen. The helper had mounted the Jesus on the post, but it was obvious nothing was going to happen. Still, I hung around until just after sunset when the preacher took the Jesus off of the pole and back into the tent that usually housed it.

I waited a moment to be sure no one could see me and moved close.

"Dammit Jesus! What the hell happened out there!" For a preacher, he had a rather foul mouth.

The voice that answered sounded like sandpaper over the eyes. I winced silently as it answered, "Don't take that tone, mortal. I was detained."

"How the hell were you detained? You're powerful!"

"There's something at work here. A woman."

"And you couldn't come and do your thing because of some stupid bitch?"

"She knows things. I could not move."

I smiled quietly to myself. So far so good. Now, if I was lucky, he would get careless.

"How can you not move?" Nelson was taking the bait.

"I cannot move."

"But you have to! You have to go out! You have to bring them in!"

"I cannot move." Was it my imagination or did I hear something… anticipatory in the voice this time?

"What do you need?" Nelson was definitely starting to sound desperate.

"I'm hungry and I cannot move." The voice of the spirit never once changed inflection, but I could feel its eagerness.

"I'll move you!" A moment later, I heard the sound of someone lifting something. There was a crashing noise and suddenly the preacher was roaring in pain. "What was that! Go! Get off of me!"

"I'm hungry and could not move – until now."

"I've been feeding you! Get away from me!" Under the orders was fear and sobbing.

"I'm hungry."

"Dammit, Jesus!"

That was the sound of the Right Reverend Pastor Timothy Michael Nelson as he realizes that the control he had over "his" spirit was fleeting – if it ever existed in the first place.

There was some screaming, followed by begging, and then, the sound of something ripping a body apart. I let it happen because the bastard deserved it for what he had allowed to grow. Once the sounds quieted down, though, once he was good and thoroughly dead, I moved inside the outer binding circle and broke the bone.

Papa Ghede was at my side before the sound of breaking bone had finished, grinning and wreathed in flames of shadow. He clapped me on the shoulder, and we both leaped toward the tent where the hunger spirit had eaten its meal.

I moved to the inner barrier I had put up and wiped a bit of it clear so Papa would have no impediments at all. The hunger spirit came roaring out, and I rolled to get out of the way, landing in a pool of blood, all that was left of the reverend. Papa laughed, deep and loud, happy to show this spirit who really ruled New Orleans. They crashed into each other with a noise that reverberated on the spirit plane, even as it was silent on the earth.

Each spirit held the other, but it only took a moment to see that Ghede had the advantage. While the other spirit took bites out of Papa with the many mouths it kept forming, it was being absorbed by the older spirit, growing smaller and smaller until there was nothing left except a morsel that Ghede popped into his mouth to chew slowly. As he licked his lips, the scars from the hunger spirit's bites sealed up, and soon he stood whole and unharmed.

"Little thing, wasn't it? Too much trouble for such a little thing, though." He cocked his head to one side and smiled lasciviously at me. "Now, you promised payment?"

"You see everything, right?" I asked as I moved to the outer binding and erased an opening. No sense in being impolite.

"Of course, sweet Violet."

"Then you know you are getting rum and not a ride tonight. Give me an hour to get it?"

He bowed. "Of course. I'll get that ride some other night."

Thing is, I think that he just might – someday.

Last Dance in Storyville

by Brent Nichols

You couldn't cross Basin Street without feeling like you were entering another world.

George Frontenac stepped over a horse plop, paused to let a police wagon pass, then stepped quickly out of the way of a gleaming red Model A as it growled its way up the street. He didn't entirely trust the newfangled machines. It was shaping up to be a noisy and boisterous new century.

He reached the far sidewalk, and just like that, all respectability was left behind. He was in Storyville now, where vice was king and the law looked the other way.

A flash of color caught his eye, and he turned to watch a young woman in an elegant blue dress making her way across the street. She wore boots with mud still clinging to them, the fancy dress at odds with the almost masculine swing of her hips. She moved like a farm girl, with a no-nonsense stride that said she meant to get where she was going and that was that.

When she reached the sidewalk near him, however, that changed. She set down a pair of dainty Mary Janes, stepping out of her boots and into the shoes. When she picked up the boots, making them look somehow delicate in her slender hand, she was suddenly an elegant lady with a willowy, swaying walk. She headed down Basin Street away from him, holding the boots well away from her dress.

George followed, since he was going the same way. When she turned on Villere, he worried she'd think he was following her. At the corner of Iberville, he watched her climb the steps to Dixon's and wondered if it was fate. He shrugged and followed her inside.

"Mr. George. You're back." The blonde in the red dress had a glint of amusement in her eyes, and George nodded politely, feeling a flush climb his cheeks. He'd spent two hours in Dixon's the night before, dancing with every lady in the place. They had to be wondering if he had mistaken the brothel for a dance hall, or if he was working up his nerve to take a girl upstairs.

He thought of Clarissa and pushed trivial concerns like embarrassment to the back of his mind. He had a mission, and a dangerous one, too. He needed to focus on the job at hand. There was an unfamiliar girl along the side wall, a brunette all in pink. He crossed to her and said, "Would you like to dance?"

The parlor of Dixon's was not made for dancing, but the band was enthusiastic, the ragtime music was lively, and the lady was willing. George moved around the room, the girl stepping and whirling in his arms, feeling as light as thistle down, her eyes bright through the paint on her face. She was a marvelous dancer, and George couldn't wait for the dance to end.

At last the music stopped, and she raised an elegant eyebrow in clear invitation. George lowered his arms and stepped back, giving her a gracious bow. He saw disappointment on her face, but she smiled pleasantly enough and moved away.

His eyes swept the room. There were two other patrons in sight, heavyset men smoking cigars on either side of the unlit fireplace, and more girls than he could count. They swept in and out like birds, delicate and beautiful, their dresses making bright splashes of color. The parlor was a dreamland, a fantasy of elegance and grace that hid the sordid reality of what went on upstairs.

Even that, George reflected, was a coy façade. Something much worse happened here.

One of these pretty doves was a merlin, and she hunted.

His gaze went to the band. It was an unusual group, a mixed-race trio, two black men and a white woman. The horn player and the man with the guitar watched over the woman like protective uncles, and with good reason. She was young and pretty enough to be one of the doves, but when her fingers danced over the keys of the piano in front of her, there was no question that her gifts lay in more elevated realms.

The music started up again and George scanned the ladies in view. A familiar blue dress caught his eye. It was the brunette from the street, looking like a young man's fantasy, every trace of farm girl gone. She was watching him, but she stood as if trying to hide behind a potted plant. She shrank a bit when she saw his eyes on her, then smiled and nodded as he gestured her forward. She was young and slim and lovely, her hair falling around her face in ringlets of pale mahogany that didn't match the sooty arcs of her eyebrows.

The woman he was hunting had brown hair, but his distant ancestor had never bothered to record the color of her eyebrows. He lifted his arms, she stepped close, and he put a hand on her waist, wondering once again if he was clasping his mortal enemy.

"I'm Ida," she murmured, batting long lashes.

"I'm George." He started to move, she stumbled, and his foot came down on her toe. They exchanged apologies, paused, and he started again. She was clumsy in his arms, doing her best, a furrow of concentration between her eyebrows. She got better with every turn around the floor, and by the end of the dance she was doing fine. As the band stopped playing, he lowered his arms.

"I'm sorry, Mr. George." There was a hint of a twang to her voice, an accent more like New York than the Deep South. "I'm not much of a dancer."

"You're marvelous," he told her. "Exactly what I'm looking for. In fact, I was wondering if you might want to accompany me upstairs?"

Her eyebrows rose. He saw a hint of unexpected color in her cheeks, and her gaze dropped for a moment. Then she met his eyes and said, "All right."

He'd expected a show of bashfulness from the ladies of Dixon's, but this looked like the real thing. How could you fake a blush, after all? That, combined with her mediocre dancing, convinced him that she was not his target. The woman he sought had too much pride to dance poorly, and she'd been around much, much too long for girlish blushes.

Ida led the way up the broad staircase at the back of the parlor and into a tiny bedroom. She was coy and flirtatious until the door closed, when she became suddenly hesitant and uncertain. She moved her hands to the buttons on her dress with the air of someone gathering her courage for an ordeal.

George reached out a hand and held her wrist. "Ida," he said. "Wait. It's all right."

The flush in her cheeks deepened. "No, it's fine, I kin–"

"That's not actually what I'm here for."

She stopped fumbling with her buttons, blinking up at him, confused. She looked vulnerable and desirable and the thought flicked through his mind that he could go through with it, put off his quest for a few minutes, find out exactly what was under that long blue gown. After all, he was playing a very dangerous game. This could be his last chance ever to know the pleasures of…

It was the nervousness in her eyes that stopped him. He smiled. "I'll still pay," he told her. "I need you to sit here quietly for a few minutes, and when we go back downstairs I need you to pretend that we, you know, that we did what people generally do here."

Ida nodded, looking uncertain.

"I just needed a chance to be alone. Well, mostly alone, here in Dixon's. Away from prying eyes while I do something." He drew a cigarette case and a box of matches from his pocket. "This may look a little strange," he said. "I promise you I'm not doing anything bad." And he opened the case.

"Is that hair?" she said, leaning forward.

"Yes." He squatted, and she sat on the end of the bed to get a better view. "Hand me that ashtray, would you?"

She handed him a thick glass one on the bed stand and he set it on the floor. He drew a scrap of paper from the cigarette case and set it in the black-stained middle.

"What's that writing?" she asked. He'd been afraid of her reaction, but there was no suspicion in her expression, no hostility. Just wonder.

"Runes," he said. "Words of power. The power gets released when I burn the paper." He set a dozen or so strands of hair on the paper. "The runes and the hair burn together, and the smoke tells me where to find the person whose hair this is."

She leaned closer, her chin almost touching her knees. "Whose hair is it?"

"A witch," he said. "A very old woman who my family has been hunting for a long time." He sighed as he thought about it. "A very long time indeed."

She turned those bright, inquisitive eyes on him. "How long?"

"Just over two hundred years, actually." He waited for her to scoff, but there was only wonder in her eyes. "My distant ancestor was a pretty big deal back in France." He chuckled. "Those days are sure long gone. But granddad was nobility."

Her eyebrows rose. "Your granddaddy was rich?"

"Well, yes." He frowned. "But the job came with responsibilities."

She smirked at that, dismissing the idea of rich men's burdens.

"Like trials," he said, wanting to wipe the smirk from her face. "There was a woman. Young and pretty. Well, he thought she was young, anyway." *Why am I telling her all this?* His answer was simple. She was lovely, and she was hanging on every word.

"She was accused of witchcraft," he continued. "She was supposed to be executed. He had to give the order. Commit her to the flames, or release her and live with the consequences."

Ida wasn't smiling any more, and he regretted that. But he couldn't stop the story now. "He locked her up," he said. "He put off the decision while he gathered more evidence. He couldn't just kill her for practicing magic." George gestured at the scrap of paper in the ashtray. "After all, he'd married a witch."

Ida's eyes went wide.

"This is her work," he said. "My grand-mam, that is. She used her magic to heal the sick. She used it to find a little boy one time who'd got lost in the forest. And she used her magic to track a murderer." He sighed. "She escaped."

"The witch?" Ida said. "Not your gran, the other one."

George nodded. "Marine. That was her name. She got free. Killed two men to do it. Grandad…" He shook his head, remembering the old diary pages he'd read. "He blamed himself. He thought their blood was on his hands. He swore to track her down, and he spent the rest of his life doing it. But he never found her."

"And all this was... two hundred years gone?"

"Yes." George nodded, searching her face for signs of doubt.

"But she can't still be alive now!"

"She gets younger," he said. "That's what the legend is, anyway. She drains the life out of people, and it makes her younger. She's been doing it for a long time." He shivered. "A very long time."

"And your family, y'all hunt her?"

He gave her a sad smile. "It's not quite that noble, I'm afraid. Granddad and his wife were quite set on scrubbing away the stain to the family honor. Granddad used his money and his position to hunt her. Grandma, she had, let's say, other resources to contribute." He gestured at the paper and the bit of hair. "Certain skills she passed on to her children, so they could carry on the hunt. There was a ring that's supposed to protect you from magic, but it's lost now. And the hair is almost used up."

Ida sat up straighter on the bed. "The hair?"

"They shaved Marine's head when they locked her up." Ida's eyebrows rose, and he shrugged. "I think they had lice in the prison. Shaved every head in the place, trying to stop it. And Grandma, she took the hair. Good thing, too." He pondered for a moment. "Actually, maybe it's a bad thing. Clarissa might still be alive at home if it wasn't for that stupid hair."

The familiar bleakness came washing over him, the guilt that he would never fully escape. He squeezed his eyes shut, and Ida's soft, warm hand closed over his.

"Clarissa's my sister," he said, not opening his eyes. "We inherited a bunch of things when my grandfather died. Not Granddad. I mean my actual grandfather. He had diaries going all the way back to France. The whole story of the hunt was laid out. There was an envelope with a little bit of hair in it." He grimaced. "There isn't much left. Not after two centuries of burning it a bit at a time."

Ida's fingers against his hand made him think of Clarissa, and how she'd squeezed his hand, her eyes dancing in excitement, as they'd gone through the chest after the funeral. Opening his eyes wasn't easy, but he made himself do it.

"My grandfather never actually hunted her," George said. "He fought in the Crimean, and maybe that was enough for one man. I don't think my father even knew the witch existed. He never told me about her, at any rate. But Clarissa and I learned everything, and she wanted me to take up the banner, renew the 'family crusade,' as she called it." He closed his eyes again, wanting to blot out the memory of her face, the glow of idealism in her eyes.

Ida's voice was gentle. "What happened?"

"I wouldn't go." It was the first time he had admitted it to anyone, and the words hurt as he spoke them. "I told her it was a fool's errand. I told her it had nothing to do with me. And when she saw that I meant it, she took her share of my grandfather's money, she took the ring and the last of the hair, and she left for Louisiana. She never came back."

He didn't tell her the rest. He didn't tell her about the sleepless nights, the worry, the growing guilt. How he'd finally realized that Clarissa wasn't ever going to return. How he'd come south, tracking down the boarding house where she'd stayed. He had a suitcase of her possessions, including an envelope with more hair than he'd expected. He'd been burning it profligately, drawing ever closer to his target. Now he knew that the woman he sought was somewhere in this very building.

Ida frowned. "How do you know it's real?" She gave an apologetic shrug. "I mean, maybe it's just a crazy story from your granddaddy."

Instead of answering her, he struck a match. The words he spoke were simple, a few quick syllables he recited over and over as he touched the match to the corner of the paper in the ashtray. The paper curled, the flames touched the little bundle of hair, and the acrid smell of burning protein teased his nose.

Smoke rose in a white stream, breaking apart and spreading as it moved through the air. As more of the paper disappeared, though, the smoke began to writhe. George spoke faster, the same gibberish syllables he'd read from Granddad's journal, and the smoke coalesced into a white ball that hovered over the ashtray. The last of the paper crumbled into ash and the flame faded away.

The little ball of smoke began to descend. George stopped speaking, barely breathing as the smoke sank into the ashtray. For a time the smoke frothed and bubbled like pale soup. Then it overflowed the edges of the glass container and gathered into a puddle on the floor. A moment later the smoke began to flow between floorboards. In a couple of heartbeats it was gone.

George stood and headed for the door. Ida was on his heels, a warm hand against the small of his back as he hurried down the stairs. The party continued in the parlor, the band playing something that sounded like an improvised, syncopated version of a Strauss waltz.

He was scanning the ceiling when Ida squeezed his forearm and whispered, "There!" He glanced at her face, then followed her gaze to the middle of the parlor floor. He was just in time to see tendrils of mist vanish through the weave of a thick rug.

A quick glance around the room reassured him that no one else had noticed. The band was focused on their instruments. The two customers from before were gone, but a trio of young men had replaced them. The men were clearly dazzled by the ladies around them, and the ladies in the room were either chatting with the men or with each other.

George retreated to a corner, Ida close beside him. "Is there a basement?" he asked softly.

Ida nodded. "There's a door in the back of the kitchen." Another nod indicated the direction. He was wondering how he could make it into the kitchen unnoticed when she said, "Get ready."

He waited, his heart thumping, as she marched up to the little raised stage where the band performed. "That ain't no way to play a waltz," she declared, and reached over the piano to bang her knuckles on the keys. The piano gave a harsh blast of sound, and the room went silent. Every eye in the place was on Ida, who planted her hands on her hips and gave the band a withering glare.

George slipped into the kitchen. He could hear her demanding that the band learn a proper waltz or give up their instruments, and he grinned to himself as he scanned the little room. A kitchen wasn't much use in a brothel, and he had the place to himself. The kettle on the stove was the only thing in the room that looked as if it had gotten any recent use. There were some battered pots hanging on the side wall, but George could see a layer of dust on the upper surfaces.

More to the point, there was a scuffed green door in one corner. He stepped to the door, twisted the handle, and pushed it open.

A staircase descended into darkness. George wanted to pause, to get his bearings and gather his nerve, but the smoke wouldn't stay visible for long. He hurried down the stairs, clutching the warped railing, his feet clumsy on the steep, narrow steps.

A beam of light followed him down the stairs, illuminating the dark expanse of the far wall. George reached the bottom and stepped to one side. As the sprawling bulk of his shadow disappeared, he caught sight of the smoke, spread thin across a section of dirt floor near the back wall. He watched as the smoke worked its way deeper and deeper into the soil and finally disappeared.

He moved to the place where the smoke had vanished, stooping to clear the low ceiling. He put his foot where the smoke had been thickest, and only then looked around. He was in a dingy cellar full of thick brick pillars, the musty air and grungy walls testifying to long years of disuse. The walls were wooden, and he could see faint lines of sunlight showing through cracks between the boards. It was a raised basement, the dirt floor no more than a foot below ground level.

He let his gaze descend to the floor beneath his feet. How could the witch be beneath him? A sense of unease tightened his stomach and grew as he knelt to examine the floor more closely. The light was poor, but it looked as if the ground had been disturbed where he stood. He swept his hand across the surface and nodded. Yes, the floor was definitely rougher where he knelt, and higher, too.

A twist of his heel left a clear scuff mark in the dirt. He left the pool of light and worked his way along the wall. The brick pillars filled the space with shadows. He stumbled along until his foot bumped something in the darkness near one corner. He found an old coal scuttle and a little scoop, no more than two feet long, designed for moving coal. He left the scuttle where it was, took the scoop, and returned to the scuff mark in the dirt.

The soil was easy to move. Someone had dug here recently. He heaped dirt against the back wall, scraping away with a mixture of anticipation and dread. He didn't know what he was going to find, but his instincts screamed that it was going to be significant, and it was going to be bad.

At last the blade of the little shovel scraped against cloth. He set the tool aside and used his fingers to brush soil away. He pulled away dirt in thick clumps, and a smell came wafting up, a rich, dark odor strong enough to overwhelm the scents of dust and dirt. George stopped breathing through his nose, but the unmistakable stench of corruption wormed its way deeper and deeper into his nostrils. *I'll wash these clothes as soon as I'm done. No, I'll burn them. And I'll spend an hour in the bath. But it won't be enough. Nothing will be enough.*

He brushed more dirt back and found himself looking down at about a square foot of fabric. The cloth was filthy and rotten, and he told himself that it didn't look familiar. There was a check pattern barely visible through the dirt. Clarissa had a dress in a check pattern, but so did thousands of women.

Three holes marred the expanse of fabric, long, thin cuts like you might get by stabbing someone with a knife. If there was blood, it was invisible in the dirt and poor light. George told himself he wasn't seeing his sister's corpse, but the twisting nausea in his stomach made a lie of his unspoken words.

One lump of dirt caught his eye, a circle too perfect to be natural. He reached for it, and had to find it by touch as tears filled his eyes. His fingers traced the familiar texture of a silver ring on a chain, at least two hundred years old. He knew that it would still gleam, untarnished, under the dirt. It hadn't protected Clarissa from the witch's knife.

He remembered her long brown hair whipping around her face as the train pulled into the station in Halifax, the last time he'd seen her alive. Her hair was always her most distinctive feature. She must have cut it, as a token disguise. And kept a few locks as a souvenir.

He blinked, tears splashed into the dirt, and he stiffened. The cellar was dark. He turned his head toward the stairs, and fingers of icy magic sank through his skin, into his flesh, into his very bones. In a heartbeat he was frozen, one knee in the dirt, his head to one side, unable to move. Only his lungs still functioned, drawing one frightened breath after another as he knelt there and watched the witch who had been the bane of his family for generations descend the stairs.

Which one is it? His brain ran through the catalog of girls as she swayed down the steps, a dark outline with the light of the kitchen behind her. When she reached the bottom of the steps, he was finally able to make out her face, and surprise made the breath catch for an instant in his throat.

It was the piano player, the slim brunette who had plied the ivory keys with such single-minded focus that he'd long since stopped noticing her. Now he could hear the guitar and trumpet playing upstairs without her. He stared at her, his eyes burning with the need to blink, and waited for his death.

"Who are you?" She had picked up the local accent during her long stay in Louisiana. Her voice was low and husky, and tinged with irritation. "Where did you come from?"

He was unable to answer. The whistle of his breath through his lips was the only sound he could make.

"Do you know this other troublemaker?" She gestured at the grave. "Are there going to be more of you?" Her gaze flicked to the ceiling. "I wish I could take the time to ask you a few questions. Oh, well." And her hand slid into a pocket in the front of her dress. Either it was a very deep pocket or it was cut to allow access to a sheath on her thigh, because the knife that she produced had a blade a good eight inches long.

George felt the frantic beat of his pulse rise to an even higher pitch as she walked through the dirt toward him. Every nerve in his body screamed at him to act, but he was utterly helpless. He couldn't even track her with his eyes. She was moving into his peripheral vision, and he found himself staring up the empty staircase toward the kitchen as she moved up beside him.

Will I even see the knife? Cold steel touched his side. *No. I won't.*

"Goodbye, Nosy," she said, and he couldn't even gasp as steel pricked his skin.

And then, like an angel of salvation, Ida appeared at the top of the stairs. She eclipsed the light from the kitchen, the witch turned her head, and George startled himself by managing to gasp, "Run, Ida!"

But Ida stood unmoving at the top of the stairs. At first, George thought she was frozen in shock or puzzlement, but he saw her left foot hovering in space over the first step. She was paralyzed, just like he was.

Except his paralysis was no longer complete. The tip of the knife moved away from his side, and he exhaled in relief. There was a stinging cut, he couldn't tell how deep, but he lived. *And I gasped.* He blinked his eyes. *Oh, that's better. What else can I do?*

He poured every scrap of willpower he possessed into lashing out at her with his left arm. And nothing happened. He shook with fury and desperation, and managed to clench his fist, but his limbs wouldn't move.

"Let me go," said Ida, her voice a low rasp. She wasn't completely frozen either, then.

"Hush," said the witch. "I'll tend to you in a moment." She turned back to George. "Why did you have to bring her into this, Nosy? I'm going to have to cut that pretty throat of hers, and for what?" Her fingertips touched George's cheek, and for an instant he was cold all the way through to his soul. "I can't even harvest you two," the woman said, sounding annoyed. "I'm full up, or close enough that it makes no difference. I'll have to flee New Orleans, and for what?" And she brought her other hand around, the blade reaching for George's throat.

He tried to hit her. He tried to twist away from the blade. He tried, as hard as he'd tried to do anything in his life, to throw himself sideways against her legs. And he achieved nothing. The blade of the knife touched his neck.

And George curled the fingers of his right hand, almost the only part of his body that he could control, and pushed the tip of his index finger through Clarissa's ring.

His paralysis vanished. The witch flinched, the blade moved away from his throat, and he rammed his left elbow into her stomach. She reeled back, and he yanked hard with his right hand, snapping the chain that went through the ring. He pushed the ring farther onto his finger, then grabbed the coal scoop and went after the witch.

He fought in a red haze of rage and fear. She backed away, slashing with the knife, muttering words of gibberish and making gestures that had no effect on him whatsoever, then falling back before the fury of his attack. He saw anger in her eyes, then frustration, and at last fear. Her face was lost to darkness by the time he backed her into a corner. A slash of the shovel connected with the back of her hand, he heard a meaty thunk, and the knife clattered against brick as it flew to the side. She cried out, clutching the injured hand to her chest, and George drew the shovel back for a killing blow.

It was a sob that stopped him. She made a raw sound of pain and terror and it froze him as effectively as her spell had done. He stood trembling, the blade of the shovel beside his face, and she said, "Please." Her face was a pale blur in the darkness. "Please, oh, please. Don't kill me. Don't do it. Please."

I have to do it. I have to! An endless second dragged past as he stood there, unmoving. Then another, and another. He gathered his determination, gathered his rage, took a deep breath, then let it trickle away. *I can't do it.*

Ida was a blur in the darkness as she reached past him and plunged the knife hilt-deep into the witch's neck. Darkness hid the expression on Marine's face as she sagged back into the corner, but George heard the wet rattle of her last breaths as blood filled her lungs, smelled the coppery tang of blood and the darker stink as the woman's sphincters let go, almost enough to wipe the smell of Clarissa's corpse from his nostrils.

After three awful breaths the woman went still, then slid an inch at a time down the wall until she was sitting in the corner of the cellar. When George took a step back she was nearly invisible in the darkness.

"Back home we get snakes sometimes," said Ida. Her voice sounded ragged. "Some of them's real pretty. Seems a shame when you got to kill one. But when a snake gets into the yard, you can't just let 'em be. Sooner or later, somebody gets bit." Her hand closed on George's forearm, her fingers hard and urgent. "Somebody dies, George. Somebody always dies. Best it be the snake."

She sounded as if she was trying to convince him, but he realized she was trying to convince herself as well, and he closed his hand over hers. "I know," he said. "You're right. Somebody was going to die." His gaze went to Clarissa's grave, partially exposed by the back wall. "Plenty of people died already, and there had to be at least one more." He moved his gaze back to the corner. His feet had kept backing up almost without him realizing. He could no longer see the witch in the shadows.

"Somebody had to die," he repeated. "Best it was her." Then he tore his gaze from the corner and led Ida back upstairs and into the light.

Normandy

by Jeff Leyco

Shawn's funeral didn't have the second line march down Bourbon Street like he always wanted. Very few people came out for it, just me, Mischa, and a few others from the Normandy Projects. I remembered them all, though it had been five years since I last saw any of them. Most of them pretended not to recognize me.

When we talked about it as kids, Shawn said he wanted his funeral to be a happy occasion. The way the sky broke open and rained down on us, everyone had flashbacks to Katrina instead.

We buried him in a plain grave, Ma and Dad on top, Shawn on the bottom left and an empty slot next to him. That was left for me.

His funeral had been closed casket, all the way through. I never got to see his face. I don't think I wanted to.

"Some sick bastard cut his brain out," Mischa said when she picked me up at the airport a day ago. I jumped into the passenger seat of her dingy old hatchback. I couldn't tell if it was used or stolen. Knowing Mischa, I could guess which one.

"Why?"

Mischa shrugged and pulled into traffic. Her constant string of curses at every driver we passed became our radio top 40, her middle finger our turn signal.

"Fuck you, by the way," she said, flicking a cigarette out the window. I always hated how her hair smelled like smoke.

"What?"

"You never said goodbye."

***

I picked up Shawn's things from the precinct the next day. The lady had a gut that gave Shawn's a good run for its money. Her name tag read DEITZ in big, blocky letters.

She handed me a small open box with the clothes, shoes, and wallet he had on him the night he died. The blood had dried on his shirt and jeans, more black-brown than red now. His wallet had all his cash still in it. I checked his pocket, a bloodstained note inside, torn from a piece of lined notepad paper.

Have you received your 30 pieces of silver yet?
I read the note again.
"Isn't this missing from evidence?" I asked Deitz.
"What are you on about, boy?"
"This." I held up the note. "Isn't someone checking it out?"
Deitz sighed. "What, are you a detective? Get outta line. There's people behind you."

The Normandies were officially condemned, even though there were still a handful of people living in them. Mischa told me most people had gotten evicted or just moved out without saying anything.

There wasn't a manager to speak of. There hadn't been one for years. Everyone who lived here took care of their own place, took care of themselves.

Graffiti lined the dirty brick walls, some still familiar from when I was a kid. Dead leaves lined the sidewalk. They would stay there until the late autumn winds blew them away. Spent cigarettes littered the entry. I picked one up off the floor and stared at it. I'd never seen cigarettes like these before. They were custom-rolled, with fresh tobacco inside. They had a dark ring around the butt, like black lipstick.

Mischa met me inside my old apartment. When I arrived the other day, I had to remove the yellow police tape myself. Shawn had been murdered, right there on the carpet, and his blood still stained the floor a deep maroon. I avoided even looking at the spot.

Mischa bit into an apple. Between chews, she said, "About a day before Shawn died, he finally signed his apartment over to Harlan Grigg–"

"Harlan who?"

"Grigg. Developer. After Katrina, he came through New Orleans like he was trying to finish what the storm started. He bought everything in sight that was cheap and broken, kicked people out, built condos."

"Sounds like New York."

"New York ain't got nothing on this fucker. Shawn signed his apartment over on one condition – Grigg agreed to include *affordable* housing, so maybe we can all buy back into it."

"Sounds like a win-win."

Mischa spat out some skins. "Sure. You say so."

"What do you care, though? You moved out of here years ago."

"Doesn't mean it ain't my home. Home is important. Home has power. If Grigg tears this place down, that's all gone. All that's left are the memories, and what the fuck good are memories?"

"The police won't investigate Shawn's death, will they?"

"When do they ever care about this part of town? Besides, I think Grigg's paying them to look the other way. He's got the cash to spend."

"What do you think happened?"

"Hell if I know," Mischa shrugged. "Guy missing his brain, killed in some grisly murder. Sounds voodoo to me. You want answers? Maybe talk to Cosme."

I paused, remembering the weird, creepy kid who lived down the hall from Shawn and me.

"I'd rather not."

Shawn and I stared at a spot on the wall. Just a second ago, a roach had crawled about halfway up. Succumbing to some poisonous concoction of roach killer, it tumbled backwards, landing with its legs over its head. It twitched for a few moments, then stopped.

Cosme smiled and brought his face closer to it. "I wonder what that feels like," he said.

"Being dead?" Shawn asked.

"Being dead without knowing why." He began humming something, an old spiritual we'd all heard at church when our parents dragged us out of bed on Sunday mornings.

"We should flush it," I said.

"No," Cosme said. "Not yet."

He touched the roach delicately with a thin, crooked finger, still humming his spiritual. The roach's legs kicked once, twice, then it flipped over and skittered away.

"It wasn't dead," Shawn said.

"It was." Cosme smiled. He watched until the roach disappeared underneath a crack.

Dad died in a car accident a few years later. He'd been out drinking with friends, at a bar where every night a small band roared out old jazz songs with a trombone that could split your brain. He tried to drive home and ended up spilling over into Bayou St. John instead.

By then, Shawn had forgotten about Cosme and the roach, but I hadn't.

After the police told Ma, Shawn, and me what happened, I found Cosme at his apartment. Strange skeletal figures etched sharp shadows that loomed at the edges of the walls. We didn't talk much anymore, and he'd stopped going to school.

"Bring him back," I said. "Bring my Dad back."

Cosme shook his head. "There are things you shouldn't change."

"Bring him back. He can't be dead. He shouldn't be dead."

Cosme shrugged. "Perhaps I'll see what I can do."

Nothing changed, or at least, not at first. Dad remained dead, and I began to forget what his voice sounded like, how boisterous his laugh could be.

When we buried him, I thought I could hear him scratching at the inside of his casket.

Cosme and I had more in common now than we'd ever had. My parents were dead. Shawn was dead. Cosme's brother Florian was dead. Their parents were dead, too, buried a few plots away from Shawn.

Cosme never moved out of his apartment, quieter now that I didn't hear his parents in another of their daily screaming matches. He'd mostly been raised by his brother, Florian, until Florian died too.

I knocked on his door. No response. For a weekday afternoon, I figured I wouldn't have any luck, but it was worth a try anyway. I didn't know what Cosme did for a living. For all I knew, he was at work.

I knocked again for good measure.

"What?" a voice growled from inside. The door nearly shook from the baritone.

"Cosme?"

"Who's there?"

"It's me. Sam. Shawn's brother."

The chain latch dropped. The lock turned. The door opened just a crack, enough to see the dingy dark inside of Cosme's apartment. If I hadn't known the walls were painted black, I would've thought his apartment was encased completely in shadow.

Eyes stared at me from behind the door, like strange lights in an abyss.

"You're shitting me," Cosme said.

"I'm back."

"You should've stayed gone."

"It's about Shawn."

"Shawn's dead. Didn't you hear?"

"I was at his funeral. You weren't."

"I was busy."

Cosme tried to close the door, but I jammed my foot in the crack before he could. He grunted, like a caged lion.

"What do you want?" he said. "I ain't got time for this."

"Shawn was murdered and his brain was cut out of his body."

"There are worse ways to go."

"Not very many."

"What do you want from me? I can't bring him back from the dead." A slight smile lingered at the edge of his mouth.

"That's not why I'm here."

"Then why?"

"Magic. You know magic. I know you have power over the dead."

Cosme laughed so hard, his lips retracted to show his pink gums and yellow teeth. His breath smelled of rum and vomit and gin. When he finally caught his breath, he said, "Are you going to go around finding every bokor you can and accusing them of killing your brother?"

"You're the only bokor I know."

"You think I killed Shawn?"

The way Cosme grinned, I was afraid he would suddenly lunge and bite my throat. I decided not to make an accusation. "Who would kill Shawn? Why would they take his brain?"

"There are some practices that require certain sacrifices. The consumption of certain organs. Stomachs, to cure a cancer. Lungs, to cure a cold. Brains, to cure ignorance."

"Are you saying someone killed him to get smarter?"

Cosme shrugged. "I'm not saying anything. Or perhaps I'm saying everything. You should have stayed gone, Sam."

"You still think I killed Florian."

"I don't *think*. I *know*."

"Pretty neat, huh?" Florian asked.

He held the pistol up, ejected the magazine cleanly into his hand. He cocked the gun back and a bullet flew from the chamber, falling onto the ground near his feet.

"Where the hell did you get that?" Shawn asked.

"Found it."

"Where?" I asked.

"Just found it."

We were in Florian and Cosme's apartment. Cosme played in the corner with a dead mouse, the way that a cat might toy with its food. It had been dead for at least three days. Cosme kept touching it, and it kept coming back to life for a few seconds, squeaking and twitching its tiny pink nose, then dying again.

"He gonna do that all day?" Shawn asked quietly.

"He's been at it for longer," Florian said. "Come on."

He reloaded the gun, then led us to the door.

"Cosme, you coming?" I asked.

But Cosme didn't respond.

We slinked through the narrow hallways, out onto the streets, empty and still damp. Florian took us to an abandoned lot. I think squatters lived here, or slept here at night. The floodwaters from Katrina had only just receded. There were lots of places to sleep if you had nowhere to go–so much was abandoned, so much was broken. And so much was still wet.

We found empty bottles, some Coke, some Abita Beer, and set them up on an orange plastic carton. Florian checked the magazine. "Nine shots," he said.

"You got anymore?" Shawn asked.

"Yeah, another two mags." He said mags like he knew what he was talking about when it came to guns. The closest I'd ever been to a pistol was holding a wooden stick, pretending it was a laser gun.

"Seriously, where'd you find it?" I asked.

Florian looked around the empty lot, eyes shifting toward the abandoned street. No one came down this way. "Drug deal gone bad, I think. Two dead bodies, in the alley. Looked like they got eaten by dogs."

"You were just in the area?" Shawn asked.

"What's it to you?"

"Innocent question."

"Yeah, I was *just in the area.* Heard a couple gunshots, went to check it out."

Shawn and I traded glances. Shawn laughed, then shook his head.

"And then you found the dead guys and the gun?"

"Yeah. There was definitely someone else there, maybe a couple more. They cleared out before I got there. But they didn't take the gun."

"Why did you?"

Florian held the gun up and posed with it. "Because it looks pretty badass, doesn't it?"

He aimed the gun at the empty bottles ahead, then squeezed the trigger. The gun boomed louder than thunder and echoed against the walls into the sky. The bottle exploded into millions of fragments of glass and crystals, sparkling as they scattered to the grass.

He gave the gun to Shawn. "Impress me."

Mischa leaned out my window, looking at the sidewalk below as rain streamed down the back of her neck. She laughed at the feeling, then brought her head back inside. She shook it from side to side, like a dog. "You and Cosme really have a fucking history, huh?"

"He still thinks I killed Florian."

"You gotta admit, it's still kinda suspicious."

"I didn't."

"And yet you left."

"I didn't have a choice."

Mischa laughed again. "He's playing you, you know. Getting into your head. I'm telling you, he killed your brother. Revenge, probably."

"Why now, though? It's been five years. What about Grigg? Would he want Shawn dead?"

"I don't see why he would. Where they left their deal off, Grigg had already won. He got Shawn to agree to move out."

I suddenly felt like I would fall through the carpet, as if it was already gone. Months from now, this room, this apartment, this complex would be rubble, replaced by something I could never afford to live in. Even the "affordable housing" sounded pricey.

"So let's follow Cosme," I said after a few moments. The rain still poured outside, tapping incessantly against the windows. "See where he goes."

Mischa yawned. "Sounds boring. You'll probably just watch him go to a bar, call a cab, and puke on the way home."

"Maybe. But what do you think about this?" I fished into my pocket and pulled the note I'd gotten from Shawn's things. 30 pieces of silver.

"It's a reference, obviously," Mischa said. "Judas betrayed Jesus for 30 silvers."

"So who did Shawn betray?"

"After he made the deal with Grigg? Just about everyone."

I stayed in my old bedroom again.

I slept, or I tried to sleep.

Howling.

One wolf, two wolves … five of them. Maybe more, maybe less.

The wolves again. I heard them on nights with a full moon. Just as when

I was a child.

How were there wolves anywhere near the Normandy?

My neighbors told stories. Mr. Cassey said the wolves patrolled the streets at night, always in the long shadows cast by a full moon. Mrs. Riley whispered, close to my ear, they would eat anyone who crossed their paths. It was why so many pets went missing around here. Mr. Armstrong lost both of his cats one night. I found dry blood, bones, and the savaged remains of something feline on the street the next morning, rotting and swarming with black flies.

I always thought they were just telling silly stories to scare the children, but a part of me knew at least some of that was true.

I'd tell Mischa about these things on the nights we stayed up in each other's beds. I never heard the wolves when I was with her, though. She always told me I was an idiot.

Shawn and I also stayed up a few times to try to find them. Sometimes we saw shadows move in the alleys, grey and brown blurs darting from one corner to another. But we never saw wolves.

Harlan Grigg.

Mischa brought over a few articles she printed out at home, plus a few back copies of newspapers she had lying around. It wasn't difficult to find out about Grigg. Change was coming to Nola, brought upon the gale force winds of the Grigg Development Co.

The blocks were all familiar to me. Touro Street, where I played baseball with Shawn and Mischa on the burning summer blacktop. I lost a ball on the roof of the building that used to be there, a long screaming foul ball that I swore disappeared into the sun. Mischa punched me in the nose after losing that ball.

Conti Street, where Ma played bridge with her girlfriends, where I'd sit and read in a hallway that smelled like ganja because she didn't want me in a room where they were smoking cigarettes. It didn't smell any worse than Mischa.

North Rampart Street, where Shawn broke his arm climbing out of a window on the second floor of an abandoned building. The place had always been abandoned, but if you climbed the big tree beside it you could jump in for a view over the French Quarter.

All these places, Grigg had torn down. He made deals with the last plucky holdouts who lived on the land he wanted, promising affordable housing, outreach, and charity to the affected populations. He smiled in all the pictures, shaking hands with the men and women who lived in the homes he was about to tear down, posing with smiling children, laughing with elders.

And in the same papers, relegated to the back pages, the corners, the footnotes of the city record, tales of gruesome and grisly murder followed. Organs missing. A full-on Jack the Ripper that the police didn't even seem interested in investigating, that the papers didn't even seem that interested in reporting about.

After all, only poor people were dying. Poor people with no connections to rich people.

Who cared?

"What if it's a serial killer?" I asked Mischa.

Mischa downed the rest of the beer bottle, then threw it into the corner. It skidded along the carpet, then bumped gently against the wall. I'd asked her not to smoke in my room.

"You're having fun with this," she said.

"What if?"

"You got something to back that up?"

I showed her the newspaper clippings.

"Too many fucking words," Mischa complained. "What's the gist?"

"Every time the last holdout in a building signs their home over to Grigg, there's some kind of crazy murder in the paper."

"People die all the time. It happens."

The last time Grigg made a deal, a firefighter was found dead in a building that burned down the night before. His lungs had been removed from his body, and not with surgical precision. The article went into detail about how messily the job was done.

His name was Gary Olson, survived by Tanya Sanders-Olson and their two children, Michael and Gabriel.

Mischa said Tanya was a friend of a friend of a friend, which was a way of just saying that she knew where they lived. We drove over when some rays of sun peeked out from behind the gray sky, a false hope for a cloudless day.

Mischa stayed in the car. "I don't do good with talking to people. Fucktards, all of them."

From the outside, it looked like a dilapidated shack, surrounded by a chain link fence with metal that had long ago rusted. Sharp, jagged points jutted out every which way. I pushed the gate open, tucking my hand behind a sleeve to avoid puncturing myself.

I knocked on the door.

"What?" a woman asked from inside.

"Tanya?" I asked. "Tanya Sanders-Olson?"

She opened the door. Gray hair flew in all directions above her head, almost like she'd been struck by lightning. Wrinkles cast long shadows over her face. From what Mischa had told me, she wasn't really that old, but it looked like she'd aged decades since her husband died.

"What you want, boy?"

"Your husband was Gary, right? He died–"

"He was murdered. Get your facts straight."

"I believe you."

"'Bout time someone did."

"My brother was murdered, too. The police aren't investigating, but he died like your husband."

"Someone take his lungs?"

"His brain."

The woman nodded. "I told the police, it sounded like voodoo to me."

"People don't practice that way."

"I don't know how they practice. Them rituals, boy. They scare me." Kids yelled inside. Michael and Gabriel, I figured. Tanya turned her head and screamed, "You boys shut up now! You shut up! Go to your rooms and shut up."

I tried to ignore the burst. "Who would want to kill your husband?"

"No one wanted him dead." She crossed her arms. "He just is."

"Why kill him, then?"

"Gary's brother Gus was the last holdout at the place on Conti Street. He was the only tenant who didn't want to move. That Grigg, he wanted that land and he'd do everything he could to tear the building down."

"Let me get this straight. You're saying, Gary was killed to intimidate his brother into selling?"

"That's the long and short of it."

"Do you have any proof?"

Tanya laughed a heavy, bitter laugh. "Of course not. And even if I did, you think it would do any good?"

The story checked out elsewhere, too. Over the next few days, Mischa drove me around Nola, from Gentilly to Carrollton, from Woodmere to Westwego. I hit some dead ends. Lots of people had fled New Orleans, or just didn't want to be found. Others gave me the story Tanya did.

The last holdouts at the places Grigg wanted to tear down faced similar tragedies. Family, friends, brutally murdered, various organs and limbs harvested from their bodies.

"I need to talk to Grigg," I said as Mischa drove over the Mississippi again. Clouds danced in gray reflections on the river.

"Heh. You have fun with that, fucktard."

I expected a large office in a building that towered over the rest of Nola. Instead, Grigg's office was in a beige and green two-story building on Decatur, on a block where rowdy jazz spilled onto the sidewalk from a nearby bar.

Mischa dropped me off at the corner. "I gotta get home," she said. "Dinner with my brothers. You need me to pick you up again?"

"I can walk home from here."

"It's far."

"I'll manage."

She drove off, and I sat down the sidewalk as graffitied walls crawled along my periphery.

I pushed aside a pristine glass door and stepped into a small lobby. The woman at the desk hardly bothered to look up.

"I'm here to see Harlan Grigg," I said, leaning over the desk. She put a cell phone away, then traced a pencil down a large paper calendar.

"You got an appointment?" she asked.

"No."

"Then get out."

"I need to speak with him."

"You and every other media outlet out there."

"I'm not a reporter."

"So you're just here to waste his time?"

"I'm Sam Calver. My brother was Shawn Calver. He was the last holdout at the Normandy."

"Then he *definitely* doesn't wanna talk to you."

"Please–"

"We read the news, Mr. Calver. We know your brother's dead."

"I just want five minutes with Grigg."

"I'll save you four minutes and fifty-nine seconds. Mr. Grigg's exact words will be, 'No comment.'"

"Just let me talk to him."

"He ain't in the office right now, and even if he was, he's not gonna talk to you. Now are you gonna leave or am I gonna call the police?"

"Fine," I muttered, then stepped back away from the desk.

The door opened behind me. Cosme strode into the lobby.

We stared at each other, neither of us speaking a word. Cosme, dressed in a nicer suit than I thought he could ever afford, his scalp shaved tight, his beard trimmed neatly.

"You're late," the woman said. "Meeting was supposed to start half an hour ago."

Cosme nodded. Very, very slowly.

"Sorry," he said. "Bus was late."

"Mr. Grigg's waiting for you."

Cosme looked past me, like I wasn't even there. He walked toward a door in the back. I watched him disappear into the shadow of the room.

"You're still here?" the woman said. She picked up the phone. "I'm gonna start dialing. Nine. Ain't moving yet? One. Last chance."

I shook my head, then went for the door, stepping out into the dying, gray afternoon.

The rain, at least, had stopped. The power had gone out, too. I found a flashlight, but the batteries were long dead and dripped acid when I picked it up.

I found candles instead, lots and lots of candles that Ma collected before she died. Most were still in their original plastic wrappings. I lit several around the room, placing them along the corners, around every surface I could find. The apartment smelled vaguely like shampoo. I never liked being in the dark for too long.

I texted Mischa. I needed to talk to her.

I waited in the living room where Shawn died, on the couch he could have been sitting on moments before he was murdered. The sun disappeared behind the horizon, and night had crept over the swampy air. I stared at a wall, sitting in the darkness, trying to put things together.

Cosme. Why was Cosme meeting with Grigg? The woman at the desk recognized him, too. Did that mean he met Grigg regularly?

Every few minutes, I went to the door so I could go to Cosme's apartment, just a short walk down the hall. Except I always just sat back down.

It would be so easy. Walk to Cosme's apartment, knock on the door, ask a simple question.

What was he doing at Grigg's office?

My phone buzzed. *Out. I'll seeya in a couple hours. Chill, dude.*

Something hit my door. It wasn't a knock. It was more like a crash, like someone didn't realize there was a solid surface right in front of them.

"Hello?" I called.

No vocal response, but whatever was on the other side of the door thudded against it again. I stood up.

"Hello?"

The door splintered open, the hinges knocked out of the frame, the wall cracking and splitting. A man pushed the debris to the side like paper and shuffled forward, one foot dragging lazily across the ground at a time. No. Not a man. A *zombie*.

I screamed as I backed away, falling on my back against the floor, near the same spot where Shawn's body had been found. A candle fell over, setting the couch alight. The carpet caught fire next, blocking the only way out into the hall.

In the burgeoning blaze behind the zombie, I still struggled to see what he even looked like. Shadows danced across a body stitched together in several places. Its arms didn't match each other, its naked legs were different heights. A Y-shaped incision where it had been sewn back together on its chest and stomach. Even the head was different from everything else, a different skin color entirely.

I crawled backward until my head thumped against the wall. I jumped to my feet, using the wall for support. The zombie approached, silent except for the dragging of its feet along the floor. I grasped an empty flower vase from the table, where Shawn and I would sometimes place lilies on Ma's birthday.

I threw the ceramic vase as hard as I could at the intruder. It smashed against its face and shattered into dozens of broken pieces. The zombie proceeded unfazed.

I tried to dash around it, but it reached out and grabbed my shirt. I fell back to the floor and it fell on top of me. I felt fire licking at my shoes, growing closer and closer. I didn't know if I was sweating because the room had turned into an oven, or because I knew I was about to die.

"Help me!" I screamed, hoping someone would hear. "Someone! Help!"

The zombie smelled like death. Rotting decay, like garbage left out in the sun for too long. Its face descended toward mine, rotting teeth on full display as it opened its mouth wide. It was going to eat me.

I struggled beneath the zombie. I got an arm free and pushed it into its face. My thumb went for its eye. I squeezed as hard as I could. The eye turned to jelly beneath the pressure, and blood oozed down my hand and onto my face. The intruder didn't even flinch. I couldn't keep it away from me for much longer.

I thought of Shawn, of his last moments. What were his final thoughts?

I got my arm in front of its mouth, trying to elbow its face, even though I knew it would probably do nothing. It caught the back of my forearm in its mouth and bit down. I screamed as it pulled his head backward, tearing a chunk of my own skin and muscle in its maw.

My arm burned as if it had been set on fire. I pushed back tears–this was it. I knew I was going to die.

Except something barreled into the intruder and knocked it off me instead. Blood still pouring from my arm, I rolled away, closer to the fire. I pushed back up onto my feet.

A wolf tore at the zombie, larger than any wolf I had ever seen. Its fur was gray and black and brown, like a mountain lit only by moonlight on a cloudy night. On all fours, it stood nearly as tall as me.

Another wolf howled down the hall, accompanied by another howl, elsewhere in the building. A furry shadow darted past the door, just beyond where the fire had spread. Behind it followed people, my neighbors, whose faces I vaguely remembered and had mostly forgotten. They looked at my apartment, ablaze as they ran past, and some shrieked in terror at the ever-growing fire.

The fight was short but brutal. After the wolf had knocked the zombie down, it circled its prey once, twice, in the narrow confines of the living room. The zombie got back to its feet, its attention still entirely on me, as if it didn't even recognize that a wolf was in the room with it.

The zombie lunged toward me, and the moment it did, the wolf pounced again, trapping the zombie underneath its weight. It struggled briefly, but the wolf brought its muzzle to his neck and bit down sharply.

When the wolf brought its head back, the zombie's head severed from its body. Its limbs still twitched and moved. The head still bit and snapped in place, as if trying to eat the air.

The wolf looked at me, and I only stared.

The wolves were real.

They protected this building.

It was true, it was all true.

The wolf charged ahead and leapt over the fire, into the hallway. I choked from the smoke, the smell of everything burning and charring around me. My eyes watered so much I could hardly see anymore. I wiped my tears with a sleeve and looked at the apartment's broken entrance.

Jump. I needed to jump.

I took a few steps away to build up momentum and leapt across the flames. Not high enough. Not far enough.

Flames licked at my clothes. My pant leg caught fire, burning my calf and my thigh. In the hall, I dropped to the ground and rolled, like all those cartoons I watched as a kid told me I should.

My leg still burned, but my clothes were no longer ablaze. I struggled back to my feet, my arm still pouring blood against my wrist, dripping from my fingertips, my leg singed and growing numb.

I took the stairs down and out of the building. The elevator was always out of service.

"Can I try?" I asked.

"No," Florian said.

"You don't want to," Shawn said. "The recoil will kick you back."

I rolled my eyes. "I'm not a kid."

"Yeah, but you can't drink yet, either."

Florian laughed. "Til you drink, you ain't a man."

"I've had Dad's rum before."

"And went right to sleep afterward."

Florian took the gun and aimed it again. He pulled the trigger, more glass shattered. Every shot he fired had hit its target. Shawn hadn't hit anything.

"Maybe you should give him a shot," Florian said. "In any case, he's better 'an you."

"Fine," Shawn spat. "Here."

I smiled and took the gun, heavier in my hand than I expected it would be. I nearly dropped it the second I had it.

Florian laughed and laughed. "You look like an idiot."

I tried to steady the gun, raising it back up. Shawn frowned. "Watch it, Sam. Don't point that thing at–"

A loud crack boomed through the air. I hadn't realized my finger was on the trigger. I didn't know how little pressure it took to pull it.

Florian fell to the ground. He wasn't laughing anymore. He was suffocating.

Blood streamed from his neck, where the bullet had whizzed through his windpipe.

"Florian!" Shawn screamed and dropped to his knees. I let the gun fall out of my hand onto the ground.

"I didn't know–" I said. "I didn't think. I didn't know–"

It didn't matter. Florian was dead in seconds.

His eyes still stared up into a hazy, cloudy sky. I knew he couldn't see anything anymore.

Shawn and I walked the streets silently. Everything empty, everything in decay.

So much of New Orleans was still off-limits after the flood. This street, there was always a band that jammed, rain or shine. Their washboard player nodded to me every time he saw me. I didn't know his name, he didn't know mine. They weren't here. They hadn't come back since the flood.

We went behind the Normandies, to the backyard that the people from City Hall always promised was going to be a patio but never was. Instead, grass and shrubs grew unchecked, and a tree dominated the center. No one ever came back here.

Shawn grabbed a broken brick and dug at the base of the tree between the roots. He took the gun and placed it in the ground, then poured the dirt back over it.

"You need to get out of town," he said.

"Where am I gonna go?" I asked.

"Away. Anywhere. Until things cool down."

"What do you mean, until things cool down? Nothing's happened yet."

"No, but people are going to ask questions. We were the last ones to see Florian. Cosme knows we were with Florian."

"We didn't do anything!"

"You *killed* someone, Sam!"

"Shhh! Not so loud."

"Sam. Florian is dead because you didn't know how to shoot a gun. That was an *illegal gun*. Someone filed the serial numbers off of it. Your fingerprints are on it. *My* fingerprints are on it. Someone's going to put two and two together."

"It was an accident."

"No one's going to care. They're going to see two poor kids from the bad part of town and they're going to lock us up and never let us go. You need to get out of here while you can."

"But … but where am I gonna go?"

"Anywhere, Sam. Anywhere but here."

"What about Ma and Dad?"

"Sam. Go. Just go now. Hitch a ride out of town. If they find out you had anything to do with this, you're gone for good."

"What about you?"

"I'll clean up this mess," Shawn said. "I always do."

"I don't have any money."

Shawn reached into his pocket, pulled out a few twenties. He stuffed them into my hand.

"Go," he said.

"Shawn, I–"

"Damn it, Sam, *go!*"

I stopped. Shawn stopped. I backed up a few steps, then hesitated. "Tell Mischa I said bye."

Shawn ignored me. He turned around, walked back to the building. I stood there, watching him, until he disappeared inside.

I left town after I murdered Florian. I didn't read the news.

Five years went by and I migrated up north.

I talked to Shawn a few times by phone, just to let him know where I was. The first time I called was a few months later, washing dishes in the back of a bar in Tennessee. Then, busing tables in Virginia. Cleaning toilets in Jersey. I called Mischa, too, but we didn't really talk about anything, and anyway she thought I was a "fucking idiot." I didn't tell her why I was gone. Shawn didn't either.

Ma died at some point. I don't know how. I don't know why. Shawn said not to come back for her funeral.

I waited tables in a cheap diner in New York, where the owner didn't care what I did before or what my name even was. All that mattered was that I had two hands and could follow directions.

The police never came for me. No one even cared that Florian was dead.

I didn't know Shawn was dead until Mischa called.

I took all the savings I had and bought a bus ticket back to New Orleans. Then I saw Mischa at the funeral, and everyone else who lived in the Normandies. Or mostly everyone else.

Cosme wasn't there.

Cosme worked with Grigg. He intimidated people to succumb to Grigg using voodoo.

He killed Shawn.

Didn't he?

The gun was still there, exactly where we left it. My fingers ached, but the bite on my arm had mostly dried. It hurt to move, but I grunted and groaned and dug out the gun.

I didn't check the clip. I didn't know how. I didn't even know if it could still shoot. It hadn't been touched in over five years except by dirt, mud, and worms.

It was enough.

Mischa found me on the street outside the building. I hid the gun in the back of my pants. I didn't even know if the safety was on. I didn't know how to operate it.

All I knew was that I just had to squeeze the trigger.

"The fuck happened to your arm?" she said.

"Cosme."

"What about Cosme?"

"He tried to kill me. Now I'm going to kill him."

"Sam, wait a fucking second–"

"Where is he?"

"How the hell would I know?"

"Grigg's office, then."

"You think so?"

"Unless he's home."

We looked up at the building, saw orange flames licking at the night sky, spreading from my apartment to the next. A few more residents shuffled out onto the street, most in their pajamas or underwear. I didn't see the wolves out here.

The fire alarm hadn't gone off, and there were no sprinklers inside to speak of. The building would burn down before the fire trucks ever reached it.

If they were even on the way at all.

"Can you give me a lift?" I asked.

Fluorescent lights bathed the sidewalk from the second floor of the office. Mischa pulled the car up to the curb.

"Hey," she said. "You sure about this?"

"No."

I got out of the car anyway.

The front door was locked. Of course it was locked. The door was made of glass, though. I pulled the gun from the back of my pants and raised it like a hammer. I slammed down on the glass, a loud clang reverberating through the air and vibrating up my arm. The glass cracked. I hit it again, and again, and again.

At some point I couldn't feel my arm anymore, but the grip on the gun stayed steady in my hand.

Finally, the glass shattered, raining onto the floor in tiny, broken crystals that crunched beneath my feet as I stepped over them. An alarm rang overhead, an overwhelming and deafening noise that could wake up the entire city.

The first floor was dark. Empty. I found the stairwell in the back and went up. The burns on my leg stung more and more, but I pressed myself upward.

I pushed the door open onto the second floor. Cosme stood near the window. Grigg sat in his chair. I'd never seen him in the flesh.

"I already called the police," Grigg said, his voice higher than I thought it would be, like he was still a teenager despite his graying hair. "They'll be here any minute."

I raised my gun up at him.

"Whoa," Grigg said. "Hey, hey now man, let's not get hasty. See this guy beside me? He's a bokor. A bokor. You understand that? He does voodoo.

He's worked a lot of magic to keep me safe. To keep people like you from killing me."

"I'm not here for you," I said.

"Oh." Grigg looked up at Cosme. "Oh. Well hell, that changes things."

Cosme's eyes widened. "What are you saying?"

"Hey look, if this thing's just between you two," Grigg said, "I'm just gonna mosey on out of here."

He stood up, slowly, hands on the table. He buttoned his slate suit and took a step away from his desk.

"Harlan," Cosme said.

"Hey, this ain't any of my business now, is it? Besides, you're replaceable. How many other bokors are there working in New Orleans, anyway?"

Grigg took a tentative step to the side, then another. When he saw that I wasn't going to shoot, he took a longer stride toward the stairwell.

"You kids have fun now," he said as he passed. I aimed at Cosme instead.

"What are you doing?" Cosme asked, backing toward the window.

"You killed Shawn."

"I didn't kill–"

"And then you tried to kill me because I knew you were working for Grigg."

"I'm not–"

"You intimidate people for him. You use your magic to murder, to make people comply. You killed Shawn. You killed Gary Olson. How many more people did you kill?"

"I didn't kill your brother–"

"And for what? *Why* were you working for Grigg?"

Cosme shook. His fists balled so tight he could turn coal to diamonds. "Because I wanted to get out of here!"

His voice was so loud it almost knocked me off my feet. I kept my gun trained on him as best as I could.

"Because this city is *sick*. Because no one is saved, and no one deserves it. After Katrina came, after you murdered Florian, I *prayed*, I prayed *every night* for another flood to come, to wash away everything. But no flood came. And I stopped praying."

"Why kill all these people? Grigg is a monster."

"Because at least Harlan is honest about his monstrosity. Everyone else hides behind a mask. Everyone wants to believe that they're better than everyone else. But no one is. We're all the same. We're all liars, we're all monsters. I'm no different. Neither are you."

"You made that zombie to do your work for you."

"I harvested its entire body from my victims. It did my bidding, it made men cower in fear, it made them cry like children as it killed them. It brought me closer and closer to getting out of this pandemonium you call home."

"You killed Shawn. You tried to kill me."

"I didn't kill your goddamn brother. *But you killed Florian*. I should have killed you a long–"

Pieces of Cosme's brain splattered against the window before I even realized I'd fired the shot. He slumped to his knees, then fell over. My ears rang from the sound of the gunshot.

So it still worked.

I threw the gun into the Mississippi River before Mischa drove us to her house, a few blocks away from the Normandies. I sat on her bed in the dark, staring at my hands. The wound on my arm had clotted, but I could hardly move it at all. My leg still burned and ached as if it was still on fire.

Mischa had her head on the pillow. We hadn't said a word to one another since I left the office.

Cosme was dead.

I killed Cosme.

"I did the right thing, right?" I asked.

Mischa shrugged. "Fuck if I know."

"He killed Shawn. He tried to kill me. Who knows how many other people he killed?"

"Sure."

"He deserved to die."

Mischa sat up and reached for the bedside table. She began rolling a cigarette. "You want one."

"Yeah."

I listened to her finish rolling it, humming a song. "La Vie en Rose," the way Louis Armstrong played it. She kissed the cigarette wrap, staining it with her dark lipstick.

She lit it in her mouth. After a long breath in, she exhaled a steady cloud of smoke. She handed the cigarette to me.

"When did you start smoking?" she asked.

"I didn't."

I inhaled some smoke as best as I could and ended up choking and coughing. Mischa laughed. The cigarette fell out of my mouth, onto the floor.

"Pick it up, fucknut."

I reached down and took the cigarette in my fingers. A dark ring encircled the wrap, like the same cigarettes I saw outside the Normandies. Cigarettes discarded on the side of the front entrance, the same ones custom made by Mischa.

Mischa had been at the apartment before I arrived.

"Hey," Mischa said. "The hell is wrong with you? Give it back."

"You were there," I said.

"Where?"

"The Normandies."

"Yeah. So?"

"You were there before I got in. I saw your cigarettes on the ground."

"I used to live there, too, you know."

"Were you there the night Shawn died?"

"I dunno, was I?"

I swallowed. I didn't want to ask the question.

But I did.

"Did you kill Shawn?"

"Yeah."

Mischa didn't even hesitate. I wasn't prepared for it.

She reached across the bed and took the cigarette from my fingers, paralyzed in place as I processed her answer. She took another long puff, calm and cold. She stared out her window onto the orange street light outside her apartment.

"Why didn't you say anything?" I finally said.

"You didn't ask."

"Why'd you kill him?"

"Fucker betrayed us all."

"But … but all he did was give up his lease! He negotiated with Grigg! He got affordable housing for the condo."

"Yeah. So? That sounds like a lost battle to me. Besides, Cosme got to him first."

"How?"

"Cosme said he was gonna kill you. He knew where you were, where you were living in New York. He could see it through the flames and the shadows of his voodoo. Said he was gonna get revenge for Florian. Shawn gave in, stopped fighting Grigg."

"So you killed him?"

"The Normandies aren't *just* the place we all grew up, you idiot. It's also where the pack got its powers."

"The pack? What are you talking about?"

"Oh, I don't know. The goddamn wolves that keep the Normandies safe? The fucking wolves that saved your ass tonight? That saved everyone else in the building, no thanks to you? We're the building's protectors. It's our territory."

"You?"

"Never eat a zombie, dude. Everything is rotting flesh and it tastes worse than ass."

"You saved me."

Mischa rolled her eyes. "I'm beginning to regret the decision."

"You didn't save Shawn."

"Shawn handed the Normandy's death sentence to Grigg. I told him not to. I begged him not to. I fucking *warned* him to hold out. When he gave up the fight, he gave up his life. Grigg gave him his 30 silvers, his affordable fucking housing and saving your miserable, worthless life from Cosme. That was the ultimate betrayal to the Normandies. To the pack."

"What the hell makes the Normandies so special?"

She sighed, then stood. "There's a spring underneath the building. It's fed directly by the bayou. There's something special in that water. It gives you power. Power beyond what people should be capable of. Me and a bunch of others, it let us become wolves, but only when you drink from it."

"You don't even live there anymore."

"None of us do–we all got evicted at one point or another. Some city official didn't like the smell of my smoking. But that didn't mean we weren't gonna do everything we could to protect it. If that stream gets polluted in any way, we could lose everything."

"So you pointed me at Cosme and had me kill him?"

"Wasn't that difficult."

"Why?"

"Because his voodoo was also keeping Grigg safe. Making it impossible to approach him. And damn it, Sam. The world's way better off without someone like Cosme around. Throwing around voodoo to do someone else's bidding? Guy was pure evil, and don't you even *begin* to try to justify that he should've lived. Yeah. I killed your fucking brother, because he caved in. May as well have betrayed us all with a kiss. Then yeah, I had you kill Cosme, because fuck that guy."

For a long time, I didn't say anything. We stayed in the room in silence, and I stared at the wall trying to comprehend everything that she'd just said.

Mischa killed Shawn.

My best friend from childhood killed my brother.

Because he betrayed everyone to save me.

I stood up and took a few steps toward the door. Everything felt numb. I couldn't feel my fingers, my toes. I couldn't even make my eyes blink.

I paused before leaving. "What are you going to do next?"

Mischa laughed. "Cosme's dead. Whatever voodoo he was working to keep Grigg safe is gone. So now? We're gonna fucking tear Grigg to shreds."

I walked all the way back to the Normandies, wandering aimlessly down streets I didn't remember. By the time I got back, the sun had already begun its slow ascent.

Most of the Normandies were still standing. The fire petered out somewhere on my floor. No firetrucks had even bothered to come. The storm was gone, for now. It was the first time I'd actually seen the sun since I arrived.

I went into the building and found the stairs leading to the basement. Nothing stirred, nothing moved.

I opened every door I found. A closet behind one. The boiler room behind another. Finally, I found another door marked DO NOT ENTER, unlocked, with footsteps in the dirt below.

Pushing it open, I descended even more stairs, down a dark hallway that I lit up with the light of my cellphone. The hallway opened up into a dark, natural cavern, directly beneath the buildings.

A small pool of water sat before me, glowing slightly with its own strange luminescence, as if lit by fireflies from below.

I knelt beside the pool and dipped a hand into the water. It was warm, and an odd tingle raced through my arm.

I cupped a handful of water and drank.

It tasted sweeter than wine.

Glass Darkly

by Paul K. Ellis

The crimson spray arched gracefully up the wall and across ceiling from the window to the overhead light. Deep, dark, almost black at the curtains to a somewhat brighter shade of maroon near the bulbs told of a day or so drying time.

If it weren't for the copper tang in the air, you might think it was paint.

Thank goodness for the cold, the coldest October in New Orleans in over one hundred fifty years. Kept the flies away. And, the maggots.

The bedroom, well, the only room in the chef's flop was tore up, and not like the bulls had given it a once over, either. That mess would've looked like it had a purpose. This mess looked like an alligator had been let loose. Except there was no bloody swath where the gator had dragged it's snack back to the bayou. And no clawed and broken door. In fact, the only thing in the room that appeared truly broken was the vanity mirror set on the wall near the window. From the smears on the cracked glass, it looked like the crimson painter had been shoved into it with significant force. Where that body was now was anyone's guess.

And yeah, the neighbors had heard nothing.

That I intuited, in large part because NOPD wasn't camped out. Which was a good thing, since my peeper's license had expired. And wasn't any good in Louisiana. I toed through the debris on the floor, shaking my head. The things we do for family.

I heard a metallic clinking while pushing a clump of wadded-up lingerie aside. I squatted on my heels and prodded at the clump with a pencil I'd pulled out of my jacket pocket. The wad fell apart, and I used the pencil to pick up a small, delicate chemise by its very thin straps. Far too small to fit on the chef's arm, much less over his head. So, Justin had a honey on the side. I'm sure his wife would be thrilled. I shook it. The noise makers fell out, and disappeared into the folds of the clothing strewn on the floor. After pawing around a little more in the unmentionables, I came up with an earring shaped like a crescent moon, with a small, stylized star nestled in the inner curve. Yeah, I recognized it. I'd seen it's mate earlier this morning.

Hooked on one of the moon's points was a tie bar. I unhooked it from the earring and gave it a gander. It was an expensive piece of frippery. 'R.' 'D.' Gaudy initials on sterling silver, and, at the time he bought it, worth more than the owner made in a month. So, his wife paid for it. Out of the food budget. 'R.' 'D.' Renny Dupre.

I swore. I wasn't being paid. Good thing; nothing was enough to put up with this.

"Lose sumting, mister?"

My skin crawled, not so much because someone snuck up on me, as my reaction to that old black magic. Contrary to Louie and Keely, it wasn't love I was feeling. No, I had felt this over a year ago in Los Angeles, when I had my unfortunate run-in with the Nain Rouge. Okay, yeah, a little because he snuck up on me, too.

I looked up from the floor to the jimmied and opened doorway. Leaning against the jam, sucking his teeth, was a short little guy. His white hair puffed around his dome like a delicate dandelion, but his hands were meat hooks. I noticed only because he was busy flexing them in time with his breathing.

"Naw, I'm good," I said, slipping the earring and tie bar into a pocket, and standing to look down on him.

He wasn't impressed. I'd had that effect a lot, lately.

"You gonna invite old Aga Bab in, mister?" His voice was a little high, but not enough to make fun of.

"Naw," I said again, around a slow smile. "I'm good."

"So, I call the cops, then?" He waved his hand in a through-away motion.

"Fine with me, sport." No, it wasn't fine with me. I was itching that "conjuring itch" all over and wanted the little prick gone. I had a feeling he wanted the cops here just about as badly as I did, so I played a hunch.

"Maybe *they* can ask you where the chef is."

He grimaced. "You don't know either? So, where's the frail?"

"What frail, sport?" I kept smiling. "You going to call the cops, or shall I?"

He stopped leaning on the doorway. "I've never seen a body in such a powerful hurry to stay the night as a guest of the state," he said.

"You do give off that air," I replied, then made a show of looking around the room. "I'll call, then. I just saw the phone a minute ago."

It was his turn to smile. "On second thought, I got other girls...younger girls to look after." He stepped backwards, out of the doorway. "You take care there, Jack. Right now, you're protected, but everything changes and we'll meet again."

He knew my name. Swell. My sinking feeling got worse when Shorty crammed a hat on his head, turned, and walked down the hall, his footsteps echoing back.

"Oh, and Balor sends his regards."

That damn hat. That red Peter Pan styled hat.

How did I get into this mess?

It's important you understand I don't hate my brother. It's just that he's a selfish ass.

For instance, yesterday, when he showed up unannounced at GrandMama's.

"C'mon Jack, just a couple of days. You come on down, I've got a place over the restaurant. You'll get meals on the house. I'm sure my chef will come staggering home in a day or two. You can treat it like a mini-vacation. What do you say?"

René Dupre. Avant-garde restaurateur, pretentious snot, unrepentant whiner, and my brother. He was nervous and fidgety. I have about as much to say to him now as I did when I found out he married Lanie. To be fair, the family thought I'd died at Pearl. By the time they found out different, old Renny had set himself up as the man-of-the-house, and left GrandMama to fend for herself, while he went to town. After the war, I came home to disabuse him of that notion. But by then it was too late. He'd already glommed onto Lanie's inheritance.

Did I mention he's self-centered? Okay, yeah, I hate him.

"Renny," I said with a sigh. "I don't want to go into the city. It makes my skin crawl. Literally. Besides, you don't need my help. You said it yourself, your chef will wander in eventually. Go on back to town." I made to close the door, and the little weasel wedged his foot between the door and the frame. I jerked it back open, preparing to slam it on his tiny foot.

"Jacques," GrandMama said. She came in from the kitchen. "Hear da boy out. He family. Family helps each other."

She means well, she truly does, but she says the damnedest things.

I looked at her over my shoulder and raised an eyebrow.

"Really?"

She waved her hand at me, dismissing all the pain and betrayal I felt, as if they didn't matter.

"Dat water's gone, *cher*. Gone on to da Gulf. Dis problem is here. In front of you. Right now."

She was right. Crazy old broad.

"You still at Casper's?" I asked, not really wanting to hear the answer.

"Yeah," he said. "So, what time should I expect you tomorrow?"

Needy. He was just so needy. And all he was offering was free food. It wasn't like my time meant anything to him.

"'Bout lunch, I expect."

He moved his foot away from the door and leaned against the outside frame.

"Could you make it sooner, I ..."

I slammed the door in his face. I would have locked it, but GrandMama had never felt the need to install any. I could still hear him talking to the closed door as I turned back to the kitchen. Could I make it sooner? Unbelievable!

She stood there, arms crossed and tapping her foot. Clearly, I had stepped over some line, but for the life of me, I didn't know where I'd crossed.

"Dat was rude boy," she said. "I done raised you better dan dat!"

I sighed again. "I was downright congenial. Rude would have been to slam my fist into his face."

"You hush, now! That boy has the troubles, but he family! You don't turn your back on family!" She was adamant, which put me in a bind, since I was staying at her place. Had been since Los Angeles.

Funny thing, the LAPD wouldn't hold me without a body, even with Kathleen babbling on about my guilt. Of course, she spent her days as a guest of California's psychiatric system. But the department made it clear I wasn't welcome, and after they spent a week "questioning" me, "Hanging" Judge Hardwick ordered me cut loose, bruises and all. That's what happens when they think you're a dirty cop that just killed their lieutenant. Well, I guess all of them didn't believe that, or plain didn't care. I was still breathing.

I heard Renny stomp off of the porch, and then heard his car door open and slam shut. He didn't start the engine though. Pity.

I relented. What choice did I have? Me and every other sane person in the bayou had a good, healthy fear of her.

"All right, GrandMama. I'll help the little bastard."

"Language!" She fumed.

"He's a bastard in action, if nothing else, and no. I don't forgive him. I'll never forgive him."

She looked worried at that pronouncement.

"You come eat," she said, going into the kitchen. "Dinner's getting cold."

I followed my nose. If you've never eaten okra fried up in a cast iron skillet, I'm here to tell you, it's very nearly a religious experience. She let me eat my okra and étouffée in silence. After I'd finished sopping the last of the gravy up with cornbread, she asked, "You want some more tea, *cher*?"

"Sure," I said.

"It's there on the counter. You pour me a glass while you is up, yah?"

I fell for it. I always fell for it.

I got up and poured. I looked out of the kitchen window, watching the wane light of the *feu follet* sparkle yellow and green on the water. The pane was dirty. I made a mental note to wash it before I left.

"Jacques, why your brother get you so riled? Dis not about Lanie."

I sat and sipped on my tea. It was almost syrup. It tasted like home.

"Of course it's about Lanie," I said. Ghislaine Delphine Boudreau. My girl. Renny's wife.

She covered my hand with her's.

"Do you blame her, for thinking you dead, and taking comfort with Rene?"

"Of course not!" I said. "It wasn't her fault!"

"As much her's as Rene's. You know dis." She took her hand away and gave me that look again. "You can't hold on to da hate, boy. It draws da dark to you."

I didn't want to agree with her. She was right, but I still didn't want to agree with her.

"*Cher*, you gotsta let that go. You can't hold that poison inside you. Ever since you got back to the bayou, I has been afeared for you. Dat hate draws da Baron to you like a lodestone."

Swamp gas, that's got to be why she says what she does. Either swamp gas, or moonshine.

"It's not da 'shine, boy! How. Many. Times. I. Gotsta. Tell. You."

She punctuated every period with a swat to my head or shoulders. She didn't really mean anything by it, other than to get my attention. Otherwise, she could've knocked me right out.

I relented. Again. That had been happening a lot.

"Look, I'm helping the stuck up little pric... prince." She was glaring. It had that effect on my speech. "I'll go and hold his hand until his chef shows back up."

She looked into my eyes and sighed.

"Bobby done tole me, you is stubborn," she said. "He say you hold on to 'dis hate for so long, it's a comfort."

Good old mouthy Bobby Tremaine. My buddy. The dead one.

"You gonna need 'dis when you goes to town to help Rene," she said, handing me an oil cloth package. "It's from the Ashcroft side of the family."

I unwrapped it.

"GrandMama, I can't take this, it's yours," I said, holding it out to her. Frankly, I didn't want it. Heirloom or not, that weathered, rust-covered Bowie knife had seen better days. It was old, plain, and in need of a good polishing. And an even better sharpening.

"It's the family's," she said. "You is going to town, to help family. You'll need it in order to face the Baron." She crossed her arms. "I have seen."

She had seen. Swell. Looks like me and the oversized letter-opener were going to town.

***

We managed the trip from Bayou Pierre to New Orleans in silence. This was due in large part to my not riding with Renny. I took my car, a black-on-chrome 1959 Dodge Coronet, and beat him to the restaurant by several hours. It hadn't opened yet, so I had to wait.

Renny managed Casper's Taste of the Bayou, ostensibly for Lanie. He liked to think he was the owner, but Casper's had been willed to her by her Great Aunt Hattie. No one really knows why. It was a smallish, cozy place, little bigger than a cafe, at the corner of Esplanade and Rampart, on the north side of the French Quarter. I remembered it being a pretty good place to eat, its menu deeply rooted in Cajun cuisine. It wasn't typical New Orleans-style fare, but I think that was part of the appeal. The joint was supposed to be "happening," whatever that meant.

Cajuns don't normally frequent cities, so when GrandMama told me that Lanie got fed up with the nightlife and asked Renny to return to Bayou Pierre, I wasn't surprised. What did surprise me was when she came back alone.

I'm no paragon of brotherly concern, but a man ought not treat his wife that way, and a smart one sure enough shouldn't treat Lanie that way. Renny abandoned family twice now. Some things you don't forgive.

I tried not to look in the mirror too hard when I thought that. It's not like I'd been around a lot for Lanie after the war. Some postcards and maybe a letter or two. Then, nothing.

I found a place to park and sat, waiting on Renny to turn up. I left the motor running so I could use the heater. I'd get too hot and turn it, and the engine, off. Then, I'd get cold. I was getting antsy. New Orleans is a locus to all manner of bizarre happenings: voodoo, hoodoo, voudon, and the like. All of that strange aggravated my "conjuring" itch, that feeling when the short hairs on my neck stand up, my goose bumps bloom, and a taste of 120 volts zaps me right between the eyes. Consequently, I didn't care much for it. My body felt a constant hum, like I was jacked into a substation.

I'd given up and was about to return to GrandMama's when Renny finally arrived.

I got out of the Coronet and met him at the door. He let us in without a word. So far, it had been a pretty good experience.

He shut the door, locked it, and cleared his throat. "Jack, I just want to thank you for helping me."

So much for that good experience.

"Yeah, about that," I said. "I'm doing it for Lanie. This is her place."

His face got all pinched. "It's not like you're going to let me forget anytime soon, is it?"

"No, it isn't," I said. I caught movement out of the corner of my eye, turned, and did a double take. "Anyone here?" I asked, walking over to the mirror by the coat room. Big, gaudy thing. A Victorian monstrosity, eight feet tall by four feet wide, or thereabouts.

"We don't open for lunch," he said. "The staff won't be here for hours. Why?"

I looked around both sides of the mirror. Nope, no one there.

"Ah, no reason. I thought I saw an old pal of mine."

"The mirror is in line with the front door," Renny said. "Maybe you saw his reflection as he walked past. It is New Orleans, after all."

"That'd be a trick, seeing how he's dead, and all."

He crossed himself. "Yah, best not to talk about it."

Who was this fellow, and what had he done with my brother? Renny wasn't usually superstitious. Normally, I'd give him the business over this lapse, but given our past history, I let it go.

The silence stretched into awkward. I broke it pretending to care about his decor. "This new?" I asked gesturing to mirror.

"That is a genuine antique from Myrtles Plantation. Got it from an estate sale for a song," he said.

"It does brighten up the area."

He frowned. "Not that I've noticed. Matter of fact, it's been a little cool." His frown deepened and he knelt to scrub at the glass with a bar rag. "Damn those kids! I find out which of 'em been leaving hand prints my mirror, I'm gonna tan their hide!"

I pulled out a nearby barstool and sat. "Why don't you lay it out for me? Who is this chef what's gone missing?"

He gave me a look like he was about to correct my grammar, but thought better of it and sat on the stool next to mine.

"Justin has been missing for about a week," he began.

"He's been gone a week and nobody thought to look for him?"

"This is New Orleans. People go missing here all the time," he said, matter-of-factly.

I geared up to say something smart when she appeared, and words failed me. Failed my mouth too, because it just hung open, catching flies.

She was upscale. Classy. Sophisticated. Chilling, and I don't mean emotionally; cold radiated off her in waves.

"Jack, allow me the pleasure of introducing Julie d'Octave, Justin's 'special' friend," Renny said, taking her hand. "I asked her to stop by and meet you, see if you had any questions for her. Julie, this is my brother, Jack."

"Charmed," she said, extending her hand to me in a courtly manner.

Did she expect me to kiss it? I snapped my mouth shut and took her hand in both of mine, giving her a firm, but not over-powering shake.

"I bet you are," I said with a wink. Then, I noticed her earring, singular. "You need to slow down there, sister. You rushed your morning ablutions, and left part of your haul behind." I pointed at her bare ear. From the other hung a silver crescent moon and star.

Renny bristled and started to unload on my manners, when she removed her hand from mine, then touched the outside of his wrist with her forefinger, shaking her head one time. No. He stopped fidgeting.

Fantastic! Only my brother would cheat on his wife with an employee's mistress.

"Oh dear," she said flatly, as if it were of little matter. "How distressing. Wherever could it have gotten to?"

"Not to worry, it's only an earring!" Renny said, quickly. Red crept up his neck.

"I do hate to run," Julie said, abruptly. "It was *so* nice making your acquaintance," she said to me, in a tone usually reserved for finding a cockroach in the pantry.

"Charmed," I replied as she turned to leave. She ignored me.

"What was that about?" Renny hissed, sounding like a busted radiator.

"Renny, what do you see in her?"

"She's ... interesting. She likes to parade around in the altogether." He winked at me again, then realized his error. "According to Justin, that is," he said hurriedly. "You know *I* would *never* step out on Lanie! Never in a million years! You must believe me!"

"Let's try something I can believe. Where does Justin live? Julie too, if you happen to know." Oh, I'd bet good money he'd happen to know.

"Justin's got her an apartment over on Royal Street, but *I've* never been there. He's been staying there most days, I hear."

I gave him the stink eye until he began to fidget.

"Fine," I said. "I'll go take a gander, and let you know what I run across."

I slid off the stool and headed for the door. I had a feeling I was going to regret this.

My mouth was dry, and I was sweating like a sinner in church.

I wouldn't say I was running back to Casper's, but I was definitely quick-stepping across the French Quarter. Any minute now, I felt like I was about to be jumped by a bunch of silver-haired nabobs in red hats. Yeah, it's been that kind of day. I paused long enough to drop three cigarettes in the gutter before finally grabbing one. My hand was shaking so badly I didn't know if I was going to light tobacco or eyebrows. Finally, I got a good, solid drag and slumped up against a light pole. I closed my eyes and exhaled. This city had my nerves frayed. I used to spend a good deal of time here when I was younger, up to general mischief and nonsense, enough so that I had a pretty good feel for the city.

I sensed a change in the street's rhythm and cracked a peeper to see what's what. Ah, a member of local constabulary was eyeing my performance. That's when it hit me.

I must've looked like a dope fiend jonesing for a fix.

I tucked the cigarette into the corner of my mouth and stood up straight, away from the pole. I fixed my hat brim, snapped my coat collar straight and calmly walked back to the cafe. The cop must've had more pressing business. I didn't see him again.

I entered through the service door with the key Renny gave me, closed it, locked it, and climbed the stairs to his apartment over the restaurant. I fingered the tie bar in my pocket. We were about to have an uncomfortable conversation. Well, he'd be uncomfortable anyway.

As I got near the landing, I heard him singing and humming along to the radio. He was cooking. It's the only time he sings. It's probably the only time he's truly happy. Good thing, too. He can't carry a tune in a bucket. We have our differences, and I pretty much consider him a waste of skin, but that boy can cook! The problem is he only does it to show off. Julie must be there. Great, they'll both have an uncomfortable conversation before Renny throws me out. I reached the top of the stairs, took a breath, and let myself in.

And there she sat on the overstuffed chair, legs tucked under her, with a highball in her hand.

"Hello, little fish," she said, with an impish smile. Actually, impish is pretty close to the truth, near as I could tell. A pained look crossed my face.

"Don't call me that, beautiful. Names like that have a tendency to stick."

No, not Julie. Maddie. Maddie Night. A smart, gorgeous, leggy brunette with a mean right hook. And I thought the Nain Rouge were trouble.

"I wanted to surprise you," she said, and sat the highball on the coffee table, bounced up off of the chair and gave me a big hug. Or, tried to. She jerked away at the last minute, like I shocked her. Serves her right. The city hammered me with continuous input, so I missed her vibe completely. Now she knew how I felt when we first met.

"I missed you," she said, rubbing her arms. Then gave me a faux pout. "You never called, you never wrote."

"I'm a terrible man," I said, with genuine laughter. "Allow me to great you properly." I held out my arms again, but she backed away.

My puzzlement was turning to aggravation. What was she doing? Teasing? Really?

"Jacques!" Renny sang, off key, from the apartment's kitchen. "Leave our guest alone, and come give me a hand."

Oh, goody.

I gave Maddie a curt nod and ambled over the four or five steps it took to reach the kitchen. "Yeah?"

Renny's eyes were shining and he grabbed my shoulders. I was starting to think this was going to get uncomfortable for me.

"She is *wonderful!*" he gushed, sotto voce. "I was so worried about you meeting Julie, until Matilda knocked on my door. I can see why you have kept her a secret! She's a treasure!"

My mouth was opened. Again. I was going to have to stop doing that. I closed it and swallowed.

"Renny, call Julie over."

"That is splendid! It'll be like a double date!"

"Yeah, except Julie ain't your wife." I gave him the stink eye. Again.

"But, I thought since you have Matilda ..."

"He doesn't really have me," Maddie said, having retaken her seat in the chair. "It's more of a lend/lease arrangement."

He started to get red in the face, and took the gumbo off the stove. It smelled great. I wondered if I'd get any. To eat that is. It looked uncomfortably warm to wear.

"First, it's Lanie that's off limits, then it's Matilda, and now you want to 'talk' to Julie?" A vein throbbed on his forehead. "No! I saw Julie first! You keep away from Julie! Julie is mine!"

I punched him right on the point of his thrust out chin. He collapsed like a sack of potatoes.

"Why did you do that?" Maddie asked from her vantage point in the chair. She wasn't in any hurry to help him. Smart girl.

"He was hysterical," I replied. "And, I felt like it. I'm more than a little angry at the moment."

"At him, or at me?"

I didn't say anything. I just started rooting around in the cabinets looking around for a clean glass. Finding one, I began filling it up at the sink. "What did you do to him?"

She looked a little hurt, but covered it up pretty quickly. "Glamour," she said, finishing off her highball. "I needed to see you, and it seemed the fastest way. Who's 'Lanie'?"

I ignored that question. "Needed to see me? Why did you 'need' to see me?"

She shrugged. "Your GrandMama got it touch with Mister Green. She was concerned about your state of mind, dealing with your brother and all. You know, the one you just knocked out."

I snorted, topping the glass off and closing the tap. "So, you just volunteered?"

"Of course," was all she said.

I let that hang between us for a moment, remembering the beatings I took for her and Green. Then I dumped the glass full of water on my brother. He woke sputtering and fuming.

"You hit me!"

I jerked him to his feet, and gave him the one-two slap; open hand, back hand. "You with me?"

He flailed for a moment. "Yes! Yes! Just don't hit me again."

"Call Julie, Renny. I need to talk to her."

"No, you don't! You ain't no cop. You ain't even a peeper anymore!"

He was scared. His pretension was slipping.

"Then, why am I here, you blistering idiot? I don't *want* to be here!"

"Boys!" Maddie said sharply. "Enough!"

Nothing like being called down in your not home by your not girlfriend to make you not care.

I took my hands off of him.

"You know, I don't need this." I backed away and headed for my bag, behind the sofa in the other room. Time to get back to the bayou. I'd just have to weather GrandMama's disappointment. I saw my reflection in the mirror that hung over the sofa. The frame was warped and my image was funny looking. You couldn't depend on what you saw in Renny's mirror.

He never had to deal with the consequences of his actions before. GrandMama always stepped in, or had me do it. My leaving would give him that opportunity to grow. It would be good for him.

It would be great for me, mind you, but also good for him.

"I'm sorry," he wailed, his head in his hands. "I don't know what came over me. When Julie is involved, I get so crazy!"

I stopped packing and swore silently. I wanted to beat him until he remembered, then beat him some more because he forgot. Lanie. My girl. His wife. But, I let him blubber on about his mistress for awhile. All the beating in the world wasn't going to shake him free of that.

I was going to regret this.

I turned back to the kitchen, all my resolve washed away by his tears. "Renny, pull yourself together, man. We need to focus. You have a problem."

He stopped and snuffled, wiping his nose on his sleeve. What was he, five?

"Another?" he said, red-eyed.

Silently, I pulled his tie bar out of my pocket and showed it to him.

"I didn't ..." he began. "We never ... Where did you find that?"

"Do the cops know you were the last person to see Justin alive?"

"What are you saying!" he demanded, backbone suddenly in place.

"What they'll be saying. Get a thicker skin because they'll be coming at you harder than this, and you'd better have the right answers!"

He looked frightened. Finally.

"You said people go missing all the time in the city, ya?" I asked.

"Y-yes," he said.

"How about here, in the Quarter? Who's been missing recently, besides Justin? Men, women?"

"Mostly men."

"Married men?"

"I suppose," he conceded.

"What are you getting at?" Maddie asked, with some asperity.

"Julie has a type," I said. "It's why she doesn't like me."

"Well, that could be 'a' reason," Maddie grinned.

I gave her a sour look. "Uh-huh." I turned back to Renny. "Call her. Tell her you have to see her tonight. Downstairs, after closing."

"What'll I tell her? What if she won't come?"

"Tell her I'm going to the cops with what I know if she doesn't," I said.

"No, tell her you're leaving your wife," Maddie said.

Renny gulped.

"That'll do it," I said, my face like stone.

"Then what?" Maddie asked.

I smiled, grim as granite.

"Oh, *cher, laissez les bon temps rouler.*"

You ever notice how time seems to lose it's mind when you have to wait?

It was long past closing. We sat at the bar nearest the coat check, sipping bourbon and slowly going insane.

After we bullied Renny into calling Julie, I pulled out the family paperweight GrandMama had foisted on me and took it to the kitchen. After several hours of dirty looks from the staff, I had sharpened and polished the blade to a keen finish, and even keener edge. Cleaning the brass took a little longer.

By the time I returned upstairs, Maddie had left word that she'd be back, just needing to change. Renny started getting ready for the evening meal. I washed up, changed, and slept on the sofa until just after closing.

I turned to face that gaudy mirror, catching sight of my reflection. I hid a chuckle when I noticed the tiny hand prints were back. I raised my glass in salute. Whoever it was doing that, I was on their side.

"*You need to pay attention,*" Bobby said, in my head.

"'Bout time," I whispered. "What took you so long?"

"*The traffic was murder,*" he replied. "*Can we move this along? I don't have a lot of time.*"

I nodded, not trusting my voice.

"*Julie d'Octave is not who you think she is.*"

"Oh, I have a pretty good idea," I whispered. "She's tangled up with the Nain Rouge, that's all I need to know."

"*It's bigger than that, Jack. You know better! It's always bigger than that.*"

"Thanks, Bobby. Now tell me something I don't already know."

"D'you say something?" Renny asked, a little bleary from the bourbon.

"Just thinking about what my old pal Bobby Tremaine would say about this."

"What did he say, Jack?" Maddie watched me intently.

"He said we've underestimated Julie. It's bigger than her. It's always been bigger."

"Is somebody here already?" Renny asked, wobbling on the stool.

"We are, we are, we are," Aga Bab said, walking up to us with Julie on his arm. They stopped in front of the mirror. He looked at me, grinning like a lunatic. "I done tole you we'd meet again!"

"Swell, who invited you?" I said, dragging a cigarette out of the pack on the bar and lighting it.

"It's important you know dis," he said. "You did. You did when you invited my Julie."

Renny slammed his glass on the bar with such force that I heard the thick bottom crack.

"No!" He staggered off of the stool and stood swaying in front of the little man. "Julie is mine!"

"Renny," I reached for him. "Kindly sit your ass down!" I grabbed his arm and the world tilted about forty-five degrees.

When I came back to myself, it was clear the crazy had been let out of the bottle. I was on the floor, crumpled up by the mirror. I uncrumpled and sat up. What is it with my jaw and dames?

I heard glass crack and realized Julie and Renny had just slammed into the mirror.

"Jack," he wheezed. "Get this bitch off of me!"

"Bitch?" she laughed, eyes wild and wide. "After all we've meant to each other?" It was the most emotion I'd seen from her. She was enjoying this.

Somehow, while I was out, Julie jumped on little brother's back and put him in a Grade A stranglehold. From the shade of blue he was turning, I'd say it was working.

She bit his ear hard enough to draw blood. He wailed and tried to hit her, but her legs had pinned his arms. "You lie, you cheat, you break your oath, and I'm the bitch? Your faithlessness condemns you. You must die!"

Okay, time to derail the crazy train. I grabbed the frame of the mirror and tried to pull myself upright. My legs were having a hard time with gravity.

Two sets of tiny hands reached through the mirror and grabbed Julie and Renny by their shoulders. I let go of the frame, allowing gravity it's victory and looked into the mirror. Two pale, dark-eyed, sunken-cheeked kids, a boy and a girl, appeared in the glass. It was almost like they were underwater, sticking their hands through the surface, except they were in the mirror. Behind them stood an equally unattractive woman. She said something I didn't hear and her kids pulled Julie and Renny through the glass with one swift jerk. They backed away until they faded from sight, leaving only the reflection of the cafe and a smear from Renny's bloody ear behind.

"Maddie," I yelled. "What just happened?"

I rolled over just in time to see Maddie high kick a surprisingly unmarked Aga Bab to the ground. His head thumped like a ripe melon on the hardwood, dandelion hair waving wildly. But, through it all, that smirk stayed on his mug.

That stupid, "you-just-did-what-I-wanted" grin.

I finally stopped rolling on the floor long enough to get my feet under me. So, I did something smart: I started pounding on the glass.

"Renny!"

"Stop!" Maddie said, grabbing a hold of my arms. "If you break the glass, you lose them forever."

I grabbed her arms and turned to face her, but every bit of my rage melted away when I saw her face. She was in agony.

"Are you hurt? What can I do?"

"Let go," she ground out from between clenched teeth.

I did and she fell to the floor. I reached for her, but she raised her hands.

"Don't touch me," she panted. "You burn."

"What?" I asked, putting my most intelligent face on.

She waved the question away. "Check on Aga Bab."

The Nain Rouge had rolled against the bar. Maddie had tied his wrists behind his back and his ankles with bar rags while I had been convalescing. Good knots. His hands were already white.

"He's fine. Still grinning like an idiot, though."

Maddie was upright and motioned for me to stay where I was. "That's my fault and it's going to cost Mister Green," she said.

"Why?"

"Because, Aga Bab will claim I attacked him unprovoked."

"They attacked first!"

"Julie did," she corrected.

"Well, we couldn't very well leave him behind us, now could we?"

"Technically, I beat your invited guest senseless at your behest."

I shook my head. I really didn't care. "Never mind, explain later. Right now, I need you to help me get Renny!"

"Even after all he has done?" She struggled to her feet.

"Well, of course! He's family."

She smiled. I felt stupid.

"I can't go with you. That isn't under the hill, but you can go. Give me the dagger," she said, extending her hand.

"Huh, oh, the Bowie knife," I said. I'd been carrying it behind my left hip, so I could cross-draw ... never mind. I unsheathed the blade and handled it to her.

She grasped it by the handle. "Turn around," she said. "A girl's got to have some secrets."

I turned my back to her and heard her gasp. Aside from my initial impulse to turn, when she barked at me like a drill instructor to stay still, I didn't move. I just listened to her gasp and softly cry out. It seemed like forever. It took less than a minute.

"Here," she said, holding the blade out to me one-handed.

I turned and took it. An intricate Celtic sigil had been etched using a dark fluid on the blade, near the heel; the sigil's knotted whirls was mesmerizing to the eye.

"It means 'Calls to protect,'" she said, and slumped back to the floor.

"Maddie!" I rushed over, and hovered, knowing I couldn't touch her without causing any more pain. That's when I noticed her other hand. The withered one.

"Why would you do that?" I asked.

She touched my cheek briefly and smiled. "The things we do for family." She sighed. "Go. You'll know how."

When I got to the mirror, Bobby was standing on the other side.

"*Grab the frame, sport.*"

I grabbed and he reached out and pulled me through.

It was cold there. Cold and sharp.

"Bobby?"

He hugged me.

"I'm so sorry, brother. I'm sorry I allowed Kathleen to drive us apart."

He smiled at me. "No apologies necessary. Thing is, here at the crossroads, everything usually works out the way it should, and everyone winds up where they ought."

"Waxing kinda philosophical, aren't we?" I said, ruefully. "I hate to ask this of you, but can you help me find Renny? Can you help me find my brother?"

He motioned behind me. "Already here."

I turned, and there was Renny and Julie. I couldn't tell if Renny was dead or out cold. The dank twilight of the place made it hard to tell just by looking.

Julie's dusky hue had turned ashen, her fingers decidedly more claw-like, and I would swear she had fangs.

I jumped a little when I felt a tiny, cool hand in mine.

"Sorry about your brother, mister," the little girl said. "He made us do it. We didn't want to."

"Hush now, cher," her mother said, pulling the children to her, and nestling in the crook of Bobby's arm.

"Everything usually works out," he said, holding the woman and children tight.

"Yes, it does!" A voice boomed from the darkness. The thing that was Julie hissed and spat, but began to back away from Renny. I took a cautious step towards him.

"Oh, I believe that is quite far enough, Jacques," the voice said. I tried to move and found I couldn't. His laughter rolled like thunder. "You are under my authority. You are here of your own free will, after all."

Baron Samedi stepped into the crossroads from the shadows. Black top hat, black tux, black glasses. And smoking a big, black stogie. It was a little at odds with the white skull tattooed on his face, but it was *his* face.

"My quarrel isn't with you, Baron," I said, trying vainly to move my feet. "I'm just here for my brother."

"So," he grinned, and blew out a ring of dense smoke. "Take him."

The thing about the Baron is, he has no natural predators in his world, so he doesn't have anything to fear. But what I saw in his face when the Bowie knife buried itself up to the hilt in Julie's head was pretty close. I know you're not supposed to be able to throw a Bowie knife, but I was desperate. My feet came free from whatever had been holding them.

The Baron's grin vanished.

"Take him."

Julie was still making mewling sounds when I planted my foot on her face and jerked the knife free. I cleaned it on her dress. It was her blood, after all. The Baron eyed the knife and looked sour.

I hoisted Renny on my shoulder. He felt cool and didn't look good. I tossed a causal waving salute to the Baron and started towards what felt like the exit. Samedi was grinning again. I felt pretty good about myself, until I saw that and realized I didn't know how to get out.

"Jacques, how about I trade you Robert for Rene? As I recall, you have a great deal more affection for the brother of your heart than the brother of your blood."

Actually, that wasn't a bad idea.

"That's a horrible idea, Jack," Bobby said. "Besides, my place is here," he said, then kissed the top of the woman's head. She leaned into him. "I can't leave."

"I can send them all," Baron said. "Then, there's no choice to make."

"What's the catch?" I asked.

"It's a little something. You won't miss it because you have no faith in it. I want your soul." He stepped backwards and puffed on that stogie. "Otherwise, take your brother and go."

"Don't answer him, Jack," Bobby said, holding his family close.

"Bobby, I've got to go. Renny ... He ain't doing so well." I tucked the Bowie into the Renny's belt, sigil pressed against his back.

"So, go!"

"I can't, Bobby! I needed Maddie's help to get here. I'm going need the Baron's to get back."

"No you don't, Jack. You opened the crossroads when you touched the frame. You're the first *traiteur* in over a hundred years to do so."

"I'm not a *traiteur*, Bobby. And, I'll do what I have to in order to get home," I replied and turned back to the Baron to give him my answer.

That's when Bobby shoved me and Renny out of the crossroads, back through the glass, and into Maddie's waiting arms.

***

Lanie gave me a hug, her hair smelling of faint sunshine and lost promise.

"Nah, cher. I'm taking what's left of Renny back home. The city is nice for a visit, but there's too much Creole cooking for a body to live here. Besides, at home I won't have to worry about him tomcatting around." She was in the process of selling Casper's. She was taking her boy home. I kissed her goodbye and watched her drive away. She was my girl.

No one talked about Renny, or Justin, or Julie. They all went on like nothing untoward happened. Maddie said it was the glamour. I had to get back to the bayou. My "conjuring itch" was making me numb.

We wandered down to the levee. Maddie slid under my arm and put her head on my chest. It seems if I'm not holding the family Bowie knife, she doesn't have any problem touching me. We know. We experimented. Her hand– what was left of it–was bandaged, and her arm was in a sling. When I asked if it could be fixed, all she said was, "I can ask." I'll never figure her out. I sighed.

She slapped my chest with her good hand. "Can I not rest, I'm injured? What now?"

"Oh, I know you're injured, I'm just trying to cotton why?"

"I was in a hurry," she said. "The Baron needed to see the sigil, so he'd know Mister Green was aware of the relationship between Balor and the Guédé. They have been trying to leave the crossroads for eons. I just wish Aga Bab hadn't gotten loose. His presence would have made it easier to explain to the Council."

"Not a magic marking, then." I let the 'Council' remark pass.

"No, it's more like 'I see you! knee-neer, knee-neer, knee-neer.'"

I laughed. It felt good. "Devil woman!"

She slid her arms around my waist. "Come under the hill with me, Jack. Come on the Wild Hunt. Come work for Mister Green."

She was serious. I held her a moment longer.

"Tell you what, we get Lanie to take over as *traiteur*, and then GrandMama can retire."

I heard GrandMama's laughter at that thought, ringing out over the Gulf.

Casket Girls

by Patrick Scaffido

New Orleans should have been my city. Every surface has a thick coat of jazz music and ghosts of other eras. But New Orleans belonged to Arcade instead. Just like she did.

I could see her in front of the Dauphine Orleans and she wasn't alone. But she was all that mattered, about to enter a hotel building dating from when this part of the French Quarter was Storyville, the short lived zone where prostitution was "not illegal." I suppose it was a fitting place for Billie to go sell herself to a monster like Valdis Arcade. But she should be mine no matter how her phantom protested.

The stones held the memory of her, coaxed out by my slowly growing power over ghosts, this the one of her black moment before she entered Arcade's clutches and couldn't turn back.

"She's not my sister," Billie said, her lightly bronzed skin shining in the moonlight, not nearly as dark as my own. "I buried her back in L.A. That thing can't be her."

Her companion stepped forward. I recognized Erica Llewellyn, a local seer masquerading as a bookstore owner. "Listen Billie. I know what she is and yes, she's dead. But you going to Arcade won't solve the problem of her. Arcade may be powerful, but he's not real." She opened a brown book titled Green's Guide of The Mystic Underground. "His powers are illusion. At best, he'll only be able to slow her down."

"Then that's more distance for me. You didn't see her. She flooded our house. My uncle is in a coma. My sister, my real sister, could never do that. That thing isn't her.

"Yes, it is. It's your sister's mind, your sister's heart, her soul, all obsessed with her greatest regret from life: failing you."

"Failing me?" Billie's eyes spun with familiar disdain. "Like she could have changed my life? She didn't even ruin it. What she did was kill my best friend, her husband, my uncle, and herself. Most of that was before she was a zombie."

Erica sighed. "She's not a zombie, Billie. She's lost. Give her a chance to be found."

"And what? Give her a chance to kill me like she killed Charlie? Or to turn me into a zombie thing like Kanda? No way."

"They're not zombies. But she came back for you. That makes you the most powerful person for her. Do this and you give that away."

"Sounds like more vague mystic nonsense from your books." Billie tossed her hands up. "I'm out. Say hi to her if you see her. I'm off to buy some real protection. People are scared of Arcade. That's worth something."

Erica sighed again and walked out of the vision to stand by me. It reset to Billie standing alone in front of the Dauphine. I wanted to watch it again, but Erica distracted me enough that I couldn't maintain it. As she spoke, the image retreated to the cobblestones from where I'd called it. "She didn't get real protection. But you saw. I tried to keep her here. It's just like I told you, Lucette."

"Lucy. Yes, you tried. You also told her I was dead, a monster. You called me 'it.' Now she's up there, hidden and unconscious, but blood calls to blood. I feel her."

"I meant everything I said to her. She didn't need Arcade to stop you and Arcade can't do anything to hurt you." She pointed at me. "Not unless you're foolish and hurt yourself."

I looked up, scanning the glass doors behind which Arcade's thugs sat complacent, not believing a threat to their boss would come calling, certainly not from someone like me. Above them, the bricked and windowed hotel facade masked a hundred plus years of racism, prostitution, and flooding. That leaves memories on a place. Memories I can use. From here, I could feel them pulsing, sleeping in the walls and the floor.

And on top all that, I saw only empty air and the night. But I felt the pulse of Billie's soul in the blank space where my companion assured me magical auras hid Arcade's headquarters. Valdis Arcade, the notorious gangster, black magician, and pool hustler making the best of post-Katrina New Orleans. I couldn't see the penthouse itself, but I could see the ghosts. The building had ghosts on every inch of it, tiny coffins holding memories of lifestyles long gone and the woman who had lived them. I could see their echoes.

"I can see it, an outline." I said.

"She knows you're dead. She knows what you are. And if you don't accept what you are, you might kill her."

I shook my head. "Acceptance is not so powerful a leash, seer."

"You know how it went last time you tried to talk to her. She knows you're dead. Convincing yourself otherwise changes nothing. She's afraid of you. That's why she's up there stuck in a devil's bargain with Valdis. Let me try another way. He's a businessman. I have friends with money. We can buy her contract and work this out without anyone getting hurt. You don't have to confront him."

My lips softened to a lie of a smile. "This isn't about him. This is about Billie. And me. I need her to know I'm sorry. I gave up on her long ago. I can't abandon her again."

"Lucy, she knows. But she also knows about you killing Charlie and what you did to Kanda. She won't forgive you. She can't even listen to the truth. It's too much for her. That's why she's running from you. You can't just force it all to go away and make things better with her. People don't work like that."

I felt the rage throughout my body. "I can." Every cell was a coffin shaking open and they spilled their contents into my eyes. Trying to blame me for the crimes of the men in her life would not be tolerated. "Kanda was a liar. He was using her like a plaything. Like she was still a whore. He deserved worse than he got and now he's been recycled. He serves us instead of her serving him. As it should be."

"No. He just serves you."

Kanda had claimed in his last free moments that he loved Billie, a married man in love with his mistress. Leaving him a walking shell was a kindness on my part. At least this Valdis would have the guts to own his baser motives. I shook my head at her implications.

"Listen, you can take her by force from Arcade. You can control her like you did Kanda. But she'll never be yours."

"I agree with my sister. That's nonsensical seer talk. Give me something useful."

"You already know how to beat Arcade. You see the ghosts of the city's past more clearly than I can." She brought the book to her face, covering her frustration.

"I don't need a lesson, Erica. I need power."

"Then why am I here? You brought me along because you want me to stop you. You don't want to do this, Lucy.. You're in pain. You know your power comes from death no matter how much you try to forget. This reunion should not happen. You have to stop this or she'll be the person paying the price."

"I have to save her. I let her stay subject to men like Arcade before. I can't do that again. That's giving up."

"There are other ways." She put her hand on my arm to stop me from leaving. "Giving up is bravery here. Trust her to find her own way. Trust me to help her."

"She's my sister. No one ever looked after here and I should have. She should be mine."

"Should she? Or should she be her own? She's selling herself to get away from you. Again."

"Selling to anyone." I tried to suppress a shiver. "It's too horrible. How could she do this? First she sells her body, now she trades her soul. Maybe.." But doubt tasted like puke. I spat it out. "I'll just break their deal. All contracts are man made and that means they can be destroyed. Everything will be fine. If you value either of us, you'll help."

I left her standing on the sidewalk alone, not turning back to her but hearing her say, "No. Nothing will be." It doesn't matter what she saw. I'd already seen the power over ghosts in my hand, the ability to command them as I will and there was no stopping me, no matter how much Erica wished there could be.

I stepped up to the glass doors. The guards hadn't noticed me. I touched the glass and felt the spirit within, older than me and lost in the years. I saw her as she saw herself, a young girl getting off at the docks. She held a casket-shaped case, hoping her new husband she'd never met would not be a violent man. Her English was poor so we spoke in her archaic French. This whole city had dreams arriving on ghost ships only we could see, but I'd never felt them this close, this self aware. She'd survived her death, she'd done things, and now she was no more than a glass wall at a tourist attraction, an original casket girl turned into nothing at all. I touched her cheek as my hand stayed on the glass. "There are men within, men who'll hurt my sister. I need entry, quick and deadly."

The glass fogged, iced over, and cracked in fractal patterns 'til it shattered. Every sharpened shard fell into the lobby of the building, littering the unaware guards with shrapnel. The first was near dead before I snapped his neck. The second gave up the card key for the penthouse in exchange for the end of his pain, and then he, too, died.

I walked up to the elevator and called it, breathing heavily. There hadn't been enough of them left to feed on. They wouldn't have been able to contain the pain and stress arguing with Erica had inflicted on me and it was starting to catch up. The doors split and I slumped against the wall, sliding the card key into the controls to make the elevator rise to Arcade's penthouse. I needed all my energy for Arcade and for Billie.

Arcade's top floor was stylized, a large meeting hall with a tall Asian screen covering the entrance to his personal quarters. The room was a pastiche of a tourist's New Orleans, the most dominant image the statues of angels stolen from cemeteries around the city. I could see the half-ghosts writhing inside, split between their marker and resting place, tortured daily when Arcade tapped them as a source for mystical energy.

He sat in his throne room, near the back. The walls were lined with his stolen memorial statues. The statues were interspersed with refrigerators, a mini bar, and a rack to hold pool cues. Rows of mirrors in brass frames stood behind, with all reflecting back down on us from a mirrored ceiling. Arcade had to see himself. The only pure thing in the room was the felt of the pool table he'd meticulously brushed clean. Valdis Arcade sat in a hand-carved oak chair covered in French Copperplate capital letters, etched like unimpressive runes. He held tightly to a golden cane with a shrunken head for a handle. Each finger held a different shade of gold ring with gemstones, none matching. They looked like wedding rings, engagement rings, all sorts of fashions, probably stolen. He was a fake, a mix of new age, hermetic, and voodoo with a cargo-cult sympathetic twist. How he'd taken over the New Orleans underground probably had more to do with personality and lack of morals than any power or skill. His hat was a large black top-hat and he wore curly black hair careening down his shoulders. Valdis Arcade, magical Russian gangster who claimed to know the secrets of immortal Rasputin, was all image and no substance.

Erica had given me the run-down on him. Arcade was part criminal and part mystic, an instrument of the universe choosing to play discordant. Just an echo of an image and an inconsistent one.

"Welcome. Please, make yourself comfortable. I can get you a drink. I have excellent taste."

"Just give me my sister." I didn't care for his hospitality. "You can't keep me from her. She owes me a debt and she's family."

He leaned forward, putting his weight and both hands on the cane. "Don't you mean you owe her a debt? No matter. She's already spoken for. She has a contract and I can't just cancel that."

"Yes. You can. You will." I stared into his eyes and watched as he tried to stare back.

"How about a game? Do you play pool?" He leaned back, reclining into his throne, feigning comfort and indifference. "I'd gladly trade her soul for the loss of an entertaining game. The pleasure of watching you leaning over the table alone might be worth it."

I smiled. He wasn't offering a good business deal. He didn't know if I was skilled or not, so something must be rigged. I didn't know if it was cursed cues, a sentient pool table, or what. Erica's reports on what his magic could do were vague. No one seemed to know. There's only one way to deal with the vague however–do something clear.

I stepped up to the rack of cues and caressed one, clearly trying to give him the wrong ideas. I pulled it down and gripped the head of the cue tightly then, with a quick flick of the wrist, the wood snapped, sending the tip and splinters to the floor. I spun and threw it towards the pool table. I could feel the presence in this room, the ghosts of the people he'd suckered and owned, their echoes crying for help. Silently, I ordered them to enhance the throw and watched as the broken cue sped toward the center of the table. The cue's tip pierced the tabletop, ruining the perfect felt cover. The table screamed. Its slate shattered, splitting the table in half. I stepped back, a little shocked at the power of the impact. The ghosts here were plentiful, upset, violent. It took a moment to calm my face before I turned to him and smiled.

"It appears I'm not willing to play a game for her. Sorry about the mess. I wasn't thinking clearly since you're holding my sister hostage."

He stood, frowning, eyes angry. "I offered you a peaceable solution and you refused me. How dare you come in here and mess with my toys."

I laughed. "Don't talk about my sister like that. I love her and I'm here to save her from you. You should expect such comments to make me angry." I could feel myself breathing heavily as I watched his eyes. I hoped he couldn't see the exertion standing was taking. He was the first man I'd met in days who didn't crumble under my will. His resistance was unexpected, but then Billie inspired people. Unlike Kanda or the others, he had something worth fighting for; he had her, and that made the difference.

He smiled.

"I love her too, you know," he said.. "Probably as well as you. You want her. I want her. But the difference is I know her. I have tasted the curves of her body and you never have. Are you jealous?"

I wasn't. This wasn't about jealousy. I had promised myself that from the start and my purpose had only wavered when I listened to Erica but...no, jealousy was not a possibility. I simply wanted to save Billie, make things right, and keep her alone with me forever. It's called love.

Arcade tapped his cane on the ground. The mirrors along the wall began to lower. Images of Billie's face, chest, and legs started moving within them like a television, then split off and began floating around the room. He gripped the head of the cane tight. "To seal her pact with me, she gave me everything. Willingly. That's exactly what you want of her, yes? Everything?"

He leaned forward, leering at me. For the first time in days I realized the clothes I wore were torn, revealing. I couldn't remember the last time I'd changed them, and he stared at my cleavage barely covered by the remains of my shirt.

He extended a hand like he held something precious out to me. "I'll give you her everything...in exchange for yours."

Embarrassment. I hadn't felt it in a long time, not since before returning to New Orleans. Not since before I changed. Despite the embarrassment, despite the pain of watching this imp in front of me using Billie, I put my hand through the images and felt for a nearby angel. Through the statue, I felt the building, the street, the very heartbeat of the city. I saw a flash of Kanda's body still blissed out in a cemetery, my uncle's mind broken from watching me first find Billie, but all I cared for now was her. It was her I needed, her I wanted. It was her fault and this pathetic man tried to block me from what was mine. I cried out to the rows of stolen angels in the room, to the stones of the street outside, to the old foundations of the hotel that still stood, the last vestige of Storyville that had once greeted arriving trains of soldiers and tourists with open arms and open legs 'til government men had tossed her aside.

I spread my fingers wide, arms wide, reaching out through the floor to the city that had birthed me. "Take what you will, Storyville, but a daughter of the Quarter is in peril at the hands of this outsider." I heard the voices of a thousand dead girls and a thousand more battered wives, the ghosts of the wives and mothers of the ancient city demanding blood.

"Valdis Arcade, you shouldn't have come to this city. She has known the touch of men like you before and it makes her sick. It is time for you to leave. Time to die."

I could see the ghosts of girls crawling from the floor and connecting with the broken spirits in each angelic statue. They began to move, slowly at first, but the stone began twisting without cracking, like scaled flesh, their fingers sharpening to points as they tore apart the images Arcade commanded, his trickery no match for the true power of ghosts. He frantically called on images of guardian dragons, made fake copies of himself, and hid in false shadows, but the nails of the angels of the Quarter tore up his every refuge and sank their teeth into his wrists.

He ran to where I stood, my hand fused to the wall and raised his cane to smash into my face. I simply pointed at him, one firm finger in his face. "No." I said.

He cried and dropped his cane. He fell to the ground, sobbing. Without his images, without his toys, his confidence vanished. "Please. You know you don't want this. I know girls like you. You need a powerful man. You need me to own you."

I shrugged. "Tempting. I've been an object before, but you just don't seem worthy to own me."

The angels ran about the room tearing up his other trophies. His throne fell to pieces. "Stop them. Please."

"You've taken what's mine. So I'm going to take everything that's yours."

He stumbled backwards, landing against his broken pool table where his hands found the sharpened pool cue. He stopped whining. His hands firmly on the shaft, he regained a look of power and confidence.

"Too bad," he said. He charged forward and I gasped as the splintered end pierced my torso.

I was bleeding. I reached my hand to the wound and felt the oozing gash. I had been cut, I had been attacked, but this was the first wound since I had awakened in New Orleans to actually bleed. It was damp and shiny in the mirrored light of Arcade's desolated hall. I laughed and reached forward, rubbing the blood on his face. "Look at what you've done. I'm bleeding," I said. "I'm alive. I'm real."

He stood transfixed, still gripping the makeshift weapon embedded in me. Armed with nothing that could hurt me, he broke.

"You are mine now, Arcade. Your blade has done nothing." I nodded his pliant head, his empty face staring through the wound I barely felt. This was victory. "Pull it out."

He complied. I caressed his face with my bloody hand. "Take my pain as you die." He nodded again and the wound closed in my side as it opened in his, transferred by the power of will and servitude.

"I'm in pain," he cried. "Please make it stop."

His smile was grateful. The angels, done shredding his possessions, began on his limbs. His skin disintegrated and he fell to the floor at my feet, a pool of self-hatred and blood. As he died, the last of his illusions dissipated. The angels returned to their new homes, standing in rows along the hall that was now mine, their spirits dormant. They waited for my next command and stood guard over me as I walked to the screen blocking the entrance to what were now my private quarters. All that was Arcade's was mine. That meant Billie.

She lay unconscious in the private room, her body broken, breathing slowly. We looked like sisters now, despite her pale skin and my darker complexion. We were covered in blood. Our clothes were torn. Her breasts were bruised and marked with teeth. Her hands were bent in a permanent spasm. She lived. She started to move, eyes almost opening before I covered them.

"Lucy? No..."

"Sleep sister. I'm here." I hushed her. "You don't want to wake up, Billie. There's nothing good here. Everything's gone and it's just us."

I reached out to her hand, summoning the spirits of a bygone era, one more recent than the time of Storyville. "We want to rest," I said. "I have you and I'm going to hold you close for a thousand years." Her body stirred and I held her close 'til she stopped moving. "Stay near, my darling. Let's go back to our childhood. That New Orleans is here, ready for us. Let's see a parade. Let's see the mother we deserved. We don't have to accept what happened anymore.

"Be at peace, my love. The world is full of terrors we need never face."

A light blossomed from the walls and spread to fold both of us in its protective petals. The light spread to the entire penthouse. Arcade's magic, the illusion that kept the penthouse invisible to those outside, was mine now. As the light spread, I sealed the spell. We didn't need to be bothered. We were hidden and guarded by angels, the nest I had built was well wrought. There was no poison in here, just us two. No pain could find us here. We would finally be able to rest, safe, just two casket girls asleep in the arms of a city that held us, but never loved us.

L'or des Fous

BY LISA-ANNE SAMUELS

The dank air in the small room was just to the edge of stifling. Nothing he had not experienced before in any of the many inns and taverns he stayed in during his recent travels across the continent. Even the language was familiar, albeit strangely accented. Then again, the young United States had a different accent from its parent nation, so why not the French Colonies?

Robert Livingston, U.S. Minister to France, shook off the wisps of thoughts clouding his mind. If all went well, the French Colonies in the Americas would become the newest part of the United States. Unfortunately, many things were no longer going well. At least, not as well as they had through October 20th. After much work, the Congress of the United States ratified the treaty sealing the purchase of the Louisiana Territories. Twenty-four senators agreed with President Jefferson that the purchase of *La Nouvelle-Orléans* and the lands stretching to the western ocean from the French was essential for the security and future of the new nation. Seven senators felt Jefferson a right fool.

That some senators did not agree with the president was not the most worrisome aspect of this entire ordeal. That lay at the foot of Congress. Specifically, the feet belonging to Mr. John Randolph, Representative from Virginia. According to Livingston's informants, Mr. Randolph had done everything in his power to first stop, then stall, Congressional approval.

The latest missive sent Livingston scuttling about his Parisian apartments throwing clothes, quills and paper into saddle bags which he then tossed over the back of his favorite steed. There had been no time for more than a quick note to his wife, nor a chance to grab his second wig. Thankfully the brine of the sea had not damaged the one he had. Amazing how vain he had grown about his appearance while working with the French. Livingston was not fond of disorder, but missives declaring $3 million in US gold missing mandated more than it's share of complete chaos. Especially when said gold was due to the French government in mere days.

Now, two months after the ratification of the Louisiana Treaty and a few days before Christmas, Livingston stood in a small room in an inn located in the heart of the city he was supposed to purchase for said $3 million. The fire was blazing and flames danced on each of the candles scattered around the room creating a cheery atmosphere, even if it was more than a bit warm for Livingston. He had to remind himself that while he found the weather in New Orleans to be warm, far warmer than Paris in December, the citizens of New Orleans would be chilled to the bone.

"*Monsieur* Livingston? May I please bring you something to eat, or drink? You must be weary after all your travels."

Livingston smiled at *Mademoiselle* Alexandra, the young, but formidable, woman who led him into the private room. "I am, *Mademoiselle*. But I am also awaiting two traveling companions."

"Do you have everything you need before they come?" The Minister gazed around the room, not wanting to offend his hostess, but wanting nothing less than to be back on the prompt time tables of America. He and Monroe had begun to joke the French had their own standard time, always late. Unfortunately, he felt as though he had fallen through a vortex. La Nouvelle-Orléans was France on a rather small scale. Only 8,000 souls lived in and around New Orleans, a drop in the bucket compared to the 600,000 counted men who lived in Paris. He knew he must say something, but what? Was she one of the 8,000 he was supposed to trust with his current predicament?

He decided upon a half truth, the one guaranteed to keep them alive for at least a while longer.

"*Oui, Mademoiselle*. I do believe I am set until my guests come. Could you keep an eye out for them, then send them my way when they arrive?"

The verbal hint from Livingston followed by a small show of cash did not entice *Mademoiselle* Alexandra as this type of largess typically did. Rather than reach for the proffered bills, she rolled his fingers back over, then shook her head. She was a rare breed, it seemed, as money was not her prime motivation. Livingston raised his eyebrows quickly before putting the money back into his pouch.

Before he could speak again, *Mademoiselle* Alexandra began speaking in a clipped, steady tone. "I rarely have time for games, *Monsieur*, but until your other guest arrives we can play that I am a mere chamber maid. I am to ensure your safety for the duration of your visit."

Livingston could do nothing but laugh at the thought of this wisp of a woman protecting him, an enemy of the English crown and landed gentleman. Raised by a father who taught him self-defense from a young age, it was absurd that he would need the protection of this very tiny, very young girl. His laugh was a jolly one, bouncing off his barrel chest before it was forced up through his throat. But it was here that his laughter betrayed him as it burst through and filled the room. Amazingly enough, his hostess did not seem offended. She didn't join in with the laughter, but neither did she grow offended by it. Instead, she started walking the room in a rather peculiar fashion. Livingston could see a small, smoking bundle held in her hands as she paced towards each corner, smelled the object in question, then moved a bit to the right, somewhat like a backwards clock.

"Have you been told what words to say?" *Mademoiselle* Alexandra said just as he was getting ready to open his mouth.

"I beg your pardon. Which words?"

"I believe you stopped on your way here in San Domingo, correct? It is home to quite a few witches who help keep us on our toes. I would wager they are the reason you are here and not, say, at the tavern around the corner."

Mademoiselle Alexandra waved smoke over her head from her herbaceous bundle. The process was ritualistic, primitive. Her lithe movements reminded him of something else, something he'd seen not long ago. Mesmerized, he stood rooted, watching as she moved from one corner of the room to another, forcing the smoke into the smallest crevices. After a few moments he began to hear words floating through the air on the back of the smoke, at least they sounded like words, but none that he had ever heard.

"That should do it. We may speak freely now." Alexandra's words pierced the fog that enveloped Livingston. He quickly shook his head, clearing his throat at the same time.

"Were we not speaking freely before?"

"No."

"Well, then please enlighten me. What do we need to speak about that we could not discuss before?"

"Ever the diplomat, *Monsieur* Minister?"

"I beg your pardon, young lady, but what makes you so sure I am here to meet with you?"

"*Monsieur* Livingston, we do not have time for such trivial games, so I will strike directly at the heart. You were sent here by Mama Massan, correct? I will take it from the look of shock upon your face that you are indeed the gentleman I am here to meet."

"But, how?"

"Birds travel faster than sails, *Monsieur*."

Livingston's mind flashed back to the day he spent on the island of San Domingo. His ship's captain was reluctant to dock at the island, but Livingston insisted. He had heard of a woman, a priestess of HooDoo, who might be able to assist him in his mission. It took most of the day, but he found her surrounded by an aerie of colorful birds. If she was the powerful priestess she was purported to be, sending a bird across an ocean would be no mean feat.

"I was told I would need a Seer and a Wind Witch. Which are you?"

"I am the best seer in the city, *Monsieur*. And Creole to boot."

"And the Wind Witch?"

"I know nothing of anyone else joining us."

Alexandra was impatient. Every second counted with her spell. At this moment, anyone watching would see, and hear, a chambermaid preparing a room for the evening. But even that did not take a long time.

"I would rather wait until the Wind Witch joins us."

"Smart move, *Monsieur* Minister." The deep voice boomed from the doorway, carrying across the room to where Alexandra and Livingston sat opposite each other at a gateleg table. The voice belonged to a tall, coffee-colored man. His dress was that of a merchant, well-made pants, shirt and vest, but his hair was close cropped, perhaps to keep his tight curls in control. Nor was this a man who would wear a wig. His clothing was his only nod to the fashions of the time.

"What are you doing here, Bertrand?" Alexandra hissed.

"There's my kitty cat."

"I am not a cat, Bertrand. No more than you are a raven, despite your desire to fly in the face of any storm."

"I thought you said we were sealed into this room, *Mademoiselle*." Livingston broke through to cut the tension as much as to retake control of the situation.

"Oh, we are, *Monsieur*. My kitty cat knows how to disguise a room quite well. It's just that I know all her tricks."

"And you are, *Monsieur*?"

"Quite sorry. Let me introduce myself. I am *Monsieur* Bertrand, as I assume we are doing this on first names only, correct?" Bertrand barely waited for Livingston to nod before plowing on. "I am the best Wind Witch in New Orleans."

"And he makes sure everyone knows it." Alexandra muttered to no one in particular.

"As though you are quiet about your skills as a seer, my love."

Livingston watched the exchange quietly. While the words Bertrand used were congenial, the tone behind them was hard as a diamond, and, like said diamond, would most likely cut through glass if attempted. He watched as Alexandra glared back at the tall man standing in the doorway. Her milk chocolate eyes stood starkly against her creamy white skin. While he was not quite sure what a seer could do, one thing Livingston knew was that her power came from her eyes. Hardened eyes did not bode well for their mission, but instead of turning on Alexandra, Livingston approached Bertrand. His eyes were just as angry, but he was a Wind Witch. Perhaps, like the wind, his attention would be fickle, and Livingston would be able to shift his direction, or, if he was lucky, dissipate the threatening storm all together.

"Do not worry, *Monsieur* Diplomat," Alexandra's voice broke through Livingston's concerns. "Bertrand and I know better than to allow our personal complaints to destroy a mission. Don't we Bertrand?"

"Of course, my love," Bertrand responded without much conviction. "Anything for Mama Massan. She did practically raise us after all."

"Yes, she did."

"Well, now that we have that settled, perhaps we can return to the matter at hand?" Livingston was beginning to become desperate. He needed to find the stolen $3 million. The gold was not going to suddenly appear just because he willed it so.

Alexandra turned slowly, away from Bertrand's heavy stare, reaching for a candle and match.

"I thought you were above props." Bertrand's voice held a mocking edge.

"In this case, the props are necessary."

"Hell must be frozen! Alexandra is finally admitting defeat!"

"Sarcasm will not change facts, Bertrand."

"And what facts are those, Alexandra?"

"ENOUGH!" Livingston's voice bounced off the spelled walls, slamming both Alexandra and Bertrand back into their seats. "Do you not know how vitally important this mission is? You both seem to be well versed in me, so much so that I would gather you also know of my mission. The last thing I need is two squabbling babes who would rather tear each other down than help stop a great injustice. Perhaps Mama Massan was wrong about you both."

"This mission," Bertrand sneered, "is important to you, *monsieur*. Your country will more than double if you succeed. Yet, have you stopped to think of whether or not it is wanted by those of us who live here?"

"I beg your problem, *monsieur*?"

"Bertrand..."

"No, he should know. *Monsieur* Livingston, when you look at me, what do you see?"

Bertrand stood and moved towards the window so Livingston could take him in fully.

"I see a strong man."

"And my skin? What color is it?"

Livingston dropped his head. He finally understood why Bertrand was acting as hostile as he was. If Livingston were true to himself, he would also be torn about who owned the Louisiana territories if his skin were the color of creamed coffee.

"Bertrand, stop."

"No, *Mademoiselle*. He is correct. I apologize, *Monsieur*."

"So, you do understand that success for you means enslavement for me?"

"Would you not be enslaved with the French? Or the Spanish?"

"Perhaps. But who says we must be governed by Europe. You, yourself, come from a country created from the forges of revolution."

"This is true, but who is to say what will happen?"

"Your own Congress would put me in shackles."

"Bertrand! Mama Massan gave us a job. God help me, she gave it to both of us. There must be a reason she chose us, and yet another reason that she chose to help this man. This is neither the time nor place to have this discussion."

"When will it be time, Alexandra? You, at least, pass for one of them."

"Bertrand!"

"My apologies, *Mademoiselle*, *Monsieur*." Bertrand said quietly. "I do not know what overtook me."

Livingston looked over the two young people in front of him. If these were the best witches New Orleans had to offer, he was even more concerned for their chances of success. He needed to find the gold before the end of the year to execute the purchase. They had to be turned over to the French before Napoleon and his lackeys changed their minds and dealt with the British or the Spanish instead. Jefferson had made it clear, no European crowns could have a foothold near their new capital. Doubling the size of the fledgling country was just a bonus as far as the President was concerned. Not only was he responsible for ensuring the return of funds to the United States and the transfer of territories from France, he now had to be an arbiter between two people who obviously had history between them. Not what he needed after traversing an ocean to step foot in New Orleans.

"*Monsieur* Livingston, regardless of our behavior, we are your best chance at finding what has been lost."

"*Mademoiselle*, if you have all you require, shall we begin?"

With a deep breath, Alexandra nodded. She lit the candle in front of her. The chant required for this level of trance was ancient and complex.

Mist began to seep in under the door, down through the chimney, penetrating the minuscule cracks in the paned windows surrounding the room. Within seconds, the floor roiled with a warm, humid white cloud. It wound its way around the room, covering every inch of the floor before it began to rise, slowly. By the time Alexandra stopped chanting, the room looked and felt more like the bayou on a murky morning than a comfortable room in a city public house.

Loosening his neckerchief, Livingston looked around the room expecting to see cypress trees and Spanish moss. He wasn't sure if he should be pleased or disappointed when he saw the walls still surrounded them. Turning his attention back towards the table, he jumped at what he saw. Alexandra's eyes were open, but where he should see liquid brown irises and ink black pupils, he only saw swirling white clouds. Bertrand's iron grasp on his forearm and stern shake of his head were the only things that kept him in his seat. While sweat beaded on Bertrand's skin, it rolled off Livingston in rivers, reminding him that he was indeed in a very different part of the world. A part of the world where the air around them was sometimes more like water than an invisible gas. A part of the world where formal attire was reserved for Sundays and other special occasions. A part of the world where a minute, young woman could control that very air and create fog in a room sealed from the outside world. Not for the first time, Livingston wondered at his friend's wisdom at wanting to include this city and it's surrounding territories into the fledgling country. Perhaps they were biting off more than they could safely chew.

Then, as suddenly as the mist filled the room, it vanished. Livingston turned his attention back towards the table to see Alexandra sitting calmly, her skin luminescent and the hue of her eyes shifting through the colors of a prism.

"I have found it" were her only words.

The following morning found Livingston awake earlier than his normal rising hour. He dressed quickly, remembering to leave off the formal attire, namely his wig. It was the rare person who saw his natural state as not even his wife was privy to that view. At the very least, he was not one of those poor blokes who had a great need for the thing. He still had access to his natural hair, but rather than grow it out to the length of the moment, he chose to shave his head and wear the more fashionable periwigs. Though, not for the first time, Livingston began to wonder if perhaps it was time to give up the custom altogether. Most of his French contemporaries no longer wore them, but it was still fashionable among the powerful men in the fledgling United States.

Bertrand was waiting for him in the public room. Like Livingston, the young man was dressed simply, shirt open at the neck and sleeves rolled up to his elbows revealing a small line of black ink running down one arm to his wrist. There was black ink leading from the open neck of his shirt. While Livingston could never think of a reason to permanently mark his skin, he understood the people of the French colonies had different views. Still, it would be difficult to meld the two cultures together into one country. At least distance would allow for limited exposure.

They left the public room, exiting quietly through the kitchen door. Outside there were three horses waiting, each built for speed with light saddles. Alexandra, dressed more like a young boy than the beautiful young lady he had met the day before, sat astride one of the horses.

"I've bespelled them," she said. "We should be be there in just a few hours."

Livingston's nod after they mounted up was all the horses needed to start. Livingston was impressed. They were traveling at great speeds as they headed south towards the delta, and yet he barely felt the motion. In just two hours, they had reached an inn at the edge of a bayou.

"From here, we travel by water. The horses will be stabled." Bertrand's voice was edgy.

The small band dismounted and walked towards the bank where a young man with pale skin, a long nose and sharp, protruding teeth waited. He wore a hat pulled low over his red eyes, and patched homespun pants and shirt. His feet were long and bare with nails that clicked against the stones as he climbed back into the small boat. If Livingston were inclined to believe in shapeshifting, he would think he were meeting a man who could change into a rat, but men did not change into animals. Yet, the more he learned about New Orleans, the more he realized there was a world roiling beneath the surface unknown to him. Looking into this world was unsettling to say the least.

As they settled into the river skiff, the young man took a position at one end and pushed off. Again, magics had been employed for speed. In this case, Bertrand's wind propelled them quickly. The rodent-faced man, a native of the bayou, was steering. The pole in his hand twitched to the right or left depending on which tributary they needed to explore. Livingston focused on the goal, not the means of achieving it.

"We are not monsters, *Monsieur*." Livingston jumped slightly when he realized Alexandra had been studying his face intently.

"I never said you were, *Mademoiselle*. I am sorry if you feel I have slighted you."

"No. You have not slighted me, *Monsieur*. But I sense your discomfort. I am amazed you have not run into more of us sooner."

"Alexandra!" Bertrand's eyes communicated a harsh warning that Livingston could not quite understand.

"Bertrand, I am merely commenting on my surprise that there are not more of us to the east."

"My apologies, *Monsieur* Livingston. Alexandra has been known to push the boundaries of polite society. Please disregard her comments."

Livingston thought quietly for a moment. He was known to be an intelligent man, a graduate of King's College in New York, an attorney. In fact, he was the Chancellor of New York and instrumental in declaring independence from Mad King George. And yet, here in this strange land he was seeing things he had never seen before. It only served to reason that there may be mysteries hidden in plain sight in his familiar world. He just hadn't seen what was strange. It was time to learn the truth.

"Alexandra, what did you truly mean just now?"

"*Monsieur*, please do not encourage her."

"I do believe the cat is out of the bag. You, sir, manipulate the wind. Alexandra can see things most cannot. And, if I am not mistaken, we are being taken to our next location by a true river rat. No offense, *Monsieur*." This last apology was directed to the young man steering their skiff who just smiled.

"Nah, that's alright. Nothing wrong with being called what you are. Cajun, river rat, just plain rat. Makes no matter to me."

"So, you are a rat?"

"Depends on the day."

Livingston smiled at the young man's relaxed manner before turning back to his companions.

"Now, *Mademoiselle*, please elaborate."

Alexandra looked closely at Livingston before nodding. "Bertrand, he deserves to know."

"I deserve to know what?"

"You have already deduced Bertrand and I are witches, correct? We were born this way, as it is not a skill you can be taught. You either have the ability to manipulate nature or not. You can train that skill, but you cannot learn it. This is what we learned from our ancestors."

Livingston nodded. He had seen too much in the past few hours to deny that his traveling companions were witches, let alone the existence of creatures he once believed to be myth.

"We are also descendents of the *Casquette* Girls."

"I must apologize," Livingston said, confused. "The *Casquette* Girls?"

Alexandra smiled. "Forgive my glee. I seldom have the opportunity to discuss our heritage with someone new to the mysteries of New Orleans.

"Our mothers' mothers came to New Orleans young. They were found in orphanages, nunneries, and in other places by agents of the King and offered passage to the new world. The only requirement was that they must marry someone established here in Louisiana. Each girl carried with them a *casquette*, something akin to a trunk, filled with everything they would need as brides in the New World, all provided by the King."

"What an interesting history, but how is that relevant to your gifts?"

"The Casquette Girls were also some of the strongest witches in France."

Livingston swallowed, hoping to moisten his suddenly dry throat. He watched as Alexandra looked out over the water, staring into her history.

"The girls came with more than just dresses, *Monsieur*," Bertrand continued. "They sewed symbols into their hems and charms onto their shoes. They each also carried their family's grimoire tucked under their clothes, away from prying eyes."

"Grimoire?"

"The spells crafted by their families, and by them, over the centuries."

"Why did they choose to come here?"

"Why did your Puritans come to this land, *Monsieur*?" Alexandra asked quietly.

"To escape religious persecution. To start a new life in a new world."

"Is it impossible to think the *Casquette* Girls came for the same reasons?"

"Point taken, *Mademoiselle*."

"Because of the *Casquette* Girls, we were born this way."

"Alright."

"And you have observed our young friend here is more creature than man."

"I would say he's a good half and half, myself, but yes."

"And what of you?"

Livingston sat upright, the quick motion almost tipping the small boat over into the swampy water of the bayou.

"Me? I...what do you mean?"

"There is a reason you were the one sent to follow this lead, *Monsieur*."

"Alexandra, he's not ready. He may never be. Please don't force this." Bertrand was pleading with her. There was genuine fear in his eyes, fear of what Livingston did not know.

"No, Bertrand. I want to know."

"*Monsieur*, there are consequences to knowing."

"To knowing one's true self? Yes, there are. I am, however, willing to take the chance."

Alexandra looked deeply into his eyes, her crooked smile grew at what she saw. "He's ready, Bertrand. And it would be better if he knew now, before we walk into that nest."

"I am assuming you mean a real nest, not a proverbial one."

Livingston was half jesting, but neither of his companions responded. Instead, they were staring intently at one another. It was almost as though they could speak without words, a notion that caused gooseflesh to rise on Livingston's arms even in the heat of the swamp. He looked away quickly, hoping to bring his concerns under control. Moments later Alexandra began speaking.

"*Monsieur*, look back through your life. You have most probably seen things others have not. Perhaps it was out of the corner of your eye, or perhaps directly in front of you, so startling you would blink and whatever you saw would vanish. You have likely dismissed what you saw as a fancy, nothing more than a waking dream."

"And you are telling me I was wrong?"

"*Oui, Monsieur.*"

Air became thick, burning as it slipped down his throat. In some ways, he had always known there was something more out there. How else could men such as Jonathan Swift create creatures small and large for "Gulliver's Travels?" Or how could William Shakespeare create his fantastical creatures for his plays? Perhaps Lilliputians, and even fairies were real. This news definitely changed his views of his traveling companions, as well as himself.

"How do I tell?"

Alexandra cocked her head before speaking. "Close your eyes. Imagine a world where anything is possible. Once you've done that, I mean truly done that, open your eyes and look around."

Livingston followed her instructions. When he opened his eyes, the world had changed. Colors and scents assaulted his senses with their strength. He took these in for a moment or two before shifting his attention to his companions.

First he gazed at Bertrand. Colors swirled about an inch from his skin. As he watched the colors changed from white to blue to grey, the color of the sky during a storm, Livingston then turned his attention to Alexandra. She was surrounded by the colors of the rainbow and beyond. There was not a color unrepresented in her aura. Her skin was also changed. Luminescent was not a strong enough word for the light pushing all other manner of colors away from her. All colors except those of Bertrand's aura. It appeared as though Bertrand and Alexandra's auras danced together. Livingston smiled quietly, imagining what this colorful dance could mean, and whether or not the two involved in the dance were even aware of it's existence.

After looking at his companions, Livingston took the opportunity to look at their captain. What he saw shocked him so much it took all his composure to not jump back. The long, thin man steering their boat stared back at him through the narrow, white face of an opossum, complete with a long, pink snout and black beady eyes. Ever the diplomat, he did his best not to break decorum.

"I tuck the tail in, less I need it of course." The opossum's lilting accent caught Livingston off guard. It was hard to imagine and even harder to actually see such a strange creature speaking.

"And do you need it often?"

"Only when I dock."

"Good to know. Thank you for alerting me."

The opossum nodded slightly before turning his attention back to the river. "Dock coming up!"

At that warning, Livingston watched their captain intently and was rewarded for his curiosity as a tail snaked out an grabbed onto the floating dock, pulling them into the shore and holding the boat steady while they disembarked. Waiting for them on the pier was a dark wolf of medium height. It was not until the wolf spoke that Livingston realized he knew the gentleman.

"Livingston." The high pitched voice did not seem to match the burly wolf, and yet Livingston had heard the voice before.

"John Randolph?"

"Of course it's me, sir. Who else would wear my face?"

"Well..."

"*Monsieur* Livingston has just discovered his gift, *Monsieur* Randolph. *Monsieur*, if you wish to see the world through normal eyes again, just close your eyes and concentrate. Although, I do believe we may need your gift again shortly."

"Then I will wait until our business is complete." It was an odd way to view the world, but Livingston couldn't say he was not enjoying this new vision.

"So, then you know you are an Observer." Randolph's snout grimaced in what Livingston could only assume was a grin. "It bloody took you long enough, Livingston."

"You knew?"

"Everyone knows. Well, almost everyone it seems."

"Perhaps when we have a moment of time, you should fill me in on what else I should expect, sir."

"We'll see. Let's survive this nest first."

Livingston stared at Randolph with hard eyes. He may be a wolf in sheep's clothing, but he was still the man with whom he had served the fledgling nation for decades.

"This is unexpected," he finally remarked.

"What is?"

"My apologies, John. When I received the message in Paris, I believed you were behind the theft. By seeing you here, I now know I was incorrect."

"That you were."

"You sent the message, correct?"

"Yes. I may not be interested in purchasing this land, but I took an oath to support our new republic. I intend to uphold it. That, and $3 million is quite a lot of money for us to lose. Not something I am interested in handing away. Are you?"

"No. That I am not."

"Then, shall we?" Randolph the wolf bowed slightly, nodding towards a planked path leading right into the tree-crowded swamp.

They traversed the walkway for quite awhile. Between the tall trees blocking the sun, the heat and the absorbing new way of seeing the world, Livingston lost track of time. If anything, his newly heightened senses were causing more headaches and hindrances than help. At least he wasn't stumbling over his own feet as he led his small team of travelers.

It was perhaps an hour or more before they reached what seemed to be their destination, a small island of land in the middle of the swamp. Livingston saw them first, thankfully stalling his reaction faster this time than he had the previous two. Two men lounged at the entrance to the island, each leaning against a tree or stump. They looked at the approaching party through slitted eyes. The larger of the two took out his boot knife and casually began to clean his nails with it, a ruse Livingston was sure. The knife would most likely find a new home in one of his party's throats in moments unless their parlay was accepted.

Livingston stopped suddenly, and turned towards Randolph. "You sent for me."

"You're the only person who can help us avoid war with that little puissant in France."

"But..."

"But how did I know you could see us as we truly are?"

Livingston nodded, wary of his response.

"There have been rumors about your family for generations. Your father was the last known wizard who could see us. He was great friends with my father, but I understood he never wanted this life for you, so you were not trained."

"But this world is no secret. I have always known of witches."

"Yet you have never known about metamorphs, other creatures, nor have you ever tapped your power. Until today."

"No."

"Today we need you. Apologies to your father, God rest his soul, but we needed to trigger your sight."

Livingston tried to digest what Randolph had just shared. That his father did not wish for him to know about this integral part of himself was disconcerting. That a man he considered a rival in politics felt the need to trigger this power was also frightening.

"What else is happening here, John?" First names seemed appropriate since they seemed to be on more familiar terms now that they shared a secret.

Randolph sighed quietly and shook his head. "The creatures who took the gold would only speak with a wizard."

"That is why you need me?"

"Yes."

"Because I am a tactical advantage."

"You give us one, yes."

Livingston stood quietly for a moment, his eyes boring into Randolph hoping for something more substantial to go on, perhaps a deeper answer or a clearer one at the very least. Realizing he could get one with his new found talent, he looked first at the wolves, then at the witches searching for something, anything, that could help him decide the veracity of their story.

"Alright. What is our strategy?"

"You're a diplomat, Livingston. Negotiate. If you need something more, we'll be here." The wolfish grin that bloomed on Randolph's face caused Livingston to shiver as though someone had just walked over his grave. Not for the first time he realized Randolph was not a person to cross.

Livingston nodded to his party before turning towards the clearing. There were wooden walkways and dirt paths connecting the small patches of dry land amongst the water. Using these pathways, Livingston picked his way carefully towards the clearing. He could see anything in there yet he could not act surprised.

The clearing was surrounded by cypresses dripping with grey-brown tendrils of Spanish moss. Between the moss and the mist swirling around his feet, chills flew up Livingston's spine regardless of the warm temperatures. There was no question, the bayou was eerie. Not especially a place to wander on one's own. And yet, here he was. True, there were men behind him to back him up if negotiations did not proceed well. However, he was walking in alone to speak to goodness knows what.

"You need not be so watchful, *Monsieur* Livingston," a voice, deep and husky, called out from the shadows. "You shall not be harmed."

Livingston did jump slightly, but then forced himself to calm his nerves. This was his first opportunity to show his true worth. During the Revolution his place had been in courtrooms and meeting rooms. Since then, he'd occupied offices with the closest thing to a confrontation being a negotiation. This was his opportunity to show the world he could stand on his own two feet in a world not surrounded by walls.

"Who do I have the honor of addressing?"

The gentleman addressing him stepped out from behind a cyprus tree. He was well dressed for a pirate, flowing white shirt, skin tight pants tucked into polished boots and a sword at his side. The only attributes distinguishing him from any merchant ship captain were the lack of a coat and the green skin. Well, the green, scaly skin, rounded snout, and razor sharp teeth. In short, Livingston was staring at a walking, talking alligator.

"Captain Holata Sobek at your service," the man before him said with a sweeping bow.

It took a moment for Livingtson to translate the two names, but once he did he laughed loudly.

"I apologize, Captain. I cannot help but laugh as both your names mean exactly the same thing, or near to it. Alligator Crocodile if I am not mistaken."

Sobek laughed as well. "I was told you were well educated. But I have never met a man who knew both Indian languages as well as Egyptian."

"Thank you, sir. May I assume your names were chosen for their attributes and not at your birth?"

Livingston sucked his breath in quickly, hoping he had not overstepped this early in the negotiations. But Sobek just nodded.

"And I assume you mean both my battlefield and negotiation skills as well as my scaly skin? Ah yes, *Monsieur* Livingston, we are aware of your particular set of skills. You are among friends here."

"Sir, I have to ask, how do you know when I, myself, did not until today?" The fact that everyone else seemed to know that Livingston came from a family of wizards was becoming more than irritating. If his father were still alive, he would seek him out for a rather tense conversation.

"Most in this land know of your father, and how he worked to keep you outside the world of creature politics. He was concerned that your involvement in the war against Mad King George would put you at enough risk, and he did not want to risk you further by bringing you into our world."

"Then why have so many people gone out of their way to go against his wishes now?"

"Your father was well respected in our community, so we did respect his wishes for many years. But now we need you."

"I keep hearing that I am needed, but not why. Will you enlighten me?"

Sobek tilted his head slightly and stared closely at Livingston. "Your new country, how does it treat those who are not British?"

Livingston bristled at that question. "Sir, none of us are British."

"Then let me change the question. How are those who are not exactly like the majority treated? Those whose skin is colored or who came here from a country other than England, such as Hessian, France or the Islands? How are the Indians, people who were here before your forefathers stepped foot on this ground, treated?"

Livingston's tongue stumbled over the words he was looking for. It was then that he realized this was not a negotiation for gold, but for the lives that would be affected by the purchase. He also realized it was a negotiation only he could partake in, as he was the only one who could offer any protection. Breathing in the mist surrounding him, he decided to take a leap.

"Captain, if I may be so bold, you seem to speak for those like yourself. Therefore, I ask you, what would you have from me?"

"Do you accept that you are like us? Perhaps that is my first request."

"Your first?"

"Oh yes, there will definitely be more than one request."

Livingston steeled himself for what could be an onslaught. "Alright. What are your requests?"

"The first is to accept yourself as one of us. There are more of us on these shores than you realize. You must count your soul as among ours if this is to work."

"I will do my best to count myself among your number."

Sobek cocked his head to the side with a toothy grin. "Thank you. Now onto the other requests. You will protect us."

"Protect you how?"

"Train others like yourself to become our magistrates and protectors. When a crime is committed in our community, only those who understand us will be permitted to judge us."

"A special court system? I am not sure that follows the line of 'all men are created equal.'"

"Ah, but we aren't equal are we? In some ways we are far superior to those who are attempting to create this country. In others we are inferior, never able to show our true selves. How would a mundane jurist understand the primal urges of a man like me, for example?" This time, Sobek showed more teeth than grin, ensuring Livingston understood his meaning.

"Noted. Again, I will do what I can."

"Not good enough."

The growl emanating from the depths of Sobek's throat was meant to frighten, and most likely did scare most people. Livingston, however, was not most people. Pulling himself up to his fullest height, he confronted the alligator-headed man.

"*Monsieur* Sobek, I can only promise those things I know the president will allow. Promising one group of individuals more rights than others, or a separate court system, I cannot do. But a judgement by one's peers? That I can promise. Jurists who can recognize who those peers would be? I can promise that as well. More than those two concessions, I cannot promise. I advise you to take what I can offer."

Livingston stood strong. He was prepared to fight for this particular line of justice if provoked, but he would not become a milch cow for an entire people. He stared into the steely, reptilian eyes of his advisory, aware of the dagger stuck in the top of his boot, within easy grasp if he needed it.

Victory came when Sobek nodded slowly, accepting the terms of their negotiation, a motion that brought forth another of his company carrying the chest filled with gold. Quietly, Sobek handed the chest over to Livingston.

"Then we place ourselves under your protection. We will send other wizards to your door for training and call upon you and your proteges to be our jurists when there issues arise."

Livingston took the gold gratefully. "May there be little need for these new jurists. But it will be there if required."

"Our business is concluded. Treat us well, Chancellor." With that nod to Livingston's preferred title, Sobek melted into the surrounding mist. Livingston did not try to follow. Instead he walked back towards his party.

"Well?" Alexandra's sharp tone broke through first. She was quite beautiful, Livingston thought quietly to himself, if a tad on edge. It was that edge that caused her waspish nature to dance across her face.

"We came to an agreement. But I believe you already knew that would happen, *Mademoiselle*."

Alexandra screwed her eyes up as she stared at him. "Nothing is certain, *Monsieur*, especially where you are involved."

"*Touché.*"

"But we do have an agreement?" Bertrand echoed Alexandra's concerns. Livingston looked at each of his companions and noted the concern across each of their faces.

"Yes. We came to an agreement. All men in this country will live under the doctrines of the land."

"So, we won't have to leave?"

Alexandra looked at Bertrand, holding her breath as she waited for Livingston's answer. Just then, Livingston realized there was so much more at stake than who would sit in judgment of those who were different. Whole lives and families relied upon this answer. These were people who had fled homes more than once because of their differences to finally land in a place that accepted them, and then found out that their new home might not be so safe after all.

Livingston smiled. As a diplomat, he loved giving good news. "Not unless you wish to."

A collective sigh of relief went up from his entire party. Bertrand quietly took Alexandra's hand and even Randolph smiled a true smile, not the smile of a politician.

"Well, Chancellor Livingston," Randolph began, "I believe you need to take that gold somewhere?"

"Yes. I am needed back in Paris for the exchange. Hopefully my absence has not been too damaging to this process." Livingston was about to pull out his non-existent hair knowing how long it would take to get back to French court.

Randolph laughed. "No worries there. You can be back in Paris by morning. In fact, you could leave now if you wished, if *Mademoiselle* Alexandra has what she needs."

Alexandra nodded, pulling her satchel off her back and starting to set up a ceremonial circle. Just one of many things Livingston realized he needed to get used to in the future, especially as the newly-anointed protector of all strange creatures in his new country. Moments later, a portal opened in the space between the candles Alexandra lit for this purpose.

"Instantaneous travel? Quite amazing," Livingston mumbled.

Randolph chuckled under his breath. "There's more, old chap. We'll talk. Soon."

Livingston nodded, took his satchel and stepped towards the portal.

"*Monsieur* Livingston?"

Livingston turned to look at his short time companions and new friends.

"*Monsieur*, thank you for everything."

"My pleasure, *Mademoiselle*, although I do not think I have done much."

"You have, *Monsieur*. You believed in us. And in yourself. Not many would do that."

"Not many would stand up to a King either, but if I can do that, how can I not stand up for those with whom, it seems, I share special qualities?"

He nodded at each of them one more time before taking a breath and stepping through the swirling doorway of light in the middle of the bayou. Without realizing it, Livingston had closed his eyes for his trip. When he opened them, he was back where he started, the salon of his Parisian quarters.

"There you are, my dear!" His wife said quietly as she walked into the salon. "I didn't hear you come in. Good trip?"

"Yes, very productive." Livingston placed the heavy chest on the floor and looked back up at his wife only to see a swirling aura of bright colors revolving around her, much in the same way as they enveloped Alexandra in New Orleans.

"Peculiar..." he said quietly as he walked over to envelop his wife in his arms with a smile. "Very peculiar."

A Gilded Fox

by Emily Karnes

"You should understand that I hate you."

That cheerful greeting flounced through a humid breeze, which was already oppressively warm for the hour. The rich, organic stench of piss invited itself into the conversation, but it dissipated almost as soon as that alleyway fell behind, bequeathing the air to the pungent scents of food vendors intermingled with the harmonic clash of dueling street musicians. The colorfully-clad speaker–Kasa Mengana, a constantly-bobbing young woman whose ambient playfulness flirted in ways her stick-straight figure could never have managed to, stretched as she wandered along, enjoying the walk and thrilled to be anywhere but an airplane. The wide mouth granted by Native American blood was perfect for broad smiles. She took full advantage of that now, tilted-almond eyes crinkling in the sunlight.

"Noted. Here." Agent Olivier Travert, a straight-backed man in a full suit– it just *had* to be ludicrously uncomfortable in this climate–held out a paper tray of vividly red spirals.

Her shriek was deafening, nabbing the attention of several passing gentlemen, each instantly prepared to pulverize whatever proponent of natural selection was accosting a woman in broad daylight. Her obvious glee dismissed any such inclination. "Tiny lobsters!"

"Crawfish," her companion corrected as he removed the preemptive earplugs. His expression didn't change as his charge tore into a shell with her canine teeth, cayenne and other spices already streaked halfway across her cheek. Not changing was what his face did best, chiseled by war or some equivalent circumstance. The same sense of servant civilian which said, "I know the lack of proper seafood in Romania caused you some distress. This seemed like an auspicious start to our latest assignment."

"Mmphnn'gd!"

He took that for a "yes." Her enthusiastic grin–mostly in the eyes and cheeks, as her mouth more closely evoked a carnivorous rampage–was perfectly clear.

"Ugh...."

Half-restrained aggression instantly clouded the young woman's expression when a third voice intruded. She closed her eyes and haughtily took another bite, unwilling to let *Agent Jackass* ruin a delightful meal.

"Disgusting. Most people don't realize how filthy you self-important creatures are." No part of Anton Jacoby's visage betrayed a thirteen-hour plane ride, fresh and coiffed as befitted his aristocratic scowl. This agent looked like the sort of man who pressed his socks and would judge any passerby who neglected the same.

"It's kind of you to be more blatant about human idiocy." Kasa stuck a finger in her mouth to suck the crustacean-juice off of it, staring pointedly at him all the while. The newcomer's lips curved with distaste, as intended.

He closed the gap between them and bent to look the vertically-challenged young lady eye-to-eye, newly unhesitant about wrinkling his suit.

"I'm smart enough to know the rules," he hissed. "Smart enough to understand that starvation is an approved method of controlling an unruly asset."

He tried to slap the crawfish out of her hand. She was faster, jerking it away at just the right angle to avoid spilling a single, precious morsel. She stuck out a food-speckled tongue.

"Did you find what you needed, Agent Jacoby?" The flat-tempered food-bringer was eager to table the children's bickering.

After a few vitriolic moments, his partner stood straight again, dismissing his pint-sized rival. "Yes." After some unspoken signal guided them away from any passersby, he reached into an unreasonably expensive briefcase–his purse, to hear the enthusiastic asset tell it–to produce a nondescript folder. "The target is Jules Villneaux, a formerly unexceptional local artist who's recently stumbled into success. Spent most of his career painting and peddling sculptures in Jackson Square. Presumably made ends meet, but little more. About nineteen months ago, his process changed dramatically: he began selling mundane items cast in pure gold. We acquired a few. They weren't produced via lost-wax casting or any other hallow method." He put a cigarette to his lips, lighting it as the other agent flipped through the dossier. "Solid, flawless 24-carat gold, every one."

Travert raised an eyebrow. "Where does a street artist get that kind of overhead?"

"And *why*, when a façade would grant the same effect." Jacoby breathed a comfortable line of smoke, turning to lean on a cool wall and keep an eye on their surroundings. "This new series earned instant favor with the fine arts community. Man's the toast of the town. At least, the rich parts; he abandoned his spot in the Square overnight. Never looked back. Thing is, he's not buying enough gold to account for the volume he's producing. Not even a sixth of it."

The girl raised an eyebrow, noticeably mimicking her keeper's expression. "Your scryers told you that?"

"Our commodity managers told him that," Travert intercepted before another spat churned up.

She sighed. "That's boring. You're boring."

"In any case," Travert continued, "this could be standard, underground fare. Drugs or other contraband, or a family connection. A fiscal idiot suddenly able to finance his vanity. "

"Could be." Jacoby glared at the interloper a moment. "But the Council is suspicious. Our first objective is to confirm the threat. If gold really is materializing out of the clear blue sky, it will devastate the economy. We have to plug that dike before people remember a gold brick is worth more than some shiny urinal cake under museum glass."

The asset, for her part, paid no further mind to the chatter, busying herself with seeking out all the delightfully varied squishy bits to be found inside a crawfish. She *definitely* liked this place better than Romania.

Jacoby gave the other agent time to peruse the documents before speaking again. "The target has an opening at the Contemporary Arts Center tonight. 'The Allure of Domesticity: a study in gold by Jules Villneaux' ."

"He isn't even playing at subtlety, then." The folder closed and found its way back to Jacoby's hands.

"Villneaux and subtlety don't get along. Ever." The paperwork disappeared into the briefcase once more. "It will be quite the black tie affair, evidently...a veritable *Who's Who* of New Orleans, with no noticeable effort to exclude the more publicly-suspected allies of the Council."

"Merrill?"

"Even Merrill."

"That supports a clueless human having stumbled onto some artifact, or else an outright mundane crime in progress."

"Agreed. Still, we have to proceed as though it's an arcane conspiracy."

Travert considered. He looked back to his charge–adult by any formal standard, though her manner made it easy to forget that–who had returned to her late lunch with gusto. "We'll need to procure suitable attire for Miss Mengana, if she's to accompany us. Something formal."

Her eyes widened, gaze snapping back to the agents. "Yes. Yes we do." Oh, she was positively hopping at the thought of some stunning gown, even as she set the tray of crawfish on a buttress. Now she could dedicate both hands to subduing these irksome shells. There just had to be a trick to this. "Ch'du nee t'way t' t'nii, doh."

Jacoby sighed, finger pressing between his eyes. "Again, if you please."

Kasa popped the shell out of her mouth and dropped it into a planter with the others. It was hard to communicate with a crustacean head in one's mouth.

A tongue licked contentedly over her teeth. "*'You don't need to wait till tonight.'* To find people who know something about him. Artists are all kinds of temperamental. If Mr. Goldstuff is really that self-important, tripped into massive success, and left the spot he'd worked for years, he must have said something unpleasant on his way out. Somewhere, someone's mad. Someone's jealous. Someone knows what led up to the change in his art. And they might even be the same person."

While the agents shared a look, a shell cracked against the silence. There *had* to be a way to do this efficiently. One that humans could do. She was *going* to find it, and the determined foodie hadn't yet repeated a method of attack.

Finally, Travert shrugged. "Shall we, Anton?"

Jacoby nodded. "Sure. We have some time before our invitations are believably engraved, anyway."

At first, it was just a distant calamity of sound, a tangled mass of a thousand colorful aural threads, interwoven too long and too tightly to ever hope for separation. And yet, as the visitors drew closer, more and more strains began to determinedly distinguish themselves: a trumpet here, a trombone there. Jazz, New Age, funky blues. A young tourist's squeal of laughter intruded, and an experimental musician poured his soul into some elaborate instrument of his own creation.

Kasa was beside herself with excitement, brown eyes wide and darting excitedly to every corner. By the time the streets opened up into the Square proper, she was hopping from foot to foot and barely restraining the squeal. Her nostrils flared, lips parting to taste the air. "This place is blessed," she murmured. "Maybe even by a muse; it's the whole place…."

Oh, it was amazing. Magicians and fortune-seers and a silver-painted man and musicians and gawking crowds and painters and...

Agent Travert pulled her back bodily, just in time for a distracted cyclist to careen past. It wasn't enough to shift her focus to the danger, and only awed glee allowed her to look back up at her savior. For now, the man ignored the implied request, turning to his partner. "Interviewing artists?"

"Yes. And…fine." After a moment, Jacoby waved dismissively. "Let the fluffbrain wander and investigate of her own accord. She may stick her nose into something interesting, and her presence with us can only complicate things."

The other two glanced to one another, then at the colorful square, then down to her equally colorful clothing. "*Really*?" That much was spoken in near-unison. "You think this," Olivier gestured vaguely to her person, "will be a disadvantage in coaxing useful discussion from street artists? As opposed to this?" He waved a hand over his anonymous suit.

"It doesn't matter," Jacoby observed, bemused. "You lost your asset."

Agent Travert's gaze darted back up just in time to see her scampering off towards a jazz band. After a few moments, two fingers pressed between his eyes. "Of course I did."

In Kasa's experience, human monuments–physical or otherwise–rarely lived up to their storied reputations. Jackson Square, however, surpassed them in every way: a churning, breathing, continuously changing testament to its city's vivacity. The cathedral and other buildings were probably impressive…but *they* hadn't captured Kasa's attention.

The visitor darted between some tourists, weaving happily through the crowd until nearly slamming into what turned out to not be a statue. She stared for a few moments at the unmoving man, who was painted like stone and frozen in time. Other people watched passively, and a few mimicked the performer's pose. All kept some respectful distance.

Except Kasa. After a few moments' thought, she poked him. Lightly.

And again.

And once more, for good measure.

To the man's credit, he didn't move, though a subtle shift in his eyes' shadows betrayed annoyance. She giggled, hopped up on a curb to kiss the performer's cheek–uninvited kisses were a perfect remedy for having invaded someone's personal space, after all–and ran off to visit a different brass band.

Sometime later, while Kasa handed some cards back to a confused street magician, a familiar hand affixed to her shoulder. "We've located a painter who used to be set up beside Villneaux," Travert informed. "Despite signs of hostility towards the name, we're having some difficulty getting any useful information out of her."

"You must have let Agent Smiley talk first."

"Just focus on what comes next."

The asset smirked before smoothing the expression into something less unkind. "'Kay." She folded her hands comfortably behind her neck. "You both need to stay away."

"Anton won't be happy."

"Results smooth his boring feathers." She shrugged. "No one who spends all her time in a place like this likes guys like him. He's *made* of pushy, vaguely threatening questions. I mean, you can pass for some PTSD insurance salesman, but everything about Jacoby screams 'I play in Big Brother's golf foursome.'"

"Anyone with eyes on us will have seen us walking together."

"That's okay. I'm adorable. It offsets."

"Some would say obnoxious."

Her smile widened. "It's a fine line."

Before long, thin arms folded over the top of a folding chair, a dainty round chin plopping down atop them. "H–"

The painter waved Kasa off before the word concluded, a sour expression curling across her face. She didn't look up from cleaning her brushes. "I saw you walkin' with them suits, sugar. And I ain't interested. I didn't get on with Villneaux, that pompous *couyon*, but artists takin' too many troubles to the authorities always ends bad for all of us. You just hurry on back to your keepers."

Kasa's lips pursed. "What if I want my picture drawn?"

An incredulous sneer found the woman's face. "You don't just want your picture drawn."

"I do."

"Then you can agree to keep yer pretty trap shut the whole time, hey?"

"I can't not talk. I would explode or have an aneurysm, I'm pretty sure. I've never actually tried."

"Sugar, you ain't fooling anyone. Just run along. Find someone with less soul invested here to tell your little stories. There are plenty of *those* 'round here."

Those. The word had bite. She filed it away. "It has to be you, though."

"Why?"

"Because you'd be drawing my picture, and all of your color schemes are high chroma versions of classical schemes that rely on temperature rather than value to express the subjects. All of the other people around here are missing the nuance. Like the guy whose grey tones are wrong to balance the accent colors he chooses or that woman smudging all her paint together until the colors' purity gets all deflowered. Also, not a single one of your pictures shows a still, relaxed face, and my face is never still."

The painter stared. The asset smiled.

Finally, the local sighed. "Havin' a good eye don't change your intentions, sugar. I ain't that soft a touch."

"It doesn't," Kasa agreed. "I'm going to ask questions. Not gonna lie about that. But I really do want you to paint my picture. Any of these others I'd just annoy until they said something to shut me up. Or bribe one. Someone has something to say. But I'd really rather it be you." She almost mentioned forcing the agents to pay for the commission, but caught herself in time to avoid offering a bribe immediately after deriding bribes. "We aren't local, promise. This isn't the kind of thing that will affect whatever keeps you and yours in business."

"Not local…" The woman's brow creased skeptically. "Your friends sounded foreign. *How* not local? What's the *couyon* gotten himself into?"

The asset beamed. "I'll happily give you the dirt on him in exchange for more of the same."

Silence.

Finally, the artist waved her towards the chair, taking up her palette. "Have a seat, sugar. I like your attitude, anyway."

It wasn't long–or maybe it was, Kasa wasn't paying attention–before the ladies were laughing like childhood friends. "So, *Couyon*, he's painting one day and George Rodrigue walks up…"

"Blue dog!"

"You don't get extra credit for what everyone should know, sugar."

Kasa huffed. "I should get a little."

"Fine, a little. Now, hold that pout a minute." The local's paintbrush dabbed at her palette, then returned to the canvas. "Anyway, this legend walks up and strikes up a conversation. Just like that! Weren't no one who didn't want to be Villneaux right about then. Amazing advice and a detailed critique from a brilliant man askin' nothing in return. The kind of brilliant that makes you feel stupid and smarter at the same time just for having talked to him. And you know what that *couyon* did?"

"He was an ass?"

"He was an *ass*!" The brush slammed down so hard that a smaller one would have snapped. The painter remembered herself halfway through–

too late to stop it–cringed, and took a moment to assess the damage. "An ass! To George Rodrigue! Oh, sugar, there was almost a riot in the Square. Man's one of ours. And Villneaux," she spat the name, "was quick to run his mouth about how Rodrigue just didn't understand his vision. You understand what I'm saying? That's like Jesus walkin' up and givin' you an ethics lesson, and you brush him off 'cause he just don't understand your morality." A paint-stained finger raised as the other hand dropped a newly-bedraggled brush into a jar of turpentine. "And if Jesus did walk up to this *couyon*, that's exactly how the conversation would go."

Another brush patted dry against a paper towel, and the painter took up the palette again. "You gotta understand, sugar…Jackson Square, for most of us, ain't a place to get your start. There's a life here all its own. This is the best school in the world for anyone with a mind to listen…and there ain't no one too old to learn. I'm still surprised no one beat Villneaux's ass that day."

The brush finally resumed its patting trail across the canvas. "Made it that much more satisfying when he did do some bleeding."

"Bleeding?" There was a marked lack of appropriate concern, there; curiosity too sunny for the subject matter. "What happened?"

"Well, this weren't long before the *couyon* had his big break. He started bringing his new little girlfriend around. Muslim, I think…not dressed like most Muslim ladies you see in America. Covered head-to-toe. Meek thing…don't think Villneaux," suddenly, the name was laced with far more vitriol, "let her talk. Controlling. Disrespectful."

Kasa's light amusement evaporated. She didn't like people being controlled by assholes. She avoided glancing towards the men in suits, leery of reminding her new friend of their presence.

"Anyway," the painter continued, "Bastien–street magician 'round here, does card tricks–was chattin' at her, tryin' to get her to open up a bit. Villneaux lost his wits, came chargin' across the square, and shoved him away. Now, Bastien didn't go after him for that …kept it to words. Angry words, but words all the same. Then, Villneaux grabbed the girl's arm. Dragged her off, sayin' something nasty in her ear. And that…"

Pause.

"Well, sugar… that was where Bastien couldn't stick to words no more.

Laid the stupid little man out. Broke his nose, I think." The local leaned back to give her newest painting a critical once-over, expression far more intense than her voice. "He offered to give the girl a place to stay if she needed it. She'd moved right in with her idiot beau, accordin' to the few words we got out of her. Bad mistake, but the punishment didn't fit the crime. I've been around the block enough times to know abuse when I see it."

"Did you ever get her name?"

"He called her 'Mel.' She never said more. Don't think she ever took Bastien up on his offer. Can only hope she left Villneaux some other way. No one's really seen her since he bought that ostentatious plantation home, so…probably? But…" a sharp wave tossed away the entire, unpleasant story. "Enough about *Couyon* and all this sad business. Come take a look, sugar. I think we're finished. And you are a darling subject."

If Kasa had any more questions, they fizzled against this particular distraction. After hopping up and nearly swinging around the painter–it was a markedly graceful movement, actually, smooth as a dancer's–a bright smile just barely preceded a shrill, drawn-out squeak of joy and a tight hug.

The artist couldn't help but smile. Genuine appreciation was a hell of a treasure.

After Olivier paid for the painting, hugs, a promise to stay in touch, and the parting of ways, Kasa rattled off what she'd learned. As the last information rolled off her tongue, Travert's brow was creased. Jacoby's eyes were thoughtfully narrow to match.

"So," Kasa concluded. "Got a mysterious new companion. Kept her totally hidden and was intensely protective of her. Became an overnight sensation *immediately* thereafter. And no one is sure who or where she is."

"Analysis isn't your job. But…in this case, I agree," Jacoby conceded. "This mystery girlfriend is everything. And I know his home has substantial land buffering it. I would wager that this woman–whomever and whatever she is–is there, somewhere. Willingly or otherwise."

"The opening gala won't just be a place to intercept him," Travert pointed out. "It also assures that the man won't be home tonight. I believe I can handle a cocktail party alone." As the implication sank in, a bright smile lit up Kasa's face.

For authority-sanctioned breaking and entering, this venture suffered from a sore lack of dramatic music. Crickets and frogs chanted in its stead, further saturating the humid, misty night air outside Villneaux's fully restored plantation home. Fireflies drifted by in wavering patterns. For once, they didn't distract the repurposed thief from her task: overriding the electronic security system near the property's fence. A faint trickle of inherent magic curled around the manifested claws on two of her fingers, racing invisibly up copper wires.

"Mundane system is decent…expensive, well-designed, but civilian. Nothing paramilitary here. Just about…*done*." She smiled at a faint, satisfying series of clicks as every gate around the perimeter unlocked. "There's a set of magic-based security strung through it. Mostly masking the property's auras, but some wards, too."

Jacoby nodded, only occasionally supervising the conscript before returning his attention to their surroundings. They were well-hidden from the road and mansion alike, shielded by bushes and trees, but one could never be too careful. "You have your mission parameters. Infiltrate, investigate, report, and await further instruction. No–"

"No 'stealing, filching, spoiliating, reclaiming, burgling, pillaging, borrowing without permission, or any other nuance of *creative appropriation*.'" A snide comment about how dismissing such nuances was akin to a colorblind toddler insisting that red and green were one and the same went unsaid. She was busy.

"You have two hours until the benefit ends. Travert will join us soon, if he feels Villneaux is securely contained by the festivities."

"He should drug him."

"He's not going to drug him. Focus, please."

Kasa knew Jacoby had no trouble seeing the gleaming, polychromatic threads her claws were methodically rearranging. Sorcerers were attuned to such things, though a lifetime of training was infuriatingly inadequate beside the natural talents of certain other creatures. Still, his kind had the advantage of increased versatility…breadth in lieu of depth.

"These wards are pretty good," Kasa murmured, meandering a few steps, finger tracing the fence and gaze unflinching. Her eyes gleamed a little too bright in the moonlight. "Would take longer if I hadn't br–*wooorked* with their maker before. Took awhile to break them the first time. Luckily, I see the same vulnerabilities here."

She started walking around the perimeter. Jacoby followed. At certain intervals–in thirds around the compass, ending at true north–the woman went back to work, uncharacteristically focused and quiet.

Suddenly, a Cheshire-bright grin split her lips. "*Eee*-hee, that's got it! It's–"

Her voice cut off abruptly as the wards failed and shattered, revealing everything beyond. As the previously concealed aura flooded over them like a noxious flood, her posture dropped: feet positioned to flee, eyes wide, and skin immediately pallid. A hand flew up to cover her burning nose.

Jacoby couldn't sense it beyond an inexplicable prickling at the back of his neck. A hand slipped into his jacket. "Miss Mengana? What is it?"

Her teeth still shone in the moonlight, but the smile was gone. This was a defensive snarl. "That's…no. I'm not going in there. I will *not*."

His jaw clenched. "Miss Mengana…"

"There's something *ancient* in there." An animalistic growl crackled beneath the claim. "Old weavings. Crafted by the kinds of beings humans call *gods*."

"Really." His eyes flicked back towards the mansion, critical and curious all at once. After a moment of contemplation, a phone found its way to his ear.

"I won't go in there!"

"I'm on the phone, Miss Mengana. Kindly shut up for a few moments."

It was more than a few moments. This tense, complicated revelation invoked certain protocols. Jacoby reported once in awhile, but spent most of his time silent while headquarters deliberated. He kept a weathered eye on the home…and devoted an unusual amount of attention to the asset.

She was shaking. She looked ready to bolt.

Interesting. You could always predict a catastrophe by watching the wildlife.

Finally, after what seemed like forever, the call ended. He returned the phone to his pocket. "You're going in, Miss Mengana."

"What!"

He shot her a chiding look, then returned his eyes to the far-off house. "The Council has decided that we need to know what's going on in there. While falling back is tempting, this initial breach may alert the powers-that-be to our presence. Unless we know what we're up against, there's no way to predict what may follow. It needs to be scouted. So, you're going in."

"I am not! I don't care what comes next. I will not cross whatever caused that stench!"

"Well, little two-tailed foxes with options never tried to break into Council headquarters," the agent observed. "You willingly chose this assignment over prison, and I believe I've been perfectly clear about your expendability. You're going in."

"Then cuff me, gov'ner. Because I'm not."

A scowl marred the man's face for just a moment. He turned to face the defiant, much smaller asset for the first time. "Miss Mengana. I will say it again. You do not have options. You are the only operative present who can accomplish this mission, and it needs to happen now. I cannot allow you to balk."

"And I will not put myself in…what are you doing?" The aggression on her face gave way to alarm before she forcefully–and imperfectly–suppressed the expression.

The sorcerer had retrieved a glassy, crystalline orb. It reflected light unnaturally, shifting and twisting as though alive…which it was. All foxes who manifested magic had one. Power, soul… life, all distilled into a single, potent droplet. This one belonged to Kasa. As long as he had this, he had her. "You will be scouting the manor."

Kasa's teeth were bared again. Every instinct screamed to grab it and run. But that wouldn't work. The same series of spells that prevented her from physically harming or using magic on her keepers also prevented contact with her own precious droplet.

"I won't." She sounded less sure, hackles further raised by the circle of sound suppression he'd woven around them while she spoke. She took a step backward, pretending she wasn't shaking.

The soul-drop hovered an inch above Jacoby's thumb. A small, red flame flickered to life at the tip of his index finger. The two drifted closer as he thoughtfully flexed his hand. "Miss Mengana, I cannot allow disobedience in this matter. We cannot afford the risk."

"Stop that." Her eyes didn't break from the droplet. She was beginning to sweat, and not just from nerves.

"You *are* going to scout the manor."

She swallowed. Once. Twice. "I won't."

Jacoby raised an eyebrow. With no more fanfare, fire flared around the gleaming little orb.

A scream consumed Kasa's next words, following her all the way to the ground. It burned to her core…heart, bones, mind, leaving her cringing and screeching and struggling to retain human form. Tears ran across swaths of black skin around her eyes, and the teeth bared towards her tormentor were far sharper than human.

"*Mortal primate.* My mother will…" she hissed, a snarl crackling beneath the voice.

"Your *mother* left you to twist the moment you were outwitted," Jacoby interrupted. "You act as though we haven't authored volumes analyzing Kitsune culture. You are not the first of your kind I've handled, Miss Mengana. And your predecessor had four tails. Literally twice the fox you are."

The flame had eased away from her drop. Although still uncomfortably warm, the girl's utterances gave way to hiccupping gasps, eyes beginning to focus and regain the façade of humanity.

At precisely that moment, his foot slammed into her gut with unnatural force, shoving a strangled gasp from her throat and sending the spindly waif slamming into a tree root several feet back. Sometime between impact and her vision returning, a strong, long-fingered hand wrapped tightly around her throat. The smaller hands darting up to pull it away stopped short of usefulness: claws had appeared on each finger, and the magicks preventing her from harming her handlers intervened.

"It ended *very poorly* for her, Miss Mengana. There is nothing to gain in defiance, no matter what awaits you in that mansion. You understand?" He held up his free hand, full weight resting on the knee he'd placed on her ribcage. The drop, suspended between the sorcerer's fingers, orbited tightly against a little ball of fire. "The only way I will not burn you to ash is through those doors."

"I...*hnnk*...I won't! Longevous foxes don't cross *ancients!*"

The orbiting spheres stopped dead, droplet planted firmly in the fire. The hand on her throat relaxed for a single moment, just long enough for her to hear her own wet scream. "Longevous foxes don't cross *me*. In there, you're mercifully uncertain as to what comes next. Be reasonable. Travert will be annoyed if I kill you."

The teary-eyed convict mouthed something, failing to force the words out. Jacoby couldn't be sure, but it looked defiant. The dull red flame brightened to orange. The otherwise weakening thrashing beneath his leg saw a burst of renewed vigor. A line of spittle wasn't the only think trailing from her mouth: threads of black smoke joined it from her throat, eyes, ears, and nostrils.

The agent regarded her with grim interest, curious as to whether he was really about to lose another one. Then, a nod accompanied whatever bitter acquiescence the fox strained to vocalize.

She could only lay there in the grass, clutching her throat and gasping and sobbing quietly, while Jacoby wandered a few steps away to straighten his suit at a leisurely pace. The droplet had already disappeared utterly. The man double-checked his tie. "This is a time-sensitive matter, Miss Mengana. I would suggest gathering yourself quickly, that whatever 'ancient forces' lurk inside have less opportunity to preemptively detect you."

A few minutes later, Olivier returned from the uptown soiree. Kasa had stripped down in front of gods and everybody, and was just finishing folding her pretty clothes into a neat pile. Her posture was sulky at best. After a pause to calculate, the handler approached her. "Miss Kasa. Is everything...."

A preternaturally quick twist evaded the hand he tried to set on her shoulder, a terribly feral snarl driving the point home. The shirt she had been folding bunched up and careened into his face instead. "*Fuck off.*"

With no further ado, the girl spun on her heel and leapt away. It was a petite fox's feet that hit the ground, sprinting full-tilt towards the bushes nearest the mansion, both tails twitching and ears laid flat.

Even under fire, a fox was still a fox… and the game of tearing through expensive security was a grand distraction. The guard dogs weren't so fun–dogs were plenty to turn her away under many circumstances–but, luckily, there were a number of sizable trees on the grounds which a gray fox had no trouble navigating. The roof wasn't safeguarded in any way, and it didn't take long to find a point of ingress by which to wiggle inside and track down the few remaining magical and electronic safeguards. That done, and with her babysitters and Villneaux all elsewhere, the place was hers.

The mansion's interior was full of quirky delights, plenty to distract a vixen from her troubles. Were it not for a little pain and the lingering smell of smoke, the little quadruped may have entirely forgotten her predicament as she poked a curious nose into a suit of armor.

She did her best to ignore the deific stench wafting around every corner.

Oh, there was plenty to see. The entire place screamed sudden wealth: the oddball flailings of a rich man trying to wedge himself into some poorly-understood mold, a caricature of the coveted one percent. There was art, of course…expensive paintings that, given the tastes showcased elsewhere, Kasa felt sure he didn't even like. A lap pool that flowed like a river. Ridiculous, mesmerizing chandeliers. And lots of those golden masterworks he was so known for.

Lots. Everywhere.

The "no stealing" directive was forgotten long enough for a roasted quail to go missing from the kitchen.

As the fox gnawed contentedly on a bone, she shifted once more to a human form and took a few seconds to coax open an irritatingly locked door. (Kasa didn't much care for locked doors, and rarely tolerated them.) It led to a home office packed with everything black-suited agents loved to rifle through: all kinds of bookkeeping and correspondence and weird golden sculptures. As she wiped her hands clean on the curtains, brown eyes flicked to an intruding glint: a golden fly on the windowsill.

Her gaze lingered.

Then she got to work, flipping quickly through various books and checking for certain key markers. She looked on the desk and in each drawer before turning her attention to the bookshelf. People always hid things in bookshelves, trusting sheer numbers for concealment even as everyone under the sun knew to check them.

One dainty hand drifted past a row of books, fingers an inch or so removed. Then, it stopped. A small, disbelieving grin edged onto the predator's face as her eyes snapped to the spot. She leaned close, nostrils flaring. *Touched often. Oil and metal. Oh, don't tell me....*

Kasa reached up to pull on the book. It was all she could do to keep from squealing when, with a click and dull groan, the bookshelf opened to reveal a door beyond. Oh, he really had taken all his ideas from movies. It was amazing.

She danced a moment.

Then, the fox breathed out to calm herself. The sudden rush of god-stench certainly helped sober her. For the sake of stealth and safety, small paws slunk around the corner in lieu of human feet, nose and ears scanning before she trotted down a utilitarian staircase, narrow and terribly dark.

Kasa loved every moment, dark eyes sparkling and vulpine heart hammering with the drama. She was indentured to an international secret society, and even they were rarely this cinematic.

The bottom of the stairs was stark, lacking any of the mansion's gaudiness. The smell of dirt hung in the air like in an unfinished basement, and a hallway comprised of cool concrete stretched out in either direction. Only one side emanated a sterile light. After an alert scamper in the opposite direction for the sake of scouting, the fox made a beeline for that room.

Inside, she stopped dead.

Whatever Kasa had expected, it wasn't this.

It wasn't a large, clear wall caging in most of the little room. It wasn't a prisoner sitting on a cot, ignoring the same audiobooks she had listened to dozens of times. It wasn't a woman whose skin was covered utterly, face and hands both bagged in odd-looking cloth that was padlocked to her wrists and neck via thick cloth bands.

It wasn't *this*.

And it wasn't the smell of old magic choking away everything else. The vixen's fur stood on end, fangs bared as self-preservation pointed in two directions at once. Ultimately, curiosity tipped the scale.

The room's resident jumped when the fox took her first steps in a woman's guise.

"Who are you?" The demand was weak. It was the tone of someone who knew she had no bargaining power.

The lady-shaped fox just observed her mark quietly, contemplating her options. Distracting as the smells may be, it would be a mistake to let danger harry her. She almost certainly had time. Ancient magic rarely rushed itself.

"I'm a lady friend of Jules." Pause. "Actually, that's a lie. I'm a burglar. Hi!"

The hooded girl could only gather herself for a moment, taken aback by the bluntness and wondering whether the claim could be taken at face value. She rose, wandering uncertainly towards Kasa until cloth-covered hands pressed against the plexiglass wall. "If you're not with him, then… then help me. Please." She wanted to say more, but it broke into a sob. "Help me. Help me…I…I can get you money. Lots of it. Just…."

Kasa stared curiously at the woman, head tilted. This was a fascinating conundrum, but her mouth was tensely serious despite niggling curiosity. She paced lackadaisically, a certain sway in her step forgetting her current lack of tails. "You're cursed."

The hooded captive recoiled a step. "W-what? That's…I mean, how do…?"

"You're cursed." The nude visitor remained perfectly matter-of-fact. "Old magic. Tell me about it."

Beneath her hood, the visitor closed her eyes. If hesitation stank as much as ancient magic, Kasa's nose may have burned off entirely. Finally, a heavy sigh trailed from the prisoner's lips. "Have you ever heard the story of King Midas?"

"Sure." The fox nodded, eternally willing to entertain odd flights of fancy. "A mostly-decent King made a stupid wish to Dionysus, and everything he touched turned to gold. Including his food and his daughter. Per Dionysus, he washed the curse off in the river and everything went back to normal. Happily ever after. Except for the peasant family downstream that picked up the curse in their bloodline. Manifests in one per-generation-and-*ohmygosh-it's-you*." An excited squeal echoed from the stone walls, followed by a gleeful laugh at not only the puzzle falling together, but the sudden and exuberant understanding that she wasn't about to be smote by an angry deity. Positively identifying the god-stench as a long-abandoned curse allowed her heart to finally resume its normal operations.

She breathed out slowly, wiping relieved tears from her eyes. "I didn't even know you were missing, gold lady!"

The young woman rubbed an arm, posture defensive. "My family probably hired someone to find me. But they don't report it if the *cursed one* goes missing. The national agency is inept, and they don't trust the Council. If the news got out, everyone would be looking for me. Mostly for bad reasons."

She went quiet. The room followed suit.

It probably wasn't kind to let the girl sweat it out on such a dire note, but it did give the fox time to evaluate additional security measures around this room–pathetically lacking; an obvious assumption that the exterior system would never fail–as well as examine the ambient magic thread-by-thread. She was humming.

"It's stuffy in here," she noted, out of the blue. Her lips parted, taking in the room's thick, ephemeral musk. "It stinks of compulsion magic."

The prisoner closed her eyes behind the veil. A line traced down her brow, darker than the surrounding shadows. "The curse was…born of greed. Greed, and all of the emotions that can arise surrounding it, are things I ambiently evoke in people around me. Almost any bad emotion. It helps… helps propagate…the…effects of the core curse."

Kasa tapped her cheek, thoughtful. "Are you suggesting that Mr. Fancy isn't to blame for all…this?"

"Am I…NO! Are you *kidding*? I'm in a cage! I have bags over my head and hands!" The voice ticked up a register when the prisoner heard Kasa playing with the door. "No…stop, no, no, please-don't-let-it…if you come in and grab me you'll…."

"Tch. Calm down, Shiny. You needn't worry about me. " The gentle, reassuring tone did wonders to offset the patronizing word choice. "A weaver's raw power–ah… *spell-weaver's*, that is to say–can only do so much to make up for the compulsion magic being an obvious afterthought. These enchantments are nothing to my mother's. I'm just investigating this lock."

For a minute, it was just quiet again. The newcomer was occupied with her work, humming thoughtfully, while the hooded girl looked afraid to ask an important question. Finally, she risked it. "Are you…going to take me home? Or just let me go home…? I've been taken and sold and used and stolen and resold so many times, I just…p-please…*please*…."

That was an interesting question, one that tugged the edges of Kasa's lips tight. Theoretically, the Council should return the captive to her family. But then, considering the asset's own experiences, used and tortured to their convenience…and even if this deity-touched unfortunate got home, how long would it be until she was kidnapped again, unwillingly put to work for someone else? What kind of life was that, anyway? Was it even worth it?

Silence.

"I'm going to make a call," the fox eventually answered, straightening back up. She nodded. "You get all that, Asshole?"

"I'm…I'm sorry?"

"Not you asshole. The guy in my earpiece asshole."

"*Affirmative.*"

"We've breached the building and are approaching your location," Jacoby informed. "Hold your position."

He arrived soon, pace predictably harried. Finding this generation's bearer of the Midas curse was big business, a serious boon to anyone's record. He swept the room once, then holstered his pistol, striding towards the cage's unlocked door. "Miss Mengana. Are you restraining the compulsion spells you reported?"

Of course he'd waltz in like he hadn't just finished torturing her. Her nose wrinkled, lips parting a moment sooner than speech demanded. "Uh-huh."

That confirmed, and with no further acknowledgement, the agent headed cautiously into the cage. "You'll be okay, Miss. The Council will take you into custody, and far from here."

Behind them, the fox's expression darkened.

The agent skipped brusquely from one vital note to the next: he'd remove her hood, but she'd understand if he left her hands covered. They would remove her from this place. Villneaux would be prosecuted by non-mundane courts. When he mentioned that, the rudimentary padlock securing the hood's thick, cloth collar clicked open, and he slipped the bag off the Grecian prisoner's head.

She blinked in the bright light.

The fox watched.

Then things happened fast.

Kasa dropped a huge section of the invisible threads she'd been holding, all at once, unleashing a torrent of greed and lust and possessive vileness. Oh, Jacoby knew compulsion magic…but the ability to fight a current didn't empower a man to stand against the battering forefront of a flash flood.

He was mortal. The power was deific.

For just an instant, the sorcerer lost himself, sense bashed away by the torrent of alien emotions. A sick smile split his face, eyes locked on the frightened prisoner, who gathered herself too slowly to cry a warning.

In that instant, covetous hands clasped each of the girl's cheeks.

The rest was quick, but not instantaneous. She screamed. He opened his mouth to protest the stabbing agony of metal racing throughout his body, starting at the veins and rapidly consuming every cell. He failed when the flash-freeze overtook his lungs. It was unbearable, all-encompassing, and mockingly silent.

The girl jerked back from the golden statue, wailing.

Kasa stared, a corner of her mouth spastically twitching upward. She didn't hear an alarmed Travert demanding a status report in her earpiece. Didn't notice in the time it took him to burst through the door.

"Anton!" At first, the agent could only stare, gun raised, breath short. His longtime partner shone dully in the fluorescent lighting. The culprit was screaming, bawling, and cowering against the back corner of her cell.

Then Kasa dropped the rest.

Fear. Anger. Possessiveness. The cacophony hit the remaining agent like a sucker punch, leaving him gasping but concealed in his shock. Anton…. His affected eyes snapped towards the cowering captive. This girl who had *killed* his partner. The gun raised, and he strode in her direction. Her snuffling cries took a different, shriller tone, gloved hands uselessly covering her face.

Suddenly, he froze, shaking his head. He was struggling visibly, gun trembling like a sniper's never should. "Kasa!"

The fox stiffened.

"Kasa!"

After a more few seconds–nearly a few seconds too long–the compulsions dissipated without a trace, contained like they should have been all the while.

Travert stumbled back, not trusting himself near the terrified prisoner just yet, gasping as the fire in his mind doused. Then, he backed into his cooling partner and jerked away. Fingers pressed to the bridge of his nose. Olivier just…breathed. Murmured a prayer beneath it. Breathed.

Breathed….

After what seemed like an age, he holstered his gun, jaw set, and turned to stalk towards the door. "Miss Mengana. A word outside."

She swallowed hard.

The underground passage was still dark. Still silent. Travert stood in the hall, and the woman-shaped fox did, too. For a long time, the only sound was the prisoner sobbing from the other room. Kasa's eyes were affixed downward. She was trying very, very hard to conceal the fear. (She was failing.) *He knew.*

Travert took a deep breath.

He knew. He knew. He KNEW.

"I have to consider what happens next." Though soft, Olivier's voice was terrifying. Oh, it was always flat. But it was never so cold. Kasa was still wearing the fox's ears. They pressed flat.

"The laws on this kind of thing, especially for a conscript, are black-and-white. It is a capital offense to murder an agent of the Council, even indirectly." Pause. He closed his eyes. "There is no… *allowance* for the agent having diverged from humane treatment of prisoners. No allowance for lashing at a torturer. Just death."

It wasn't until the end, his tone at the end, that she had any hope. She started to breathe. When he opened his eyes, she recoiled again.

"Of course, Anton was my partner. And besides that, whatever grace I may have extended has been severely threatened by your apparent decision to… what? Put that poor girl out of her misery?" Finally, a frustrated grimace bared his teeth. "We'll handle this internally. I don't know yet what that will mean." After a moment of indecisive silence, Olivier turned on a heel to head back into the room.

Then, he paused.

"I understand that foxes are predators. But this wasn't predation. You used and tortured that girl. I need you to understand that. Now, get back to work. Figure out a way to move Agent Jacoby. If you can't, sand down his fingerprints and dental records." Then, ignoring the stunned brown eyes affixed to his back, Olivier headed back into the room, removing his jacket and draping it over the girl's shoulders.

The whole, quiet proclamation had unfurled inches from Kasa's face. And yet, there was no fire. No cuff. Not so much as a grabbed shoulder. She watched the gloved agent murmur reassuring things to their sobbing objective: that they were going to take her back to her family. That it wasn't her fault. That she was safe. That they were going to take her home.

The fox watched, ears pressed low.

For a moment, she wished Olivier had just burned her.

Blood On The Quarter

by Riley James Keith

Report Number: QT-175 (personal record)
Bentley, Alton, Detective NOPD
Blood on the Quarter Caper
New Orleans, Louisiana 1931

Crime always happens in the middle of the night. Never fails. It's always on time and always when I'm in the middle of something else. Sleeping, or sometimes a drink. Or two. Or a girl. Or two.

Never am I by the phone, anxiously waiting for the call. When it does come, it takes my tired brain a few minutes to register what's going on while the guy on the other line blabs on about someone did something to someone else. Maybe there's an arm draped around my waist. Maybe the arm in question is black, maybe it's white, maybe it's a mix of both. Maybe it has scales or a jewel or two. Sometimes I'll get lucky and the girl will have wings.

I don't discriminate.

The call came in at 12:30 a.m. New Year's Eve day, later than usual for a murder.

It was raining, and my head felt like someone had stuffed it full of cotton. My hand ran into three different bottles, which then made their acquaintance with the floor. At least one of them shattered, and I smelled bourbon.

Not my favorite alcohol. The Rakshana beside me, however, is particular to sweet things.

The phone screamed into my ear. I answered it on the fifth ring, pushing off the striped arm circling my waist.

"Bentley," I said.

"Alton, it's Walter."

"What are you doing up at this hour?"

"Our job."

I sat up, swung my feet over the edge. The sole of my right foot met glass. I yelped.

"What was that? You got a girl with you?"

"Yes," I said, pulling a piece of glass from my foot. "But a girl didn't make that noise."

"For your benefit, I'll pretend she did."

"Where are you?"

"French Quarter. Bourbon Street."

I frowned. "What's a stiff doing in the Quarter?"

I could hear the shrug on the other end. "Better come and see."

I put the receiver down and stood up carefully.

"What was that?" Agni asked, her large red eyes half-lidded with sleep.

"Day job," I said.

"Do you have to go?"

I grinned at her. "Someone has to pay the bills, honey."

My clothes waited for me on the floor and I slumped into them. I fumbled around for the coat rack, found it, and snatched my trench and fedora from it. My keys jangled in the pocket, thank God. For a minute, I had the idea I'd left them at the bar.

Wouldn't be the first time.

Rain pattered on the windshield as I drove. Lightning flashed overhead, followed by halfhearted thunder claps. Seemed like the weather was putting in as much effort as I was. I commiserated and hoped it would continue to half-ass the storm. Nothing worse than trying to commune with the dead in a downpour. I drove as close to the scene as the crowd of gawkers would let me. I killed the engine and honked. One of the officers keeping the onlookers back spotted me and waved me over. I opened the door.

"Make some room!" he shouted.

Like all good people do, they looked at me, spotted the shiny badge I flashed them behind the windshield, then moved out of the way with more than a little bit of grumbling. People were more interested in the shape under the blanket than a half-drunk detective with his hands in his pockets. Walter Robison, red-faced and bleating, his bald head covered by his trench, met me halfway.

"Hi, Walt."

He grunted a greeting.

"Nothing's been moved," he said.

"Good to know. Have an ID?"

"Clarissa Charbonneau."

"The Temperance Union dame?"

"The same."

"What's she doing wandering the Quarter at midnight?"

"Witnesses says she was handing out flyers."

"Flyers?"

"Something about Prohibition."

"It's New Year's Eve." I said.

He pursed his lips, shrugged back into his trench coat. "You know how they are."

"Radio is full of it," I agreed. "Why was she handing them out at midnight?"

Walter had no answer. We walked to the body. Coroner Wilson Sheffield, a short man with a long nose and antennae, paid absolutely no attention to us. I looked at the body over his shoulder.

Miss Clarissa Charbonneau was once a person with hopes, dreams, and no doubt a fanatical belief in the safety and security of the city of New Orleans. A Joe Brooks if I ever saw one.

"Mind pulling the blanket down?" I asked.

Wilson looked up at me, his slanted eyes honeycombed with a thin membrane.

"Would it help?" His voice carried a slight buzz.

"Wouldn't hurt."

He did as I asked without complaint. "This isn't going to be pretty, detective."

"It never is," I said.

He pulled the blanket back. Bile rose in my throat. Walter swore and crossed himself. She was pretty once. I'd seen her picture in the paper enough times to know that. Now? Now she was a heap of skirts, blood, and organs that belonged in her abdomen.

"Looks like something took a bite out of her," I said, pointed to her neck. The dress she wore had a long collar neatly ripped in a diagonal line. Long, deep scratches in her skin told me that whatever decided to go after her wasn't human.

We looked at the coroner.

"It's out of my hands," he said. "Dynphna will run some tests when she gets it."

"Why don't you find out what got at her?" Walter asked me.

"Yeah, yeah, pipe down," I snapped. From my breast pocket I pulled out a pack of cigarettes and lit one.

"You want the crowd around?"

"You want to try and make them go away when the gettin's good?"

Walter grunted. I took a long drag from the cigarette. Didn't get the ash quite down to the butt, but I was close. I kneeled at Clarissa's head. Blonde hair spilled out from an impossible hairstyle and feathered in the puddle under her.

Another puddle, this one of blood, tangoed with the water which two-stepped with the reflected street lamps, a pretty picture. Lucky me got to stare at it until the blood leeched all of the color out of the streetlamp and began to glow.

I sighed. I don't have to call on any particular god or Loa or saint to do this little trick. Or any of them in my arsenal. I'm not that kind of Wielder. I was born with the ability to converse with the dead. After Dad got his fill of booze and carting me around every carnival and fair in Louisiana, Texas, and Alabama and after mom served him the divorce papers and took me away, I grew up with shorter, nastier kids calling me all kinds of names. They ranged from freak to others I daren't utter aloud for any of the sensitive types. Eventually I got sick of running away and decided some education was better than none. I couldn't cut it as a lawyer, and I liked women too much to be an accountant. Couldn't keep running from my ability either. That presented a problem for most respectable jobs.

Police officer it was.

The choice made my mom proud and my dad roll over in his shallow grave. Money would have been better as an accountant.

"You gonna do this or what?" Walter demanded. "It's pouring down."

"You want to dry up for a minute?"

I scooped up the glowing blood bubbles. They floated on a thin skein of water before deciding they liked the moisture-laden air better. I closed my eyes and blew out the smoke in a long, gentle exhale. It swirled around the bubbles. Clarissa came up screaming. I put my hand over the shade's lips, put a finger to mine. The crowd gasped. I ignored them.

"Don't scream," I told her. She looked at me, the glowing bubbles serving as her eyes. I smiled, trying to be as handsomely reassuring as possible. "Just answer one question for me, alright?"

Clarissa nodded, her eyes flicked frantically from left to right before meeting mine again.

"Who did this to you?"

Her lips worked against my hand. I removed it, repeated my question.

"Wolf," she said, the bubbles popped. She disappeared in a bolt of lightning and grumble of thunder.

"Well," I said, lighting another cigarette. "There's our answer."

"Tell it to Sweeney," Walter said, crossing his arms over his considerable stomach. "You know Charbonneau is her father?"

I nodded.

"He is the only wolf we got in the city. The other stations would have told us if one of theirs decided to take up residence. Not that they would get the chance."

"True," I said. "Check and see if out of state came into the city."

Walter pouted. "We would have been told. Charbonneau knows the rules. He can scent them coming off the Ponchartrain."

"He's rich," I countered. "The rich have their own rule book. Maybe someone decided to settle an old debt, and Charbonneau decided we didn't need to know about it."

Walter raised a thick eyebrow. "Even though his daughter is dead?"

"Would you just do it?"

His salute was terrible. "You want me to fetch your slippers and a pipe while I'm at it?"

"Fuzzy slippers," I told my partner. "If they're pink, I'll kill you."

The problem with Louisiana is the same problem that weighs on the rest of the country: people who think they know what's good for others won't shut up and leave people alone. One of those people waited for me in a chair outside my office. Her hair was done up so tight I swear the follicles screamed for mercy. She was dressed to the nines in a long dress with a tight waist jacket and a wide brimmed hat. I wanted to say her legs went on for miles, but my view was impeded by tweed and ankle-high boots. Her eyes were dark and her lips were red. She wore pearls and just enough make-up to show her femininity. The rest of her, excluding her hard expression and bright white Women's Christian Temperance Union bow pin, was a mystery I wasn't sure I wanted to solve.

"Detective Bentley?"

"Yes," I said. "Won't you come in, Miss..."

She stood. "Abigail O'Brien."

I closed the door behind us. She sat down at the business end of my untidy desk. I took my seat and wondered why my typewriter had something that might be blood or raspberry preserves on six of its keys.

"What can I help you with, Miss O'Brien?"

She sat so straight it made my spine ache to look at her.

"I would like to report a missing person," she said.

I liked looking at her, even if her spine seemed ready to snap. Under her cap, her hair was a bright red, and jewels embedded beside her right eye trailed down her cheek, cupped her jawbone and would swirl in an intricate pattern, hugging her right breast. I knew what she was and it surprised me how much she tried to hide it.

"I know there is a time limit," she said, digging into her purse, "on when to report a missing person, but she didn't come back to the apartment last night and she is never, ever late."

"Who are we talking about?"

She looked up, her gold eyes catching mine. I sank into them willingly. She produced a photograph, thrust it at me and broke the spell.

"Her name is Clarissa Marie Charbonneau."

I studied the picture, met Abigail's eyes again and managed not to sink this time. "I hate to be the one to tell you this, Miss O'Brien, but Clarissa was found dead on Bourbon Street last night."

Abigail blinked at me. "Dead? What do you mean dead?"

"She's deceased, Miss O'Brien."

"No," Abigail said. "No, that isn't right. She was alive when she left. She said she would be home at exactly ten o'clock. Clarissa is never late and she never lies. This must be some mistake."

"It isn't a mistake, ma'am. I'm sorry, but she was taken to the mortuary at one o'clock this morning."

Abigail's frigid exterior melted in a rush of tears. Her jewels dimmed, her body shook, and I pushed a box of tissues toward her. She pulled three from the dilapidated container and blew her nose.

"No," she said. "We were going to see her father this morning. That's why I got worried, you see? She never misses an appointment with him, or her little sister."

"I see," I said and fumbled around my desk for a notebook and pen. "What was the nature of the visit?"

She sniffed, blew her nose again. "Her sister is Antoinette Charbonneau, the ballet dancer. Do you know her?"

"I've heard of her."

"She is in town this week, from Paris. Clarissa was supposed to meet Antoinette and her father to discuss a conflict of interests."

"Oh?" I asked.

Abigail nodded, dabbing under her eyes. "The Temperance Union is having its annual rally. Antoinette wanted Clarissa to come to Paris with her on the same day. Clarissa was hoping to talk about a reschedule."

She collapsed into sobs.

"Miss O'Brien, what is the nature of your relationship to Miss

Charbonneau?"

Abigail gulped. "She was like a sister to me."

"Did Clarissa have any enemies?"

Abigail blinked. "No, none at all. Apart from those who are against the League, of course. And there are plenty of them. But none that are violent."

"Do you know why she might have been in the Quarter at night?"

As Abigail's stranglehold on the tissues loosened, she frowned at me. The skin between her eyebrows puckered in confusion. "No. I don't understand why she would be. The city is dangerous at night." She paused, rummaged in her purse. It fell out of her shaking hands and tumbled to the floor. She moaned. I jumped up, she kneeled, and together we put her purse back in order.

"That is mine," she smiled. "It's too small for your hand, don't you think?" She took a single glove from my hand and traded it for a yellow square of paper. "It's a receipt from the printing office. I found it on the accent table this morning. It might be the reason she was down in the Vieux Carre."

I looked at the neat typescript. "One order for two hundred flyers, pick up yesterday at twelve o'clock."

Abigail nodded.

"I'm afraid I don't understand."

"Clarissa sometimes acted as secretary for the Union. She had to place and pick up orders for any propaganda. I assume this is one of those orders."

"Aren't you part of the Union?"

"I am," she agreed, "but Clarissa and I kept separate schedules. She had her to-do list and I had mine. We might have lived together, Detective, but we weren't without our need for privacy."

"Thank you, Miss O'Brien, you've been very helpful."

She stood, straightened wrinkles in her dress that I couldn't see and looked at me. Her eyes bored into mine.

"Please find who killed her, Detective. For her family's sake and mine."

"Anything about werewolves?" I asked my partner.

Walter shook his head. "Not a damn thing. I was up all night making calls, I'll have you know."

"I owe you one," I said. "No one slinked into the city?"

"Not one. Charbonneau has people, Alton, like spiders. They tell him when someone comes in when they're not supposed to be within a half mile of the State line. You know how territorial werewolves are."

I nodded. "Thanks."

He grunted, his way of saying "you're welcome." I brought him along with me to the printer's office. Not because I liked my partner, but in spite of the fat blooming around his middle, he was an imposing guy, good when answers are needed in a timely manner.

"What are we doing here?" He asked in-between slurps from his coffee cup.

"I've got a receipt for two hundred flyers due to be picked up yesterday."

"Victim?"

"Her roommate delivered the receipt personally."

He nodded, slurped from his cup and got out of the car. A bell rang when I pushed open the door. The place smelled of old paper and fresh ink, a nostalgic smell, reminding me of my childhood spent hiding from mean kids who gave any place with books a wide berth.

A tall, slim, bespectacled man looked up from an open book. He smiled, revealing white, even teeth. They shone like searchlights from his coal black skin.

"Can I help you?"

I showed him my badge. "I'm Detective Bentley and this is my partner, Detective Robison."

The man straightened, his easy expression faded. "What can I do for you gentlemen?"

I pushed the yellow receipt across the table. He looked at it.

"Did a woman come in yesterday?"

He nodded, "Plenty of them. Is there one in particular you want me to remember?"

I pulled out Clarissa's picture. His honey eyes softened.

"She came in," he said, handing the picture back with reluctance. "Picked up two hundred flyers for the Temperance Union."

"Did she say where she was going?"

The man pursed his lips and shook his head. "I'm afraid not. I didn't ask, anyway."

"Did she look like there was anything wrong?"

He shook his head. "Not particularly."

"Was she in a hurry?"

"I guess she might have been."

We questioned ourselves into a circle, left with a smile. Walter lit two cigarettes, handed me one.

"He's hiding something."

"Like a squirrel hides nuts for the winter."

"You need to work on your similes, Alton."

"My what?"

"Never mind. Charbonneau?"

"Might as well get it over with."

I drove to the Garden District. The sun was hot and Walter was moody. Didn't make mine any better.

"Stop being moody," I told him. "You're worse than my mother."

"Have you called your mother lately?"

"No."

"Maybe that's why she's moody."

My mood did not improve.

We arrived at the St. Charles Avenue mansion right with afternoon guests. Undeterred by the show of money, we walked right up the cascading stairs. The butler stopped us, but showing him our badges changed his tone.

Gordon Charbonneau was not known for a jovial disposition. The mustachioed oil baron made his money with a stern look and a strong arm. The death of his daughter rendered him mute. We got nothing out of him but grunts and monosyllabic answers.

Antoinette Charbonneau was a different story. She sat us down for sweet tea and scones, told us not to mind the mourners pouring into her house.

"Everyone thinks funerals are such a sad affair. Papa should have thrown Clarissa a party, you know? But he does not. He is too broken hearted."

"And you aren't?" Walter asked.

She blinked at him. Her pretty face melted into a smile that would make the sun weep. "But of course, *monsieur*. I miss my sister more than I could possibly say. But the best way to honor the dead is to continue living, no? So, that is what I am doing. I shall create a dance in the ballet for my sister, I think. Something delicate and sweet."

"What can you tell us about your sister?" Walter asked.

I was too busy climbing her legs. Metaphorically. They were good legs. She watched me out of the corner of her eye and smiled.

"My sister was strange," Antoinette admitted. "But I loved her. She was always so, what is the word? Prudish. There were things she would not do, even when we were girls."

"Such as?"

She pursed her lips. "I would run and jump with the boys where we were raised. We were not raised in the city, but on Papa's plantation further south. This house was not purchased until I had left for France the first time, but that is not important. While I would run and jump, Clarissa would entertain herself with tea parties and solitary walks. Her dresses were long and her hair, her beautiful hair was never far from that awful style. A nun has more style than my sister did. And those gloves." She shuddered.

"Gloves?"

Antoinette made a face. "She was afraid of germs. Always wore them. Awful things."

"Did she know anyone that would have wanted to hurt her?" I asked.

She turned her full attention on me. "She was married once. I do not think he liked the divorce papers Papa forced on him."

"Married?" Walter asked. "To who?"

"To whom, my pudgy *pâtisserie*. You mean to say, to whom."

Walter flushed to put a beet to shame.

"He is a printing man, I think. Black as the night is long and very handsome. Papa would have none of it."

Tall, black, handsome, and very dead.

"That's him," I said. "That's the man from the printing office."

Walter nodded. "Poor bastard. Neck ripped open in the middle of the

French Quarter for God and all the world to see."

"What the hell was he doing out here?"

Walter shrugged. "No family to speak of."

"None?"

"None that we could find. He's William Moody of Charleston, West Virginia. Mother died when he was fourteen, father dead long before that. No brothers or sisters."

For the first time in a long time, I didn't have a witty quip. No one deserves to die like William did.

Union flyers scattered around William's body. They made the halo and soaked up his blood, not his cropped hair.

At least it wasn't raining.

"Any witnesses?" I asked, beginning to sober up and wanting to get reacquainted with the whiskey bottle at home. "Or do I have to perform my little trick?"

Walter, significantly more sober than I, shook his head. "Not this time. We got the guy who did it." He pointed.

I looked. A man sat in the open bed of an ambulance, half soaked in blood and sporting a thousand yard stare. Gordon Charbonneau, looking like he'd been through hell. I walked over, fully intent on adding insult to injury.

He glanced up at me and went back to looking at the body.

"Mister Charbonneau, do you remember me?"

"I do," he said.

"I need to know what happened."

"He killed my daughter," he said, nodding at the body. "He killed my daughter, so I came to return the favor."

Redundant question. "Mister Charbonneau, did you kill William?" Then I noticed his hands. The one not covered by the blanket sported very long, very nasty claws. They receded as I looked. Gordon Charbonneau caught my gaze.

"I didn't kill him," Gordon said. "I came too late. Found the sonofabitch like that when I got here."

His claws turned back into fingers. I met his gaze.

"I didn't kill him."

***

I spent the evening in my office, having a staring contest with a bootleg bottle I kept in my bottom drawer for just such an occasion. On the wall to my left, a clock slowly ticked down the minutes to midnight.

"I got registered werewolves, Temperance Union flyers, two people killed in the same way, and one very rich man who says he didn't do it. Am I missing anything?"

The bottle had no answer. I don't normally touch bootleg, but I'd take anything within reach. I grabbed the bottle and took a swig, declaring myself the winner of the staring contest. The stacks of evidence in front of me didn't tell me anything I didn't already know. Time to talk to William and see if I could learn anything new.

Lucky for me that the morgue is a short walk away and that William was still on the slab. It's harder to talk to spirits once the embalming process starts, but not impossible. Just takes a lot more concentration. The clock stood at fifteen minutes until midnight when I finally managed to pull enough of William together to talk to him.

"Who killed you?" I asked.

He blinked at me, a slow, lazy blink of someone just waking up.

"Glove," he said. And in the blink of an eye, he was gone.

I sighed. One and done, that's the rules. Sometimes I'm lucky and the dead know who did them in. Other times, I'm not and they say something completely useless. Like this time.

"Any luck?" The mortician Dynphna, a woman with spectacles and lovely brown hair, asked.

"I think my number's run out."

"Too bad. I wish I could do something for you, Alton, but you know how these things go."

I nodded. "At least you get to have a conversation with them."

"If you can call having their ghost stand over your shoulder and scream about how you're desecrating their body a conversation, sure."

I smiled. Dynphna and I have the same kind of gift. But where I pull spirits from their dead bodies to demand answers with smoke and an occasional mirror, she uses formaldehyde and other chemicals. Where I can talk to the ghosts, she can make them move on. And she does, quickly. Ghosts aren't exactly sane and Dynphna isn't exactly the run of the mill mortician. Saint Dynphna, patron of the insane, New Orleans mortician. I watched her work for a while, mulling over the case.

"Can I get you anything?" I asked.

She pushed her glasses up the bridge of her nose. "That's sweet, but no, thanks. What did he tell you, anyway?"

"Glove," I said.

"Glove?"

"Whatever that means."

She shrugged and pulled her hair back into a loose bun. Curly tendrils framed her face quite nicely. Not for the first time I thought about pushing one of those tendrils back behind her ear. She and I could be something, if I could work up the courage to ask.

"Wish I could help," she said again and pulled a medical mask over her mouth.

"Yeah," I said, "I'll bring a bottle around for you. Might not be at midnight, but I'll try my best."

Her eyes crinkled. I left the examination room and stumbled back toward my office. Something about William's words made my head hurt. The facts weren't adding up. I had papers strewn around two bodies, both were in the Quarter, and both knew each other. Gordon Charbonneau said he didn't do it, but there was nothing to prove that. The man was a werewolf; both bodies looked like product of a changing gone wrong. There was no reason not to book him and throw him in the pen for the murder of William Moody and Clarissa Charbonneau.

Except that Gordon might have had a reason to kill William, but none to kill his daughter. And William had said 'glove' and Clarissa had said 'wolf'.

I got back to my office and sat down behind my desk.

"Hello moonshine," I mumbled. "Did you miss me?"

"Yes," a woman's voice purred from a dark corner. "It did, and so did I."

I looked up. Abigail appeared out of the shadows, slowly, as if to make the moment last. First came one long, unclad leg, then a hip, a shoulder, and finally her head.

"Hello," I said.

"Hello yourself," she said, a hand on her round hip.

"Can I help you with something, Miss O'Brien?" I asked.

She smiled at me, "I wanted to ask why you put Gordon in prison. You weren't here, so I decided to wait."

"He attacked a man. Did you know that Clarissa was married?"

Her eyes widened. "No, I didn't."

I grunted, took a sip from the bottle. "Her sister told me."

"Poor Antoinette. She must be devastated."

"If she is, she has a funny way of showing it."

"Was Clarissa's ex black?"

I looked at her. "How did you know?"

Abigail's smile was gentle. "Gordon is racist, Detective. The other question would be to ask if her ex-husband was human. Either one would get a man killed for even thinking to touch his daughter. Do you mind if I smoke?" She asked, shifting her weight from one foot to the other. "I was at a party and the mistress of the house doesn't enjoy cigarette smoke."

"Go ahead," I said. "Only if you share."

She pulled out two from a gold case and lit them.

"A Union member who smokes," I said, faking surprise.

She smiled and sat on the corner of my desk, passed me a cigarette. "It's a secret. Don't tell anyone."

I smiled and took a long drag.

"Are you going to keep Gordon in prison?"

"For a little while," I said. My head started to feel light, my body like it was floating. "At least until he gets the money to pay his bail."

"Shouldn't be too long. Poor Gordon. He cared deeply for Clarissa, you know. She was his favorite."

"That so?"

Abigail pulled her long hair to one side. "It is. He would never say so, of course, what with Antoinette making the family name so big no one would dare ignore a Charbonneau, but Clarissa was his oldest. And fathers dote on their oldest daughters."

"I see," I said. "Does Antoinette know?"

"I suspect so. It isn't difficult to see."

The floating feeling disappeared. I wanted it back.

"Would you like a drink?"

She shook her head. "I don't drink, detective."

"What fun do you have on New Year's Eve, then?"

Her gaze flitted to the clock, lips turned down in a frown. "It is past midnight."

"Show me anyway."

Her kiss was sweet and soft and untrained. I fixed that. Her giggle turned into a moan. Sometime during the kiss, I had stood up and fixed our positions on the desk.

"Here?" she asked, pushing my suspenders from my shoulders.

I smiled against her mouth. Her jewels burned with an inner fire, and I really wanted to see the design they made on her breast. The thought tortured me. I kissed her again, added my tongue to the equation.

"Unless you'd be more comfortable somewhere else."

She slid off the desk and gave me her answer.

I smelled moonshine all over me. It stung my nose and made me wince. The sudden sensation of ice made me yelp and jump to my feet. Laughter turned some of the cold water warm.

"Looks like someone had fun," Walter said through his laughter.

The day shift joined him. I looked down. At least Abigail had left me my trousers.

"I don't want to know what you did," Walter said and held up a hand, stalling any explanation I would have given him. "You sober?"

"Unfortunately."

"Good," he said. "Antoinette is in the hospital. Critical condition. Her old man took the opportunity of a drunk guard and a drunk detective to slip out of his cell. He's in the hospital with her."

I struggled with what he was saying. "What?" I asked. My head felt like someone had taken a hot poker to it unconcerned about the results. My body felt about the same.

"What happened to Antoinette?" I asked.

Walter tossed me my shirt and someone else tossed me a bar of deodorant. "You need it," that someone said. I didn't argue. "I got mouthwash too."

"Do I need that?"

"Does the Pope wear a tall hat?"

I made myself presentable. Walter waited until we walked out of the station door to answer my question.

"She was attacked," he said.

"By what?"

"Same thing that got her sister, looks like."

"Will they even let us in?"

"They wouldn't when she was first brought in, but we can try."

We hurried into the car, put on the siren and blasted through traffic. It was the shortest hospital run I've ever made in the passenger's seat. Walter didn't ask how I was doing, or what happened, and I felt a little put out at that.

"Aren't you going to ask?"

He grunted.

I felt sick to my stomach and more than a little embarrassed about being found at my desk blacked out half naked with my mouth wide open. My head still felt fuzzy and I had a taste in my mouth that was half moonshine, half almonds. I scrubbed my unshaven face.

"What happened last night?" He asked, swinging the car into the first spot he saw.

"You only asked because I said something," I pouted.

He grunted, "Let's go."

Charity Hospital was full to the gunnels. The staff all wore varying degrees of exhaustion and irritation. Every manner of person filled the seats. Some wore tentacles, others sparked and sizzled as their abilities got out of hand with their hangover. The air smelled of sanitation and burnt hair.

"Can I help you?" A male nurse asked without looking up.

"New Orleans Police," Walter said. My head hurt too much to talk. The almond taste grew worse on my tongue. I resisted the urge to gag and draw unwanted medical attention. The nurse looked up, unimpressed.

"We're here to see Antoinette Charbonneau," Walter clarified.

"You'll have to wait until I can get someone to escort you."

"We–"

"Doesn't matter who you are. You could be the President or the ghat damned Pope, and you'd still have to be escorted. Wait over there, out of the way, and I'll get someone to you as fast as I can."

"As fast as I can" turned into an hour wait. Walter got us coffee. I sobered up enough to think straight. When we were finally led up to Antoinette's room, she was awake but wasn't talking much.

"Five minutes," her doctor, a man with beer eyes and a long nose, said. "That's all you're getting. She has pretty severe injuries."

"Is she talking?" I asked.

He shook his head, ginger curls bouncing playfully. "Her throat was cut deep enough to sever the vocal chords."

Walter winced, looking green.

"Can she move at all?"

"If you mean can she answer the questions you no doubt have in store for her, the answer should be no."

"We need to know who did this," I said.

"There is a clipboard with paper and a pencil on her nightstand. If you need them so desperately, have her write them down. She's at least able to do that." His glare was shiver-inducing. He wasn't a big man, but he was in charge of pointy things and plenty of drugs. I stepped back behind Walter, away from the small doctor.

"Five minutes," I promised. "We don't need to know that much."

He left us. We walked into her room, Walter in front. Gordon looked up, his eyes wet and red-rimmed.

"I didn't do this," he said immediately.

"We don't think you did," I agreed. "But you will need to come back to jail."

He nodded. His broad shoulders slumped as he held onto his daughter's hand. Antoinette blinked up at us. She looked thin and frail against the white of the hospital bed. Her face was a mess of bruises and lacerations and her beautiful hair was shorn to the quick. I could see the head of the long, deep cut at her throat peeking above the bandage. She managed a smile. I smiled back. Walter looked sick.

"Hello, Antoinette," I said.

Her tight smile tried to grow. I asked her the same question I asked every single ghost I've ever resurrected.

"Do you know who did this to you?"

Her beautiful blue eyes watered. Her throat worked. She winced and motioned for the clipboard and pen. A female nurse, her guardian while we were in the room, handed them to her.

What the beautiful woman wrote on the piece of paper didn't break my heart. Coffee helped to put the world–and the taste of almonds–into perspective. Still, a little piece of me wanted to disbelieve. Gordon gasped. His eyes went wide and his free hand went to his mouth.

"She didn't."

"She did," I said. "Do you know why?" I asked Antoinette, taking advantage of her spirit still being tethered to her physical shell.

She wrote again. *Difference*?

"No," I said. "I don't think it does make a difference."

Get her for me. Reward.

She held the notepad up to her father. He nodded.

"I will make a generous donation to the police department for whatever materials you need," he said.

"Do you know where she lives?" I asked.

Gordon gave me her address.

"Someone will be here to take you back to Orleans Parish Prison," Walter said.

I thanked Antoinette and walked out of the hospital room. Coffee burned hot rivulets down my fingers. I'd crushed the coffee cup without realizing it.

We pulled up to her shotgun apartment in the Irish Channel. Walter and I decided against back up. Abigail was one woman and Walter was big enough to block the door if necessary, and tough enough to knock her out. If necessary. I decided to do the kind thing and knock on her door. Not that there was any answer, even when I announced that the New Orleans Police Department was calling.

"Kick it in," I told Walter. "I feel like I'm going to fall over."

"What happened to you?" He asked and raised his tree trunk leg.

"Poison. Arsenic, I think. That's the one that tastes like almonds, right?"

"Smells like almonds," he said and gave the door a good, hard kick.

It flew open. Abigail screamed. She was in the middle of packing a large suitcase. Sticking out of the struggling seams were flyers and she was sporting a brand new, very deep cut right across her pretty face. Four of her jewels were missing; ripped right from her skin. Ten years or so and they'll they'd start to grow back.

Walter whistled.

"Detectives," she said. "I–I wasn't expecting company."

"A cab, maybe?"

She smiled at me. Her hands tried to smooth creases that weren't there. "Yes, I've been called to New York as it turns out."

"Oh? Why for?"

She straightened. "Well, if you must know, the Union is looking for a new chairwoman and they've decided I am the best fit."

"Ain't there an interview process?" Walter wondered aloud.

Bless him, he did the thing I brought him along for and blocked the door. Abigail's eyes flicked toward the only other exit. She glanced at the window.

"Don't do it," I said. "You don't have wings. You're not that kind of Faerie. Unseelie have jewels. Seelie have wings. Faerie anatomy 101."

Her shoulders stiffened, "There's a stairwell."

"I'm quick on my feet."

"I wouldn't be so sure." Her smile turned nasty.

"Why'd you do it, Abigail?" I asked, tired of the game she was trying to play.

She raised her chin. "I have no idea what you're talking about. I'm going to New York, just as I said."

I nodded, went to her bed, and flipped open the luggage. It gave with a grateful yawn. She screeched and lunged for me. Walter took two quick steps, snatched her by the collar and held her still.

"Thank you."

I took a handkerchief that managed to cling to my jacket's breast pocket. I used it as a buffer between skin and evidence and rifled through her clothes until I got to the thing I wanted. I held up the glove by one of the clawed fingers.

"Clever," I said. "Charbonneau was the only registered werewolf in New Orleans. Too bad for you Charbonneau would have alerted us if anyone decided to step on his turf. You should have killed more people besides the family and the ex-husband, Abigail. We might have believed that. The papers were a nice touch, though. Threw me for a loop."

"I tried," she said. Her voice was saccharine sweet.

"Why did you do it?"

She wet her lips. "Clarissa was going to leave me. She was going to leave the Union. For *him* and for *Paris*."

Walter raised an eyebrow, looked at me.

"William," I clarified. "Printing man, you remember him."

"The stiff on the Quarter?" Walter said.

I nodded and sighed. The pieces fit. "Clarissa was going to go to Paris with Antoinette. She wasn't going anywhere near the Union, was she?"

Abigail refused to answer. I continued.

"She told you and you got angry. You didn't kill her in the Quarter, you killed her in here with this nifty little glove of yours. Somehow, I'm not exactly sure how, you got her to the Quarter and placed her smack in the middle. The flyers were just a decoy; a good reason for her to be out in the middle of the night. Good for the ex-husband, too. A printer taken down on the way to a delivery, maybe. I'm sorry I told you about him."

"Don't flatter yourself," she said. "I already knew. Why do you think I went after him? They were going to meet in Paris a few months apart." Her lips drew down into an ugly expression of hurt and irony. "Clarissa was in love with him and Antoinette was in love with the idea of forbidden romance. The whole thing was Antoinette's doing. Their father had no idea."

"Why didn't you tell Gordon?" Walter asked.

"I did," she said. "He didn't believe me. When he confronted Antoinette, she lied to him. Clarissa lied to him, too. They said it was all in my head, that Clarissa was done with William, they hadn't spoken. They didn't have contact with each other. But of course they did. William's shop was the only one Clarissa would do business with. So, I killed them all."

There was no remorse in her eyes, nothing in her voice but triumph. I pulled out my handcuffs. She held out her hands, caught my gaze. Her eyes smoldered. What jewels she had, flashed in the room's muted light.

"Do you think you could go easy on me? For old times' sake?"

I caught her lips with mine, enjoyed the kiss. "Sorry, honey," I said.

I cuffed her with all the care and attention of a man presenting a wedding ring to his beloved. She snarled at me. I snarled right back.

"Let's go," I told Walter. "We've got a report to write."

"What do you mean 'we'?" he asked, wheeling Abigail around. "I made the calls about the werewolves that weren't necessary. You get to do the paperwork."

"And that's the Blood on the Quarter Caper," I told Dynphna.

"Sounds exciting," she said. "Too bad about Abigail."

"Not really," I said. From behind my back, I produced a handsome bottle tied with a purple ribbon. "Here."

She looked at me, eyebrow raised. "What's this?"

"I promised you a bottle, didn't I?"

"On New Year's," she said.

I shrugged. "You got something to drink out of in this cave of yours?"

"I've got beakers in the next room," she said and took the bottle from my hand, admiring it. "You didn't have to do this, Alton."

"I made a promise."

"I didn't think you'd come through."

I took a chance. "For you, I'd pull down the moon."

She snorted, but there was a smile on her lips. I cracked an idiot grin and rushed off to the next room. There were beakers stacked neatly amongst a configuration of clear tubes and Bunsen burners I didn't pretend to understand. I took the first beakers I spotted.

"Are these clean?" I asked, coming out of the room, two of them in hand.

"I just washed them this morning."

She opened the bottle and poured us each a measure. She capped the bottle and I handed her one of the beakers.

"To New Orleans," I said, raising my beaker. "A city full of surprises. Like a puppy on Christmas Day."

"You need to work on your similes, Alton," she said, tapping my beaker with hers.

We drank.

"Happy New Year, Dynphna," I said and poured myself another.

"Happy New Year, Alton."

Butler's Last Stand

by Michell Plested

I cannot remember the last time I slept at night. Not because I'm a vampire; I am a normal human being.

I think.

There was a time when I could have definitively stated I was 100% normal. Mind you, I also slept when normal people slept.

Like I said a moment ago, I cannot remember when that was.

That's part of the problem with being a detective. Whenever a crime happens, you get called. In this city, that's usually at night.

Lately, that seems to be more and more often. Crime happens. You go to the scene and talk to anyone who will meet your eyes and more than a few who don't. When you're investigating whatever the crime du jour happens to be, you need to be up and about when your suspects and witnesses are.

You guessed it. That's usually at night too.

Not that I mind. I don't have any family. In truth, I belong to this city. It's been my mother and my father for almost as long as I remember. That's why I want to keep it safe. Some people are born to reach the sky. Me, I exist to keep the gutters clean.

"Hey Rafael, come over here. I want you to take a look at this."

That is my partner, Jean. He's been doing this job for almost as long as I've been alive. In fact, he's the reason I'm doing this job at all. He pulled me out of that rathole orphanage I called home and gave me a life.

"What's up, Jean," I asked, walking over to him.

"What do you make of this?" He pointed up to the roof of the building we were checking out on Canal Street in Mid-City, one of those old double houses converted into offices. I couldn't quite make out what was hanging off one of the gable brackets.

I shook my head. "I dunno, Jean. I can go up and have a closer look at it, if you like."

Jean rubbed at his right leg. "Yeah, that's a good idea, Raf. My leg's acting up again. It's that old football injury."

I grinned. Whenever Jean talks about his "old football injury," I know he's just covering for something he doesn't want to do. Knowing his fear of heights, I didn't have any trouble knowing I was being voluntold to do the job.

"Sure thing. You stay down here and talk to any witnesses. I'll see what I can find up in the heights."

I entered the old building and climbed the stairs up to the roof access. I opened the creaking window and stepped out onto the slate-tiled roof. Looking down, I didn't really blame Jean for not wanting to be there. The ground looked a long ways away.

I patted the hidden Butler medal I kept tucked under my shirt. It was just about the only thing I had left tying me to parents who had died when I was too young. It was my lucky charm. I hoped it would keep me from doing something stupid like falling off the roof.

The only saving grace if I did? Jean wouldn't be able to give me a hard time about it.

The roof was slick with moisture, making footing treacherous. I inched my way toward the mystery object.

The closer I got, the fuzzier it seemed to be. I had to practically lean over top of it to get any idea what it was. When I saw it, there was no doubt though.

It was a head. More precisely, the head of a black man. Some sick bastard had impaled it on a piece of metalwork protruding from the eaves. It still looked all fuzzy, even up close. I could only guess that was because it was dark and foggy.

I took a pair of gloves out of my breast pocket and pulled them on. Then I carefully reached down to retrieve the grisly piece of evidence.

My hand went right through the thing like it wasn't even there. I almost did a header off the roof.

As my hand passed through it, the head made a tiny popping sound and disappeared.

Now what? Jean would never believe it. I wasn't sure I believed it and I was the one who found it.

I made my way back down to the ground where Jean waited.

"So, what did you find up there, Raf?" Jean asked.

What to tell him? That I found a ghost head? He'd have me checked into Charity Hospital as crazy for certain. My story had to be believable, whatever I told him. "It was a balloon, I think," I said. "Popped when I touched it. Must have been a leftover from someone's birthday party, or whatever."

Jean nodded. "Makes sense. What do you say to calling it a night. Nobody here seems to have heard anything like the reported gunfire and I could use some shut eye."

"Sounds good. I could use a little sleep myself. All these late nights are making me see things."

***

Jean dropped me off at my place. I went up the stairs to my little apartment and tried to relax before I went to bed. I cracked a beer and sat down on my couch to think.

I couldn't get the image of the ghostly head out of my mind. It had looked so solid right up until the moment I reached out to touch it. Then it had disappeared in a puff of smoke.

The features had been those of a black man. No real discerning marks on the face. It wasn't a face I had ever seen before, that was certain.

I pulled the Butler medal out of my pocket and gently rolled it between my fingers. An old nervous habit, it often helped me to focus my thoughts.

I thought I saw something out of the corner of my eye. I turned my head, draining my beer as I did so.

Nothing.

I shook my head. It wasn't bad enough that I was seeing things out on the street, but now it was happening at home?

I thrust the medal back in my pocket, grabbed my jacket and keys and headed back out of the apartment. Maybe all I needed was to clear my head a little.

The night still held some of the heat of the day so I threw my jacket over my shoulder and started walking down Bienville Street. Even at this time of night, the French Quarter was alive with people. I walked past the Kerry Irish Pub, ducking around crowds of people, toward Jackson Square. Maybe I could find a little peace and quiet there.

The park was locked up tight in the evening, but I had an ace in the hole: a key from my beat cop days. It was one of the reasons I lived where I did. I let myself into the park and locked the gate behind me.

As I walked through the gate into the park, the sounds of the street faded and I finally found the solitude I was looking for. A light fog covered the ground giving the entire area a surreal feeling.

So what exactly was going on? I tried to think of anything that might give me a clue to the most recent investigation. There hadn't been any reports of headless bodies that I knew of. No odd murders or criminal activities. If anything, the city had been quieter than usual. The feeling in the air, if I were to put an emotion to it, was expectation. Almost like New Orleans was waiting for the other shoe to drop.

A tree loomed on my right decorated with some ghoulish hanging for Mardi Gras. I shook my head. The festivities were still weeks away. Some local, or more likely some tourist eager for a photo opp must have put it up already.

Except the closer I got, the clearer it became. I was almost beside it when I could see this was no decoration. Hanging by the neck, and clearly very dead, was a black man. A black man garbed in what looked like tattered canvas and linen.

I looked around to see if the killers were still in the park. At the same time, I moved to try and lift the unfortunate soul down from the tree.

As my hands wrapped around his legs, I felt a distinct chill and then the body vanished.

"What the hell?"

My eyes searched the night for the perpetrators of this hoax. This vile joke. Again, nothing. Except a few yards down the path was another piece of the vile, rotting fruit hanging from yet another tree.

I hurried toward it wondering what I would find. Similar to the first, but not the same, another man swung gently at the end of a rope. Again, I reached out to the body and it vanished at my touch.

This was getting to be too much for me. What in heaven's name was going on?

"Whoever you are, this isn't funny! Show yourself!" I watched the darkness, but still saw nothing. Nothing but what appeared to be yet a third corpse hanging some yards down the pathway.

I moved toward it, more cautiously this time, hoping to catch the prankster who was having a laugh at my expense. My hand went into my pocket and touched my Butler medal.

A jab of cold raced up my arm and a feeling of dread and malice surrounded me. Instinctively, I started to run. Whatever was around me, it was evil and I had to get away. But where?

I spied the hulking mass of St. Louis Cathedral and turned toward it. I could only hope and pray whatever was after me wouldn't follow me there.

I raced across the grounds of Jackson Square and through the cast iron gate into the walkway. The feeling lessened but still seemed to be following me. I went up the stone steps of the cathedral and tried the door.

Locked, but whatever had been pursuing me was gone. I sat down, my back against the door of the church and tried to catch my breath.

"It won't stop looking for you, you know."

The voice was so unexpected I may have screamed then. Someone certainly did and, as I looked back, I'm pretty sure it was me.

"Hey! Calm down. I didn't intend to frighten you." The speaker moved closer so I could just make him out.

That didn't actually do anything to ease my nerves. The speaker, besides being an older, portly bald man, also appeared highly translucent. If that wasn't enough of a clue, the fact his feet didn't touch the ground convinced me I was dealing with yet another spirit.

"Who...who are you," I asked after several moments.

The spirit bowed. "Major General Benjamin Franklin Butler, at your service. Er, retired, as you may have guessed."

The name sounded familiar, but I didn't immediately place it. "Why are you here, General?"

"Son, there is wickedness happening in this city that must be stopped and it appears you might be the man to do it."

Now, I'm no stranger to trouble – I am a police detective after all – but to be told by a ghost that it is your job to stop some evil? That took a minute to get used to.

I shook my head. "I'm sorry, General, but I don't follow. Why do you think I'm the person you're looking for?"

"You are carrying one of these aren't you?" he asked, holding up a small object.

Despite my better judgement, I stood and moved closer to the spirit to get a better look.

"Is that...is that a Butler medal?" That's when I realized why I knew his name.

"Indeed it is, son. I gave these medals out myself back in the day. You have one, do you not?"

I pulled my medal out of my pocket and showed it to the general. "Yes, sir. My father gave it to me."

"Well, there you have it. You come from a line of goodly men. You are indeed the man I have been looking for!"

"I still don't understand, sir. How can my possession of an old Civil War medal prove I'm your man."

"I only gave that medal to men of good character and grit. I have no doubt you embody the same characteristics your ancestors did," the general said firmly.

I shrugged. "I don't know anything about that, sir. I was orphaned as a baby and never had the chance to know my parents."

"What do you do now? What is your chosen profession?"

Finally a question I knew the answer to. "I am a police detective."

"Would I be correct in believing that your profession helps other people. Perhaps even serves the people?"

"Yes."

"Then, you are my man. New Orleans is under threat, sir, and needs the protection of men of fortitude. Men of the people. Men such as yourself."

"Let's say, just for a moment, that I believe you. What exactly would you have me do? I can't fight ghosts." It seemed so surreal to be discussing a battle with the dead with someone who himself had been so for more than a century.

The general floated closer to me. "Son...."

"Raphael. Or simply Raf, general. My name is Raf."

"Well met, sir," the general said, bowing once more. "As I was about to say, Raphael, I can deal with the spirit world if you will handle the living. Together we can overcome the threat."

"What is the threat you're talking about?"

"An undead power by the name of Marie Laveau is trying to raise a spirit army to overtake New Orleans. What I hear is she feels she was denied her right to rule the city."

"Marie Laveau?" I said. "Everybody knows who she is. Are you certain?"

"Absolutely! Will you help me?" General Butler said.

"It's all so fantastic. I don't know what to think." I shook my head. "I deal in the real, not the imaginary."

"Am I imaginary, young Raphael? Would you call me an enfeeblement of your mind?"

"Enfeeblement? No! I believe you are here." I thought about his request. What would it hurt for me to follow this spirit to see if he told the truth? "Very well, General. I will accompany you. But what will we do first?"

"First, we go to the place where this Voodoo Queen is buried. I believe her followers are trying to free her as we speak."

I heard the sound of shovels before we even entered St. Louis No. 1 cemetery, just into the Treme across Rampart Street from the Quarter. I crouched down behind a granite tomb. The general floated somewhere behind me, choosing to go invisible. Four men were busy breaking into a grave in an older area of the cemetery.

Even if I had been carrying my gun, four was more than I ordinarily went up against. In point of fact, as a detective, I rarely had to face a large number of men without backup. It was time to call in the calvary.

I dug my cell phone out of my pocket and placed the call.

"Dispatch?"

"This is Detective Raphael LaCroix. I have a 10-211 at the St. Louis No. 1 cemetery. Four suspects. Request immediate assistance."

"Roger that, Detective LaCroix. Dispatching officers immediately."

I put my phone away and continued to kneel behind the tomb to watch. The men had only scratched the surface of the front and would still be a while.

It wasn't long before I heard the sound of sirens. The grave robbers heard them too. They scattered, running in all different directions. One came running toward my hiding spot. A well-placed foot tripped him up. He banged his head into a granite cross and knocked himself out.

Then all I had to do was wait.

Fifteen minutes later, I was being interviewed by the duty sergeant.

"So, detective, what exactly were you doing in a cemetery this time of night?" the sergeant asked, his clipboard and pen poised. From his voice and stance, he was clearly saying I had better make my story a good one.

It wasn't a good way to start; I watched the grave robbers being led off, thinking furiously how best to answer the man's question. "Well, sergeant, I had just come home from an investigation and I was still pretty wired. I decided to take a walk to knock down the adrenalin levels a little."

"You live around here, LaCroix?"

I nodded. "Over on Bienville Street. As I was saying, I was out for a walk and ended up on Rampart Street. I saw these fellows acting suspiciously and decided to follow them."

"Suspicious how, detective?" He was still trying to intimidate me, but I've had better men try. I wasn't exactly sure what his problem was. Getting up on the wrong side of the duty desk was my best guess.

"Well, for starters, they were all carrying shovels and pickaxes on the street. I considered that pretty suspicious." I didn't bother hiding the annoyance from my voice.

"You've made your point, detective. Carry on with your report."

"As I said, I followed them. They came into this cemetery and started digging into that grave over there." I pointed to the oven-style grave decorated with graffiti and x marks. "They didn't hesitate or look around, so

I would guess it was their target all along."

"Apparently they were trying to break into Marie Laveau's tomb..." The sergeant looked at his notes, "They aren't even the first to try this week. Probably some fool tourists hoping to get their wishes granted." The sergeant closed his notebook and stuffed it into his jacket. "Anything else, detective?"

I didn't feel like arguing with the sergeant. Clearly he had it all worked out in his mind. "No, that's pretty much it. I didn't hear them say anything to each other. They scattered when they heard y'all coming and I managed to trip one of them up as he went by."

"And you didn't bother trying to stop them before we came?" Again with the attitude.

"With what, sergeant? I don't carry my sidearm when I'm in my civvies. I'm not about to take four men on without backup. What would you have done?"

He finally thawed at that. "I probably would have done exactly what you did, detective. Nice work. We may have further questions for you later. I'm going to have to ask you not to leave town over the next few days."

A joke? Wow! "Sure thing, sergeant. I'll be around."

I didn't see anything of the general again until I was back in my apartment. As I pulled the medal out of my pocket, he reappeared.

"You don't believe in decorations, do you?" he asked, looking around my bare abode with a critical eye.

"I wondered where you had gone," I said. "Come to say good-bye?"

"Good-bye? I don't understand," the general said.

"We stopped the bad guys. New Orleans is safe."

The general's expression was solemn. "I wish you were correct, Raphael. Alas, the forces in the spiritual plane continue to gather."

"So, what can we do, general? I doubt my gun will have any effect on ghosts."

The general nodded. "Physical weapons cannot harm spirits. But just like one man's strength can best another's, in the spirit world, one being's power or essence can defeat another if he or she is strong enough."

"Are you strong enough?" I asked. "Because if you aren't, I hope you have an army to help us."

"No, I don't." He turned away from me. "If I did, I would never have approached you."

"But, what can I do? You already said my gun can't help."

The general went silent for several moments. When he finally faced me, his expression was sad. "You know how the light of the moon is a pale reflection of the sun? It carries no heat, only illumination?"

He waited for my nod before continuing. "The spirit world is much the same. It is a pale reflection of the real world with little power to change or affect anything living. To a spirit, the living appear to blaze with the power of the sun. Your essence is thousands of times stronger than ours."

It made sense. "Is that why so few people ever see ghosts?"

"It is. And it is also the reason I have come to you. Your physical presence can help me defeat the evil that seeks New Orleans."

"How?"

If the general had been standing on the ground instead of floating, he would have shuffled his feet. He did not meet my eyes as he spoke. "I need you to lend me your body. I need you to lend me your strength."

I froze. I really had no idea what to say. All I got out was, "Why me?"

"You carry one of my medals. I feel a connection to you through it."

I sat down. "I…I don't know what to say. I mean, what would I have to do?"

"You wouldn't have to do much. By agreeing to host my spirit in your body, you are letting me exist alongside your own spirit and mind. You would be able to communicate directly with me, see what I see and hear what I hear."

"Would I be able to control my own body?"

The general came closer. "Raphael, if you agree, you must relinquish total control of your body to me. Otherwise we would be battling each other at every turn. That would be disastrous."

"I don't know. Can I have some time to think about it?" I asked.

He shook his head. "I'm afraid not. The evil that would overwhelm New Orleans is already on the move. If you don't agree now, I'm not sure I will have time to find someone else."

"So, there is someone else you could approach," I asked, seizing what little hope I could find.

"No," the general said. "I know of no others in the city who could both see me and might have the skills to serve the people. You holding my medal and being a police detective are the ideal candidate."

I thought about his words for several moments. If not me, then who? Nobody else, if the general were to be believed. Could I turn my back on my beloved city?

I knew I couldn't.

"Very well, general. What do I have to do?" I said with more than a hint of a sigh.

"You have already done it. You have agreed to let me in. You have shown yourself to be the courageous, caring individual I suspected you to be."

I felt better hearing his praise, but at the same time I was still worried. What the general was proposing was not normal. I closed my eyes for a moment and leaned back in my chair, trying to prepare myself.

"Okay, what next?"

"*It is already done,*" said the general's voice in my mind. My eyes opened of their own accord and I could see the spirit was no longer in my apartment. My body stood up.

"*General?*" The words, intended to be spoken, were in my mind only.

"*Don't worry, Raphael. I have control of your body now. I can still exit it now if you wish, but once we leave this apartment, I will not release control until we are done. Is that understood?*"

"*Yes general. Let's get this over with. I don't like feeling helpless like this.*"

We left my apartment then and walked for several minutes, first down North Broad Street, then Lafitte Avenue and finally onto North Johnson Street until we arrived at St. Ann Street. It was a route I had taken before; I was surprised the possible doom of New Orleans could be so close to my own home.

"*We are here,*" General Butler said. I had gathered that much considering we had stopped walking in front of an old, nondescript Creole cottage. The building, like many of its neighbors, had been renovated many times in its life. The last time looked to have been in the 1970s judging by the crumbling stucco on the exterior.

"This place? Are you certain?"

"Oh yes. I can feel the evil emanating from the building." We took a step forward and stopped again. *"I'm going to give you back temporary control of your body. I want you to go up to the door and knock. When the door is answered, tell whoever comes that you are here for the ceremony."*

"The ceremony? What kind of ceremony?"

"I believe it is some sort of voodoo, resurrection-type ceremony. That is not important. Getting inside is."

I nodded, surprised and delighted to actually have control of my head back. I walked up to the door and knocked three times.

I waited a good minute. Nothing. I knocked again.

This time, the door creaked open a very little. "What do you want?" asked a female voice from within.

I cleared my throat. "I'm here for the ceremony."

"Ain't no ceremony here. Go away!" The door started to close.

"Wait!" I cried, trying to stop the door from closing.

"Tell her you are here for the Queen's resurrection ceremony."

"I'm here for the Queen's resurrection ceremony," I said. The pressure to close the door stopped.

"You're here for the Queen?" the voice asked. Doubt colored her voice.

"That's right," I said. "Please let me in."

The door opened wide this time. The speaker was revealed to be a small black woman, no more than a girl. She looked suspiciously at me. "Where did you hear about a ceremony?"

"Tell her some of your friends referred you. You were to say you came for the gris-gris."

"A couple of my boys sent me for the gris-gris," I said.

The girl smiled and stepped aside. "Come in. We are just getting started."

I followed her into the house and stopped as she closed the door. With the light from the street blocked, the room was dark. I took a few moments to let my eyes adjust.

"Follow me," she said, beckoning me to follow her down a dark hallway.

"I'm going to take over your body again," the general said. *"You have done*

very well, but I need to be able to channel your energy when we get down there."

We stumbled on uneven flooring, almost falling onto our guide, as the general took over my body once again.

The girl stopped. "Are you all right?"

"Sorry about that. I tripped," the general said through me.

"Very well. Take it slow. We are almost there."

A few more feet down the hallway and and we were at the back door of the house. We stepped into a fenced courtyard filled with glowing candles and more than a dozen people dressed in white, all heads wrapped in scarlet. The middle of the yard was clear with a pentagram laid out in chalk on the exposed dirt. A small wooden box sat directly in the middle of the pentagram with what looked like a finger bone on it.

"Take your place against a wall," the girl said to me. "We will get started."

I went to stand at the place indicated and the girl drew a cloak over her head. She faced the penitents from the opposite side of the pentagram from me. "Tonight we are here to raise the Voodoo Queen. Marie Laveau was wrongfully treated at the height of her power. Now she will come back to right those wrongs and take her rightful place as Queen of this city."

"General, what is going on here? I stopped the grave robbers. It looks like they still have a bone for this raising."

"I suspect they always had the bone. They likely wanted more of her body to have a stronger connection between the spiritual and living world," the general's voice replied silently.

The girl had started to chant and writhe while the general and I were speaking. I could feel the hair on my neck and scalp standing up as if some static charge was building around me.

She stopped and stared directly at me, raising her hand to point me out. "You! You have brought an unwelcome spirit into this gathering."

The feeling of static intensified.

"I must draw upon your essence now, Raphael. The priestess is preparing to attack you with spiritual power."

I suddenly felt weak. The general raised my left arm. "You will not finish this foul rite, girl. I will not allow you to raise your Queen!"

"Not allow?" the girl said, her eyes fiery. "We shall see what you will not allow!" A beam of…something flashed toward me from her fingertips. At the very same moment, a similar stream of energy erupted from my left hand.

The two bursts of energy met midway between us and an incandescent ball of fire formed. It grew larger and larger as she and the general poured more energy into it.

It felt like minutes had passed when in truth it was only seconds. The ball continued to grow until it was big enough to touch the bone on the box.

A small explosion flashed and I was thrown back against the wall. I banged my head and briefly blacked out.

I woke moments later to find the courtyard and house engulfed in flames. People were screaming and running for the exits – some through the door I had used earlier and others fled out a gate in the back of the yard. I couldn't reach the house – flames blocked that exit – so I followed the crowd out the back way.

I fled the scene along with the rest of the crowd. I tried to reach the general with my mind as I ran. *"General? General are you there?"*

When I didn't get a response, I pulled my Butler medal out and gently rubbed it, hoping it would connect me once more the the spirit. Still nothing. I stopped running then. I was starting to stumble from fatigue and I was well away from the burning house. I looked back at the glow, thinking I should call it in. I pulled out my cell phone, but it was smashed.

I shrugged. The authorities would have to find out the normal way.

Then I saw glowing somethings falling from the sky. I held out my hand to catch one. It touched my skin and it disintegrated away in a small puff of fog, leaving my hand tingling.

I couldn't be sure. Was the Voodoo Queen really gone? Had her essence been destroyed, leaving New Orleans safe for another day? I might never know.

I started walking again, back into the Quarter towards St. Louis Cathedral. It just felt right. As I entered the grounds, I saw a figure making a lonely walk near the cathedral.

"Père Antoine," I said by way of greeting, nodding my head toward him.

He looked startled but nodded back to me and continued his walk.

Then I realized something. I knew who this displaced spirit was without thinking about it. Somehow, the general had left me a gift in the battle. He was gone, but I had the ability to sense other spirits. Maybe I would know if New Orleans was safe after all. But learning what I could do would have to wait for another time. Right now, I needed to get home and finally get some sleep.

Prompt Succor

by Hugh O'Donnell

The name is Terry O'Byrne. Folks that know me call me "Sharp." I have a keen eye, keener than most people believe. I was born in Ireland back at the turn of the century. My Gran said my generation was going to be something special,that we had a fate touched by the fair folk. She was a bit soft, my old Gran, but she was right, in the end. I have what she would've called "the sight." I can see things other people cannot, or maybe just willfully ignore. I see ghosts, naturally, but I've spotted many things as well: faeries, angels, demons, and a thousand others. When it first began, I thought I was going mad, and in a panic, I fled the country. In my haste, I took some favors and made some promises to some men I would have been smarter to avoid. I hoped that leaving would cure my condition, but the sight has only gotten stronger, and my new friends began making some serious demands.

That is how I ended up in New Orleans, running a charming little curio shop in the Vieux Carre. I play to the tourists, ask no questions about where my merchandise comes from, and I take on other odd jobs as my sharp eyes earn me. My primary employer is William "Big Willie" MacCarthy, boss of the Irish mob and the man that supplies the water of life that keeps The Big Muddy flowing. I take other odd jobs and requests from time to time, but the oddest one of all was in January, 1925.

It was the feast of the three kings, and New Orleans was celebrating in its own particular fashion. I was just about to close up for the night when a walking shadow stomped in. He wore an oilskin coat and a low-crowned hat, but I could see his black shirt and white collar clearly enough. Although he came in by himself, he wasn't exactly alone. He was followed by a line of ghosts, each one soft and indistinct, and as colorless as a film projection. That's usually how it is with spirits. I get the image, but most of the time, it's like a moving picture. No color, no sound. I've never been able to communicate with one. The priest's ghosts were a line of little old ladies who clung weakly to him like mist.

The regular ghosts in the shop made themselves scarce. I haven't had many priests in the shop, but they seemed genuinely terrified of him. I wondered what they saw that I didn't.

"What can I do for you, Father?" I inquired as he stomped his way up to the counter. Even for a man of the cloth, he had a dour expression. The hair under his hat was white, but he didn't look much older than thirty. But there was something about his eyes that I couldn't put my finger on, just then.

He stared straight into me and hurried to the front, as though trying to avoid seeing any of my wares. I knew there were rumors about my store. I started most of them myself. An air of mystery is good for business in New Orleans, and the more "legitimate" sales I made, the less on the hook I was to my benefactors.

"You're O'Byrne?"

"So I've been called."

He reached into his coat pocket and thrust a letter at me the way one of Willie's goons draws a roscoe. I took the slightly damp envelope and flipped it over. "This is the Archbishop's seal," I said.

"Aye." The priest continued to stare, so I pulled out my pocket knife and broke it. The letter was not very long, but it was from Archbishop Shaw himself. I read it twice, and looked the holy man in the eye.

"He might have telephoned, or used the post. This is all rather cloak and dagger."

He grimaced at me with a most unholy look on his face. "If it was up to me, we wouldn't be calling on someone like you at all. But your services are required by the Church. I am told that you fought for the liberation of Catholic Ireland, but no one has ever seen you at Mass. If you were a parishioner, this all could be handled quietly, but as that is not the case, we've taken extraordinary methods."

"I'm a shopkeeper, not an exorcist," I protested, which did nothing to break the thunderclouds settled on his brow.

"Then I suggest you inform the Archbishop when you see him and save us all more wasted time." With that, he spun on his heel and disappeared into the rainy afternoon, trailing his ghosts behind him.

The next day, at the appointed time, I closed up the shop and headed out in the bustling streets of the Vieux Carre. I had on my accustomed uniform for these sorts of meetings: a white linen suit, green vest, and a gold tie. I wore a emerald four-leaf clover tie pin, and wide-brimmed straw hat with a green and white band. After much internal debate, I brought my revolver, keeping it hidden in my jacket. It was not completely inconspicuous, but while I didn't want to be seen carrying a gun in church, I didn't want to be without one on the long walk from the shop to the Square.

Last summer, I was given a job by Big Willie. While I owe the boss much for my current state of residence and employment, I was not able to satisfactorily complete the task. A night of mucking through the Louisiana swamp and emptying an entire drum of a Thompson machine gun into the hide of what I can only describe as a swamp monster leaves me thinking nobody could. But although Willie assured me he was not angry, he did explain that he was "disappointed" in me. Things had been tense and quiet between us ever since. Part of me wishes he had just been mad. The waiting, knowing the hammer was still raised, was more bothersome. I had seen what happened to people who disappointed Willie in the past.

St. Louis Cathedral rises like a white wave above the statue of Andrew Jackson in the middle of his Square. High, whitewashed and imposing, I had never entered it before that day. Since leaving home, God and I hadn't been speaking.

On my way to the cathedral, I watched the ghost of Père Antoine, pacing in the alley named after him. The little monk wore a placid expression, and, not for the first time, I wondered what was the view from his side of the world. His calm demeanor showed he was unaware that he had been denied the heavenly gates he had devoted his life to someday reaching. Did he know he was dead? Or was he even denied them? Was I looking at his soul, or the echo of something long departed, like the reverberation of a church bell? I still could not say.

I slipped into the cathedral through a side entrance and knelt in a pew near the confessionals. I went through the motions of prayer with cold, leaden heaviness.

At the proper time, I rose, bowed, and entered the tiny confessional. I muttered the proper phrases in half-remembered church Latin. "My last confession was five years, two months and six days ago." I said.

"That's a long time to go without seeking the absolution of the Lord, Mr. O'Byrne." The voice from the screen was thin, weak, with a southern American accent distinct from the city natives. I guessed the Archbishop was from Mississippi or Alabama. I considered making a joke of it, but decided against it. Better to get down to business.

"Yes, sir. I'm not sure I want my sins to be absolved just yet. That isn't why I'm here today, either, I understand."

"I hope you'll forgive the theatrics, but a man of my position sees many enemies, and if it were common knowledge that I were to be seen conversing with a..." he paused, either for emphasis, or to find a polite word for the kind of man I was. "A sinner such as yourself, things would be complicated."

"I understand, but what can a sinner do for you, Archbishop Shaw?"

"I'm told you have sharp eyes, a sort of intuition. Is that right?"

"Something like that, Your Eminence."

"I'd like you to find a ghost for me, and get rid of her, if you can. It is of the utmost importance." It was a bit more than I expected. I hoped he couldn't see my expression through the screen the same way he was invisible to me.

"Not to be impertinent, but don't you have exorcists for this sort of thing?"

"We do, but he failed. This is a very different sort of ghost, I'm given to understand. We needed to find outside help."

"And how did you find me?"

"Your name came up several times, but I'll be honest with you. You weren't our first choice. When she turned us down, she recommended you." I stared doggedly at the wooden carvings. That would be Mercy, then.

Mercy Laveau was a psychic, socialite, and most of all, a con artist. She had much of the upper crust of the city wrapped around her finger, but she certainly wasn't the descendant of the city's famous Voodoo Queen, as she claimed. However, she did know more about the city and it's secrets, and that gave her a precarious sort of status. She knew where all the bodies were buried, but she certainly didn't believe in ghosts. I'd have to have a talk with her later.

"What sort of ghost will I be looking for?" I asked. Some ghosts haunted places, others haunted people. Others clung to objects or ideas. I've used ghosts to find hidden objects, or figure out some secret, but I'd never actually hunted for one before.

"An Ursuline nun. She appears every year around this time at the old convent. Every year she gets more active, more violent. Mass is tomorrow, and, well, there is a concern." January 8th. The anniversary of the Battle of New Orleans. There was a mass said every year at St. Mary's, next to the Old Convent. It was a big to-do, but I didn't know much more about it than that.

"I'm not really an exorcist. I can see the dead, but I don't know if I can help you."

"Just go tonight and see what you can see. The power of Christ did little for her, but maybe you can spot something we missed." There was defeat in his voice.

"Alright. I'll do what I can."

I left the Cathedral into the drizzling damp crowd of Jackson Square feeling rather queer. I passed through unnoticed, another lost soul in the Crescent City, unremarkable. And yet I was being called upon by the Church, as though I were some gallant knight. I didn't feel comfortable in either set of skin, so I made my way over to Mme. Mercy Laveau's two-story studio. As usual, I had the uncanny luck to find her with a client, a tall, black man in a severe black suit sitting at a desk in the waiting room, writing in a book. He looked up sharply when I stepped in. I tipped my hat to him, gave him a wink, and he went back about his business.

Mercy is a Medium at Large. Which is to say that she's a con artist who ran from some trouble up north, and made a new life for herself as the long-lost direct descendant of the original Voodoo Queen. She tells the future, contacts deceased relatives, and gives vague but generally pleasant advice to rich old white women who pay handsomely for the privilege. But that mostly harmless con aside, her real asset is in information. I can't find a record of her older than ten years in the city, but in that time, she made friends in all the right places, mostly low. The tall young man, a chauffeur by the look of him, is one of her friends, and though I didn't know him by sight, he recognized me. Mercy knew every secret, dirty and otherwise, in New Orleans. A dangerous woman, and a dear friend.

I waited patiently while she finished her session upstairs, employing every confidence trick she knew to reassure her client, while the real profit of the day was written down by her friend in his little book. Anyone with an ounce of street smarts knew, or at least suspected, her game. Thus, nobody crossed her if they could help it. Me, I had nothing to lose. She'd already spread my second-greatest secret to the Archbishop. And my worst was buried an ocean away, in a home I'd likely never see again.

After the matron made her way downstairs, was helped into her expensive, and entirely inappropriate, fur coat by the chauffeur, and escorted out to her automobile, I headed upstairs to the parlor where Mercy was cleaning up a deck of tarot cards.

"Care to have your fortune told?" She asked with a smirk. She palmed a card and pulled it seemingly out of thin air. She showed me The Wheel of Fortune with a flourish, the card flashing white in her dark hands.

"It's the past I have questions about." I took a chair opposite her and gestured for her to sit. I didn't pull out the revolver, but she saw the lump of it under my coat, and her face froze in a mask of hesitation, for just an instant. Then she sat, all mystery and power once again. I stared fixedly at the wraith behind her, a boy of maybe fifteen shivering as monochromatic blood poured out of a chest wound. He was the same as always, at least.

"All may be revealed, if the spirits are willing. They know many things that are hidden from mortal sight."

"Like how the Archbishop of New Orleans, of all people, came to hire my services?"

She broke into a wicked grin, losing character completely. "I was wondering if he would call on you. They came early this week looking for my help. Obviously, I'm far too busy, and it would do much damage to my bad reputation as a fortune teller if I was caught assisting the church."

"In other words, you couldn't bring yourself to scam the Catholics, but you thought I'd be more than happy to."

Her smile widened, exposing sharp white incisors. "You're the one complaining last week that you were hard up since Big Willie's disappointment."

"I'm not so hard up that I want to scam the Vatican."

She leaned back and crossed her arms like she was a chess champion who knew her victory was assured.

"So you admit that it's a scam, then?" Mercy didn't believe in ghosts, and was certain I was lying about the sight, as much a con artist as she was. I never told her about the boy I saw bleeding behind her. I think she was happier not knowing.

"I admit no such thing, but I'm not an exorcist," I protested. "Why didn't you just turn them down?" She gave me a level look.

"Because these are the Ursulines, Terry. They have something of a history here, and I do owe the nuns a few favors. I'm sure you'll figure something out. You always do. Take me to brunch on Saturday and tell me all about it."

I got up, accepting the dismissal. I already took the job, and confirming my suspicions about where it ultimately came from didn't change anything.

She called out to me as I stomped peevishly down the stairs. "By the way, if you see Fr. Willem, do me a favor and go easy on him, will you? He's had it rough since the war." I thought about the rude priest that brought me Shaw's message and made no promise as I left.

The Old Ursuline Convent is one of the oldest buildings in the city. It has served as a home, a shelter from fire and a sanctuary from war, as the Archbishop's Palace, and now as office space to the church next door. The next day, it would serve for the 110th Mass in thanksgiving of Her protection during the Battle of New Orleans.

A novice nun, who couldn't have been more than nineteen, met me at the gate and escorted me to an office, where I was met by a white-haired, and familiarly unhappy priest.

"Father Willem, I presume?" I took off my hat and hung it by the door.

"I thought you weren't going to take this job. Sister Natalie, you may go." The nun silently departed, her wimple trailing behind her like wings.

"I wasn't, but Archbishop Shaw was rather insistent. I haven't a clue how to do exorcisms."

"No, you don't. Have a seat, Mr. O'Byrne, and tell me, are you a con artist, or merely an amateur?"

I sat in a hard-backed chair and stared back at him. "What do you mean?"

"We're alone, so let me speak frankly. We both know what kind of woman 'Mercy Laveau' is. She talks a good game, and knows just about every secret this city has, but I don't think she's ever so much as set foot on Hispaniola."

"I know that it's smarter to count her as a friend than an enemy."

He gave me a queer look, not quite a sneer, but with disgust behind it, and grudging respect. "Tell me, Mr. O'Byrne, have you seen the boy?" I raised an eyebrow.

"Colored, in a winter coat, with a sucking chest wound? That boy?"

"Amateur it is, then. Have you spoken to him?"

"I, that is to say, I can't exactly talk to spirits. I have the sight, but not much else."

"A pity. I bet he would have some interesting things to say. But tell me, how did you come by your sight?"

"You first, Father."

"Fair enough. I was a chaplain on the Western Front, fresh out of seminary. When America entered the War, I was filled with fervor, certain the Lord would guide me and let me shepherd my flock through the storm. I had heard of the Angel of Mons, and other legends of Divine Providence on the Battlefield, and I was hungry to witness a miracle. And the Lord, in his infinite wisdom, granted my foolish wish.

"I don't recall when I first noticed. Most men in the trenches looked like ghosts already. But the Lord, and my training, let me send them on, the confused, and the frightened, the lost."

"And what about them?" I asked, gesturing to the apparitions floating around him. "Why haven't you sent them on?"

"O'Byrne, I have a lot of duties as a priest. One of them is confession, and another is last rites. Let me put it to you this way: If you could do what I do, if you could call on the Lord to send his wayward souls onward, but you knew they would only receive the torments of Hell for your trouble, would you do it?"

"I don't know. I've never thought about it that way."

"So when did you first see the dead?"

"I grew up poor, in Dublin. I've seen death my whole life. But it was at a football match in 1919. It's a long story."

"I've heard enough of it. His Holiness called you in, frankly, because I failed. I haven't been able to exorcize either of them."

"Either of them? There's more than one?"

"Take a look around, but remember I'm watching you." Sensing my dismissal, I stood. I'd have to play whatever game Willem had planned, but for now, I took a look around the compound. The buildings were old, and beautiful, a maze of stucco and dark wood. It was full of ghosts, most places with any sort of history are, but the two I was looking for weren't hard to find.

I found the first one in the chapel. She was a nun weeping softly in the apse, kneeling in supplication. Even faded out and fuzzed at the edges, it was easy to discern her habit and dress. And the tell-tale bulge of her pregnancy.

The soldier, his uniform bloody and ragged, was wandering the grounds, lost, or looking for something. He seemed to see me, but if he could do anything to harm me, he took no action. Even faded and translucent, the uniform of a British Redcoat was unmistakable. Night had fallen, and the site was mostly empty. Which is how I was able to tell I was being followed. Whoever they were, they had a light step, but were inexperienced. I reached for the gun in my coat and turned to stare directly into Sister Natalie's frightened brown eyes.

"*Mon Dieu!*" She cried, glancing from me to the revolver. I uncocked it and put it away.

"I'm sorry, sister, but I get a bit twitchy. What can I do for you?"

"It is I who should apologize. I was following you."

"Why?" She looked at the ground, ashamed.

"It was a request of Father Willem. I think he suspects you mean to steal the candlesticks." We shared a grin, but she immediately blushed and turned away. These were not holy thoughts. The ghost, whoever he was, was gone, and I led the novice back inside. The church was already decorated, the altar covered in candles and flowers. I bowed before the host, following Natalie's lead. I had never been in so grand a church as this at home, and I'd never stepped foot in once since coming to America.

"Tomorrow's the mass," I said, and she nodded.

"Our Lady of Prompt Succor. We will pray in thanks for the nights she protected New Orleans, and for the souls of those who were lost."

"Those who were lost…" I looked at the saints in stained glass above me, and the crucifix above the altar. Surely, it couldn't be as simple as that, could it?

"Tell me about the lovers," I said.

"Whatever do you mean, Mister O'Byrne?"

"Surely there's a story, and you must know it. A nun, and a soldier, with a tragic destiny?" Her eyes went wide.

"How did you know about, that is, it is only a legend, and it is not something that should be talked about, here of all places."

"I think it might be important," I said.

"Very well. It is like you said. There was a nun, here, who forgot her vows. She met the eye of an English solider, during the War of 1812, in fact. He was wounded, and she was his nurse. The devil tempted them, and they forgot their promises. Hers to God, and his to a fianceé far away. She broke her, um, vows with him." She swallowed, fearing even that hint of a taboo.

"What happened to them?"

"When she discovered her condition, he pledged to marry her, and she prepared to leave the convent. But he was killed in the Battle, and she could not keep her condition secret. She drowned herself, with her baby still inside her. Damning both herself and her unborn child. It is a horrible story. Some have claimed to see her, but I think she must surely be in Hell."

I watched the apparition weeping silent tears. "I think you may be right, Sister. Excuse me."

It wasn't hard to find a record of the story. Daniel Gilliam, an English Sargent, wounded in the leg, and Sister St. Francis Marguerite Du Champlain, his nursemaid. He healed, and returned to the English forces, a week before the battle. She was listed as dying "suddenly" a month later. Theirs was the only case that matched. I copied down the names and discovered Father Willem watching me from the doorway.

"I've identified the ghosts," I said.

"And what will you do, now that you know their names?" He asked. "I have tried everything to remove them, but the power of Christ could not push them out. Sister Marguerite is only made angry by it. Do you think I didn't try that already?"

I considered my response very carefully.

"While I agree with you that Ms. Laveau is more in the business of separating widows from their inheritances than speaking with the dead, there is one thing she has said that always struck me, even if she doesn't believe in ghosts."

"What is that?"

"She said that the thing that connects us to the dead is a need. Every client of hers needs reassurance. Needs to find out some secret that their loved one took with them. Needs to know that there is something beyond this life. And, where she can, she satisfies that need. I've often wondered if it works the other way. What do you think Sister Marguerite and Sargent Gilliam need?"

He smirked, a most unholy gesture. "I understand, but what they want is impossible. A philanderer and suicide don't deserve the forgiveness of God."

"Maybe not. But what about mankind? I have an idea."

The next morning, I attended Mass for the first time in five years. My Latin was rustier even than I remembered, and I was distracted, watching the weeping sister and the wandering soldier who followed the crowd into the chapel. I missed a few steps, but the routines and refrains of my childhood, and something that had been so important to me in my youth, came back easily enough.

As the service and the prayers went on, the ghosts became more and more agitated. Candles began to flicker from an unfelt breeze. I felt a sense of heaviness in the air like a thunderstorm could break out any minute. Gilliam hoisted a spectral rifle as though he were taking aim. Willem, assisting Shaw, stared nervously at them, and myself. There was a huge crowd, and he was taking a chance on me, I realized. And finally, the

Archbishop reached the prayers of the faithful. He prayed for the souls of the dead, and for the city, and for the Holy Church.

And then, he said, "And for Sister St. Francis Marguerite Du Champlain and Daniel Gilliam, we pray." Both ghosts froze, and as though they saw each other for the first time, ran through the aisle toward one another. They embraced, and I was blinded in a single ray of light. For a moment, Marguerite turned to me, I saw her mouth whisper something, and almost thought I heard someone say, "Thank you." Then, they were gone, like they were never there.

"Wait, you prayed for them, and it sent them on?" Mercy was incredulous. We were sitting in a corner table of the Cafe Du Monde. I could feel the Cathedral looming behind me like an iceberg, but I ignored the feeling. I had taken a job, gotten paid for it, and was determined to feel proud of myself, but a prickling of Catholic guilt, like a long-healed scar, itched in my brain. I took a long sip of coffee. "If that's the case, why couldn't Willem exorcize them?"

"If I had to guess, I'd say that's the difference between praying at someone, and praying for them. The power of Christ couldn't compel them, but it could welcome them home."

Mercy bit into a beignet and brushed powdered sugar from her fingers. "So is this what you do now, ghost hunting?"

"I don't know about that, but the substantial consideration for my services to the parish hasn't hurt. But does that mean you believe me?"

"Not a chance," she said. "Speaking of lost lambs, though, does this mean you're back to Mother Church?"

I stared down at my dregs.

"I don't know about that, either. Marguerite and Daniel just wanted a little bit of forgiveness. But one hundred and ten years is a long time to wait for prompt succor."

The Sacred Marriage of Etienne McCray

by Kirsten M. Corby

Officer Steve McCray hated patrolling the French Quarter.

Alone, on foot, jostled by drunken tourists and locals alike, it was a rough beat for any cop. But for Steve it was – too much. Too much like his own neighborhood, the Marigny – the narrow streets, the townhouses with their shuttered windows, blind to the streets. Just like his overpriced apartment that Rosemary had wanted, but Rosemary was gone now. Too close to home, too apt to remind him of better times. And too much chance of running into Rosemary.

His request for transfer to the Seventh District in the East had been denied. The force was severely understaffed, still struggling after Katrina, and officers were needed in the money-making parts of town. Had to keep the brand up there, protect the tourists, keep the conventions coming. And so he and a good twenty percent of his brothers in blue kept rustling the streets of the Quarter and the Central Business District, running off the shoeshine kids and the pettiest of the petty drug dealers, and giving directions to flushed, wine-soaked tourists.

One of them was speaking to him now, tugging on his arm. "Officer, officer." Steve tensed. Sweet Jesus, didn't they know in whatever podunk town she was from not to touch a cop?

"Officer," the woman continued, having got his attention. "I believe that … person is a prostitute."

"What?" he said.

"There." She pointed down the street to a leggy redhead who was, yes, loitering under a streetlight on the corner. A little too leggy and a little too red to be altogether natural, Steve thought. And a little too much Adam's apple, too, if the shadows from the streetlamp weren't confusing matters.

So yes, a hooker, a real New Orleans tranny hooker, a regular Lady Marmalade. But still he looked at the woman, the tourist, bemused. Didn't people come to the Quarter, to New Orleans, precisely to see such sights?

"She's not bothering you, ma'am, is she?"

The woman's nostrils flared as she sucked in her breath. "She is plying her *trade*," she hissed in a stage whisper, jabbing a bony finger at the working girl. "On the *street*. It's *illegal*."

Her indignation was genuine. He looked at her afresh: face mostly devoid of makeup, modest slacks and a blouse buttoned higher than the weather demanded. The Baptists, he realized. There was a big church convention in town this week. They were more apt to come into the Quarter to testify to the revelers than join them. But apparently a street hooker was beneath even that.

Steve wondered what this godly matron would say if she saw all the whores in Saint Louis Cathedral on Ash Wednesday morning.

But "I'll take care of it, ma'am" was all he said.

He trudged down the sidewalk toward the working girl.

"Oh, fuck no," she said when she saw him coming. She straightened up, dropped her cigarette and ground it out with one Lucite heel.

"Beat it," Steve said.

"Bite me, pig," she said. "I ain't doin' nothing."

"Go on. You're scaring the tourists."

The streetwalker looked over his shoulder at the church lady, then tossed her red mane of hair. "Who, her? I bet I could show her a better time than that dishrag husband of hers, even without my johnson anymore. You want a date, baby?" she yelled at the tourist, who gasped in mortification and clutched said dishrag's arm.

Goddammit, Steve thought. He grabbed the whore, spun her around against the lamp post. "You're under arrest."

"No! I ain't done nothing!"

"Solicitation, for Christ's sake," Steve said, pulling the handcuffs off his belt. "You just propositioned a missionary. Now shut up, you just earned a trip to Tulane and Broad."

But before he could get the cuffs on her, she sagged in his grip and then suddenly lunged up, pushing against him. She was, of course, stronger than she looked, johnson or not. Steve stumbled backwards, and the hooker took off down the street.

Fuck, Steve thought as he gave chase.

Long legs aside, she couldn't get far in those stripper heels, and within a block Steve caught her. He felt an evil flush of pleasure as he grabbed her from behind and flung her against the wall.

"Resisting arrest, too, you cunt," he said. "Assume the position."

He frisked her, taking an extra moment to cop a feel of perfectly respectable breasts, running his hands up under her spangled miniskirt, wondering what really was between her legs. The thought both disgusted and excited him. Even without the heels, she was taller than him. She was Creole, like he was, a high yella bitch, but for some reason that made him feel more anger toward her than kinship.

"No," she pleaded, resistance gone, "I can't go there. Please officer, no." She looked down at him with big wet eyes, glistening in the lamplight.

"Then stop turning fucking tricks," he said. "You have the right to remain silent."

"My pimp is in there," she begged. "OPP. I can't see him."

"So what, you won't," Steve said. "You have the right to an attorney, bitch."

"I was just talking, earlier," she said in a whisper. "I ain't had the operation." She took Steve's hand, guided it to her crotch. She was no woman. Again he felt the same mix of arousal and revulsion. "They'll put me in the man's side, no matter what I say. When Lil T finds out I've been freelancing, he'll hurt me. He'll cut me. For real." Her voice trembled. She really was scared.

Everyone was scared and pitiful when they were facing time in the notoriously violent and lawless Orleans Parish Prison. "Not my problem," Steve said.

"Please," she whimpered, "Officer McCray. I can make it worth your while." She arched her back, thrusting up her hormonally enhanced breasts.

"I'm no queer!" Steve lashed out, shoving her back against the wall. Personally he didn't give a shit who put what where, but it never did to look weak in front of the perps.

"No, baby, not like that," she said.   "Just my mouth, that's not queer, everybody does that." She put her hands on his chest, ran them up to his shoulders and down his arms. "Just a blow job, baby, and we'll call it even, hey?"

"Okay, even," he said, and dragged her into the nearest alley. It was narrow and dark, reeking of garbage and old piss. An appropriate venue for such a transaction.

"Bite me and I'll blow your head off," he said as he fisted his hand in her hair and pushed her down.

"Never, baby," she said, and unzipped his uniform pants.

It was good at first. He groaned at the first touch – so hot and wet, slickness of tongue and throat and the flashing risk of teeth. He used to love it when Rosemary went down on him. Thoughts of her made him realize he wasn't using a condom, but he let it slide – what did it matter? Who else would he be fucking anytime soon? He leaned back against the brick wall and surrendered to the rhythm of it, hands clutched in the hooker's hennaed hair.

But then things got weird. As he came closer to orgasm, a wave of dizziness overcame him, beyond anything he'd ever felt from sex. Vertigo whirled him around. Colored lights popped in front of his eyes. He heard a babel of sounds and voices in his ears, coming from everywhere and nowhere – jazz traditional and progressive, women screaming, babies laughing and crying. Sirens, gunshots, whispers in the dark, frenzied drumming, the hiss of blackened fish hitting the pan. The rush of the river several blocks distant.

His knees buckled and he slid down the wall, but the hooker held him up, hands strong on his waist and thighs, mouth tight now, working him. He smelled church incense and crab boil and the funky lakewater smell of the bayou. Jesus, was he having a seizure?

"Stop, " he grunted, "stop –"

It was too late. With a final strong stroke, she swallowed him, and he came, bursting into her mouth and throat with a pleasure so strong it tipped into pain.

A soundless, blinding flash of light went off. He felt things crawling all over his skin, like electric ants. The streetlight outside the alley sparked and went out. He felt himself falling – but no, he was still standing, his body was good, but his mind, his mind was – spreading out , expanding, leaving his body behind. Hovering over the Quarter, spreading, uptown, downtown, back of town – he saw it, he felt it all. He saw New Orleans, everyone and everything in it.

Then it was over. The whore screamed and jumped back, and Steve fell to the slimy pavement, his cock still hanging out. The smell of frankincense filled the little alleyway, for real.

"What did you do to me?" he gasped.

"*Ifreann na Fola*! What did I do? Who are you, human?" the hooker said, with a changed voice.

Steve looked up. The person who had recently been pleasuring him was gone. Before him stood a being like something out of a costume designer's wet dream: taller, no longer Creole, but with milk-white skin. Hair no longer hennaed but blazing electric blue, thickly braided and twined with feathers, crystals and shells. No longer a slutty skirt and tank top but garb of brilliant green silk, tight at the waist and flaring out in flowing skirts or trousers.

"What the fuck?" he said weakly.

"Who are you?" It bent down closer to him. Its eyes – purple – had vertical slit pupils like a cat's. "What is your name, mortal?"

"Steve," he blurted.

She – she? – was still wearing the Lucite stilettos. She jabbed one into Steve's sternum, grinding it in. He screamed at the pain. "Your *full* name, son of Adam!"

"Etienne – Etienne McCray…"

A stream of words came out of her in some unknown language that sounded like a cross between silver birdsong and pots and pans clanging together. She kicked him in the stomach, the head. Finally, in English she screamed, "What have you done? What have you *done*, Etienne McCray?"

Winded, undone, he fumbled for his gun, but his nerveless fingers wouldn't grasp it. He tried for his radio, but it wouldn't work: dead silent, not even the click of the channel kicking in. Fried somehow.

The being towered over him. Unfolding from her back came wings: huge, transparent, shimmering in the moonlight and veined like a dragonfly's. They arched above her, straining to catch the air.

"All the realms will rue this day, you foolish mortal," she said.

The last thing he saw was that stiletto heel coming for his face again.

He woke up in the alley, lying spread out. Instinct made him check, and his junk was still untrousered. He zipped up, pinching himself in his haste.

"Ah, shit!" he said, flailing to an upright position.

Steve checked his watch. Three a.m. shift was almost over. Slipping down Exchange Alley, Steve crept to the back door of the precinct house. Sneaking toward the stairs, he stopped, puzzled.

Directly across the alley from the precinct house entrance was a door in an otherwise blank wall. He stared at it, mystified. It was weird, even for the Quarter – low, with a rounded top, made of heavy oak or cypress, bound with big iron hinges and an ancient-looking skeleton lock. He had never noticed it before.

He stared at it a moment, then shook his head, dismissing it. Maybe he had forgotten it. He just had a blow to the head after all. He slipped in the back door of the District and skulked around the evidence locker until it was shift change. Avoiding the desk sergeant, he clocked out and went home.

The next couple of days were weird. He was off the next day, and called in sick the day after. He wouldn't be able to avoid work forever, but maybe by the time he went back the bruises would go down.

But that wasn't the real issue. He kept seeing things. Hearing things. The city had changed. Or he had. Or he was going crazy.

A building in the middle of Royal Street that had collapsed the year before was suddenly standing again – or an image of it was, the building as it had once been, clean new brick and fresh whitewash, instead of the crumbled ruin. He found if he tried hard enough he could still see the empty lot, the piles of neglected bricks no one had hauled away. But when his concentration lapsed, the ghost building was there again.

Other buildings had upper stories they hadn't had; alleys that never existed opened off streets he had walked his whole life. And there were … people in those streets. Creatures. A businessman with a briefcase, a bespoke suit, and arching white angel's wings on his back, rustling softly as he hurried down Iberville Street. At the mouth of one of the alleys, a *vévé*, a voodoo sigil, was scrawled in white chalk – he saw something hovering about it, a shadowy cloud watching him with perfectly human brown eyes.

Snakes crawled out of the sewers and climbed the wrought iron lampposts downtown, hissing softly, watching him as he passed, their eyes glowing like fire.

On some crazed impulse, he went at midnight to the door in Exchange Alley, across from the precinct – the door that had never been there before – and banged on it for several minutes.

The being that answered could only be called a *loup-garou*. Bipedal, towering over him, covered in a thick gray pelt, with the body of a man and the head of a wolf.

Its red tongue lolled out between its sharp white teeth. "Been expecting you," it growled.

Steve's nerve broke and he ran, ran all the way back to Frenchmen Street, his own neighborhood. He didn't sleep that night, but spent it taking scalding hot showers and forcing himself to throw up, trying to purge this madness from his body.

The next day, there was no help for it. He had to go back to work.

His radio shrilled, the caterwauling double tone that meant an all-units call. "Eighth District, all units report to 1400 block of Burgundy Street. Fire reported in residence at 1425 Burgundy. Support NOFD with crowd control and material assistance. All units acknowledge."

Holy shit, that was just a couple blocks away. Adrenaline pushed back the dread that had come to fill him. He turned; already he could see the thick black column of smoke rising over the low roofs of the buildings.

Fire was something to be feared in the French Quarter: a densely packed neighborhood of ancient wood and plaster buildings built cheek by jowl along narrow, crumbling streets. Fire leaped quickly from building to building, and modern fire trucks couldn't negotiate many of the tiny, Old

World streets. Blazes had leveled the old quarters of the city more than once in the past, and could do so again.

Arriving at the scene, he set up a cordon with other officers, controlling the crowd of tourists and locals pressing close to get a view, drawn by humanity's ancient and perverse fascination with fiery destruction. The building was already burning steadily, an old galleried house in the Greek Revival style – flames and nasty black smoke pouring out of the tall narrow windows. The front of the home was scorched black in an ugly starburst pattern, the windows blown in, the trumpet vines that graced the balconies a crisp, blackened tracery.

"What the hell happened?" he asked a fellow officer.

"Fire captain says it looks like arson," she said, nodding toward the black starburst.

"Damn!"

She nodded. "Yeah, it's bad. They think there's people still in there. It's some kind of group home."

Teams of firefighters swarmed in and out through the front door, insectile looking in their plastic facemasks and oxygen tanks. One emerged, carrying a body shrouded in a thermal blanket. As he ran down the steps, Steve saw an arm flop from within the blanket – an arm as blackened and crisped as the trumpet vines.

Steve's gut twisted at the sight. Several onlookers in the crowd screamed; the crowd became much more restless, surging at the barriers. A crowd, Steve realized, that was composed largely of regular humans. There were few of the nightmarish creatures that thronged the streets in the rest of the Quarter.

Scanning the throng, he did see one. A jolt of adrenaline shocked him. It was another *loup-garou* – or some kind of wolf-man: smaller than the first one had been, tawny brown instead of gray. A coyote maybe? It was watching the burning house avidly.

Steve darted over and grabbed its arm. "Hey!" it growled in a dog-like voice.

"What do you know about this?"

"Nothing, officer," the thing said, trying to pull its arm out of his grip. "I'm just watching." For a moment, he saw the creature as the rest of the world must see it: a skinny little black man with ashy skin and ratty dreads, hands clasped around the police barrier. Then the vision was gone, as if it had tried to assert the illusion against his new crazy vision, and failed.

"Where are all the others?" Steve demanded.

"What others?" the dog-thing asked.

Steve jerked its muscular little arm practically out of its socket. "The others like you!"

The coyote-man hissed in surprise. "So it's you!" he said. "The rumors are true."

"What rumors?"

It grinned, exposing snaggly little canines. "Welcome to the Otherside, Tanist," it said, and laughed a sniggering little laugh like a dog whining.

Steve shook the thing so hard its teeth rattled. "What the fuck is going on here?"

The creature pointed back to the burning building. "You wanna know? Ask that."

Steve turned, and in an upper window he could see a black and red form, shimmering as if it gave off tremendous heat, human-shaped but small, two eyes glowing like pits of lava.

"There!" he shouted to the firemen, pointing. "Up there! It's alive!"

The firemen responded, racing up the steps of the inferno, just as a great gout of flame and smoke burst out of the front doors, knocking them back, and the upper story of the building collapsed, showering sparks, flame, and burning timbers across the street. The rubbernecking crowd screamed and scattered. In the ensuing chaos, Steve lost track of the dog-creature.

In the end the FD had to let the building immolate itself in a barely controlled burn, while they soaked the adjoining buildings with water and chased down any floating cinders. When it was finally done, late in the evening, Steve prowled around the scorched perimeter, looking for – what? Some sign of the thing he had seen in the window. He found nothing, but he kept at it until the fire marshals ran him off with a threat to report him to his superiors.

The next day, Steve pored through the arrest records on solicitation. That red-headed tranny must have been picked up for turning tricks before. He had to find her. He needed answers.

He found her at last, a street name of Strawberry Fields – of course – her last known down off St. Claude past the railroad tracks. He checked out a cruiser and drove down there. In the judgment call between a show of force and a soft touch, he felt the need for cracking skulls.

It was a shotgun shack on Piety Street, oh irony, the windows crusted with dirt and a BEWARE OF DOG sign on the gate. The titular dog started barking madly when he pounded on the door. He did not identify as police. After some minutes, he heard an indistinct voice from the back of the house, and a moment later the door cracked open.

It was her, the shock of red hair even more garish in the daylight. "The fuck you want?" she started. "People tryin' to sleep up in here –"
Then she recognized him and darted back inside.
Steve yanked the door open, plunging in after her. She fled down the narrow length of the shadowy house from room to room. The dog, a shaggy black thing, leaped at him and he kicked it, sending it away with a yelp.

He caught her in the back bedroom, right before the back door, tackling her and driving her down to the grubby carpet. She writhed under him, kicking and squirming. He had a hard time holding her down. She seemed much stronger than a skinny whore had any right to be, weirdly supple and with seemingly too many limbs, a twisting snarl of flesh and bone. She almost got away until he pulled his Glock and jammed it into her face. "Lie the fuck down!"

She did, going completely limp under him. She flinched away from the gun and he pressed it harder against her cheek. It seemed to hurt her, and he kept it there, enjoying her pain, feeling a distinct rush from hurting her. Payback.
"What did you do to me?"
She said nothing, her full lips trembling. Her eyes darted around.
The dog came barreling back, snarling and drooling. He shifted, pressing one knee into her chest to keep her down, and pistol-whipped the thing as it leaped for him, striking it across the muzzle. It howled, then lay limp. As he watched, it quivered and changed, losing its fur and muzzle shortening,

until what lay before him looked like a tiny little withered old man, bald-headed, naked, but still with the canine fangs of a dog, and glisteny wings like a dragonfly's on its back.

He clicked the safety off and pointed the gun back at the hooker. "*What are you?*"

There was a cherry-red welt on her cheek where the gun had lay. It smoked slightly.

"The Good Neighbors," she said. "The Fair Folk. The Gentry."

He had no idea what that meant. "What did you do to me?"

A look of genuine dismay crossed her face. "Not what I did, Tanist," she said. "What *we* did."

Tanist. That dog-thing at the fire had called him that. What did it mean?

"And both worlds will be the sorrier for it," Strawberry Fields said.

"I keep seeing things," Steve said.

"You see things as they truly are, Etienne McCray."

He remembered her as he had seen her in the alley, after – whatever had happened. "Show me what *you* truly are," he said.

She sighed. "As you wish, Tanist."

And she changed. No longer the skanky transsexual, she became something more truly androgynous, lithe but sensuous, tall and slim, with milk-white skin and purple eyes.

Just like in the alley.

Her hair was pale lilac this time. She shifted slightly, and the wings unfolded from her back, part butterfly and part bird, peacock green and blue, casting shards of iridescence around the dim bedroom.

He remembered the old wives' tales Great-Grandmother McCray had been so fond of. "You're – a fairy?" he said.

She inclined her head. "The Fair Folk, as you say."

It was broad daylight, and he wasn't drugged, or drunk, as far as he knew. He had to accept it. "What did you do to me? That night?"

"I did nothing *to* you, Tanist," she said. "We both did that deed through our own free will. And so the ancient bond was sealed."

"Why do you keep calling me that?"

"Because it's what you are," she said. "Now."

He leveled the gun at her. "I need answers, goddammit, not riddles!"

"Three days hence it was, when we came together," the fairy said. "What day was that?"

He thought back, feeling a flush of shame at the memory. "April 31."

"May Eve."

"So?"

She shook her head. "You mortals of the Information Age. The knowledge of all history at your very fingertips, and you are all so ignorant.

"May Eve is the ancient spring fertility rite, the blessing of the fields to receive the crops. The marriage of the Lady and the Lord, the King and the Land. The *hieros gamos* – the Sacred Marriage."

Despite himself, Steve laughed. "Whatever that was, sister, it wasn't sacred."

"Not to you, perhaps, but to the old powers, certainly it was. A rite that has not been acted for generations, centuries, in this New World. Not by the true heir."

That just made him angry. He was heir to nothing but a deedless house in the Lower Ninth seized after the storm, and the continuous unanswered question that was his mother's absence.

"Bullshit," he said. "Make it stop."

She smiled, an inhuman smile that chilled his blood. "I cannot. It is what you are now."

"I'm no one's heir," he said. "Take it away."

"But you are," Strawberry said. "Etienne Alphonse McCray, son of Julius and Delia. Son of Africa and Europe, the Sahel and the Black Forest. Son of an ancient bloodline, the Kings of Tara of the Emerald Isle. Son, also, of the kings of Dahomey in Mother Africa. Two bloodlines, one scion.

"When you came in my mouth you made the Sacred Marriage with the land, Etienne McCray, and you are the Tanist now, the heir to the King."

"The King of *what*?" Steve asked, too baffled to argue anything else.

"*La Nouvelle Orleans*, of course." Her wings and raiment changed, became purple, green and gold. "Really, what else is there?"

"Why me?" Steve asked. "If I'm the heir, then where's the King?"

A guarded look came over her inhuman face. "The King is gone," she said.

"Lo these many years. Not dead, but elsewhere. At last, we of the fey felt ourselves free from mortal interference. Believe me, your accession is quite a surprise." She touched her mouth, as if she was remembering what they had done.

King of the city. It made no sense. It jumbled in his head, crazy talk from a crazy thing.

"I can't live like this," he said.

She reached out, brazenly tilted the barrel of his gun up toward his face. "Then end it."

He hastily pulled the gun away to the side. "Suicide is a mortal sin," he said automatically, a shard of catechism drilled into him since smallest childhood.

She laughed. "Mortal indeed. See, you do know the things of the spirit. You have the sight now; you always had the potential. Or the Marriage would not have been made. So use it."

She sat up suddenly, tumbling him off her like a rag doll. He realized that she could have overpowered him at any time, if she had wanted to.

The dog-fairy thing was waking up, stirring and groaning, its wings making a cicada-like buzzing against its back.

"And now, Tanist, you must leave my house. My Hound will be much less gentle when it sees you have hurt me." She touched the rosy welt on her cheek where the gun had touched her.

"What is that?"

"Cold iron," Strawberry said. "Anathema to the things of the Otherside. "

True to her word, the dog-thing rose up, snarling, hackles stiff. Steve pointed the gun at it and her, got up, and backed away.

"Don't leave town," he said.

She smiled. "Never."

At the end of the shift, he stopped by the ruin of the burned home. Slipping under the crime tape, he prowled the smoky wreckage, looking for...something. There was more to this fire than just mere pyromania, or even straight arson. No one would benefit from the destruction of a cash-strapped non-profit like that. And he had seen that...thing. With the burning eyes, in the fire.

On the rear wall, he found something, a symbol scrawled on the wall: three upward-pointing triangles, nested within each other, but it glowed; orange light seemed to shift and move within it, as if it were scribed in flame.

He touched it. Ah! It was hot! He shook his hand, blowing on his singed fingers. He had no idea what it meant. But it was something.

As he stood there in the dark wondering, a crash came from within the ruins of the house. Someone – some *thing* – was in there!

Disregarding the danger of the crumbled ruins, he plunged inside.

The smell of burned wood – and worse – hung thick and acrid in the air. The orange glow of the streetlights threw tricky shadows throughout the wreckage as Steve stumbled from room to roofless room, looking for an unknown foe.

As he came through a door it attacked him, a dark shape barreling down upon him, knocking him over.

Its rank smell washed over him; it growled in his ear, an almost subsonic rumble, no human sound. It lashed out at him and claws left a line of fire along his chest, shredding his shirt. Steve screamed. He reached out blindly, and his hands closed on both hard muscle and soft, pillowy flesh. A breast – the thing was a female! He yanked, and the she-thing tumbled off him.

In the chiaroscuro light, he saw its canine muzzle, long and lean, slaver dripping off its jaws. The *loup-garou*! A blaze of white fur ran along its muzzle up past its ear. He drew his gun, but before he could get it out all the way its huge taloned hand clasped around his wrist, squeezing, grinding the bones. Agony flared up his arm and the gun slipped from his grasp. He was a dead man.

Then the death grip fell away and the thing said, in a surprisingly mellifluous human voice, "You!"

Then its weight was gone, off him, and the beast backed away. Before his eyes, it changed, assuming a truly wolfish shape, four-legged and low, huge head hung from a thick furred neck. Before he could move or shoot, it turned and bounded away, out of the ruined house, into the night.

He drew his gun fully and scrabbled up to put his back against a wall, lungs heaving, the gashes in his chest burning like fire. He readied himself, but the werewolf did not return.

It scared him stupid, but he banged again on the creepy hidden door in the alley behind the station house.

The door opened. The *loup-garou* stood there, towering over him, red tongue lolling. Its rank, meaty scent washed over him again. Steve had to clench to keep from pissing his pants in fear.

Its fur was steel grey, and it had no white blaze on its toothy muzzle. It was male. This was not the beast who had attacked him in the burned house.

"Welcome, Tanist," it growled.

It stood back to let him in.

Tanist. He had looked the word up on the Internet; it meant the designated heir of a Celtic High King. How did it know? They all knew, all these creatures of the Otherside, as the fairy had called it.

He stepped through the door.

Inside was a traditional French Quarter courtyard, a pavement of ancient flagstones surrounded by luxurious trees and vines in pots and planters. A fountain chuckled in the center. The stucco walls of the buildings crowded close, gas lamps flickering in sconces.

He swallowed down a sense of vertigo, because he knew full well that what really lay across Exchange Alley from the precinct house was the garage for the motor fleet and a warehouse that stocked cheap Oriental trinkets for Mardi Gras parades. You could look down from the second floor of the District onto the corrugated roof of the warehouse. This courtyard wasn't there, wasn't real. It struck him forcibly for the first time that he really had crossed over; he was on the *other side* –

"May I offer you my hospitality, Tanist?" The werewolf growled, holding up a bottle of whiskey and two highball glasses. A fragment of Great-Grandmother McCray's lore flitted through his memory – *never eat the food of the fairies.*

"No, thanks."

The beast skinned its lips back from its fangs in what he supposed was a smile. "It's too late for that, Etienne McCray. You have already crossed over; you will never cross back."

"I didn't come here to drink," he snapped.

The creature put the bottle down on a tiny wrought-iron table below a rambling bougainvillea. "As you wish. Then how may I serve you, Tanist?"

Steve crossed his arms. "You have me at a disadvantage." Something his mother used to say, part of her Garden District upbringing.

The *loup-garou* bowed. "Allow me to introduce myself," it said. When it straightened up it had changed, just like that – no longer beast but man, an olive-skinned male with a neat beard on the jawline, slightly almond eyes, wearing a linen suit and a straw Panama hat. Stocky, a bit of a Cajun look to him, not the languid yellowness of the old New Orleans Creoles, like Steve's father's kin.

"I am Delaunde Doucet. I am the alpha of the Bayou Sauvage pack of the *loup-garou* of *La Louisianne.*"

"Why are you being so polite to me?"

"Why have I not torn your throat out and quenched my thirst with your blood, do you mean?" He smiled, just as disconcerting on his human face as the grin of the wolf. "We *loup-garou* are not like the Slavic werefolk of Hollywood fame. We are civilized beings – to an extent. There are laws. You are my sovereign now, after all."

Steve didn't know what to make of that. Sovereign?

"Not every being on this side will feel the same way," Doucet said.

A memory floated up from the jumble of impression he had about that night. "She said, 'Both realms will rue this day.'"

"Indeed," the *loup-garou* said. "For many years the denizens of this side have traveled the streets of this city unchallenged, unobserved. But now you are here, watching us. Judging. There are those who will resent it."

"And you?" Steve asked, aware of the weight of his sidearm on his hip. But he had no silver bullets.

"What good would it do me to make an enemy of you at first blush? No, we garou are pack animals. We follow the rightful leader."

A discussion of werewolf ethics was not really why he had come, Steve thought.

"You have come about the fire," Doucet said, taking the words right out of Steve's mouth.

"Why were you there?"

"It was not I, but one of my kind. We also wonder. Even the mundane denizens of the Quarter know that was no ordinary fire."

"I saw things," Steve said.

"Please elaborate," Doucet said.

So Steve told him about the fiery sign on the wall, the triangles, and the coal-eyed burning thing in the window upstairs.

Doucet stroked his chin. "The triangle pointing upwards is the elemental sign of fire. The beast, then, would be a salamander."

"Like, a gecko?" Steve said, confused.

"Not really. Those sort of salamanders are actually amphibians. No, *this* sort is an elemental spirit of fire – fire made physical, and conscious. Very dangerous, hard to control. It's concerning that someone would choose to summon one. They do not mean well."

"Four people died in that fire," Steve said.

"Doubtless that was the intent."

"A sacrifice?" That rocked him. *Human sacrifice?*

"It seems likely. One could summon a salamander by burning down any old building, not one full of people."

"But why? Who would do that?"

"Not anyone I know. Perhaps, a new faction in town. There has been quite the influx since the storm, as I'm sure you know."

The thought of hordes of carpetbagging supernatural monsters descending on his hometown just the like the yankees put a cold lump in the pit of Steve's stomach.

"Such people seldom stop at one such outrage," Doucet said. "There will doubtless be others."

"I can't take any of this to my bosses," Steve said. "I can't show them evidence that's invisible."

"I would visit the Awakened Eye bookshop," the *loup-garou* said. He pulled a card and flashy gold pen from his suit pocket and scrawled an address deep in the Quarter. "It is frequented by those of the arts more newly come to the city, and who tend to follow the left-hand path."

"Left-hand?" Steve asked.

"Bad guys," Doucet said. "As you would say. Be wary; they will know you are coming."

"How?"

"We all know."

The Awakened Eye turned out to be a tatty occult bookshop on St. Phillip Street on the downriver side of the Quarter. After his shift was over, Steve changed and went to stake it out.

The sign over the door, a creepy gilded eye in a pyramid, creaked in the breeze. The windows were dusty and had not had their stock rearranged in months, if not years. It looked like a front for a drug ring – or worse. God knew what sort of insane intoxicants *these people* were prone to use.

Hardly anyone came in or out. Nerving himself up, Steve went to check it out from the inside.

The bell on the door jingled as he opened it. Inside was a crowded maze of bookshelves, chests and little tables cluttered with peculiar merchandise – bags of dubious herbs, dusty crystals, statuettes of pagan-looking deities.

The bell on the door jingled again.

"Namaste, Tobias," the newcomer said to the clerk.

At the sound of that voice Steve's stomach bottomed out, right to the floor. He turned.

"Hello, Rosemary."

Her already pale face went even paler. "Steve!"

He just started at her. Of all the creepy magic joints in the all the world, why did she have to walk into this one? She was wearing one of her customary long print dresses, but she had cut her hair into a pixieish bob instead of the long tawny locks he remembered. Otherwise she was exactly the same – the bangles on her wrists, the scattering of freckles across her nose, the vetiver perfume, which was the only kind she wore.

"What are you doing here, Steve?"

How could he even begin to answer that? He turned it around, a customary tactic between them. "What are *you* doing here, Ro? This doesn't seem like your kind of place." Rosemary, the Maiden of a traditional witches' coven, was no fluffy-bunny Wiccan, but she did tend to prefer things to be clean, bright, and colorful instead of grimy and dark.

"They have a book I'm looking for, *Morning of the Magicians.*" She stepped closer to him, searching his eyes. "What's happened, Steve?"

"Huh?"

"Something's changed. What is it?"

He clamped his mouth shut, aghast that she could sense a change in him after a few moments' acquaintance. The one person he knew who might understand what he had gone through. He was damned if he'd tell her.

"I'm working a case."

She frowned dubiously. "Which case?"

"The arson on Burgundy Street."

Her eyes widened. "We didn't have anything to do with that."

Steve felt pretty confident of that – he knew Ro's friends, a bunch of well-meaning stoners and trustafarians. They had trouble organizing a potluck; felony arson would be beyond them. But they were on that side. He was on the Otherside now.

"Do you recognize this?" he asked, her. He took out his pad and drew the sign he had seen, the nested triangles.

Rosemary nodded. "Fire. Fire within fire, within fire. This was at the crime scene?"

"What does it mean?"

She shrugged. "I saw it in a book once on Semitic magic."

"Semitic?" Steve doubted the Jews of New Orleans had anything to do with the arson. It just wasn't their style.

"Middle Eastern," she clarified. "It represents purification of the material world, through fire. I think it belonged to a Persian sect? It was a long time ago."

Persian? Could this be the work of a terrorist cell? The thought made him cold. New Orleans was a port city, people and goods came there from all over the world. Terrorism was an acknowledged risk; the Department had plans.

But what about the fire thing in the window, the salamander? Al-Qaeda wasn't into conjuring up demonic creatures.

Rosemary moved closer to him; the cloud of her perfume enclosed him, bringing a flood of memories. He had ended it between them, but not because he didn't care.

"What's going on, Steve? You're not a detective. What are you mixed up in?"

"Police business."

Rosemary scowled. She had never really cared for his chosen profession. It had been one of the things between them. "Well, don't expect me to inform on any of my people, Etienne." She always called him that when she was pissed. At first it had amused him. Before the end, it had started to grate.

"Did I ask you to?"

Her lower lip thrust out sullenly. There was a time when he loved that pout, it drove him crazy with desire, but those times were gone. He held up the slip of paper. "Just tell me, Ro, if anyone was practicing this – Persian magic, what would it look like?"

Silently, he laughed at himself. Magic! Five days ago he wouldn't have been caught dead asking such a question. But it was his only lead.

Rosemary took the paper, looked at it thoughtfully. "Well, fire. Lots of fire, big fires. In that mythos, fire symbolizes strength, order, purification. It represents the divine essence."

"Like the arson?"

She shook her head, handing the paper back to him. "I just don't know, Etienne. I hope not. It's never good for any of us if some group goes too far down the left-hand path."

Left-hand path, right-hand path. As far as Steve could see there was no path on this Otherside, just a wilderness of crazy.

"You shouldn't be here, Rosemary," he blurted. "This is a bad place."

Her mouth set in a line of disgust. "You don't know anything about it, Steve. You're the one who shouldn't be here."

"I wouldn't be, except it's the only lead I have. Where would these fire magicians meet?"

Rosemary smirked. "Someplace fireproof, I suppose. The docks? A warehouse? I don't know."

"Is there anything else you can tell me?"

"Why should I?"

Steve took a breath and throttled down his impatience. The arguing, that was another thing he had had enough of. He needed to remember that. "You said it's not good for your people if others take things too far."

"Well, if anyone's planning anything, they'll do it soon. It's currently the planting festival in the Persian calendar. Big fire festival then – offerings to make the crops grow. Will be for two more days."

Two days. Not much time. "Thanks, Rosemary."

She eyed him strangely. "I wish you would tell me what's going on with you."

Her insight unnerved him. If she could see…what had happened to him, who else could? "It's this case," he said. "Four people are dead. And you know I don't put much faith in all this hoodoo crap."

"Don't I know it," she said. She rooted around for a moment in her big purse, drew something out. "Here," she said, putting it in his hand. It was a smooth, rounded, glossy black stone, just large enough to nestle in his palm.

"It's obsidian. For protection. It absorbs negative energies."

He looked at it dubiously. He put less truck in that than in his grandmother's beads and holy water.

"Just in case," she said.

He pocketed it just to be polite. "Thanks, Rosemary."

There was a moment of awkward silence. "Goodbye, Steve," Rosemary said finally.

"Bye." He left the store, hoping he would never have to go back.

Fire magic. It was a thin enough lead, and by day's end it petered out. New Orleans was a port town – there were hundreds of warehouses in every neighborhood, abandoned and in use. And that didn't include old factories, or the blighted housing in the flooded neighborhoods – thousands of places where such criminals could hide. He drove around, checking those he could when he got off duty. It was hard to do without the resources of the department, but he couldn't bring his suspicions to the brass. He'd be the one they locked up as crazy.

He drove the streets that night, looking for – something.

And that was how he found Strawberry Fields again, plying her trade on Airline Highway by the parish line.

"Aw, hell no," she said when she saw who it was.

"Get in," he said, popping the door lock.

After a moment she did, flinging herself sulkily into the passenger seat, and Steve pulled away.

"You avoiding me?" he asked her.

She sneered. "Of course, pig."

"You should have moved farther."

"I can't. I was born in this place. New Orleans is where I came to be. It is where I stay."

"Well, ain't that some shit," Steve said. Even the fairies were too provincial to leave New Orleans.

"What do you want?"

"Persian fire magic. What do you know about it?"

She tossed her blonde mane. "Nothing. That is human magic; it doesn't concern us."

"Human sacrifice, in broad daylight, right in your – as you say – hometown, and it doesn't concern you? That sort of thing calls attention to the whole scene, I'd say. And the one thing I know about you, Strawberry Fields, is that you don't want attention."

She shifted uncomfortably in the seat; he had hit close to home. "The Black Phoenix; the dark side of Zoroastrianism. Zoroaster preached of two gods: Ahura Mazda and Ahriman – one light, one dark, in eternal struggle for possession of the world."

"Like God and the Devil," Steve said.

"Much older, and more true. Your Christian stories draw from the older stream of Persian myth. Your Lucifer is a pale imitation of Ahriman, the Deceiver. True Zoroastrians follow the side of the light, and seek to do good in the world. The Black Phoenix swear loyalty to Ahriman. To evil. The fire that scorches and destroys, instead of shedding light and warmth.

"Of course, the two sides are one. You humans never seem to learn that, down through the ages. Victims of your limited nature."

"Whatever," Steve said. "So where are they?"

"Why ask me?" Strawberry said. "You should know, Tanist."

"What? How should I know?"

The fairy sighed as if she were talking to someone extremely stupid. "Because of the *gamos*. The Prince and the Land are one. That is the *point*. Like any wedding, the two become one flesh. This dark fire burns you, Etienne McCray. It wounds you. So…feel it."

Steve remembered the babel of voices, images, and scents he had experienced during their unfortunate encounter. Was that what that was?

"How the hell do I do that?"

"Just close your eyes. And feel it."

He pulled the car over. Could it really be that simple?

Clutching the steering wheel, he closed his eyes. He didn't see anything but the darkness behind his eyelids.

Lacking any other avenue, he listened instead, tried to still his mind and let the sounds of the city wash over him. The whoosh of the cars on the highway beside them, the buzzing of streetlights, the chatter of the working girls on the street corner. A snatch of honky-tonk music from a bar. The soft hush of wind in the big oak trees that lined even the side streets in New Orleans.

Other sounds began to come to him from farther away, sounds he rightly shouldn't be able to hear: a lone saxophone player somewhere downtown; the chug and clang of the St. Charles streetcar. The lowing of a foghorn down on the river – past the Point, at the Harmony Street Wharf. How he knew that, he couldn't say, but he did.

And finally, the hiss and crackle of a fire burning – a large fire, and getting larger.

"Fire," he said, eyes still closed.

"Where?" Strawberry asked.

He could smell it now, a rank burning smell – an accelerant, burning greasy rags, ancient wood burning brightly. There. A confused jumble of impressions – a big echoing space, the smell of dirt and motor oil under the fire, flickering light in the darkness, the smell of fear –

He even knew the exact place, a crumbling warehouse on Conti Street in

Mid-City. He could feel it burning like a boil on his own flesh.

He reached over and opened the passenger side door. "Get out."

The fairy smiled wryly. "Perhaps having a reigning Tanist will not be so bad after all." She slipped out of the car. "Be wary, Tanist. The tides of the Otherside run high this time of year. Their magic will be strong."

"Yeah, yeah." Magic. He whipped the car around and sped back to the city.

Back down Airline to Carrollton, out to Mid-City, that was the fastest way. He debated calling it in, but what the fuck would he actually say? Evil cultists were burning down an abandoned warehouse for black magic mojo? That would get him a one-way trip to the department shrink.

Better to wait until he had something to report.

He turned right on Conti. It was down there, he felt it, a tension like a rubber band between him and – and the magic, he guessed. Sweat suddenly flushed his face; he could feel the heat from the fire somehow, but he couldn't see it yet.

There. A low hulk of a building, a falling-down warehouse, not yet gentrified in this rapidly developing neighborhood. Steve parked a block away, sat there for a moment, his heart thudding in his chest. It was late; the street was quiet, no foot traffic, nice family cars parked in front of flood-restored bungalows. What was he going to do? This was ridiculous. He was alone and going up against – he had no idea who. Or what.

From the outside the building showed no signs of life, but he knew something bad was going down in there.

He pulled his off-duty weapon from the glove box and clicked off the safety. Jamming it in the back of his jeans, he got out of the car.

As he got closer he could detect a flicker of light in the grimy windows of the warehouse under the roofline. Fire. The wide front doors were securely locked with a huge, rusty padlock. There had to be another way in.

Gun at the ready, he crept along the side of the warehouse, through the tall grass, looking for a side door. He mopped at sweat running down his forehead, stinging his eyes. He could feel the fire as if he was already in the building, smell it even, an acrid stink of burning trash and maybe something worse.

Just around the back corner, on the bayou side, he found a door. Orange light flickered from the dirty window at the top. Locked from the inside. He kicked it in, and dived in after, rolling and coming up with his gun out.

Before him, in the middle of the empty concrete floor, he saw figures moving around a huge fire, their shadows flaring huge and unsteady on the walls. But he could hardly hear them, neither the pounding of the drums nor the roaring of the fire nor the yells of the revelers. A wall of shimmering heat enclosed them, some kind of boundary between the everyday world and the space of the ceremony. It was an eerie feeling; he could not hear what was right in front of him, except as a distant echo in his inner ear, more like a memory of the sound than the real thing. Behind the shimmering heat waves the forms of dancing men and women wavered – men and women and, other things – tiny, bipedal, tailed and glowing like coals. Like that thing he had seen before, at the first fire. *Salamanders.*

For a second he just gaped, undone by the weirdness of it all – the berobed men and women whirling around the central fire, the capering little monsters burning bright, the weird unnatural shapes the bonfire warped itself into – a flaming bird with spreading wings, a sneering mask-like visage with black sockets for eyes, a tall tower like an Old World castle, flames shooting out its windows. This couldn't be real. He doubted his own sanity.

Then he saw the victims, tied up and piled together like kindling at the edge of the circle.

Kids, teens, gutterpunks by the look of them, all colorful mismatched clothing and facial tattoos. The lost boys, kids no one would miss, no one would look for. The disposable.

The cold-bloodedness of that, among all this heat and frenzy, was what got him moving. He raised his gun and fired at the one of the cultists.

The shot echoed weirdly in the impossibly silent space. The bullet pinged away from the fire circle and ricocheted through the room. Steve hit the deck. That weird heat barrier had blocked a bullet! Now what?

The cultists noticed. The salamanders went into a leaping frenzy, sparks shooting off them like bottle rockets. The human cultists went into overdrive, the drummers' hands blurring into invisibility. The one who looked like the lead cultist, a woman in a scarlet robe and a tall horned hat, tossed some fluid into the fire that made it flare ever higher. Steve could hear the roar now even through the magic barrier. The rest grabbed the bound kids and dragged them toward the fire.

If even his gun couldn't breach that barrier, what the hell else could he do? He'd seen enough. He yanked his cellphone out of his pocket and dialed 911.

"Officer Steve McCray, badge number 954472, on the scene of an attempted murder and arson, 3112 Conti Street, requesting backup. Suspects are..."

– fire monsters –

"...uh, armed and dangerous. Situation still evolving. Request immediate assistance."

Shoving his phone back into his pocket, he felt it click against something. He dug it out.

That black stone, the talisman Rosemary had given him. He clutched it in his hand, feeling its coldness in the fiery warehouse. Obsidian. She said it absorbed negative energies.

In the fire circle, the gutterpunks struggled and kicked as the cultists dragged them to the flames.

He cupped the obsidian in his hands, trying to *feel it*, as Strawberry and Rosemary had both advised him, trying to get clear his intent. *I'm the Tanist. Let me in there. I – well, I command it!*

He threw the rock toward the fire.

With a *pop* it crossed the shimmering heat-magic barrier. The barrier collapsed and suddenly the warehouse was a maelstrom of heat and sound – the roar of the fire, the screams of the captives, the demoniacal hissing of the salamanders.

Outside, the wail of police sirens approached along the bayou.

"Police!" Steve shouted, raising his gun. "Everybody on the ground! Hands on your heads!"

Some cultists did as he said, while others ran for the exits. The salamanders climbed the walls in a reptilian frenzy, their paws sparking fires where they ran. The tall woman in the scarlet robes grabbed a bound captive and, with an incredible display of strength, raised him above her head, and pitched him screaming into the fire.

Steve shot her, across the fire, right between the eyes.

She dropped like a stone.

As the sorceress fell, everything changed. The fire dwindled from a raging inferno to a normal bonfire burning in a crude pit. With squeals of rage, the salamanders disappeared with hissing pops from the walls, although their fiery tracks remained. The cultists broke and scattered; some dropped to the ground and put their hands up, the fight leaching out of them with the violent death of their leader.

The hapless sacrificial victim fell into the edge of the dwindling fire and rolled out, screaming. His fellow captives, still bound, rolled and crawled to him and covered him with their bodies, extinguishing the fire catching in his clothes.

Steve stared, stunned, his gun still pointing where he had fired. He had never discharged his weapon before.

As he watched, the Black Phoenix sorceress's body *shifted* as she died, assuming an unsettlingly familiar shape: taller, hairy, her face lengthening into a lupine muzzle with blazing yellow eyes and wicked fangs.

She was a *loup-garou.*

A blaze of white fur streaked along her muzzle, up behind her ear. He had seen her before, in the burned house on Burgundy Street.

She died, and the light went out of those eyes, and her body reverted back to a human shape, the blood beneath her blasted head as scarlet as her robes.

Steve staggered to a corner and puked as the NOPD finally swarmed the warehouse, dome lights whirling, radios crackling, batons cracking the heads of fleeing cultists.

The next hours were a blur. He identified as police and was taken outside to an ambulance. They swabbed his hands for gunshot residue; an EMT checked him for injuries. People talked to him, but he could barely understand what they were saying – why did he enter the warehouse? How did he know? He couldn't even begin to fashion a reasonable answer for that. After a while the brass seemed to get that, and left him alone, for now. They sent over his union rep, but he couldn't talk to her, either.

When he closed his eyes, he saw the color red – red fire, red blood. It was a good shoot, they told him; he had saved that kid's life, who had escaped with minor burns. But still.

"Someone to see you, McCray," the union rep said after a long time. She brought a civilian up through the crime scene tape to where Steve sat in the back of the ambulance.

He looked up into the eyes of Delaunde Doucette, still wearing a smart linen suit and that Panama hat.

"I just wanted to thank you personally, Officer McCray," the *loup-garou* said smoothly.

"What?" Steve said, stunned.

"Mr. Doucette is on the board of the Police Foundation," the rep said. "The Foundation always sends a representative to the scene of major incidents."

Steve lashed out and grabbed Doucette's wrist, dragging him closer. "You son of a bitch, you knew your people were involved!"

"Give us a moment," Doucette said to the union rep, sending her away with a flick of the hand.

"I had my suspicions," Doucette said. "But Veronica Belmont – the dead woman – was not a member of my pack. My options to discipline her were limited. So I steered the problem toward you."

"Why me?" Steve gritted out, enraged. "Why should I have to do your dirty work?"

Doucette smiled that frightening lupine smile. "Why, my dear boy, you are the Tanist now. Prince of the Otherside – *all* of the Otherside, by the Oldest Law known to man and fey. It is your responsibility. And you have met it mightily."

Steve let go of the werewolf's wrist, slumping back in the ambulance. "I didn't ask for any of this. I don't want this."

"My dear Etienne. Did Arthur wish to become the True King when he drew Excalibur from the stone? Did Christ wish to drink of the cup that was passed him? Of course not." He smiled again, more genuinely this time. "Destiny is what happens when you are making other plans."

"That's life," Steve sighed, remembering the song lyric.

"They're the same thing, my boy," Doucette said. "The same thing."

Charlie Brown is a writer and filmmaker from New Orleans. He currently lives in Los Angeles, where he recently received his Masters in Professional Writing from the University of Southern California and also runs Lucky Mojo Press and Mojotooth Productions. He has made two feature films: "Angels Die Slowly" and "Never A Dull Moment: 20 Years of the Rebirth Brass Band." His fiction has appeared in Oddville Press, Writing Disorder, Jersey Devil Press, The Menacing Hedge, Aethlon, and what?? Magazine. This is the second book he has edited in the "Dirty Magick" series.

Kirsten Corby is a writer and librarian who works for the public library and lives in the Irish Channel in New Orleans.

Paul Ellis is an avid reader and chronic procrastinator. He bides his time producing and voicing podcasts for MythBehaving.com, CityNewsNet, and the Dark Justice Podcast. He has taken a turn at The Roundtable Podcast here and here, written a nifty short story about a detective's run in with a bunch of Celtic gods in 1950's Los Angeles in the Dirty Magick: LA anthology, and plans a run at the presidency. Well that's not completely true however, he and his wife **are** raising three lovely daughters in the Central Virginian Piedmont. When not not otherwise engaged, he lurks on Facebook, Twitter, and occasionally at his own site, paulkellis.com.

Rhonda Eudaly lives in Arlington, Texas where she's ventured into several industries and occupations for a wide variety of experience. She's married with dogs and a rapidly growing Minion© army. Her two passions are writing and music, which is evident in her increasing horde of writing instruments. Rhonda has a well-rounded publication history in fiction, non-fiction and script writing. Check out her website - www.RhondaEudaly.com - for her latest publications and downloads.

Michael Ashleigh Finn writes his shorts from Houston, Texas. The protagonist here can also be found getting into trouble in "Dirty Magick: Los Angeles", and is worming his way into a nascent novel. In addition to his shorts, he's a consultant for the "Jim Butcher's The Dresden Files" comics from Dynamite Press and the "Mana Punk" role-playing game from Hot Goblin Press.

Emily Karnes would like to get a good night's sleep without her imagination intervening. With a BFA in studio art, a career in illustration and comics, and a light background in anthropology that markedly affects her writing, there's always some wild inkling to be sketched at three a.m.

Riley James Keith, under a super secret normal name that no one but the world, the IRS, and the Social Security Office knows, spends her time as a college student. Exiled to the abyss of the American Midwest, she spends time between art classes to write books. When she must do other things, she can be found walking her dog or reading. Sometimes at the movies. Her sanity is kept at accessoriesnotincluded.com

Jeff Leyco does more things than he knows how to keep track of. When he's not writing stories, he's swinging out to Count Basie. When he's not dancing, he's making maps and geeking out. Jeff currently lives in New York with all the Chinese food he can handle.

Terry Mixon, co-host of the Parsec Award finalist writing podcast The Dead Robots' Society, is the author of "Command Decisions," book 3 in The Empire of Bones Saga. A former non-commissioned officer with the United States Army 101st Airborne Division, he also dedicated sixteen years to providing direct computer support to the flight controllers in the Mission Control Center at the NASA Johnson Space Center supporting the Space Shuttle program, the International Space Station and other spaceflight projects. More information at terrymixon.com

Brent Nichols is a Canadian writer of science fiction, fantasy, and steampunk. His stories appear in a bunch of anthologies, such as Shanghai Steam, Blood and Water, Here Be Monsters, and Tesseracts. He's also the author of several novels and novellas, including Lord of Fire, Bert the Barbarian, and Gears of a Mad God.

Hugh J. O'Donnell is a writer and podcast producer living in Western New York. He is the host and editor of the Way of the Buffalo podcast, which features interviews and fiction from writers working in digital formats. His fiction has appeared in Bards and Sages Quarterly, Over My Dead Body! and others. He is also the author of "140 Characters," a series of novellas updated daily at hughjodonnell.com.

Michell (Mike) Plested is an author, editor, blogger, closet superhero (not to mention sock herder and cat wrangler) and podcaster living in Calgary, Alberta, Canada. He is the host of several podcasts including the writing podcast, Get Published, (2009, 2011, 2013 & 2014 Parsec Finalist). His debut novel, *Mik Murdoch, Boy Superhero* was shortlisted for the Prix Aurora Award for Best YA Novel and its sequel, *Mik Murdoch: The Power Within* was launched August 2014. He has stories and several novels coming out in 2015 including *Scouts of the Apocalypse* (May) and a collaborative steampunk work, *Jack Kane & the Statue of Liberty*(June).

Some creatures feed on blood and revel in the screams of their prey. **Scott Roche** craves only caffeine and the clacking of keys. He pays his bills doing the grunt work no one else wants to take, bringing dead electronics back to life and working arcane wonders with software. His true passion is hammering out words that become anything from tales that terrify to futuristic worlds of wonder. All that and turning three children into a private mercenary army make for a life filled with adventure.

Patrick Scaffido writes and performs The Horde, a musical and spoken word podcast novel available at www.thehordewilleat.us. He is currently coordinating the literary and new media programs for Balticon and editing The Horde for print publication. He majored in historical uses of semiotics and media and has taught both English and History to the uncaring masses. Find more about his songs, stories, poems, and machinations at www.thousandheads.com.

Claudia Smith is a freelancer, author, editor, and general renaissance woman with credits in a couple of gaming magazines as well as CHUD Stories. This is her first appearance in an anthology, and she hopes to use it as a stepping stone to her ultimate goal of trying to take over the world. When not researching her stories, she can be found in the weird alleyways and back streets of different cities she visits, doing something clever to add to her author's bio.

Also available from Lucky Mojo Press on Amazon.com:

www.ingramcontent.com/pod-product-compliance
Lightning Source LLC
Chambersburg PA
CBHW020228260626

47156CB00002B/586